A DAUGHTER'S JOURNEY

Jo Melling has arrived in Birch End from Australia, still grieving her father's recent death. She's not intending to stay long, but after tracking down her distant family, Jo becomes more involved in village life than she could ever have imagined – and suddenly in danger too. Jo also finds herself drawn to Nick, a handsome newcomer to the village. Nick had planned to settle in Birch End and start a business, but as he grows closer to Jo, he realises he may have to choose between his dreams and a chance at love.

A DAUGHTER'S JOURNEY

A DAUGHTER'S JOURNEY

by

Anna Jacobs

Magna Large Print Books
Anstey,
Leicestershire

British Library Cataloguing in Publication Data.

A catalogue record of this book is
available from the British Library

ISBN   978-0-7505-4794-9

First published in Great Britain in 2019 by Hodder & Stoughton
an Hachette UK company

Cover illustration © Jasenka Arbanas/Arcangel by arrangement with
Arcangel Images Ltd.

Published in Large Print 2019 by arrangement with
Hodder & Stoughton Ltd.

Magna Large Print is an imprint of Library Magna Books Ltd.

Printed and bound in Great Britain by
T.J. (International) Ltd., Cornwall, PL28 8RW

Dear readers,

Here is the first book in my new series. I do hope you enjoy reading it as much as I've enjoyed writing it.

I'm still lingering in the Ellin Valley to give you the Birch End series, set in the middle village in my imaginary Pennine valley.

If you'd like a list of books in each series, please visit my website, where there is a complete list of my books and also a list of which books are in each series. Just go to:

www.annajacobs.com/seriesList.aspx

This book introduces a heroine who's come all the way from Australia to Lancashire, a voyage taking several weeks in the days before air travel. It took several days even in the early days of air travel. It's a long way from England to Australia.

This is an imaginary valley, but it feels so real to me now, after several years of setting my stories there, that I even walk round it in my dreams!

I hope you enjoy my new series and the new characters who've turned up in my story. And of course, you'll again meet characters from other series set in the valley.

Happy reading!
Anna

1

Lancashire: June 1934

Jo Melling and her stepmother had to change trains at Manchester and only made their connection thanks to a kindly porter who whisked their luggage across the station on a big trolley, calling out to people to get out of the way, please.

As he stacked their trunks and suitcases in the luggage wagon at the rear of the slow, stopping train that would take them to Rivenshaw, Jo tugged the older woman towards the nearest compartment. Edna, who was too plump to run easily, panted and protested.

Thank goodness this would be the last stage in their long journey from Western Australia by sea and rail. Ten thousand miles of her stepmother's fussing and the need for them to share a cabin on the ship had nearly driven Jo mad.

Nearby, the guard was holding his whistle to his lips ready to send the train on its way. He scowled and jerked his head at them to tell them to hurry up. It was lucky that a stranger who was already on the train saw their need and opened the door again. He helped Edna into the compartment then turned to offer Jo an unnecessary hand up.

She waved him back. 'I'm fine, thank you.' She was about to make sure the door was closed properly, but the porter was there to slam it shut

11

with a final bang. The guard's whistle sounded immediately it was closed.

The train jerked into motion as she was reaching up to put her hand luggage in the overhead rack, and that sent her bumping into the stranger, who was about to move his newspaper out of her way. He steadied her with a smile, and she murmured her thanks.

He was taller than her and perhaps slightly older, about thirty or so, and had a lean, muscular look to him. He wasn't good-looking exactly, but had a pleasant face and lovely dark auburn hair. He had good manners, too, and picked up her bag, ready to put it into the net for her.

She stretched out her hand to stop him. 'Just a minute. Is it far to Rivenshaw? It's not worth putting the bag up and pulling it down again if we're only a few minutes away.'

'It's about an hour, I'm afraid, because there are a few stops before we reach it, but I doubt anyone else will get on the train at this time of day.'

'I'll leave my bag on the seat then, if you don't mind. It has all our travel papers in it and I like to keep it close by.'

'There you are, then.' He put it beside her, picked up his own bag and went to sit in the far corner of the compartment near the corridor, leaving the two ladies to settle into the window seats.

Jo stole another glance at the stranger. He was neatly if rather shabbily dressed and had been nothing but polite and helpful, but when she looked across at her stepmother, she saw that

12

Edna was eyeing him suspiciously. Typical! The woman seemed to think any young man who spoke to Jo would be a threat to her stepdaughter's virtue and they'd had several sharp quarrels about that on the ship.

As if Jo would behave in an immoral way. What's more, she could look after herself, if a man got too frisky, and had proved it more than once in the past few years!

'Don't encourage him,' Edna whispered.

Jo didn't waste her breath responding. It would do no good. Her stepmother had what their stockman in Australia called 'tin ears'.

Jo had been horrified when her father married this foolish woman a few years ago. She was pretty, yes, her hair only lightly sprinkled with grey, but she was rather stupid and Jo found her conversation focused mainly on clothes and food. The only reason she could think of was that Edna must be good at pleasing men in bed, or why else would he have married her? You couldn't help knowing about things like that when you lived on a farm, whether you were married yourself or not.

After Edna took over the house, Jo soon moved away from the farm to work in the city, because no one was going to treat her like an unpaid drudge. Or constantly carp and criticise. Her father had understood, thank goodness.

Her stepmother, however, had complained to everyone in the neighbourhood about how ungrateful and badly behaved the girl was. As if friends and neighbours who'd known Jo for years would believe her.

Jobs were in short supply in such times, but

13

since Jo had been doing the farm's accounts and ordering groceries, goods and stock feed for years, she'd used her contacts to find a job working as a bookkeeper in an office in Perth, the capital city of Western Australia. She'd shared lodgings with a friend and life there had been very pleasant, even though she'd missed the farm and her father dreadfully at first.

When he fell ill and was given only a few months to live, Jo of course left her job and went back home to Beeniup. She loved her father dearly and wanted to be with him. As it turned out, she found herself doing nearly all the nursing, especially when he grew weaker, because Edna was useless about such things, not to mention bone idle.

Her father had been wonderful right until the end. He'd done everything to make their life easier 'afterwards', which included selling the farm to Harry, the neighbour who was his closest friend, and also making him the executor of his will.

He'd secured Jo's promise to escort his widow back to England to live near her family 'afterwards', because Edna had come to Australia with her first husband and never really settled there. Some people didn't. Of course Jo had given him her word. No need to tell her that Edna would be useless at organising anything.

She didn't want to make the long journey, especially with Edna, but she'd do it for him.

Since Jo had no intention of living with the woman for one day longer than necessary, she'd set to work organising the journey immediately after the funeral, using the money he'd provided.

As soon as she'd seen Edna settled somewhere near her remaining family members in England, Jo intended to have a look at Buckingham Palace and a few other famous places, after which she'd return to Australia, where she had a few distant relatives and several good friends. She probably had relatives in England, too, and from the same part of the country as her stepmother's family, because her father's family had been from Lancashire as well, so she might see if she could find some of them.

She was jerked out of her reverie by a sob, and turned to see Edna dabbing at her eyes again. What now?

The stranger had hidden behind his newspaper. Jo wished she could hide away, too.

'Why are you ignoring me?' Edna asked, with another of her easily summoned sobs. 'You know how sad this is making me.'

'I was just ... thinking.'

Edna lowered her voice. 'You weren't too deep in thought to be talking to that young man! You wouldn't have behaved like that in Australia when your father was alive.'

Jo kept her voice even lower. 'I was only being polite. And so was he.'

As her stepmother opened her mouth to argue, Jo said, 'Not now! Shh!'

With a scowl, Edna subsided, but a minute later she found something else to complain about. 'Look at that ugly scenery. Mills and smoke and dirty old canals. Why did you insist on bringing me here? We could have settled in Perth and had sunny weather.'

15

Jo wasn't going to put up with these lies, whether the stranger overheard their latest quarrel or not. '*You* were the one who wanted to come and live near your family. I only came with you because I promised Dad as he was dying that I'd see you safely settled here. This isn't *my* country and I shan't be staying here after we've found you somewhere to live.'

'You're heartless, absolutely heartless! It's your duty as an unmarried daughter to live with me and look after me.'

'I'm not your daughter! And you're perfectly capable of looking after yourself.'

'But I–'

'Will you please keep your voice down!'

But Edna didn't care who heard her when she was upset and continued to complain about her stepdaughter's unkindness in her usual shrill tones.

The stranger had let the newspaper sink a little and was watching them with a shocked expression on his face. Jo felt her face flush with embarrassment.

She wondered if her father had realised how difficult the task of taking Edna 'home' would be, especially this last part of the journey. Jo didn't know much about life in this country and felt rather nervous about the task of finding a home for her stepmother. Edna would be hard to please, she was sure, since the money she'd been left wasn't unlimited.

To make the whole situation worse, this was the second time Edna had been widowed and that had thrown her into genuinely low spirits about the future, something Jo tried to make allowances for.

As the train continued to rattle along, stopping four times at places whose names meant nothing to her, Jo shivered, still not used to the cooler weather in Britain. She would have to buy some warmer clothes and if this was summer, she dreaded to think what the winter would be like. She hoped she'd be long gone by then.

A couple of times she caught the man watching her and didn't know whether to say something or ignore him. When he winked and rolled his eyes at the older woman, she couldn't help smiling at him.

Edna had subsided into a miserable heap, sniffling into her handkerchief occasionally or varying that by dabbing at eyes that were leaking no tears that Jo could see.

As they came out of a tunnel, the man leaned forward.

'Excuse me, miss, but you've dropped one of your gloves.'

'Oh. Thank you.' She bent to pick it up. Stupid things! In Australia she had only worn gloves in cooler weather. Edna, however, had tried to impose what she called 'ladylike standards' on her stepdaughter but Jo had refused to be dictated to or to obey such silly social rules as ladies wearing gloves every time they went out of the house.

At twenty-six, she wasn't a child and didn't intend to behave like one.

A few minutes later, the man said, 'You might like to get your things ready, ladies. Rivenshaw is the next stop.'

'Thanks.' Jo made sure Edna gathered everything together and waited impatiently to get out of the train. She was so very tired of being shut up in small spaces with people.

As soon as she left the train Jo beckoned urgently to a porter, telling him about their luggage. Then she helped Edna get out while the porter hurried to unload their things from the rear luggage wagon, piling them haphazardly on the platform. As the train pulled away, he called out that he'd fetch a trolley to move them near the station entrance as soon as he'd seen the disembarking passengers away.

The two women showed the porter their tickets and walked across to the entrance, passing the man who'd shared their compartment, who was talking to another man.

There was no one there to meet them, which upset Edna. 'Where's my cousin? What shall I do if he's died? I need help settling back into English life.'

'He'll be here soon, or if not him someone else from your family will. You sent him a telegram to give him our time of arrival as soon as we got off the ship.'

They waited a few minutes but there was still no sign of anyone. 'Perhaps we should get a taxi to his house, Jo, and leave our luggage to follow.'

'You can do that if you want, but I'm not going to turn up at your cousin's house uninvited. He's a stranger to me and even you haven't seen him for a good many years.'

'He was a close friend of my brother's as well as

18

being our favourite cousin. Why, I've known Clarence all my life. *Of course* he'll want me to go to him, and you too, if only for my sake, until you've found me somewhere of my own to live.'

'I've told you before: your cousin can do that for you. He'll know the town far better than I do. I'm going back to Australia quite soon.'

'Your father must be turning in his grave at the way you're breaking your promise to him.'

Jo began pacing up and down to avoid going through the same old arguments.

A few minutes later, with still no sign of anyone coming to meet them, she decided to prepare for the worst and signalled to the taxi parked to one side of the station forecourt. When it drove across to them, she asked the driver if there was some small hotel where they could find rooms for a night or two.

He studied them and nodded as if satisfied by what he saw. 'Mrs Tucker's lodging house is very respectable and she only takes ladies. You'll be quite comfortable there and I hear she keeps a good table, too.'

But just as he was about to load their luggage into his taxi, a large saloon car drew up and a man got out of it, well-dressed and in his middle years.

Edna clutched Jo's arm. 'I'm sure that's my cousin Clarence! Goodness, he's grown very plump. He was such a good-looking young man, too.'

Well, he wasn't a good-looking older man, Jo thought. In fact, she found him quite repulsive, she couldn't work out why. Maybe it was the

19

arrogant expression on his rather podgy face. She preferred to study his car, which was a shiny black Rover.

He strode towards them. 'Edna? We got your telegram but I'm a town councillor and had to attend a meeting at the town hall today. I'm afraid it took longer than I'd expected.' He looked towards Jo, clearly waiting for a proper introduction.

'This is my stepdaughter, Josephine. I told you about her in my letter. Josephine, this is my cousin, Clarence Rathley.'

'It's Jo, not Josephine,' she corrected.

He studied the younger woman from head to toe and inclined his head. 'Miss Melling.' He didn't wait for her to reply but turned back to his cousin. 'You haven't changed much, my dear. You're as pretty as ever.'

'And you're still a fine figure of a man, Clarry.'

It sickened Jo how Edna fluttered her eyelashes at her cousin – she was nearly fifty and should be past that sort of girlish trick. And she'd just told a blatant lie. The 'fine figure of a man' had a large belly, very little hair left and his mean, pinched little mouth was almost hidden by his puffy jowls. He strutted about as if he owned the world, arrogance personified.

He still didn't address her, but he looked. Oh, my, how he looked! His eyes lingered on her breasts in a way which made her feel as if she was undressed. She hated men who treated women like that.

'Is that your luggage, Edna? My goodness, what a lot there is! We'll send it to the house by taxi

20

and I'll take you and your stepdaughter home with me in the car.'

'I'd better stay and make sure they bring everything,' Jo said. 'If you give the taxi driver your address, he can bring me along shortly, Mr Rathley.' *She* wasn't going to call him cousin.

Clarence looked down his nose at her. 'The fellow knows exactly who I am, believe me. I have a respected position in this town. And a young lady like yourself should leave those with older and wiser heads to make the arrangements.'

Edna made a tutting sound and shook her head at Jo, before turning back to her cousin, 'I'm afraid young ladies in the colonies are rather independent in their behaviour, but perhaps it might be better if Josephine did keep an eye on our luggage. She's very capable about everyday matters. There are quite a few pieces of luggage because I don't intend to return to Australia, and I'd hate to lose anything.'

'Very well, then. Let her do it. You can come with me, Edna. Welcome to Birch End, my dear.' He offered his cousin his arm and his chauffeur moved quickly to open the rear car doors for him and Edna.

Clarence hadn't welcomed her to Birch End, Jo thought, or even given her a farewell nod before walking away. All his attention now was for his cousin. Could he be one of those people who despised colonials, and considered them inferior? She'd met such an attitude on the ship and if they'd been rude to her, she'd treated them in a similar way.

Here, however, she wasn't sure how best to deal

21

with it and didn't want to start off on the wrong foot with Edna's family, so she said nothing.

His booming voice floated back to her. He must be slightly deaf to speak so loudly.

'It's good to see you back in civilised parts, Edna. I never did like your first husband taking you out to the colonies and what were you thinking of to marry a colonial when he died? Life must have been very hard out there for a delicately bred lady like you.'

Jo let out a scornful huff. Delicately bred, indeed. Edna was a plump, indolent woman who ate heartily and never lifted a finger to help anyone but herself.

The last thing she heard was Clarence asking Edna if her second husband had done the right thing by her financially and she paused to listen before getting into the taxi.

'Oh, yes! I have an income for life, and a generous one, too. The money is being managed by a gentleman in Australia who is the executor, and it doesn't go to Jo till I die or remarry.'

'What did *she* get?'

'I believe she has what's left from the sale of the farm.'

'We'll have to look into that. It doesn't seem a fair arrangement to me. You should be entitled to a permanent share in his estate, Edna, and I'm sure a British lawyer would be able to deal with the capital more efficiently than a colonial chappie.'

She dabbed at her eyes. 'I never could understand money.'

The driver closed the door of the big black car just then, so that was all Jo heard. She watched it

22

drive away. It looked expensive and Clarence had got into the back as if he were a duke, with a chauffeur fussing over him and his passenger, so he couldn't be short of money.

What a strange thing to ask a cousin you hadn't seen for over a decade before you'd even got her home: how much money she'd been left. Was that all Rathley cared about?

She was glad she hadn't told her stepmother the full details about the financial arrangements her father had made for his daughter. He'd been right about that being best kept quiet, as he had been about so many things – except his need for female company. In between her mother dying and him re-marrying he had been seen with a series of women in Perth, and spiteful people hadn't hesitated to tell her about that.

Well, that was all water under the bridge now and even though the money situation wasn't fully settled yet, she had easily enough to manage on, thanks to an inheritance from her mother's parents. She wasn't sure Edna knew about that and she certainly didn't intend to tell her.

Now that she'd met him, she wished she didn't have to go and stay with Mr Rathley. She didn't know when she'd taken such an instant dislike to anyone. And yet she'd taken an instant liking to the stranger sharing their compartment. How strange!

As the car vanished round a corner, Jo turned to the taxi driver, who was still waiting patiently. 'Sorry about the delay. You must add something to your charge to cover the lost opportunities for

23

more fares.'

'Thank you, miss, but Mr Rathley wouldn't like that. He knows the taxi rates to a penny.'

'Well, I'm the one who'll be paying you, so it's up to me what I give you.'

The man looked at her warily. 'You're paying?'

'Yes.' She grinned at him. 'Us Australians are rather independent-minded.'

He hesitated, then said, 'Well, if you'll take my advice, miss, you'll not cross that man. Mr Rathley is very much king of the castle in his own home, as everyone in Birch End knows. Anyway, I doubt there will be any more people looking for taxis until the next train arrives, so I'm not in any hurry. Dick Simpson, that's my name. Do you have a list of your luggage, miss?'

She tapped her forehead. 'In here. Those are our things over there, that pile of bags just inside the entrance. Will they all fit into your taxi?'

'Probably. I'd better get out the longer straps for the rear luggage rack, though, if you'll excuse me for a moment.'

She nodded. 'I'll go and check that they've unloaded everything. I should have checked before now really.'

That wasn't like her. She'd been a bit distracted by her stepmother's fussing and then the arrival of the arrogant cousin. She headed off to check that everything was in order.

She couldn't get out of going to Rathley's home for one night, but she doubted she'd stay longer, not if she could help it. But what was she going to do? It would look so rude if she were to leave her stepmother so abruptly.

2

Nick Howarth had helped the two women into his compartment on the train automatically when he saw them rushing to get on board quickly. He'd been hoping for a peaceful journey at this time of day, but there you were. You didn't always get what you wanted. He helped them settle down then sat as far away from them as he could, hiding behind his newspaper.

He couldn't help overhearing what they were saying, though, and if they'd been men, he'd have got talking to them about Australia because he liked to find out about the world. But you couldn't do that with ladies.

As the journey passed, the older one started berating her companion for what sounded to him like a series of imaginary faults, including flirting with him. He was astonished at that, it was so patently untrue, and the newspaper slipped down. The younger lady had been pleasant enough, yes, but not in the way the older female was suggesting, and there had been no sign of her wanting to flirt with him.

Actually, that made a change from what had been happening to him lately, with one woman where he used to live trying to compromise him so that he'd marry her. He had been engaged once, years ago, and poor Dulcie had died of pneumonia before they could marry. Since then he'd not met a woman he wanted to spend his life with.

Mind you, he did find this younger woman attractive, in what he thought of as an outdoor way. She had dark hair, rosy cheeks and eyes that sparkled with interest as she gazed out of the window and tried to ignore her companion. She reminded him of a friend's sister, who was a farmer's wife and a hard worker. He respected such women much more than the ladies he thought of as 'butterflies', who were no use to man or beast that he could see.

He sighed. Even if he had met someone, the hard times people were experiencing, especially in the north, would have made it difficult to make a home together. He'd gone to work in the Midlands after Dulcie died, lodging with his older brother, who'd moved there first, because you could get a job there. Times weren't as hard in the southern half of the country. Sometimes it seemed as if there were two completely separate parts to England.

When the train stopped, he let the two ladies get out first, helped by the porter, then lifted his own suitcases out of the train. He paused on the platform to stare along towards the open square in the town centre, part of which was visible outside the entrance.

Living in Rivenshaw again, eh? The neat station with its two boxes bright with flowers didn't seem to have changed at all, but he had. Life did that to you.

He held back, not wanting the older woman to accuse her companion of encouraging him. Half hidden by a big advertising poster on a stand, he watched the porter make sure all the outgoing passengers were safely on the train before giving the signal to the engine driver that it was safe to leave.

Only when the ladies had moved out through the entrance did Nick pick up his own suitcases again. But on his way out of the station he got talking to the porter, who was now stacking the ladies' luggage in the entrance. They were standing outside as if expecting someone to meet them, but no one had.

'Do you need directions, sir?' the porter asked.

'No, thanks. I used to live in Rivenshaw about ten years ago. Do you think the place has changed much?'

'Not really. People grow older, buildings grow a little shabbier, but we're getting by. Not as bad as some places.' He hesitated, then asked, 'Do you have somewhere to go, sir?'

Nick smiled. 'Yes. Todd Selby is letting me have a room. Do you know him?'

'Everyone does. Nice, friendly gentleman. Married Mrs Willcox from Ellindale last year and he's a partner of Charlie Willcox.'

Nick saw an opportunity to spread the word about his new business. 'Well, Todd's an army acquaintance of my older brother and he's going to help me set up to teach driving. It'll benefit us both. The customers who buy his cars can learn to drive from me; my customers can buy cars from him.'

The porter chatted for a few moments, but kept an eye on the station clock and after a while excused himself to prepare for the arrival of the next train.

As Nick turned to leave, the loop of his shoelace caught on a nail protruding from the leg of a wooden bench and came undone. He bent to refasten it and from where he was kneeling, saw a young lad peep round a corner once the porter had left the area.

The boy mustn't have been able to see Nick because he ran across and snatched one of the smaller bags, running towards Nick to get away. It was instinctive to lunge forward and grab him by the shoulder.

'What the hell do you think you're doing?' he roared.

The lad dropped the bag and kicked out, desperately trying to wriggle out of Nick's grasp.

'Stand still, you!'

At that moment the young woman came back into the station and hearing the lad pleading to be let go, hurried across to join them.

'What's the matter?'

'This boy was trying to pinch one of your bags.' He indicated the bag lying on the ground nearby. The lad was still a child really and his gaunt face told its own story. The famine look, people called it.

She turned towards the scrawny youngster and her features softened. 'Why did you do that?'

The boy jerked as far away from her as he could, holding his free arm in front of his face as if expecting her to thump him. Even when it was clear that she wasn't going to do that, he made no attempt to answer. He was shivering now and trying not to cry, all resistance gone out of him,

'Times are hard round here,' Nick said quietly. 'He's probably hungry. But that's still no excuse for thieving. *No excuse!*' He shook the lad again, not hard, just to emphasise what he'd said, then looked round. 'Isn't your mother with you, miss?'

'She's my *stepmother*, not my mother,' Jo corrected automatically, but her attention remained on the lad. 'She's gone ahead with her cousin. I've been ordered to take the luggage to his house by taxi.'

The sharp way she spoke made him guess she wasn't best pleased with how she'd been treated. Well, he'd heard the stepmother berating her for nothing on the train, hadn't he?

The taxi driver came back on to the platform just then, took one look at the lad and hurried across to the small group. 'What's the matter?'

Nick explained and the man sighed. 'Jimmy, you promised me you'd stop thieving.'

'I was hungry an' so was my mam, Mr Simpson. We've had nothing to eat today an' only a slice of stale bread yesterday.'

'What happened to her job?'

'She's been ill again, comes over all dizzy if she stands up, can't do the heavy scrubbing.'

The taxi driver looked pleadingly at Nick. 'Please don't call in the police, sir. If he's taken anything, I'll pay for it. I grew up in the same street as his mam and she'd be horrified by this. He isn't a bad lad, but the father ran off with another woman last year and Jimmy's mam has been struggling ever since to put bread on the table. They'll be sent to the poorhouse – or worse

29

– if the authorities catch him stealing.'

Nick fumbled in his pocket and produced a shilling but held it out of reach. 'If you'll promise me never to steal again, Jimmy, I'll give you this.' He'd sometimes been hungry as a lad, knew how awful it felt.

The boy gaped at him then at the shilling coin as if unable to believe what he'd heard.

'Do as the gentleman says, Jimmy,' the taxi driver said. 'And thank him for his help. Mind you take that money straight to your mam. She'll get more food for it than you could. I'm sure you can help her round to the corner shop to buy something.'

The boy looked at Nick as if he was a god. 'Thanks, mister.' He looked at the taxi driver. 'I won't do it again, Mr Simpson.' He made a swift gesture of crossing his heart.

Nick let go of his shoulder and gave him the coin. 'You should say sorry to the lady, too. It was her bag you tried to steal.'

He sniffed and nodded. 'Sorry, missus. Only I was that hungry an' someone said they'd give me money for the bag.'

The taxi driver shook his head at Nick as if to warn him not to pursue this, so he didn't ask who'd been pushing the lad to steal.

'Here.' Jo pulled the remains of a squashed Fry's chocolate bar out of her handbag and gave it to Jimmy. 'This'll put you on a bit till you get some proper food.'

'Oooh, thanks, missus!'

He was already cramming a piece into his mouth as he ran off.

'I'll deal with them as are trying to lead him astray,' the taxi driver said grimly. 'They're not going to mess about with *my* passengers.'

Nick turned back to the young woman. 'I hope you don't mind me letting him go?'

'Of course not. It isn't the first time I've seen such things. Some people are having a tough time in Australia as well. Hunger can drive folk to do things they'd not do with full bellies. And he's only a lad. Did you see how thin he was, poor thing? Well done for helping him.'

She offered her hand to Nick to shake. 'I'm Jo Melling, by the way. We didn't introduce our-selves properly on the train. I've just arrived from Australia.'

He'd taken her hand before it sank in how un-usual her action was for a lady to shake hands as a man would have done. 'I'm Nick Howarth, newly returned to Rivenshaw, to start up a busi-ness giving driving lessons.' He'd promised him-self to mention it to as many people as he could so that word would get around.

She gave him a sunny smile. 'I saw an article about plans for driving tests to be required in yesterday's newspaper. I found it lying on the seat in the first train and I've read most of it now. I've still got it in my bag, if you'd like it to read.'

'I'd be interested in seeing the article. I think everyone should have driving lessons before they take to the roads. Some people are downright dangerous when they get behind the wheel of a car. Um, I hope you don't mind me asking but have they left you behind? I hope you've got

31

somewhere to stay.'

'I'm to accompany the luggage. I'm assuming I'll be staying with my stepmother at her cousin's house – at least, that was the plan. I didn't take to Mr Rathley, though, however important *he* thinks he is, so I doubt I'll want to stay there for long. He obviously doesn't like colonials and the way he looks at women, well, it's not decent.'

She rolled her eyes to emphasise this and Nick could guess what she meant. Still, she'd surprised him again. He'd never met a lady so open about everything. She was obviously respectable, but so frank. He liked that. You knew where you stood.

The taxi driver joined in. 'It's not just colonials, miss. He doesn't like anyone as hasn't got money, looks down on ordinary folk, *he* does. Only don't tell anyone I said that or he'll find a way to stop me running my taxi.'

'Is he that spiteful?'

The man shrugged.

'I won't tell anyone. Look, you mentioned a respectable lodging house for ladies only. I may need to go there. Could you tell me where it is, please?'

'Mrs Tucker on Alma Road, Number Twenty-one. Anyone will tell you where that is. It's quite near the town centre. Shall I start loading the luggage now?'

Jo frowned and said slowly, 'Yes ... um, no!'

He stopped and looked at her in puzzlement.

'On second thoughts, how about we visit Mrs Tucker first and leave my trunk and big suitcase there? I can pay her in advance for the room and I'll move there after a couple of days.' She couldn't help shuddering at the memory of how that man had looked at her.

She saw that they were both staring and gave them a rueful smile. 'I really don't want to stay with Rathley at all, but it's only polite. As for Edna, I'm fed up to the teeth with her and her silly mock-genteel ways. I definitely think it'll be good to have an escape route planned in case I have to leave suddenly. I don't know anyone in Rivenshaw, you see, so I'll have no one to turn to if there's a problem.'

The taxi driver was looking at her sympathetically as if he understood, but Nick was frowning. 'Why are you so sure there's going to be a problem? After all your stepmother will be there to protect you.'

She flushed. 'She couldn't protect a flea! It was – well, the way Mr Rathley was staring at me made me feel extremely uncomfortable. I've had to protect myself before in that way. Some men are not – not nice to women. There had better be a lock on my bedroom door or I'll be out of there tonight.'

The taxi driver hesitated, then said, 'Oh, dear. Mr Rathley has got a name for pestering young women, the younger the better as far as he's concerned. You will definitely be better keeping your bedroom door locked. Tell Mrs Tucker why you need the room. She'll understand. She's a very sensible woman.'

Nick scowled. He hated men who preyed on poorer women. He hoped this lady from Australia wasn't short of money. She did sound confident about being able to pay for a room elsewhere, though.

'Well, Rathley has the wrong person if he thinks he can behave like that with me,' Miss Melling said.

'Are you sure your stepmother won't protect you?'

'Not against her relative. She'd blame me for anything that happened. You saw what she was like on the train, accusing me of flirting with you. She only sees what she wants to see and she seems to see faults in me which don't exist. It was just the same on the ship. And now that my father's not there to protect me, she's become spiteful and bossy. I don't know how I've held my tongue at times. Oh well, I can cope with her for another day or two.'

'Why did you come with her, then?'

'I promised my father when he was dying that I'd bring her here. She was at her best with him. It's the only good thing about her. She really did love him, well, as much as she's capable of loving anyone.'

'Ah. I see. What will you be doing when you leave? Will you be staying in the valley?' Nick had asked that before he could stop himself.

'No. But my father's family came from this area originally, so I thought I'd see if I could find any of them. After that, I'm going back to Australia. I don't know anyone here and I've got some good friends there.' She sighed. 'Though I can't go home because Dad sold the farm before he died.'

'I know most families here in the valley,' the driver volunteered. 'Maybe I can help you find your relatives.'

She squared her shoulders and changed the subject. 'What do you mean by "the valley"?'

'Rivenshaw is at the foot of the valley of the River Elm, there's a big village called Birch End a couple of miles up the hill from the town, then Ellindale at the top, though that's only a small place. Mr Rathley lives in Birch End, the higher part, where the nobs have big houses with gardens. The lower end has the worst slums in the valley, Backshaw Moss that part's called and it's where young Jimmy lives. My house is in between the two places, where it's respectable but not fancy, an' most of us just have terraced houses with backyards but no gardens.'

'That's very helpful to know.'

Nick looked at the station clock, unable to think of any excuse for keeping her talking, surprised he wanted to. 'I'd better be getting along now. I hope you enjoy your stay in the valley, Miss Melling.' He couldn't resist adding, 'And if I can ever be of service, if you ever need help suddenly, I'm staying at Willcox and Selby Motor Cars, which is just outside the town centre on the corner of Crimea Street.'

He tipped his hat and moved off. Pity she wasn't staying around for longer. He'd have liked to get to know her better. She seemed such a wholesome young woman with no false airs and graces. Ah well, there you were. You met people and then they were gone.

How must it have been for lads fighting in the Great War, with friends being killed all around them? His brother wouldn't talk about those days, but Nick knew Stan sometimes had nightmares still.

What Nick needed now was to concentrate on setting up his business. He needed to get to know the valley all over again, every single street and where it led, if he was to make his living going round it giving driving lessons.

But first he had to see his brother's old friend Todd, who was providing the car for his new job at a good price and his initial accommodation in a house attached to the car sales yard. Clever business move for both of them, that.

Since his marriage, Todd had moved up to his wife's house in Ellindale, so the one behind the car sales yard and workshop was unoccupied. He wasn't charging rent, thank goodness, and said Nick living there would make his stock of cars safer.

Once he got the car and could find his way round again, Nick would need to start advertising his services, probably in the local newspaper. Maybe Todd would let him put up a sign outside the house, too. There would be even more demand for driving lessons soon if the driving test became compulsory as people said it would.

He'd been saving his money for a while now, wanting to start up a business, planning how best to do it. He enjoyed anything to do with cars and was pretty good at doing smaller repairs on them, too, which would save him money.

His brother, who'd been a driver in the army during the Great War, had taught him to drive as soon as he was old enough. Stan was staying in Leicester, driving a delivery truck, with no ambitions to do anything but lead a quiet life there with his wife, family and the friends he'd made. Nick would miss having him nearby. But this was his big chance.

One day, nearly every family would own a car, he was sure. Not yet. Not till cars could be made more cheaply, not till jobs became plentiful again all over the country and people had money to spare. But that time would come and he meant to be one of the people to profit from it. People laughed when he talked about ordinary people owning cars, but he knew he was right, just knew it, was staking his whole life on it, in fact.

He found a lad outside the station with a hand-cart to trundle his heavy suitcases to Todd's car yard and set off with him. His other things would arrive in a day or two, his tools and various bits and pieces of equipment.

He hoped he could stay in Todd's house for a while. He smiled. He was daring to hope for many things. But he was willing to work hard, and it wouldn't be his fault if he didn't succeed.

3

Mrs Tucker studied Jo carefully after she'd explained what she wanted. 'Let me get this straight: you need a room and you won't be using it at first, but you'll still pay for it?'

'Yes. You see, I was born in Australia and when my father died, I had to bring my stepmother here to England to live near her family. She'll be staying with Mr Rathley, who's her cousin, and I suppose I'll be staying there for a day or two. Only...'

She hesitated, not sure how to put this into words, 'Well, the fact is I didn't take to him, he made me feel, um, uncomfortable, the way he looked at me. So if I want to leave suddenly, I'll need somewhere to stay. I'd like to be prepared. In case.'

The woman looked at her and nodded slowly, as if she understood exactly what lay behind the words.

Jo took a deep breath and risked asking, 'Would you let me in, even in the middle of the night?'

'Oh, yes. And stop looking so anxious. I know why you're asking that.'

'You do?'

'Yes. He has a bit of a reputation round here. With women, I mean.'

Jo nodded slowly. 'Someone else told me that. I hope it wouldn't bring trouble down on you if I came here, Mrs Tucker.'

'He wouldn't dare. Unlike you, I've got good friends and family nearby. What I don't understand is why you would even want to stay in the town if you don't know anyone here?'

'My father said I had distant relatives somewhere nearby and I thought I'd like to meet them before I return to Australia.'

'Ah!' Mrs Tucker looked at her more sympathetically. 'Melling... Could you be a relative of Kath Melling, do you think?'

'I don't know. But Melling isn't a common

name, is it?'

'No, it isn't. Kath's a friend of mine so I'll introduce you, if you like. And I'll give you a reduced rate for the room till you start needing food and other services.'

'Thank you.'

When they'd taken her two largest pieces of luggage into the house, she was left with only a suitcase, her handbag and a Gladstone bag, which contained all sorts of bits and pieces.

When they arrived in Birch End, the taxi driver went through the village to a group of large houses at its northern end. He stopped at the front door of a redbrick house, which looked raw and new, surprisingly ugly too, for all its size and immaculate surrounding gardens.

'If you get out here, I'll take the luggage round to the back, miss. He's a bit of a stickler about only family using the front door.'

'I'll come round the back too, then.'

'Better not, miss. That's just for servants and tradesmen. He has a side door as well, but that's only for people who come to see him on business.'

When she hesitated, he added, 'Trust me on that.' So she moved to get out.

As she reached for the car door handle, he added hastily, 'If you don't mind, I'll come round and open that for you.'

It seemed a silly way to behave to her, but clearly the driver was afraid of upsetting Mr Rathley, so she let him deal with the door, then walked up the three shallow steps at the front as he drove off round the house. When she rang the bell, the door was opened so quickly the maid must have seen her coming. Why had she waited to open it, then? And why was she frowning? What a way to greet a visitor!

'I'm Miss Melling, come to join my step-mother.'

'Ah.' The maid's expression immediately cleared and she stepped back. 'You're expected, miss. Please come in and I'll show you to your room.'

'Shouldn't I meet Mrs Rathley first? I don't want to seem lacking in manners towards my hostess.'

'Mrs Rathley is changing for dinner.' She lowered her voice. 'If you don't mind my saying so, it'd be best if you changed quickly to be in time, Miss Melling.'

'All right.' Jo bent to pick up her suitcase.

'The boot boy will carry that up for you.'

'It's only small. I can easily manage it.'

The maid said even more quietly, 'Mr Rathley wouldn't like that.'

Another person afraid of him. Jo sighed and left her suitcase there, following the maid up two flights of stairs, the second of which were creaky and had only a thin carpet runner on them.

Even crossing the landing had shown her that the first floor was much more lavishly furnished than this one, and must have had at least eight bedrooms. She smiled as it suddenly occurred to her that if Rathley was so fussy about social standing, she was probably being relegated to 'poorer relative' status. How amusing!

To check that, she asked, 'Where is my step-mother's room?'

'On the floor below, next to Mrs Rathley's suite. Did you wish to see her? I believe she's changing for dinner.'

'No, no. I just wondered where she was. I'm sure she'll be very comfortable there.'

'Oh, yes. The bedrooms below all have their own washbasins. The house is very modern in that way. Here you are.' She opened the door to a neat but not very large room. 'The bathroom for this floor is at the end of the corridor. Will you need help unpacking?'

'No, thank you.' She didn't intend to do much unpacking. There was something very unwelcoming about this house, and a heavy feeling, as if unhappiness had seeped into the walls. Oh, she shouldn't be so fanciful!

'The dinner bell will be rung twice when it's time to gather in the drawing room, miss.'

'I see.'

When the maid had left her, Jo went to stare out of the window, which looked down on what was probably the kitchen garden. Cabbages and beans. Definitely a poor relative's view. She chuckled.

There was a tap on the door and she found a youth there with her suitcase. He left it just inside the door and hurried away with a quick nod.

She put the case on the bed and flung it open. No need to worry about what to wear. There wasn't much choice if you were in mourning. She got out her best black crepe dress, which didn't show the wrinkles too badly, and gave it a good shake. She was tired of wearing black. Her father had told her not to bother, but she knew Edna

41

would make a fuss if she wore anything else.

It had been over three months now since her father died, and she was going to make changes to what she wore as soon as she parted company with the silly woman. As if she needed dark clothes to grieve for her father!

Putting a black cardigan round her shoulders and fastening her mother's pearls round her neck, she stared at herself in the mirror, tidying her hair quickly. Buns might not be fashionable but they were easier to manage with straight hair like hers. Back on the farm she'd simply tied her hair back. She blinked away a sudden tear at that thought. Those days were over. You had to carry on.

When she was ready she waited with the door half open till she heard a bell ring twice somewhere below, then made her way downstairs. She hesitated in the hall till the same maid appeared from the rear and opened a door for her. It led into a large, comfortably furnished room, where three people were sitting in armchairs set cosily around the fireplace. As the door closed behind her, she stood waiting, not sure what to do next.

Her stepmother looked up and then sideways at Mr Rathley as if asking for permission to speak. 'This is my stepdaughter, Josephine. You've met Mr Rathley at the station, Josephine, but you've not met my cousin's wife.'

'Pleased to meet you, Mrs Rathley.' She frowned at her stepmother, puzzled at how she'd been introduced. 'I'm always called Jo, not Josephine. You know that, Edna.'

'I do not believe in shortening names,' Mr

Rathley announced. 'It's a very low-class thing to do.'

Jo immediately decided to forget to answer sometimes. How dared they tell her what she should be called!

Mrs Rathley hadn't joined in this name changing or shown any sign of animation in her narrow face. She had her hair tightly drawn back into a bun, which didn't flatter her. When she indicated a chair, Jo sat down.

From their empty teacups it looked as if the three people had been sitting in here chatting for a while, not changing their clothes. Why had she been kept waiting to join them? So that they could talk about her? Probably, and knowing her stepmother, what had been said wouldn't have been complimentary.

They carried on chatting about the town, without really including her, so she studied them. They were snobs. Definitely. As well as ill-mannered to a guest.

'We can go in for dinner now if you're ready, dear,' Mr Rathley announced a few minutes later.

His wife inclined her head, so he rang the servants' bell.

When Mrs Rathley stood up, he offered her his arm and as if by magic, doors to one side were opened. The two of them led the way through.

What a silly way to behave, Jo thought. She joined Edna when beckoned across but before they got to the dining room, she whispered, 'Please stop introducing me as Josephine. You know I never use that name.'

'I agree with my cousins. It's common to shorten

people's names.'

'Too bad. I'm *not* Josephine.'

Edna glared at her, but she didn't care, just took the chair Mr Rathley had indicated as the maid pulled it out for her then sat back to watch what the others did and imitate it.

She decided this was rather fancy behaviour for a man who had started life owning a shop, from what Edna had said about him. Was he imitating the real upper classes – well, imitating the way they were shown behaving in films – or did he consider himself to be superior to others in the town?

Jo didn't say much during the meal. Well, how could she when they talked about their families and the old days, ignoring her most of the time? She listened and watched, though, catching Mr Rathley eyeing her speculatively once or twice, his eyes undoubtedly lingering on her bosom again as they had at the station. This made her feel as if something dirty had touched her and she shuddered.

Her stepmother and Mrs Rathley didn't notice because the horrible man chose his moments carefully.

She suddenly realised that she hadn't checked whether there was a lock on her bedroom door. Bother! If there wasn't, she'd have to find some way to stop it being opened. No, he wouldn't try to come into her bedroom unless he was sure she was the sort to accept his advances. Even her stepmother couldn't have led him to believe that, surely.

Or could she? Had Edna been complaining to

44

him about her unladylike behaviour, exaggerating, as usual? If so, he might consider her fair game, and if he thought her a poor relative, might think her afraid to speak out. Yes, of course Edna would have complained about her 'free colonial ways'.

The dratted woman had been openly disapproving of how Jo behaved when she first married her father, only he had gently stopped her criticising his daughter. After he died, however, she had started doing so again, not exactly telling lies, but exaggerating greatly.

Oh dear! Jo wished she hadn't come to stay here, only it had seemed the polite thing to do. Could she move out tomorrow? She might have to.

Mr Rathley's voice cut into her thoughts. 'Josephine, my wife has addressed a remark to you.'

'Oh, sorry. I was just admiring your tableware. Such pretty crockery.'

Mrs Rathley smiled at her but *he* shot a quick suspicious glance at her, which deepened into a scowl as she added, 'And I'm afraid that after twenty-six years of being addressed as Jo, I can't think of myself as "Josephine" so with the best will in the world I won't always notice that it's me you're talking to.'

His colour deepened to a dark red and he breathed deeply, looking angry. The dirty look he gave her seemed to promise retribution for the way she'd responded to him. That did it! She was definitely going to leave the following day.

The meal dragged on and after it ended and

they left the table, Jo pretended to yawn. 'I hope you'll excuse me, Mr and Mrs Rathley, but the travelling has exhausted me and I can hardly keep my eyes open. Goodnight, everyone.'

She could still hear his voice when she stopped for a moment at the top of the stairs to the second floor. My goodness, he did speak loudly!

'You're right, Edna, she is an impudent young madam and needs teaching a few manners, not to mention respect for her betters.'

Betters, indeed! He was an arrogant snob – and probably far worse than that, from the way people talked about him or reacted to his name.

When she got up to her room, the first thing Jo did was check for a key. There was none, nor was there a bolt. What on earth was she going to do?

The house had electric lighting even upstairs in this part used by inferior persons, so she did a quick tour of the other bedrooms, flicking light switches on and off. When she found a room that did have a key in the door lock, she breathed a sigh of relief and moved her things there without asking permission or informing the maid.

She didn't understand why she felt so unsafe about going to bed. She'd disliked the way he looked at her when they first met, and several times since, but other men had done that. Only, there was something particularly nasty about Clarence Rathley that made her unusually wary and her father had taught her always to listen to her instincts, especially where men were concerned.

She left the curtains half open, not liking to be in the complete dark in a strange room. The bed

46

was comfortable enough but she tossed and turned, sleeping only lightly. Suddenly she was jerked fully awake by a noise outside her door. Sliding quickly out of bed, she saw the door handle turn and heard the door bump against its frame as if someone had tried to open it.

Anger filled her. She wasn't going to put up with that in silence, so she called out, 'Whoever is out there, I'm holding a heavy candlestick and will be ready to hit you over the head if you break into my bedroom.' For some reason she didn't use his name, though she was quite sure who was trying to get in.

There was silence, but the door handle turned back into its normal position and didn't move again. She tiptoed across to the door and thought she heard the faint whisper of footsteps moving away and then yes, that was definitely a stair creaking.

Surely she wasn't the only one to have heard him come upstairs? But if she'd called for help, she wondered whether the maids would have dared come to her aid.

Unable to get to sleep after that, she started thinking what to do in the morning. It would look bad if she simply left the house without a good excuse but she could place no reliance on her stepmother supporting her. However, Jo didn't feel safe staying here, so she'd just have to go anyway. She wouldn't be staying long in the area, so what did it really matter?

As the first pale shades of dawn lit the morning sky, she slipped out of bed and went to stand by the window and stare out. There was a lovely view over the moors.

Maybe she should just leave the town altogether and not look for her relatives.

Would that be cowardly or sensible?

4

When he left the station, Nick followed the boy he'd hired whose noisy, rattling handcart easily carried the two heavy suitcases. That would be well worth paying sixpence for, even with a short walk to Willcox & Selby Motors.

'Stop here for a minute while I check it's the right entrance!' Nick studied what must once have been the front garden. It was covered in asphalt, on which stood five used cars in a neat row facing passers-by. Todd was chatting to a gentleman next to the end vehicle, an immaculate Wolseley Nine saloon. As it might be someone buying a car, Nick didn't interrupt their conversation.

Todd winked at him and gestured towards the rather shabby-looking house standing behind the sales yard, then turned back to his customer.

At the door, the lad helped lift the suitcases from the trolley, then went on his way whistling happily with the sixpence stowed carefully in the pocket of his ragged waistcoat.

Nick heaved the suitcases into the house and left them in the hall. Since his brother's friend was still talking earnestly to the customer, he strolled round the place, finding it larger than you'd guess from outside, with four big rooms on the ground floor, two on either side of the central hall and two behind them. One rear room was a large kitchen with a scullery, pantry and storeroom at the far side of it.

He went back, noting that the front room to the right of the entrance was used as an office and shaking his head at the untidy piles of papers on the desk. He couldn't operate like that, always preferred to have everything neat and tidy.

Upstairs he found four bedrooms, a small box room and a very old-fashioned bathroom with a gas water heater over the end of the bath. One of the front bedrooms contained a single bed, with blankets and sheets folded in a neat pile at the bottom end. The room also contained a huge, old-fashioned wardrobe and a chest of drawers, both empty. As the other bedrooms had beds with thin flock mattresses on them and no blankets or sheets to be seen, he assumed he'd be using this one, which overlooked the row of cars.

He went downstairs again and out into the backyard, mainly bare earth with a path made of uneven slabs of stone, some cracked, with weeds sprouting here and there. It had a coal store and old-fashioned outside lavatory, and a gate leading out into a laneway between the backyards of two rows of houses.

He peeped into the lavatory, where he found a small shelf with a candle and box of matches standing ready on it, and some torn pieces of newspaper neatly threaded on a string hanging from a nail at one end of the shelf. He grimaced. His grandfather had had a convenience like this.

Damned cold in winter, an ordeal in rainy weather.

Still, he needed to use it. Afterwards Nick went back into the house, hearing Todd's voice coming from the office at the front, and the deeper voice of the customer.

His friend poked his head out. 'I thought I heard you come in, Nick! Can you spare us a minute or two?'

'Yes, of course.'

As he went inside the office, Todd gestured to the stranger. 'This is Mr Slater, who is buying the Wolseley from me but who needs some driving lessons before he takes to the roads. I told him he was in luck, because you've just arrived in town and are offering a special rate for your first customer.' He cocked one eyebrow and winked without the customer noticing.

'I am indeed,' Nick said at once. 'Pleased to meet you, Mr Slater.'

As he shook hands, excitement rose in him. He had not only been making plans for setting up his own driving school for years and saving every penny he could to buy a suitable car, but had even visited a branch of the British School of Motoring in a nearby town to see how they did the job. This organisation had opened branches in many English towns over the past two decades, so it stood to reason they must be doing things well.

He'd pretended to be making enquiries about taking driving lessons from them and had found out that these cost ten shillings an hour. When he said this was a lot of money, the man had assured him that the lessons were well worth that, since

50

they covered all necessary basic skills. Further questions produced a printed list of what they undertook to teach customers, which included starting the car engine, controlling the vehicle, changing gear and giving the necessary hand signals, as well as hints on driving safely once their pupils were turned loose on the roads.

He hadn't gone as far as booking a lesson, didn't think he could pretend not to know how to drive, because he'd been doing it for ten years, ever since he was eighteen.

A few weeks after that visit he'd been lucky enough to obtain a job as instructor in a small driving school nearby, whose owner had more customers than he could handle on his own. During his year working there Nick had found he enjoyed sharing his skills with others and was good at it – and the owner said he was, too.

However, he had his own views of what was needed and intended to cover more than the basic skills necessary to drive a vehicle. To his mind, it was essential to be able to interact with other traffic, yes, and with pedestrians. And that took practice.

Of course, driving in a small town like Rivenshaw wouldn't be as difficult as it would in a busy city. But you could never be quite sure what other drivers would do, let alone where you'd be driving, so you should be prepared. A lot of people had been killed on the roads in the past few years, the accidents often caused by pedestrians' lack of understanding about how fast cars could go or by drivers' lack of skills in handling a vehicle in busy traffic. And there were still plenty of horse-drawn vehicles and bicycles on the roads you needed to be careful with. Yes, a lot to cover.

Now that it was likely some sort of driving test would be made compulsory by the government, Nick hoped this would be a good time to start a business of his own. When Todd had made him an offer of help via his brother, who must have told his friend about his efforts, he'd snapped up the chance to make a real start.

He realised the customer was still waiting for an answer. 'The standard price of lessons is around ten shillings an hour everywhere, sir, but as you'd be the first customer in my new business, I'd offer the lessons to you at seven shillings and sixpence for the first five hours – which is usually enough to get most people driving safely.'

The man frowned. 'That still seems rather expensive. Have you had experience of teaching people to drive?'

'Oh, yes. I worked for a small driving school in the Midlands until recently.'

'It's a lot of money for only an hour's work.'

'If you consider my expenses before a client even gets into my car, you'll see that my charges are reasonable. I have to cover the cost of buying my own vehicle and providing petrol, not to mention paying higher insurance fees for the vehicle because of the greater risk of learners having accidents.'

'Ah. I never thought of all those.'

Todd joined in. 'And since you'll be spending a lot of money on your own car and you won't want to damage it, Mr Slater, I'm sure you will want to learn to drive *safely,* so for several reasons, it will be money well spent. My friend here is a very capable chap or I'd not be recommending him. It's only because you're his first customer that you're getting a discount. It'll be ten shillings an hour for everyone else from now on.'

Mr Slater nodded reluctantly. 'Well, when you put it that way, I see what you mean. I'll definitely take a few lessons with you, Mr Howarth. Anyway, I understand I'll need to show I've taken some instruction before I'll be allowed to buy a driving licence at the post office.' He shook his head sadly. 'That will cost five shillings just for a piece of paper! The government must be making a lot of money from motorists.'

Nick knew the signs: this man wouldn't be an easy pupil. 'Well, at least the Highway Code book costs only a penny, sir. You have got one?'

'I bought one yesterday.'

'You should read it very carefully before you get into a vehicle, then you'll know what to expect.'

'Yes, yes. I'll read it tonight.'

Todd added slyly, 'Think how wonderful you'll feel once you've learned to drive and are free to go where you please at the drop of a hat, Mr Slater. Little outings into the countryside or across the Pennines into Yorkshire.'

The customer's expression brightened. 'Yes, indeed. I must say my wife and I are looking forward to that.' Then his smile faded and he sighed. 'She's even talking about learning to drive as well, but I'm not sure women should be allowed to. They're much too excitable. What do you two gentlemen think?'

'A lot of women drove during the war,' Todd

said. 'They even drove large vehicles, lorries and buses, which are much more difficult to handle, and did it as well as the men, too. And we in the forces were glad to have them doing it, I can tell you.'

Nick could see from Mr Slater's expression that this didn't help much. 'If they're carefully taught, women are perfectly safe on the roads, I promise you, sir.'

Todd added quickly, 'I've heard that there is a lady intending to give driving lessons to other ladies in our town, which will be much more comfortable for all concerned.'

'My goodness! Just imagine that! Wait till I tell Mrs Slater! She can be very headstrong when she wants something, but if she's carefully taught, well, it may be all right, as you say, Mr Howarth.' He turned back to Todd. 'Now, I'll just write you a cheque for the car.'

Hiding a smile, Nick left them to it and went to put the kettle on. Ten minutes later he heard the customer leaving.

Todd came to join him in the back room. 'I've had that man fussing about the car for well over an hour today, even though it's a Sunday. I had to come in specially for him. He came to inspect the car yesterday and stayed just as long, but he likes to be fussed over. I thought he'd never come to the point. He's been going over and over the same ground with his questions. If he's such a ditherer, I reckon he's the one who'll not make a good driver, rather than his wife, so I don't envy you teaching him.'

'I've taught ditherers before. I'll manage.'

'Yes. Your brother said you had a good reputation as an instructor. Anyway, Slater's coming at two o'clock tomorrow afternoon for his first lesson.'

Nick looked at him in dismay. 'But I haven't bought myself a car yet.'

'I said I'd find one for you and I have done. You won't get a better bargain than this one, I promise you. It's waiting for you in the workshop. I've been checking the engine over carefully, and haven't found a thing wrong with it. It's a Ford, a Model A saloon, made in 1930, and it's hardly been driven. Good as new, it is.'

'How much?'

'Nothing till you start earning.'

'I can't accept that.'

'Why not? I know you'll pay me back in time; you're Stan's brother. Look, lad, you're better having a bit of money behind you at first when you start a business. You can pay me once you're more settled.'

They haggled for a few moments then Nick gave in. His brother's friend was determined to help him set up. He'd find a way to repay his companion for this generosity one day, though.

Todd patted the upper pocket in his jacket. 'I'm looking forward to paying this cheque into the bank after all the patience it took to earn it. When I've had my cup of tea, we'll try out your new vehicle.'

Nick would rather have gone to look at it immediately, because he wasn't buying the car until he'd tried it out, even on such favourable terms.

He'd had a little van until recently and it had been a good runner. He'd sold it to an eager friend in Leicester before he came here, because it wouldn't have been suitable for teaching driving in. But he'd loved that van.

Todd took a mouthful of tea and waved one hand at their surroundings. 'The house is rather old-fashioned, I'm afraid, Nick lad, but you can bring in any furniture you please and you can use the other front room as your office, if you like, as well. There's plenty of room in it for a clerk.'

'I shan't be able to afford a clerk at first. I'm not certain how I'll manage the bookings. Maybe take bookings in the evenings.'

'No, that won't do. You'll lose opportunities that way. I've been thinking about it. How about we share the cost of a woman to do our paperwork and make appointments for your driving school as well as sorting out my mess? I definitely need help in my office. What do you think?'

'It sounds like a good idea.'

'And you can definitely share the cost of her wages.'

Nick nodded, relieved. He didn't want to feel like a charity case. 'I must pay some rent, though.'

'Well, I'd rather you paid it in kind. Three ways, actually. First, you know enough about cars to deal with queries when I'm not here. People come knocking on the door at all hours, and you can contact me at home if it's urgent. Second, I reckon it'll help my sales if I have a driving school on the spot. And third, the cars will be more secure overnight if someone's living here.'

'I don't know what to say.'

'Say yes. It's a poor lookout if we can't help one another.'

Then Todd grinned, drained his cup of tea and stood up again. 'Come on. I can see you're dying to check the car. Let me show it to you.'

Nick followed him eagerly, giving the workshop only a quick glance, his attention all on the only car in it, whose bonnet was still raised.

It was a very neat-looking vehicle, and as Todd said, it had clearly been looked after. It wasn't too big but big enough to fit people of all sizes and ages. And it had four doors. A two-door vehicle wouldn't have done at all.

Todd gestured like a magician producing something magical. 'I know for certain this car hasn't been driven much. The old man who owned it just went to and from the shops and to visit friends nearby. No long journeys. He believed in looking after his machine and I've checked it for him regularly, changing the oil and so on as necessary.'

'Why is he selling it now, then?'

'He dropped dead a month ago, poor chap. And his sister can't drive, so she's sold it to me. She's moving to Morecambe to live with a friend. If you don't want it, I can always sell it to someone else.'

Nick walked round the car twice, sat in the driving seat and sighed happily. 'I've driven this type of car a few times. Couldn't be better for beginners.'

'That's what I thought. Let's start her up and you can have a tootle round.'

The car started first time after which the engine

chugged gently as if happy with its task in life.

Todd let Nick check it out for a few minutes then glanced at his watch. 'We've just got time to take it for a drive round the block, then I have to go and see someone. After that, I'm going home. Leah said we could go for a stroll on the moors if I got back early. It's grand up in Ellindale. You can see for miles.'

He was still talking as he fumbled in his pocket. 'Nearly forgot to give you the keys to the workshop and front door in case you want to get your car out tomorrow morning before I arrive. I've locked all the vehicles and the keys are in the bottom drawer of the desk in my office.'

'Just one thing that's occurred to me: what if someone wants to buy a car while you're out?'

He clapped Nick on the back. 'You can show the cars and I'll give you commission on any sales. I've left a list of prices in the top drawer of my desk. Now stop worrying. Everything's going to work out well.'

By the time they returned to the house, Nick was utterly convinced about this car. 'I'll take it.'

'Good. I'll get off home now.' Todd stopped again and snapped his fingers. 'Oops. Nearly forgot. You'll need to buy some groceries. Leah said to tell you there's a little shop round the corner. Very convenient and Mrs Nottage who runs it is extremely obliging. There's a fish and chip shop further along the street as well. I used to go there two or three times a week till I got married. Wonderful invention for bachelors, fish and chip shops.'

Nick stood in the doorway watching him lock

up the workshop. 'Drat! I should have thought of that. I think I'd better go and buy some food before I go for any more drives.'

'It's Sunday.'

'Ah. Looks like I'm going to go hungry, then.'

'No need. Go and knock on her back door and explain that this is an emergency. She's very obliging.'

'Thank you. I will.'

'One final thing. Leah says would you like to come to dinner next Sunday – midday dinner, that is? We don't live in a fancy way, mind. It'll just be good home cooking.'

'I'd love to come. How do I get there? I never had much to do with Ellindale when I was living nearby as a lad.'

'Easy. Just drive up the valley, stay on the main road and go straight past Birch End, then on to Ellindale village. Continue straight through that till the road ends at an old track. We're on the right. The sign on our wall says *Spring Cottage Mineral Waters*. There's the house at one side, the business and youth hostel at the other.'

'Fizzy drinks?'

Todd grinned. 'Yes. Only we call them mineral waters. My wife started making them when her first husband took her up there to live, and the business is doing well, even in these times. She sells to a lot of posh folk. Clever woman, my Leah.'

'I'd love to come to dinner. Thanks.'

After Todd had left, Nick looked regretfully at the workshop, but refrained from going for another gloat over the car. He had to buy some food. Indeed, he was suddenly aware of feeling ravenous. He locked everywhere up carefully and walked round the corner, where he found the little grocery shop and made his way round the back.

He endeared himself immediately to the owner by explaining his predicament and asking her help to buy all the basic groceries she thought necessary for a man living on his own. She was beaming by the time he'd added a pound of ginger nut biscuits, a big crusty loaf and a wedge of cheese for his tea and finally he bought two hessian shopping bags to carry his purchases in.

'You just let me know if you want me to save you a loaf,' she called as he walked out of the back door.

Back at the house, he put away the groceries, then unpacked his clothes and set the house and bedroom to rights before it grew fully dark. Todd might be happy in untidy surroundings but Nick wasn't.

The house was shabby and neglected, but it had a nice welcoming feel to it and he sighed happily as he ate a rather late tea and sat on at the table to read the Sunday newspaper he'd purchased at the station.

Well, he tried to read it but he found himself staring into space, wondering how Miss Melling was going on. She had such a vivid face, he could see it clearly still in his mind's eye. Then he wondered why he kept thinking of her. She'd made it plain she wasn't staying in Birch End. Pity. It was years since he'd met a woman who attracted him so strongly.

5

For the rest of the night, Jo only dozed and as soon as it was light enough to see what she was doing, she got up. As she washed and dressed, she listened carefully for the sounds of anyone coming to this floor. She shuddered. She would never feel safe in this house again, even with the bedroom door safely locked, not as long as *he* was there.

She'd made up her mind to leave today, so after she'd used the bathroom, she packed all her clothes in the suitcase. Padlocking it, she left it behind the bedroom door and moved her bag of oddments to join it, then tiptoed down the stairs.

To her relief, no one seemed to be stirring on the first floor, so she continued to the ground floor. If the way was clear, she'd go back for her suitcase and leave the house for good. Mrs Tucker had said she could turn up at any time, after all.

When she reached the ground floor, Jo stopped again to listen. The front part of the house seemed deserted but she heard a noise from the rear and was standing in full view as a young maid peered out of a doorway. How annoying!

'Ooh, miss! I didn't realise anyone was up yet. Did you want something?'

'I'm an early riser and since no one else seems to be around, I thought I'd go out for a walk. It's such a lovely morning. What time is breakfast?'

'Eight thirty, miss. The family eat it in here.' She pointed behind her to the room she'd been working in.

'All right. If anyone asks for me, tell them I'm out for a breath of fresh air. Otherwise, don't bother them.'

The maid hesitated. 'Um. Excuse me saying so, but Mr Rathley likes people to be on time.'

'Yes. I was told that. I'll do my best, but after sitting in a train all day yesterday I really do need to stretch my legs.'

'Yes, miss. Let me unlock the front door for you.'

'Don't bother. I can go out through the kitchen.'

'Please, miss, let me do it. Mr Rathley wouldn't like a guest to go out through the servants' quarters.'

'Very well.' She didn't want to get anyone in trouble.

As she left the house, she closed the door behind her as quietly as she could. It was still early. She was a fast walker and would surely have time to see Mrs Tucker before breakfast and arrange to move in today. The thought of leaving this place made her feel as if a load had been removed from her shoulders.

On a sudden thought she moved back to the top of the steps to peer into the hall through the windows set on either side of the front door. As she watched, the maid appeared in the doorway of the breakfast room carrying a basket of household cleaning equipment and walked through to the servants' quarters at the back.

The girl must have finished that job, so Jo decided to risk going back for her case and bag. She opened the front door again and slipped back inside, creeping as quickly as she could up the two flights of stairs to get her belongings. It took two journeys but she managed to come down without bumping into anyone.

She closed the front door quietly and picked up the suitcase, but found it awkward to walk quickly while holding it as well as her bag of oddments and her handbag. After a quick study of the garden, she hid the two pieces of luggage in some bushes. She'd find a taxi to come back in and retrieve them once she'd checked with Mrs Tucker.

She kept an eye on the house, but no one opened the front door and called to her to come back and the curtains all remained closed and motionless on the first floor, so she didn't think anyone had seen her hide the bags.

Relieved, she hurried out of the front gate and turned towards the town.

Was she being foolish?

No, the mere thought of another poor night's sleep and constant worrying about *him* made her sure that her decision to leave here today was the right one.

And if that upset certain people, too bad. It wasn't as if she was fond of her stepmother, and who but Edna could have said something to give Rathley the idea that his younger visitor had loose morals?

Jo walked down the hill towards Rivenshaw at a brisk pace, enjoying the fresh morning air. The

63

road from Birch End was gently curving and bordered by farms. She remembered the way to Mrs Tucker's house.

What a contrast it seemed to Rathley's home when she arrived there! She felt instantly welcome. The maid who answered the door greeted her with a cheerful smile and showed her through to the kitchen, which smelled delicious. There was a new loaf sitting on a breadboard, with another nearby.

Mrs Tucker looked up and smiled across the room at her. 'Hello, love. What can I do for you?'

When Jo saw the kindly expression on the landlady's face, she felt like weeping in sheer relief. 'Can I come here today, please, Mrs Tucker? This morning, in fact.'

'Call me Mrs T. Everyone else does. And of course you can move in today. You're paying for a room, after all.' The older woman studied her more carefully, her smile fading. 'What's happened to put that look of anxiety on your face?'

Jo had trouble saying anything for a moment. 'Someone tried to get into my bedroom last night. It must have been him.'

'Eh, lass. He didn't reach you, did he?' She dropped her breadknife and moved round the table.

'No.' Jo shook her head, shuddering involuntarily.

'Eh, come here, love.'

As Mrs Tucker put her arms round her and gave her a hug, Jo leaned against the older woman for a minute or two, feeling comforted in a way she hadn't experienced since her father died, then she pulled away and tried to smile.

'When exactly do you want to come? I have to go out shopping this morning, but I'll leave the back door open and Janey will be here.'

'I need to find a taxi, because I have two bags to bring. I'll come as soon as I've retrieved my things, Mrs T.'

'Will they let you do that?'

She explained what she'd done. If no one noticed her getting the bags, she would send round a note to her stepmother later.

'No need for a taxi. Hard to find one at this hour, anyway. My Peter can go with you to carry the bags. He's a strong lad and he'll make sure they don't try to stop you leaving.'

'What? They wouldn't try to keep me there forcibly, surely?'

'Who knows how far that man would go? He has a bad reputation in this town about women and his servants are terrified of him, won't open their mouths to say anything about the family at the shops.' She frowned. 'He doesn't usually attack women in his own home, though.'

'I'm afraid my stepmother may have given him the wrong impression. She considers my behaviour improper – mainly because I say what I think, not because of anything bad that I've done, I promise you. And he's her cousin. She's depending on him to help her settle here, so she'll take his side and blame me for anything that happens, I'm sure.' Look at how she'd accused Jo of flirting with the man on the train who'd opened the carriage door for them.

'Well, you'll fit in well in Lancashire if you say

what you think. We're a bit blunt-spoken round here, too. But do let my Peter go with you, just to be safe. Sit yourself down for a few minutes while he gets ready and have a cup of tea. There's some in the pot.' She went to the door and yelled up the stairs, 'Peter, hurry up. You're needed.'

When both women were settled at the kitchen table, Mrs Tucker leaned back, looking thoughtful. 'What exactly are you going to tell Rathley about why you're leaving? It'd be easier if you had an excuse.'

Jo shook her head. She hadn't been able to think of any credible reason.

'Why not tell him I'm taking you to meet your Melling cousins? And why don't I do exactly that?'

'Could you? Would you mind?'

'Of course not. I'll send Kath Melling a postcard if you'll drop it off at the post office on the way back. There's just time for it to catch the early morning post and then it'll be delivered to her by noon. I'll invite her to come round here and meet you this afternoon, so that you can work out whether you're related or not.'

'You're very kind. I can't tell you how grateful I am.'

'Between you, me and the gatepost, I have a daughter and she's pretty, like you. *That man* tried it on her, took a nasty fancy to her, he did. Luckily my Peter was around to keep an eye on his sister but Meg still moved away from the valley when she got married because she never felt safe again. I miss her.'

'*Didn't feel safe?* What happened?'

Mrs T took out a handkerchief and blew her nose. 'Meg slapped Rathley's face when he said something disgusting to her in the street, and she had a couple of accidents after that, you see. She got badly bruised in one of them, because someone shoved her in front of a moving car. Good thing it was only going slowly.'

Jo could only stare in shock.

'That's how bad he is. So maybe you might be better leaving this town, too, once you've met your relatives.'

And some people thought colonials were uncivilised! She was amazed that a man could get away with such behaviour Just because he was rich. This was the 1930s, after all, not the 1830s!

Mrs T gave her a sympathetic smile. 'Most folk in the valley aren't like that, love, but there are bad people everywhere, no denying it. He and his cronies between them own most of the slums in Backshaw Moss. Just down the road from Rathley's house, that place is. The landlords cram tenants into their hovels, shovel rent money into their pockets and never repair a thing. It's a wonder some of those places haven't fallen down.'

She lowered her voice to add, 'And they let a few houses out to be used for immoral purposes. I won't go into what that means, you not being a married woman, but believe me, it's bad.'

'I have a fair idea, being a country lass.' Her father had always explained such things to her, however embarrassing, because of her not having a mother at an age where a girl most needed one. Edna had been scandalised at that frankness.

'Well, there you are, lass. Eh, listen to me run

on, only I was talking about them slums just yesterday to my friend and we've been wondering what's going to happen to them. We had council elections in the valley recently, you see, and some decent people got elected for a change, so everyone's hoping they'll clear up some of them slums. Who wants places like that on their doorsteps? Let alone they haven't got proper drains and that can spread disease.'

She glanced towards the clock and opened a drawer, taking out a postcard and a pencil. 'I'll just scribble a quick note to Kath.'

That done, she licked a stamp and placed it neatly in a corner, then passed the card to Jo. 'I'll get Peter to take you past the main post office on the way back to Birch End. It's not far out of your way.'

Her son came in just then, a tall, healthy-looking man of about Jo's age. When his mother told him Rathley was causing trouble again, his smile vanished and a grim look took its place. 'What's he doing now?'

She explained and suggested he escort their new guest back to Rathley's house to pick up her things.

'You can count on my help, miss. By heck you can!'

Jo thanked him and added, 'Do call me Jo. We don't stand on ceremony in Australia.'

'Jo, it is. And I'm Peter. I'll definitely come with you, glad to, and what's more, we'll call at my friend's house on the way and ask him to come with us as well. Two escorts are better than one, just in case we need witnesses.'

Was Mr Rathley really so powerful people didn't want to face him on their own? Jo wondered as they left the house. The man must be mad to behave like that. Why hadn't someone stopped him?

She gave the postcard a quick kiss for luck before she dropped it into the slot in the post office wall, then strode out at a fast pace with Peter. She did hope these Mellings would prove to be her relatives. You felt so alone in a strange country where you knew no one. Especially when someone behaved like that to you.

6

When she and her two escorts arrived at Rathley's house, Jo left them outside in the street and went into the house alone. She'd decided it was best to be open about leaving because it would be rude to go without thanking her hostess. Mrs Rathley had done nothing wrong, after all.

She pushed open the front door without knocking and the older maid appeared at the back of the hall, looking surprised to see her.

'Just been out to stretch my legs,' she said cheerfully.

She went into the breakfast parlour and found the family there, about to start their meal. Her stepmother frowned and pointed to a chair, but something made Jo stay where she was, perhaps because she felt intimidated by the way Mr

Rathley was scowling at her. Already she had a feeling that this wasn't going to go well and was regretting making the effort to be polite.

'Where on earth have you been?' Edna demanded. 'We were worried when the maid told us you'd gone out. In a strange town! All on your own! Did you get lost?'

'No, of course not. I bumped into a lady I was introduced to yesterday. She knows a cousin of mine on my father's side and is going to introduce me to her this afternoon. She's invited me to stay with her, so I'll thank you for your hospitality, Mr and Mrs Rathley, and move to her house.'

'You're planning to stay with a stranger we don't know anything about?' Edna exclaimed. 'What on earth has got into you?'

'I may stay with this lady. It depends on this possible cousin. I may stay with her instead. This lady is very respectable, though.'

'You can't possibly go off like that! How many times must I tell you that an unmarried young lady has to be particularly careful of how she behaves. How can you possibly know that this woman is respectable when you've only spoken to her once? Who is she and who introduced you?'

Jo didn't even try to answer that. 'I think I'll be safe with my own relatives.'

'Your father didn't tell *me* you still had relatives here, though he did say his family came from the area originally.'

'He told me about them when he knew he was dying and made me promise to look up my English family while I was here.'

Instead of answering, Edna looked pleadingly

at her cousin. 'Clarrie, tell her this isn't right.'

'A young lady can get into trouble going off with strangers,' Rathley said at once. 'I'm afraid I must forbid it.'

Jo looked at him in shock. 'You can't forbid it. You have no authority over me.'

'I can do as I think best in my own house.' He began to push his chair back.

She'd experienced it before, this sense that something bad was going to happen and she knew better than to ignore it. Not waiting for him to get up, she ran to the front door. But though she got it open, it took a few moments and he caught up with her before she could leave. He grabbed her arm, trying to yank her back into the hall.

'Help me, Peter!' She kicked Rathley and slapped his face as hard as she could with her free hand. But it wasn't enough to get away from him.

Fortunately, Peter had run across the garden and up the stone steps before Rathley, struggling to hold Jo, could close the door on him. He pushed the door fully open. 'Let go of her!'

She wrenched away as Rathley's hold slackened and went to stand beside Peter, her heart pounding. What would have happened if she'd been on her own?

The older man scowled at them from the doorway. 'If you touch me, fellow, I'll call the police!'

Peter moved down the steps with her, keeping an eye on Rathley. 'Go ahead and call them. Seems to me, you're the one who's been touching people. This lass doesn't want to stay here.'

'I'll just get my bags.' Jo moved towards the bushes.

Keeping well away from the burly young man, Rathley followed her down the side of the stone steps and blocked her way. 'What do you think you're doing in my garden?'

'I packed my bags and brought them out here this morning. I'm taking them and leaving.'

'I'm not aiding and abetting you in this immorality. Do as your mother wishes and come back into the house this instant.'

The other young man joined them. *'Immorality!* You know who I am, Mr Rathley. As the son of the Methodist minister, is it likely I'd be involved in something immoral? I'm concerned about this young lady, who is a stranger here, and my mother and father are too. What right have you to force her to stay with you?'

'Her mother has asked me to keep an eye on her, if it's any of your business.'

'Where exactly are the bags?' Peter asked her in a low voice.

'Behind those bushes.' The trouble was, Rathley was now between her and the case.

'Potterton!' he yelled suddenly. 'Help me! Potterton!'

Jo saw a man who looked like a gardener peep round the corner of the house at his employer's call, then bob quickly back out of sight again before his master could turn that way and see him.

Another man was walking along the street and when the gardener didn't answer his call, Rathley turned towards him and once again shouted loudly. 'Help me! These people are trying to rob me.'

The man stopped dead, gaping at them.

Wilf Pollard cursed under his breath when he saw that it was Rathley who'd called out to him. This man was the last person he'd ever want to help, but he didn't like to turn away from anyone in trouble so he stopped and tried to work out exactly what was going on.

He suddenly realised that the young man with his back to the street, who looked to be in a threatening position towards Rathley, was Peter Tucker. That surprised him. Peter was a decent young chap employed by a carpenter in the town. And wasn't that the minister's son? Yes, it was definitely young Fernby.

That settled it in Wilf's mind. It was more likely that they were the ones in trouble if they were dealing with Rathley. Or perhaps it was the young woman standing to one side of the three men who was in trouble and they'd come to her rescue? She certainty looked upset.

He had problems of his own so it was with great reluctance that he moved towards the group, stopping nearby and waiting for Rathley to explain why he'd called out for help.

'These fellows are stealing from me, Pollard,' Rathley said. 'Help me get those bags back into the house.'

He couldn't even see any bags. What on earth was going on here?

'That's not true!' the young woman exclaimed. 'That's *my* suitcase and bag, and all I'm doing is trying to leave this house and take my possessions with me.' She darted behind a big bush and started dragging out a battered suitcase.

Wilf was still more confused. Why would a suitcase be hidden out here? But as Rathley took a step towards the woman, he looked so threatening that Wilf moved too. He didn't blame her for wanting to leave, and could make a good guess as to why she was upset: for the same reason as other young women in the town had been.

He was surprised that Rathley would do something to upset a young woman staying in his own house, though, given how fiercely respectable Mrs Rathley was known to be. He gestured to Peter and his friend to stand back. The three of them mustn't look as if they were threatening Rathley.

To his relief a car drove along the street just then. Recognising it, he yelled, 'Stop that car, Fernby!'

The minister's son flagged it down, arms waving wildly, and it screeched to a halt.

As Charlie Willcox got out, Wilf sighed in relief and beckoned to him. No one would be able to accuse such a well-known figure in the town of trying to steal from anyone.

Charlie got out of the car and came to join them. 'What's up, lad?'

Wilf had to move quickly to stop Rathley going up to the young woman. 'Stay back.'

'Have you run mad?' Rathley asked. 'This is my own house. I can go where I like.'

Charlie stared from one to the other, mouth falling open in shock.

Wilf spoke quickly. 'Mr Rathley stopped me as I was walking past and asked me to help him. He claims this lass is stealing from him. *She* says these are her own bags and she's just trying to leave the house with them. Will you help me sort it out?'

'Yes, of course.'

'You can send those two fellows away for a start,' Rathley said loudly. 'They've been threatening me and I've told them to leave my property.'

'What are you two doing here?' Charlie asked.

'My mother sent us to escort Miss Melling and carry her suitcase. This young lady is going to stay with us. Rathley tried to stop her forcibly from leaving. I saw him grab her and try to drag her inside.'

'*Mr* Rathley to such as you! And you're mistaken. She stumbled and I was merely helping her.'

'He'd grabbed me to pull me into his house. Who does he think he is?' Jo said loudly.

Charlie looked at Rathley suspiciously, wondering what the hell was going on. All he was sure of was that he didn't trust the fellow one inch, never had, never would. 'If she wants to leave you have no right to stop her.'

Glaring at them all, Rathley stayed where he was. 'I didn't ask for *your* help, thank you, Willcox, so if you're going to try to interfere, you can just leave my property as well. I can deal with this person myself if Pollard will keep those two from attacking me. She's trying to steal from me.'

'You liar!' Jo yelled.

Charlie was intrigued. He studied the young woman, liking her fresh face and neat clothes. You could usually tell whether people were decent or

75

not, and she surely was. He couldn't quite place her accent, though. 'What's your explanation, Miss, um...?'

'My name's Melling. I escorted Mr Rathley's cousin from Australia to England and we stayed here last night, as arranged. Someone tried to get into my bedroom during the night, so I decided to move out earlier than planned. Only my suitcase is heavy so I left it and the bag in the bushes till I could check whether Mrs Tucker would let me go to stay with her. She sent her son to help me carry the bags, and his friend came with us.'

That sounded reasonable enough to Charlie. 'Go on, miss.'

'Mr Rathley tried to stop me leaving and is now accusing me of stealing my own suitcase.' She held out her arm to show him the red marks on her wrist.

'All lies!' Rathley said at once.

Charlie looked at the case and asked the obvious question. 'Do you have a key for that padlock, miss?'

'Yes, of course I do.' She fumbled in her handbag and produced it, unlocking the padlock.

'She's stolen the key from the hook in the hall,' Rathley said at once.

She turned on him. 'Another of your lies! What sort of man are you?'

Charlie managed not to grin openly at that, because Rathley was known to tell lies about anything and everything.

She flung open the case. 'Have a look at what this contains, Mr Willcox. Those are hardly a man's possessions. And you'll find an embroidered pouch underneath the clothes, one my mother made for me when I was little. Ask him what's embroidered on it. He won't know because he's never seen it.'

Charlie took a quick glance inside the case, lifting the edge of the neatly folded garments to find the pouch. 'Well, Rathley? What's embroidered on this pouch?'

'I have no need to prove anything to you. I think I'm well enough known and respected in this town for you to take my word against that of a complete stranger.'

Charlie couldn't hold back a scornful snort. Respected! Only by his cronies, who were just as bad as him. He turned back to the young woman. 'I believe you, miss.'

That voice boomed out again behind him. 'You'll regret insulting me, Willcox.'

Charlie swung round. 'Oh no, I won't. You're well known for avoiding the truth if it suits you. And if any accidents happen to me or mine, I won't wait for the police, I'll retaliate in kind.'

Rathley let out a gobbling sound that sounded like an indignant turkey, drew a deep breath and started to speak.

Jo interrupted him. 'I'd rather you checked all the contents of this suitcase while you're at it, Mr Willcox, in case there are any accusations later from this liar. And then you can check the bag as well. I can tell you what's in it before you open it, a fairy with a wand.'

The other three men were standing behind Charlie, grinning broadly now.

'Good idea.' It was, but that didn't stop Charlie

flushing with embarrassment as he did what she'd asked. He found only outer clothing and beneath it underwear, as well as the sort of personal possessions a young woman would need. 'Nothing likely to be yours here, Rathley, unless you've taken to wearing women's clothes. And you'd be too big to fit into these, anyway.'

The three young men chuckled at that.

Rathley drew himself up, glaring at them all impartially. 'I can see that I shall have to be frank about this unfortunate matter, then. My cousin is this young person's mother and she is concerned about Miss Melling's immoral behaviour on the way here from Australia. She has asked me to help her deal with it by guiding her daughter's actions from now on.'

'That's another lie! His cousin is *not* my mother, she's my stepmother – unfortunately for me!' Jo exclaimed. 'And I've never done anything immoral in my life, let alone on the ship.'

Charlie was shocked by these accusations from Rathley, but once again he knew who he believed. 'I think you'd better come round to my house for the time being, miss. You'll be safe there with my wife till we sort this out and nobody had better accuse *us* of condoning immorality.'

He turned to add sharply, 'What's more, if what you've said about her is untrue, it might be called slander, Rathley, in which case, I shall take Miss Melling to consult my lawyer.'

Allan Fernby stepped forward. 'I think we should ask my mother to get involved in this as well, Mr Willcox. As a minister's wife, she has a particular interest in young women whose virtue is being threatened by those who should know better.' He stared pointedly at Rathley as he said this.

'Her virtue is not being threatened! On the contrary. I'm trying to *protect* her from her own foolishness.'

Charlie's snort of disbelief was echoed by, 'He's lying again!' from the young woman.

'I shall wash my hands of this whole business,' Rathley said loudly. 'But you will regret helping her, Willcox, without my needing to lift a finger. That sort of person is not to be trusted. She'll soon be known for what she is.' He turned and walked into the house, slamming the door hard behind him.

Charlie let out his breath in a long whoosh. 'What on earth did you do to upset him, Miss Melling?'

'Apart from trying to leave this morning, what I did was lock my bedroom door last night and threaten to hit him with a brass candlestick if he kept trying to get in.'

Charlie frowned as her name suddenly sank in. 'Melling? Are you any relation to the Mellings of Barcup Farm?'

'I might be. I'm hoping so. I may be from Australia but my grandfather's family came from round here originally. I've arranged to stay in Mrs Tucker's lodging house and she's going to introduce me to Kath Melling later today.'

'You'd be welcome to take refuge any time at my mother's house, if you need to,' Allan said. 'It's next to the Methodist chapel. And we'd look after you, I promise.'

Charlie stepped back. 'Well, I hope things go well for you, Miss Melling. But remember, if you need any more help, Peter and his mother know where I live, or you can catch me at one of my shops. I'm well known in this town and I'm quite sure no one would ever accuse me or my wife of condoning immorality.'

'You're all very kind. Thank you so much. I hope it won't be necessary to ask for further help. I doubt I'll be staying long in this town, especially after what happened today.'

As she turned towards Peter, he picked up her suitcase and they set off. Allan fell in beside them carrying the bag.

Jo let out her breath in a long whoosh of relief as they walked away from Rathley's house.

When the trio had disappeared in the direction of the town, Charlie exchanged glances with Wilf that said a lot more than mere words. 'Rathley's getting worse.'

'I've heard a couple of tales of his womanising lately. They say he visits a woman in that place in Backshaw Moss regularly, you know the one I mean.'

'Packman Alley?'

Charlie let out a little growl of disgust. 'Yes. It's an open secret what goes on in those three houses. Only it's hard to know what to do about that, given that *he* hasn't openly broken the law and there have been no fights or other trouble there. Sergeant Deemer isn't happy about the situation, though.'

'The whole of Backshaw Moss is a disgrace, the

worst slum in the whole valley.'

'Well, just between you and me for the moment, the place is on a list some of us have made of things we intend to draw to the new council's attention. It's more than time those slums were cleaned up, and there's been legislation passed by the government to help us in recent years. Why haven't they taken advantage of the grants available?'

Wilf nodded. 'Good to hear. Everyone's saying how furious Rathley and his cronies are at how the recent council elections went. It's a miracle he got elected again as a councillor. Must have paid out a small fortune in bribes to do it, and even so, it was a close call, the counters said. I'm glad we've got you on the council now. They won't be able to push you around.'

Charlie rolled his eyes. 'It's not a job I ever wanted, but the mayor was rather persuasive about a few of us standing for office and supporting his initiatives for improving our town.'

'I'm sure we'll see a few changes for the better now. Apart from anything else, Backshaw Moss is a health hazard, the drains are so bad. Have you walked round it lately?'

'Well, no.'

'Try it. The place stinks. It's been bad for a while, but it's getting worse rapidly. And diseases from poor drainage spread to the better areas, you know. My Enid wouldn't even move to a house in Birch End because it was at the far end of the terraces near Backshaw Moss and she was worried for the children's health.'

Wilf sighed at that thought. His wife was so

obsessed with the children they'd adopted, she was hardly a wife to him these days, she so doted on them. That's what ten years of trying in vain for a child of her own did to a woman. But he was at a loss as to how to deal with the situation. He realised Charlie was waiting for his attention. 'Sorry. Just thinking about something.'

'While I've got you, can we talk about something more pleasant? I've been meaning to speak to you for a while, Wilf lad. My wife wants a few little changes made to our house. Well, not so little. She wants a room with big windows adding to the back of the house for her to use as an art studio. She loves her design work.'

Wilf was all attention now. Did this mean what he hoped?

'So I got that new young architect to draw up a plan, and it's gone to council and been approved. There's plenty of room for a studio because we've got a big back garden.'

He paused then added, 'I thought, and she did too, that you'd be just the chap to supervise the building of the studio. We'd not want Higgerson's company doing it. They made a right old mess of a conservatory at her friend's house and I've heard that they skimp on quality of materials.'

'I've heard that too, from chaps who've worked for them.'

'There you are, then. So how about it?'

As it sank in what this offer would mean to him, Wilf swallowed hard and excitement ran through him. This would be his big chance to take a step up in the world. He didn't hesitate because he knew he was good at anything to do with building and making things. 'I'd love to do that job for you, Mr Willcox. I wouldn't let you down, I promise you.'

'I know you wouldn't. I've been hearing good things about the smaller jobs you've done for people recently. I'm sure you're more than capable of tackling something bigger. Have you finished the renovations on Heythorpe House yet? Finn's really pleased with what you've done there.'

'Not completely. But I've not been doing everything myself or it'd take too long. I've got a couple of lads I know doing most of the final work there. They're good carpenters, and there are only cupboards and shelves in the servants' area left to sort out now, then a bit of painting. I could come and look at what you need, though I've not done an estimate for a big job before.'

'My wife suggests you do the job and we'll pay the costs as we go along. Subject to everything being satisfactory, we'll pay you ten per cent on top of what it costs.'

Wilf's voice was husky. 'That's very generous of you.'

Charlie shrugged, looking embarrassed. 'We've all had help along the way. And anyhow, we need another builder in the valley. I'd not trust Higgerson to do a job for me and Roy Tyler's getting on a bit. It was sad, him losing his only son. They say he's a shadow of his old self.'

'He's a good worker, Tyler is.'

'No better than you, lad.'

Wilf took a deep breath and held out his hand. After they'd shaken on the bargain, he said, 'When can I see the plans?'

'We've got a copy at home. Why don't you come round after tea tonight, look at the part of the house where she wants to put the studio, and study the new plans? You can see what you think and talk to Mrs Willcox about details. About seven o'clock, say? It'll still be light then. My wife is rather impatient to get it done.' His Marion always wanted things doing quickly, bless her.

'Happy to do that. And Mr Willcox ... thanks again for giving me the chance.'

Charlie nodded in satisfaction as he watched Wilf walk away. He'd been keeping an eye on Pollard and seen him go from strength to strength, given half a chance. It was good to keep an eye out for likely younger chaps and help them on their way through life, especially in times like these when it was even harder for poorer men with ability to get a start.

He grinned and admitted to himself that there was a more selfish reason for doing this: apart from anything else, they usually did jobs more cheaply than established tradesmen, and were so eager to get on that they did a far better job than certain people he could name, especially Higgerson.

He could definitely be sure of good workmanship with Wilf Pollard in charge. And if ever a man *deserved* to have worked his way out of poverty, it was that chap, who was increasingly in demand for small building and repair jobs: a new shed here, a wall rebuilt there. And a whole range of minor renovations at Heythorpe House had been well done and, just as importantly, well managed too, his friend who owned it said.

Charlie wouldn't be surprised to see Wilf end up as a full-time builder, with a proper company of his own. The man had a talent for practical jobs, a real talent.

In fact, it might be worth investing in Wilf, as he had in Todd Selby at Willcox & Selby Motors. That business was bringing in a steady income now. Not a fortune, but every extra pound was a nice bonus when you didn't have to do the hard work to earn it, only shell out a little money.

Thank goodness for the pawnshops he'd started up years ago, when he was trying to make good. They still brought in more money than anything else. That sort of business didn't sit well with some of the snobby types in town, but who cared about them? Not Charlie. Well, not much.

He had a busy life, a wife he loved, though he wished she didn't insist on running a business, and a child of his own, too. He smiled fondly at the thought of little Arthur, who was a lively youngster.

The only real sorrow in his life was his brother, who had been gassed in the war and never really recovered. Jonah had died last year, but at least he had left a son and heir. And his widow had recently married Todd, which had pleased Charlie. Connections were important. They were what made the world go round more smoothly. You could never know too many people if you were a businessman.

He missed having a close friend, though, someone with no axe to grind, a friend like his brother had been.

Charlie blinked furiously, glancing furtively round and hoping no one had seen his momentary weakness. If you couldn't mourn for your brother, who could you mourn for, but what did it look like, a grown man standing crying in the street? Life went on and you either went with it or you sat in a corner on your own and went nowhere.

He had a few ambitions still waiting to be realised, some of them for improvements to his town, some of them for himself and his family. Realising he'd been standing there like an idiot at a fair, lost in thought, Charlie got back into his car.

The Ellin Valley and its inhabitants had been coping with the hard times for years now, but things were improving in other parts of Britain. Why shouldn't they improve here in Lancashire, too?

The council really should look into taking action and using the Greenwood Housing Act to help things along. He'd been reading about it since he got elected to the town council. It had been passed in 1930 to encourage towns to clear out their slums. The previous members of the town council had made only a token effort, with most of their so-called slum clearance aimed at improving the property of corrupt officials. They'd been clever and not many people had realised what they were doing, or if they did, they couldn't prove anything.

Well, things were going to change. Charlie smiled. He tried not to show it but he was rather proud of being a town councillor. Just let him hear of certain people, whose closest friends were dodgy builders, trying to subvert public money from now on. There were enough honest people on the council this time to make a difference.

And there were a couple of lady councillors, too, including his sister-in-law Leah. You had to move with the times and since the war, women were doing all sorts of things. Well, look at his own wife starting a business. Not that the lady council members would know much about building, but Leah was nobody's fool and she'd quickly learn.

He was so lost in thought that he scraped the car on the gatepost as he turned into his own drive and that made him curse under his breath. They didn't build gateposts far enough apart, if you asked his opinion. This wasn't the first one he'd hit.

Marion kept telling him he needed stronger glasses, but he didn't. It was bad enough having to wear any glasses. He didn't want great big ones with thick lenses that looked like the bottoms of bottles, and he wasn't going to buy any either, whatever she said.

7

Jo walked briskly down to Rivenshaw from Birch End with her two protectors, glad to be away from that unhappy house. 'Thank you for helping me.'

'It's our pleasure,' Peter said in his deep rumbling voice. 'A word of warning, though: you'd best watch how you go from now on. People who have upset Rathley find bad things happening to them.'

'I shall avoid him like the plague, believe me.' But would that be enough? Jo was more than a bit concerned that Rathley might do something to blacken her name and could think of no way to prevent him.

What would her new relatives think of her then?

No, surely he wouldn't go that far? What good would it do him? He hardly knew her and if he blackened her name, it might reflect on Edna.

She pushed that worry aside, thinking of her mother's old saying: *Never trouble trouble till trouble troubles you.* It had amused her as a child, still guided her sometimes as she grew older. One thing had surprised her. 'Will the postcard we sent this morning really reach this Kath Melling by lunchtime, Peter?'

'Aye. They're very efficient at the central post office. Pride themselves on getting the early mail out to people quickly. Don't they do that in Australia?'

'I think the distances between our towns are too great to deliver anything that quickly, except in the capital cities, perhaps. It takes over two days non-stop to go by train from Perth in the west to Sydney on the east coast, you know. I was really surprised how close together the towns and villages were here when I first saw them from the train.'

'Over two days? Non-stop?' Allan shook his head as if finding that hard to take in.

Just before they got to the Tucker house in Rivenshaw, Peter stopped. 'You turn off here, lad. We can manage the rest of the way.'

Jo took her bag from him. 'It's not too heavy. Thanks for your help.'

Still Allan hesitated. 'If you need my help again, don't hesitate to ask for it, Peter.'

'I won't. You were a big help when my sister had trouble with Rathley. I shan't forget that.'

'It took a few of us to keep your Meg safe, didn't it?'

Jo looked from one grim face to the other and a shiver ran down her spine. What had she fallen into? Should she leave Rivenshaw straight away? No. That would be cowardly. And anyway, she really wanted to find her father's relatives after coming so far. She had so few blood relatives. She'd always wished she had a brother or sister, but there you were. You made the best of what life gave you and she'd had wonderful parents.

Peter led the way into the house, hefting the heavy suitcase as if it weighed nothing and setting it down in the hall.

As she put the bag next to it, she heard the sound of voices and cutlery clinking on plates from a room to one side.

Peter jerked his head in that direction. 'The lodgers will be finishing breakfast soon. Let's go into the kitchen and tell Ma what happened. Your bags will be safe here.'

Jo followed him; she felt suddenly weak. The lack of sleep was catching up with her, not to mention the sheer exhaustion of living in close quarters with a foolish woman for all those weeks and needing to be mentally on guard all that time. Her father had brought out the best in Edna; she seemed to bring out the worst.

They told Mrs T about the events at Rathley's house and she patted Peter's shoulder. 'Well done, son.'

Then she studied Jo and patted her shoulder as well. 'You look tired out, love.'

'I didn't sleep much last night.'

'Let me take you up to your room and you can have a rest. Would you like a cup of tea first?'

'No, thank you. Just a drink of water, perhaps. You're right. I am tired.'

Peter said, 'I'll take her suitcase and bag up.'

He was down again almost immediately and his mother shoved a plate in front of him. 'I made you some bacon butties. You're not going off to work without some food inside you.'

As he picked up the first of the sandwiches and took a huge bite, Jo drained the glass of water quickly and followed Mrs T up to the pleasant bedroom she'd seen briefly the previous day.

She stared round it again, seeing her trunk and suitcases waiting for her like old friends, then checked instinctively that there was a way to lock the door.

'You won't need a lock in my house.'

'No. Of course not, Mrs T.'

The older woman's eyes were shrewd but understanding. 'If it'll help you sleep more soundly, I'll find you a key. Now, you have a nap. There's plenty of time. If Kath comes to see you, it won't be till later in the afternoon.'

'I will have a rest, if you don't mind. And thank

you for everything, Mrs T.'

'You're welcome.'

She came back a couple of minutes later with a key, putting it into Jo's hand and folding the young woman's fingers round it. Then she left without another word.

Jo fitted the key in the lock, trying to resist the temptation to turn it because surely she was safe here. But in the end she admitted to herself that she'd rest easier with the door locked, so turned the key.

After that, she stood frowning at her luggage, which took up most of the floor space. You had to bring a lot of things when you were travelling for weeks on a ship. She'd need to get some washing done, once she'd sorted everything out.

She didn't expect to sleep, rarely did so in the daytime, and wondered whether she should start unpacking now. If she hung up her clothes, it'd let the creases start to drop out.

A yawn took her by surprise and she gave in to her tiredness, lying down and pulling the eiderdown over herself. Just for a few minutes…

Mrs Tucker frowned as she went back into the kitchen to join her son. 'That lass has made a bad enemy, Peter love. And she has no family to protect her. I hope she really is related to Kath.'

'Aye.' He glanced at the clock and put the last piece of sandwich into his mouth, saying indistinctly, 'Thanks for that. If you can just squeeze another half cup of tea out of that pot, I'll get off to work.'

He gave her one of his serious glances. 'I reckon

things are going to change in the valley now we've got a new town council, as them greedy devils like Rathley will find out. It's a pity all the folk with money aren't more like Mr Willcox, who doesn't look down his nose at anyone and helps folk when he can.'

'Well, he's on the council now and some other good folk with him. I hope they'll get to work quickly. Those houses in Backshaw Moss are a disgrace. It's a wonder they haven't fallen down. And maybe they can stop Rathley and his cronies from preying on people. It still upsets me that our Meg had to move away from the valley when she got married, so she'd be safe.'

She dragged out her handkerchief and blew her nose loudly, then poked her finger into her son's chest by way of emphasis. 'Yes, and it's about time *you* found yourself a lass and got wed, more than time, Peter Tucker.'

He picked her up till her face was level with his and plonked a smacking big kiss on the end of her nose. 'I will only get wed if I meet someone who can cook as well as you, Ma.'

When he put her down, she flapped one hand at him. 'Stop joking. I meant what I said, son.'

'I'm not getting serious about any woman yet. I won't *let* that happen. Not till jobs are more secure. I'm not bringing children into the world to see them go hungry.'

'You've got a good job and it's not likely to vanish overnight. And my business isn't going to go away. Any children you had would be sure of having bread on the table.'

'For the moment I've got a job. But what would

I do to support a family if Mr Cooper dropped dead and that nephew of his took over the business, eh? You tell me that! Vincent Cooper would sell the business in a flash and the person who bought it could chuck me out just as quickly.'

After Peter had gone to work, Mrs T had a little cry while her maid was doing the dining and sitting rooms. She so badly wanted grandchildren to love, as her friends had, and Meg's were too far away to see very often, even if there wasn't the boarding house to look after, a seven-day-a-week job.

Rathley was a wicked man, downright wicked he was, and she prayed every Sunday at chapel that he and those like him in the valley would get their come-uppance. Her prayers hadn't been answered yet, but surely the recent council elections were a sign of hope?

At midday, after the incident with Rathley, Charlie smiled at his wife across the table. Marion was looking very pretty today and when she smiled back, he ventured to ask, 'When can the doctor confirm that you're expecting again, my dear?'

'Not yet. I'm quite sure I am, which is what matters most. I've felt queasy in the mornings as I did last time and a bit sore here.' She pressed a hand against her chest.

He beamed at her. 'That's wonderful!'

'Me feeling queasy?' she teased.

'No. You having another baby. Um ... you'll give up your business now, surely?'

She stiffened and glared at him across the table.

'I knew you'd say that, and I'm not going to do it, thank you very much. As I *keep on* telling you, I *enjoy* my design work, you know I do, Charlie.'

'But people will think I can't afford to keep you.'

'No, they won't. You've only to complain to your friends that I refuse to give up working because I enjoy creating my little designs and they'll sympathise with you for being married to such a terrible woman.'

'They'll think I can't control my own wife,' he said gloomily.

'Of course they will.'

He blinked in shock at this.

'And none of them can control their own wives, either. Well, the decent men can't. I'm not talking about bullies like Rathley or his cronies. I deeply pity *their* wives.'

He tried to get the conversation back on track. 'Marion, please think of me. I'm a councillor now. It'll look bad if you don't stop work and–'

'Of course it won't! In fact, it'll probably be useful to you as a councillor, because women who have to go out to work will come to ask my advice about whether to trouble you with their problems. And *you* will ask my advice about what to suggest to them.'

'Well, you're not to go out and about meeting people when you're all – you know.' He made a gesture suggestive of a big belly.

'What do you think I should do, then? Hide under the table till it's all over?'

'Rest more. Get up later, take a nap in the afternoons.'

'Hah! I'd go mad from boredom. You're talking like my grandfather, who was a bossy old man and how my grandmother put up with him, I'll never know. Now, are you going to let this silly idea drop or do I have to go and wait in my sitting room till you've gone to *your* work, so that I can eat my breakfast in peace before I get on with *my* work.'

He breathed deeply. 'But Marion–'

She leaned forward, thumping one hand down on the table. 'I will *not* give up work, Charlie. Not for this baby and not for the next one, if we do have any more children, that is. Though I won't agree to have any more if you start trying to boss me about like this. I do believe you're worse than you were last time!'

'But I–'

'I'm well aware of how ladies can prevent babies, you know. I've been reading about it lately because I don't want to bear babies non-stop. One of my aunts had ten of them.' She shuddered at the thought. 'A friend told me that Dr Marie Stopes is planning to open Mothers' Clinics all round the country, one of them possibly in Leeds, where my friend lives. I could visit her and get help from them.'

His shock showed in his face.

'Stop looking like that, Charlie. This is 1934, not 1534! Surely you didn't think I was ignorant about that sort of thing. That's real progress as far as us women are concerned.'

You could never win against Marion when she got that challenging look on her face, he decided. And actually the fierceness and the way her eyes sparkled with life made her more attractive to him, as usual. Abandoning the argument, he captured her hand. 'Oh, very well. Do as you please. You will anyway. I hate it when we argue.'

She raised their joined hands to her lips and kissed his hand in that lingering way which always made him breathe deeply.

'I do love you, Charlie, but I can't turn myself into a cabbage.' She tapped her head. 'I have a brain and it needs things to occupy it.'

He knew when he was beaten, so pulled her hand towards his lips and returned the long, slow kiss – satisfied when it affected her in a similar way, making her draw in her breath sharply.

Smiling at this minor triumph, he turned at the door to remind her, 'Don't forget it's the council meeting this afternoon. I may be late home. And Wilf Pollard is coming round to see about building your studio this evening.'

'I'm looking forward to seeing Wilf and I wish I could be a fly on the wall at the meeting. How do the numbers stand?'

'Just about even, with two unknowns, but don't worry. We won't let the people you're thinking about carry on as they have been doing. We want to look after our town, not treat people badly and milk them dry of money.'

8

Nick woke early after his first night in his new home. For a moment he couldn't think where he was, then it all came flooding back. He was back in Rivenshaw, with a new car and a new business of his own, something he'd dreamed about for years.

Though that was exciting, it was also more than a little daunting.

He picked up his watch from the bedside table and squinted at the dial in the paler light of early morning. Six o'clock. Earlier than he usually got up, but there was a lot to do, so he flung the covers aside.

He had a quick bath in the old-fashioned bathroom, revelling in having it to himself with no one knocking on the door and telling him to hurry up.

There was no hot water downstairs because he hadn't lit the fire in the kitchen range last night to heat any. He wondered if Todd ever bothered to use the kitchen fire at this time of year. He'd ask him later. Thank goodness there was a gas stove.

He lit the fire in the range, relieved when it took hold quickly and didn't seem prone to smoking. He'd try to keep the fire burning low all day so that he could sit in front of it in the evening. He loved a cheerful blaze.

He thought about his day: so much to learn

about and organise, and Mr Slater was coming this very afternoon for his first driving lesson. Why on earth had he agreed to do that so soon? he wondered. Well, he knew why – because he was grateful to Todd, whose generosity had given him the chance of owning his own business.

The two of them would be sending customers to one another regularly, he had no doubt. That was how things worked in both life and business: you looked after your friends and associates.

First things first, though. Before he gave a driving lesson, Nick needed to be conversant with every aspect of driving his new car, and also to renew his acquaintance with the main streets of the town. Surely Rivenshaw couldn't have changed all that much? Thank goodness he'd driven that sort of car before, but each vehicle had its quirks.

He smiled wryly. And he had to plan out where exactly to take Mr Slater for his first lesson. Somewhere very quiet with little traffic of any sort, but with reasonably wide roads.

After the kettle had boiled on the gas cooker, he toasted some bread on the fire as best he could, muttering in annoyance as one piece fell off the long metal toasting fork into the flames and refused to be tugged out before it turned black. He cut another slice and took more care how he put the prongs of the toaster into it, then fried up a couple of eggs to put on his rather patchily browned toast.

Once he'd eaten, he cleared up the kitchen quickly, banked up the fire and went out to his car.

Men and women were walking along the street to

work by now, some of them yawning and looking heavy-eyed. Nick felt to be bursting with energy as he unlocked his new car.

He didn't get in straight away because he couldn't help stroking the bonnet then walking slowly round it, gloating at how good the bodywork looked. He couldn't resist walking round it a second time and trying all the doors, sitting in the passenger and back seats. Anyone watching would think him daft! He should stop messing about. Locking up the house, he took a deep, happy breath and got into the driving seat.

As it had done yesterday, the car started first time, a good omen, he felt. He set off to drive round Rivenshaw town centre.

He'd guessed correctly about one thing. The town hadn't changed much since he'd lived here, though some buildings were looking rather shabby. He remembered the layout of the main streets clearly even after several years away from the area because when he was younger, he'd come into the town regularly on his bicycle to visit friends. His family hadn't lived in the town itself but in a small hamlet to the south-east of the valley.

He decided to drive up the hill next, to explore Birch End, which he had only visited a couple of times before and couldn't remember. Kids went where their friends were, didn't they, and he hadn't had any friends who lived in Birch End.

He didn't meet any other cars as he drove up and down the terraces of small but decent dwellings, with older cottages dotted about here and there in the centre of the village. He found a road that led further up the slope and turned on to it, whistling softly as he came to some expensive-looking houses with large gardens. He supposed this was still Birch End but what a difference! He couldn't remember seeing this area before.

When he returned to the terraces in the village centre, he carried on eastwards, slowing down as he came to a very run-down part, which must be Backshaw Moss. He stopped to stare round. Run-down! It was a slum. He'd not bring his customers driving to this part of the valley.

Backshaw Moss consisted of only a few short streets and yards, which ended at an unmade road, more like a lane really, leading to open countryside. He turned the car and headed towards the main road that led up the valley, relieved to get away from the faint smell of bad drains that had hung over the slum dwellings.

He stopped to pull out his watch. It was still quite early in the morning. Why not revisit the whole valley while he was at it, then he'd have a mental map of it? He carried on slowly up the hill to Ellindale, enjoying the more rural scenery. This stretch would be good practice for hill starts, but he'd not do that for the first lesson or two.

As he was driving into Ellindale, he stopped to look at a railway carriage that had obviously been turned into a dwelling. He'd seen that sort of thing before at the seaside, but not out in the countryside. It looked well cared for with a neat little vegetable garden just visible to the rear.

Time was getting on, so he turned round in the open area in the centre of the village and drove slowly back down the hill. He'd enjoyed his outing, wished he didn't have to give a driving lesson today, there were so many business details to arrange.

All of a sudden he realised he'd not insured the car yet and could have kicked himself for being so careless. He drove even more slowly and carefully back to Rivenshaw and parked the car in front of his new home again.

He could see that the workshop was open now but he didn't try to say hello to Todd, who looked to be working on a car engine, just waved to him. Anxious to insure his car, he walked into the town centre, remembering seeing an insurance agency not far away. To his relief it was open.

Only when he'd paid his money and signed the various papers did he relax again.

When he got back to the car yard, he patted the car and murmured, 'Well done!'

He was all set to give Mr Slater his lesson. He'd had it planned out in his head for a long time how he would start with a beginner, based on his previous work as a driving instructor, but with a few details improved. Well, he felt they'd be an improvement and he was going to enjoy the freedom of choosing how to teach people to drive safely.

After Jo had left, Edna looked at her cousin Clarence apprehensively. He hadn't said anything to her about the incident, but was concentrating on his breakfast, methodically working his way through a huge plateful of food. She'd seen how furiously angry he was, though, and that made her lose her appetite completely. His wife had said nothing and was also concentrating on her plate.

Pushing her remaining food to one side, Edna aligned her knife and fork neatly, and waited for Clarrie to finish. She glanced at Gertrude but she was still eating as well. He seemed to go on eating for a long time, so she clasped her hands in her lap and stared down at her white knuckles. She could feel her heart going pitter-patter in her chest.

Why did Douglas have to die on her? She needed him so badly to look after her.

When at last he put down his knife and fork, Clarence looked across the table at her. 'Could I speak to you in my study, please, Edna?'

To her relief, his wife intervened, her voice quiet but firm. 'I think anything you say to our cousin would be better said in front of me, Clarence, so that I can be of help to you both in the future. And given the delicate circumstances, we should go into the small sitting room and close the door first. We don't want the maids accidentally over-hearing what we're saying, do we? You have a very clear voice and it carries a long way.'

Which was a polite way of saying he had a loud voice, Edna thought. He did. Very loud.

He hesitated then shrugged. 'As you wish, Gertrude.'

His wife led the way into the room she sat in during the day and gestured to a seat nearby. 'I think you'll find that chair comfortable, Cousin Edna.'

When they were all seated, Gertrude looked at her husband and waited, head slightly tilted to one side.

Clarence cleared his throat. 'You didn't tell us how troublesome your stepdaughter could be,

Edna. All you did was hint that her behaviour could be extremely unladylike and that she rode out without escort, staying away all day, not to mention hobnobbing with stable lads and farm-hands, and so on.'

'Well, yes. She's not only rather headstrong, but downright unladylike sometimes, well, *most* of the time by English standards. Australian young ladies brought up in the country are – well, un-supervised so often, it's not to be wondered at, I suppose. But she nursed her father devotedly, I have to grant her that.'

He spoke slowly and emphatically. 'What exactly do you mean by headstrong? Did I – we misunderstand you? You seemed to be hinting yesterday that she was immoral?'

'Oh, no! Good heavens, no! Douglas wouldn't have stood for that.'

'What, then?'

'Well, um, she went her own way without seeking my permission or her father's when he was alive. She even went off to work in Perth, though I told her it wasn't the right thing to do. A capital city is not a good place for a young lady on her own, you know, but her landlady did *seem* respectable, if a trifle brusque – well, very brusque actually. Even in the towns, young women in Aus-tralia have more freedom than here, I'm afraid. A lowering of standards, if you ask me, and–'

He interrupted her. 'Hmm. I see. We'll leave it at that for the moment, since Josephine is no longer living under my roof and will not be allowed to visit. There's another thing I've been concerned about and that's your welfare. Perhaps you could tell us again how your husband's money has been left, so that I can help you with your finances if needed.'

Edna looked at him in shock. 'I couldn't tell Douglas what to do about his finances. He wouldn't have stood for it. And well ... I don't always understand figures. But I *do* know, because he explained it several times, that he's left me the income from his money and investments, and that his Australian lawyer will look after it for me and remit it to me here in England quarterly. Mr Pakefield is a very capable gentleman, so I won't need to trouble you, Clarrie. Not that I'm not grateful for your offer to help. I am, very.'

'Are there any restrictions on what you do with that income?'

'Oh, no.' She recited the words her late husband had made her learn by heart, saying it was too important for her to get it muddled as she sometimes did with business details. 'Douglas told me that the income is all mine to enjoy until I die. But if I get married again, I'll get a lump sum of a thousand pounds and the rest will go to Josephine, as it will after my death.'

'So she's without money until then, dependent upon you?'

'Um. Not exactly.'

He looked at her in exasperation and was about to say something sharp when his wife intervened again, clearing her throat and shooting him a warning glance before asking, 'What do you mean by that, Edna dear?'

'Well, Josephine has some money that came to her from her mother. I don't think it's a lot, or

104

why would she have had to get a job when she went to live in Perth? I'm sure *I* have never gone out to work, even before my first marriage. But I don't know exactly how much it is. When I asked Douglas, he said his daughter was very well able to manage her money and I was not to worry about her. And I don't, because she's always been good at figures and her job was something to do with accounting.'

She looked to her cousin anxiously and he scowled at her again, so she turned a pleading gaze on his wife.

'Is Josephine's income enough to live on comfortably, do you think, Edna, or just to manage on?' Gertrude prompted.

'I don't know for certain, but she doesn't buy a lot of clothes. She mostly makes her own and she re-made her mother's old clothes for herself as she grew up – just imagine that – so she can't have a lot of money to play with, can she?'

'One would guess not,' Gertrude said in a soothing tone.

'I had better keep an eye on what that young woman is doing, if she stays in the valley,' Clarence declared. 'If only to make sure she doesn't land the family in a scandal or get into debt.'

'I don't think she intends to stay long in Lancashire, Clarrie, just till she's found her father's relatives.'

His voice was sharp. 'I presume they'll be the local Mellings bunch?'

'I'm not sure. Her relatives can't all be Mellings, can they? I mean, women change their names when they marry – why, I've done that twice already myself. Her father always said she probably had relatives here on her mother's side.'

Gertrude glanced at her husband and again interrupted hastily. 'I think that's enough questions for now, Clarence. I'm sure you have plenty to keep you busy at work. I shall take your cousin into Rivenshaw today and show her our shops. You'll enjoy that, won't you, Edna?'

'Oh, yes. I love shopping.'

'And I'll introduce you to some other ladies during the next few days.'

'I shall look forward to making new friends.'

'Next week we can give a dinner party to welcome her, Clarence. I'll draw up a guest list for you to approve. Then I'll help Edna find a new home to live in.'

On that thought she turned again to Edna. 'Shall you have enough income coming in to rent a nice home and hire a couple of maids, do you think, or will you have to live in rooms?'

'Well, Douglas said I would have more than enough to live on and *he* ought to know, but I'm not sure exactly how much will be coming in, only that it'll be paid into my bank account in Australia every quarter and then transferred to my English bank account. I'm to write to Mr Pakefield once I've visited the bank here and set up a new account. But I'd be truly grateful if you could help me do that.'

'Of course I'll help you,' Clarence tried to hide his irritation. His cousin was proving to be amazingly stupid. But she was a pretty woman, much nicer to look at than his wife. And blood was thicker than water. But if he could get hold of her money and manage it for her, he would. Why should some Australian lawyer benefit from the interest it could earn?

He'd also see if something could be done about the stepdaughter taking nearly all the money if Edna remarried. Apart from the fact that he'd like to keep the money in the family, he didn't like the thought of a young woman controlling large sums of money. Women didn't know how to manage their finances. And Douglas Melling had clearly been well off, because the ladies had sailed to England first class.

How well off? He'd have to find out.

He caught his wife's eye and stood up. He wasn't pleased at Gertrude's intervention but he knew better than to cross her in any household or social matter. If he did, his life inevitably became very uncomfortable.

They lived comfortably separate lives, because she was a cold fish in bed. He'd not have put up with her interfering in his business matters, but it kept her happily busy to manage the house and keep in touch with ladies from other useful families. And her family had some very useful connections, which was why he'd married her in the first place.

He had somehow never managed to control her social life, though, because she also regularly visited one or two ladies from families he'd rather not deal with. When he'd protested about this, she'd insisted it wouldn't do to get on bad terms with people from those particular county families. He could understand that but unfortunately, women didn't always think of the implications of careless sharing of information when they were gossiping with their friends, especially when those same women had been at school together.

He scowled as he considered how his cousin had misled him about Josephine's character and morals. He'd made a bad mistake there. Thank goodness that young woman hadn't accused him of anything this morning. Well, she couldn't have done, because she hadn't seen who was at her bedroom door.

She'd guessed it was him, though, damn her! What else could have made her change bedrooms? He'd told the maid which one to put her in, and the girl had said this morning that she'd done as instructed. She hadn't known Miss Melling had changed to another bedroom until he mentioned it.

Surely all that meant his original suspicion that Josephine was not an innocent young woman was correct?

The incident had left him feeling edgy and unsatisfied, needing a woman. If his wife suspected that he had this driving need for the services of other women in bed, she had never shown it. Gertrude had never been much fun in bed, not even when she was younger and quite pretty. Strange how plain she'd become as she grew older, and she dressed frumpishly, too, stupid bitch.

The two of them hadn't shared a bedroom for years, not since the birth of their second child – a son, thank goodness. After that Gertrude had begun having severe headaches, which the doctor had said might have been caused by bearing children.

That had turned out better than he'd expected. Having his own bedroom had rather suited Clarence. He was a man who liked a little liveliness in bed, of the sort to be found only among the lower classes, he had come to realise.

He also had his own room downstairs with French windows on to the side garden. That made it easy to come and go late at night without anyone else in the house knowing about it.

Now, that was enough thinking about personal matters. He had work to do and the first meeting of the new town council was this afternoon. That was another serious worry. Its new members had to be made to toe the line and not betray their class. There was usually a way to bring them to heel. Everyone had a weakness or two. Thank goodness the mayor's group hadn't won an outright majority. He'd have to make sure the two independent councillors didn't vote the wrong way.

9

Jo woke with a start, then realised where she was and that someone was knocking on her bedroom door. 'Yes?'

'You'd better get up now, lass. It's nearly two o'clock.'

She glanced at her bedside travel clock and gasped. She *never* normally slept in the daytime, let alone for several hours. 'Yes, right. Thanks for waking me up, Mrs T. I'll only be a few minutes.'

'Good. I'll have something ready for you to eat.'

'I can wait till teatime.'

'Not in *my* house, you can't. I feed my lodgers properly.'

There was the sound of footsteps going heavily down the stairs and fading into the nether regions. Jo rushed to the bathroom, studied herself in the mirror and sighed over how crumpled her skirt was. Well, there wasn't time to iron it now.

When she went down to the kitchen, Mrs T turned to give her a sunny, welcoming smile. 'There. You look a bit better now.'

Jo had to swallow hard at those kind words. Such a contrast to Edna's behaviour towards her.

'Sit down, love. I made you a cheese sandwich and there's a piece of my fruit cake to finish off with.'

'Thank you. You're so kind.'

'Am I? Well, it's a poor lookout if we can't help a stranger from a faraway land – or someone who lives next door.' She turned back to take a quick peep into the oven, which, judging by the wonderful smell emanating from it, contained another cake.

When Jo had finished she carried the dirty plate and cup into the scullery and called, 'Shall I wipe these dishes for you?'

'That'd be a help, if you don't mind. It's the girl's afternoon off and I'm a bit behind.'

Twenty minutes later the front door knocker went.

'That'll be Kath.' Mrs T wiped her hands on a

towel and disappeared up the stairs to the front door.

There was the sound of voices but the women were speaking too quietly for Jo to make out what they were saying. She couldn't help wondering if they were talking about her, but she wasn't the sort to eavesdrop, so stayed in the kitchen.

When they came downstairs she eagerly studied the woman who'd come to meet her and was disappointed to find no resemblance whatsoever to her father or his parents.

'Kath, this is Jo. Sit down and I'll make us all a fresh cup of tea, then we'll have a chat about her family, see if you could be related to one another.'

The visitor sat opposite Jo, studying her. 'You've come all the way from Australia, eh? Is it as sunny as they say?'

'The weather's different in each state. At this time of year, it's winter where I come from in the west near Perth, so it'll be cold and rainy, but with intermittent sunny spells. It's hot in summer and hardly ever rains then for months.'

'Fancy that.' She bent to fumble in her shopping bag. 'I was talking to my mother about you. Wonderful memory she has still, for all she's nearly ninety.' She pulled out a large and very handsome leather-bound book and put it on the table, patting it as if it was an old friend. 'This is our family tree. It's been used for nearly two hundred years. We write down everyone we know about, so we'll be able to add your name to a branch now if we can find a connection.'

She opened the book carefully at a page where a piece of red ribbon stuck out. 'We think we've

found some possibilities. What was your grandfather's full name? There are two John Mellings
of roughly the right age who left Lancashire, and
we've never been sure what happened to either of
them.'

'He was John Tayner Melling.'

'Aha! That's one of them, so no need to even
look at the other, because he's John Henry Melling.' She pushed out the chair next to hers and
patted it. 'You'll see better if you come round and
sit by me.'

Jo did as she asked and stared at the beautifully
written names. So many connections were tapped
and mentioned as Kath took her through the
pages. How she envied the English side of her
family having that record!

'John Tayner Melling was a second cousin once
removed, and he would be distantly related to
both your father and mother. Most of that branch
of the family went to live in the south in the
middle of the nineteenth century.' Kath paused
for a moment, looking suddenly disapproving.
'There are only a few Tayners in the valley still,
and they'll be your closest relatives, but they're
the black sheep of our family connections, I'm
afraid. We don't speak to them, not even to say
good morning.'

'Why? What have they done?'

'Freddie Tayner was a drunkard. He beat his
wife and spent most of what money he did earn
on boozing and betting. He was brought up
before the magistrates a few times, and jailed for
a few weeks here and there, too. He's dead now,
didn't make old bones, but his daughter still lives

in Backshaw Moss, and she's ... um, not respectable. Which just goes to show that the apple doesn't fall far from the tree, does it?'

'I don't know much about this Backshaw Moss, except I gather it's a slum.'

'That's the point! It's the worst place in the whole valley. That branch of the family don't care about whether you're a relative or not: all they'd want from us would be money to gamble away or waste.'

'Oh dear.'

Kath waited a moment or two, then said gently, 'Now, where were we? Oh yes, your grandfather. Was your father his only child in Australia?'

'Yes. His full name was Douglas Matthew Melling, and my mother was Catherine Jayne born a Charter.'

Kath was scribbling on a scrap of paper. 'Well, I'm sorry you and I aren't more closely related but that won't stop us accepting you as a distant member of the family. You must come out to visit the farm one day. I'll get back to you in a week or two, when we're not so busy.'

'What about the remaining Tayners? How do I find them?'

'You won't want to have anything to do with them two, I promise you. In fact, you should stay away from Backshaw Moss if you value your purse and safety.' She changed the subject firmly and Mrs T shook her head warningly, so Jo didn't pursue the point.

The three of them chatted for a little longer then Kath said she had another appointment and left.

Jo felt very let down.

When Mrs T came back from showing her guest out, Jo asked, 'Why didn't you want me to ask for more information about the Tayners?'

'There's bad blood between them and Kath's family. It'd only upset her.'

'Do *you* know their names and addresses?'

Mrs T hesitated.

'I've come so far. I'd like at least to meet them.'

'Well, Freddie's daughter is called Moira – her mother was Irish – and Moira's got a daughter called Tess, I think. Yes, definitely Tess. She'd be a fair bit younger than you, about fourteen now, I should think.'

'That makes her twelve years younger than me. Where exactly do they live and what's so bad about them?'

Mrs T shrugged. 'Who knows exactly where they live? The houses in Backshaw Moss are mostly let out by the room, and people move about a lot.'

When Jo looked at her sceptically, Mrs T flushed and said, 'I really don't know for certain, but what Kath didn't tell you is that Moira is – well, she's a – you know – fallen woman.' She flushed scarlet as she added, 'I don't know any-thing about the daughter. They start that sort of thing young, though.'

'Oh.' That was the last thing Jo had expected.

Mrs T hesitated, then said, 'You could speak to Allan's mother, just to confirm it. Mrs Fernby will know more about them, if anyone will. She helps run a home for women like that who want to make a new start.'

'I see.' Jo didn't think she'd get anything more

out of Mrs T, so let the matter drop. She might want to find out more about these Tayners, or she might not. She'd have to think about it.

She let out a gurgle of sudden laughter when she realised how outraged her stepmother and Rathley would be at the news of this connection but was glad that Mrs T didn't hear her laugh, as she didn't want to seem to be making light of such a shocking state of affairs.

Mr Slater turned up at the car yard for his driving lesson at a couple of minutes before two o'clock, as arranged, beaming like a child expecting a treat. Nick began the introductory talk and questions that he'd carefully worked out to make sure a pupil understood the rules of the road.

But this pupil didn't seem to be concentrating. Well, the man wasn't going to get behind the wheel of Nick's new car until he'd listened properly and demonstrated a sound knowledge of the rules. What sort of chaos would there be if everyone went their own way on public roads? The world had changed, many vehicles moved faster, but some people thought they could still amble about without looking where they were going and especially without watching out for cars. You read about road accidents in the newspapers all the time.

In the end he said bluntly, 'I'm afraid you're not listening to me, Mr Slater.'

His pupil made a little huffing noise. 'Well, I've come here to learn to drive a car, not listen to you talk at me.'

'The Highway Code is more important than you

seem to realise. I won't let you into my car until I'm sure you have a sound understanding of the basics,' Nick said firmly. 'I can understand that you're eager to start the actual driving, but it's more complicated than you seem to realise. Until you understand the rules, you won't know what to do yourself or what to expect other drivers to do.'

When the man scowled and said nothing, he added slowly and emphatically, 'People can get *killed* in car accidents, Mr Slater. How would you feel if someone killed your wife by driving care-lessly or doing something the other drivers weren't expecting? Or if you killed some other person's child because you hadn't done what was expected at a road junction?'

There was dead silence as Nick waited for this to sink in.

'By gum, you don't mince your words, do you? I'm the one as is paying for driving lessons, though, and I know what I want from you. I can take care of the rest in my own time.'

'And I bear the responsibility of teaching you to drive *safely!* For your own and everyone else's sake.' Once again, Nick waited, seeing the exact moment when the older man's shoulders sagged and he gave in.

Fifteen minutes later, they went outside. Nick got into the driving seat and, explaining exactly what he was doing and why, took them to a place he'd noted on the outskirts of town, a fairly wide stretch of road near a scrubby piece of open land. 'Right. You can have your first try at driving the car here.'

The enormity of what he was about to do

116

seemed to strike Mr Slater all of a sudden and he hesitated by the open car door before getting into the driving seat and clasping the steering wheel so tightly his fingers seemed bloodless.

Patiently, Nick outlined again what to do then waved his hand. 'You've watched me drive. Now you start the engine and let's see how you go.'

After a few attempts, Mr Slater managed not to stall the car engine as he tried to put the car into gear. As the minutes passed, he managed to drive along the quiet road very slowly indeed, mostly in second gear.

When Nick said to stop, he noticed that his pupil was sweating.

Mr Slater pulled out a big handkerchief and mopped his forehead. 'It's harder than it looks, isn't it?'

'Yes. Much harder. But you did quite well.'

'I did?' He looked astonished.

'Yes. Definitely.'

'Oh. Well. That's all right, then.' He relaxed visibly, then said, 'I was wrong to want to rush it.'

'Yes. But you're not alone in that. I'll drive us back today and talk about what I'm doing again, so listen carefully now you know how it feels and watch what other drivers are doing. Tomorrow I'll take you somewhere else for a longer practice drive if you'll promise to read your Highway Code again tonight. I'll be asking you some questions tomorrow to check.'

'Right.'

'But I'll still drive in the centre of town tomorrow. The day after that, if you're doing all right with the driving, you can take us back to the car yard. Then the day after we'll drive round the town centre mainly for you to get used to meeting a lot more vehicles, buses and lorries as well as cars.'

Mr Slater nodded.

When they got back to the car yard, he was about to walk away, so Nick called, 'You haven't paid me.'

'Eh, sorry! I were that nervous I forgot.'

His pupil might or might not have forgotten, but this incident made Nick decide to ask for payment *before* any lessons were given in future.

He went inside and made himself a strong pot of tea to share with Todd. He needed it. Mr Slater hadn't been the only nervous person in the car.

10

Later that afternoon, the members of the town council began to assemble for their first meeting since the election. Charlie Willcox peeped in and saw that the council chamber was still almost empty so waited outside in the lobby for someone he knew to arrive.

Leaning against the wall, he watched others come in, people he knew only by sight, members in the middle of their six-year term as councill ors. They moved into the main chamber confidently, but he still waited near the doorway.

He half wished he hadn't taken this on. He reckoned most people only used their council

118

positions to further their own interests. He didn't intend to do that, but was suddenly feeling unsure of what he'd be able to contribute.

The mayor, Reginald Kirby, was already in place at the far end of the big chamber, sitting at the head of a shorter table set crosswise between two longer tables. His had been a surprise appointment last time, because he wasn't allied to the entrenched group, but he hadn't been able to do much to help the town without a majority of the council behind him. He was attended by a clerk ready to take notes for the minutes.

Thank you for dragging me into this, Reg, Charlie thought as he stared sourly at the mayor.

One of the town's two lawyers, also newly elected as a councillor, strolled into the antechamber and stopped beside him. 'Looking forward to it, old chap?'

He knew Henry Lloyd well enough to tell the truth. 'No.'

With a chuckle, Henry moved on. He didn't seem in the least nervous, damn him.

Charlie was about to follow him inside when a couple came into the antechamber: his sister-in-law, Leah, and her second husband, Todd. He gave Leah a hug and shook Todd's hand, then fell in behind them, feeling better.

That didn't last long. As he walked through the big doors, he felt swallowed up by the large, wood-panelled room with its row of high, stained-glass windows along the outer wall of the building. The afternoon light was still shining through these and that made him feel as if he were in church.

Todd went to sit next to the top table, with Leah beside him. They beckoned Charlie to take the seat between her and the lawyer, who was busy straightening some papers and aligning a small notepad very precisely in front of himself.

Well, at least he'd be among friends there, Charlie thought as he joined them.

Henry leaned towards him and whispered, 'Do you think we'll get much done today, Charlie?'

'I doubt it. But whatever we do or don't do during our sessions, it won't be as little as the last council achieved. That's one of the few things I'm sure of. Trouble is, we've still got some of *them* left to deal with. See if they don't try to hinder us if we put forward ideas for improvements to our town.'

The lawyer nodded and his expression turned grim as he saw who was coming in.

'Talk of the devil. Here's the leader of their merry band.' Charlie watched Clarence Rathley walk into the council chamber as if he owned it, followed closely by two of his cronies. All three of them stopped just inside the door, blocking the entrance for a few moments, then sauntering forward a short distance to take seats at the door end of the table, as if deliberately sitting as far away from the mayor as they could.

'They look like three fat turkeys ready to be roasted,' Charlie whispered to his neighbour.

Henry let out a splutter of laughter, which he tried in vain to disguise as a cough. 'I think they look more like dogs that have been marking out their territory for years and are ready to do it again to frighten away new arrivals.'

As if to confirm this summary, the newcomers scowled across the room, their eyes lingering on Charlie and his companions but sliding over Leah as if she were invisible. When they had noisily settled themselves, interrupting everyone else's conversations, they began whispering to one another.

Charlie tried to hear what they were saying, but for once Rathley was speaking quietly.

Two more of the town's businessmen appeared, one sitting next to Rathley's group, smiling and nodding at them, the other, who gave only a vague nod to those already in the room, sitting next to Henry but saying nothing.

Finally the three last members of the council arrived, a woman and two men. The men sat at the end of Rathley's group and the woman went to sit on her own in the last empty chair, which was at the door end of Charlie's side. She gave everyone a quick nod, then stared down at her clasped hands.

'It's going to prove interesting when we're voting,' Henry whispered. 'Reg didn't quite get the numbers he wanted. Nor did Rathley.'

The mayor tapped a little silver gavel to gain their attention. 'Now that everyone is here, I have pleasure in declaring this meeting of the new town council open. When I've finished speaking, perhaps you'll each say your name and that of the ward you represent, plus briefly what your occupation is.'

As he paused for another look round, Rathley stood up.

The mayor held up one hand to stop him speaking. 'I haven't finished yet, Mr Rathley. We'll do this in an orderly manner, if you don't mind, starting with the row on my left and then going along it and coming back to me down the row on my right.'

Scowling, Rathley sat down again, saying loudly to the man next to him, 'As if we don't all know one another, by sight at least.' He reshuffled his papers loudly.

The mayor waited till he'd stopped fidgeting with them then continued, 'First I'd like to welcome all the new members and hope you'll do well by our town. In times like these, the people who live in the valley need all the help and support we can give them, not just those who pay rates.'

There was a murmur of voices as some responded with 'Hear, hear.'

Charlie noticed that Rathley had not joined in.

'I think you all know our new chief clerk, Maurice Jefferson, who is taking the minutes today. His newly promoted deputy is Mrs Helen Westing, who will be in charge of staff and records. We couldn't have a better pair for understanding how things are done in Rivenshaw. Sadly, as you probably know, our former deputy clerk proved untrustworthy and is currently in police custody awaiting trial.'

There was dead silence for a few moments, then the mayor gestured to Todd, who was sitting nearest to him. 'Mr Selby, perhaps you'll begin? And since you're a relative newcomer to our town, perhaps you'd outline briefly your background before you came here and add any information you consider pertinent to your new role.'

Todd stood up, smiling quickly down at his wife then letting his smile fade as his gaze lingered on Rathley and his group at the door end of the table. 'I'm Todd Selby. I served in the army during the war and when it ended I went off to see a bit of the world, going as far as Australia. I'm sure this experience will be of benefit to the valley. It's good to know about different ways of doing things. I represent the Rivenshaw West ward and I currently sell and repair motor cars.'

The mayor inclined his head. 'Mrs Selby.'

His wife introduced herself next. 'I'm Leah Selby. I own the fizzy drinks factory and also the youth hostel there in Ellindale, which is also the ward I represent. I hope to be able to contribute most to matters affecting employment, women's and families' needs.'

Rathley made a loud disgusted sound at this.

Leah studied him as if he were an insect crawling across her plate, a cool look that said a lot more than words about her opinion of him.

Charlie saw him flush slightly as she outstared him and smiled slowly. His sister-in-law was a quiet person, but she had a calm dignity that somehow made people listen to her, and she got things done.

'Mr Willcox?'

Charlie didn't waste time on a long introduction. Everyone knew him. 'I own two pawnshops, the electrical goods shop and a few pieces of property in town. I represent the Birch End ward and it's where I live. I'd like to think I can speak for businesses and I'm particularly interested in improving the town's amenities.'

'Mr Lloyd?'

The lawyer spoke briefly, but in a beautifully modulated voice that figured prominently in the church choir, ending, 'I represent the Rivenshaw East ward.'

One by one, the others stood up and introduced themselves. The other female councillor spoke quietly but clearly, looking calm in spite of Rathley and his friends rudely gazing elsewhere during her introduction.

Charlie had heard Rathley and the man next to him rant on, even during the Great War, about a woman's place being in the home. They said very little about themselves when it was their turn, and their scorn, not only for the two women councillors but for all the people on the other side of the table was all too obvious.

When the introductions were over, the mayor took over again. 'Just to recapitulate for the benefit of the new councillors, when we ended our last term of office, we were in the middle of discussing, and not for the first time, how we can use the provisions of the Greenwood Housing Act of 1930 to improve or replace certain tumbledown dwellings in our valley. There was, as I recall, considerable dissension about how to do that, if at all.'

'There was no need for it, that's why,' one man said scornfully. 'There are slums in every town. They're part of life. We have only one real slum in our valley, and I see no need to spend ratepayers' money on rehousing the shiftless, idle people who live in Backshaw Moss.'

'Even though we would be helped financially by the government to do that and make a big difference to people's lives?' the mayor asked.

Rathley and his cronies made such loud remarks expressing their antipathy that it was a few moments before the mayor could make himself heard.

'Make no mistake,' he said coldly, 'from now on I shall exclude from the meeting anyone preventing others from speaking, as you gentlemen have just done.'

There was dead silence at that and Charlie had to hide a grin as Rathley's mouth literally dropped open in shock.

'To our town's shame,' the mayor continued, 'Rivenshaw Council also previously failed to take proper advantage of the Housing and Town Planning Act of 1919. Indeed, our town has hardly built any new dwellings for our poorer neighbours in the past two decades. Building has focused on privately funded homes for the better-class people in Birch End.'

He paused for a moment, then continued, not hiding his disapproval, 'Sadly, the few houses the council did manage to build for less affluent families had rents so high that those most in need of decent housing couldn't afford to pay them. And those houses were so shoddily built that they are already showing signs of serious wear and tear.'

Charlie watched one of Rathley's colleagues stiffen at this, open his mouth to reply, then shut it again as an elbow was dug sharply into his side. It didn't matter how much Gareth Higgerson protested, Charlie thought. The poor standard of buildings erected by his company was known to people in the valley.

Pity he himself hadn't known about that when he bought his own house. He'd had to spend good money putting right certain things like a leaking roof.

He'd been ambivalent before but suddenly he felt deep-down glad he'd done as the mayor urged and stood for council. This was *his* valley and he wanted to be proud of it and he wanted its people to live decently. Times were slowly improving in the country and if he had any say in it, Rivenshaw was going to improve with them. He straightened and listened even more carefully as the mayor continued to speak.

'If I achieve one thing during my tenure as mayor, it will be to get rid of Backshaw Moss completely and replace it with decent and affordable housing for our poorer neighbours.'

Rathley let out a snort and whispered to the man next to him, who rolled his eyes and gave a shrill whinny of laughter.

Kirby paused then nodded to the town clerk, who passed out sets of papers. 'As you will see, this is a summary of what we are permitted – encouraged even – to do under the 1930 housing act and how much help we can gain from government funding to improve our valley. The money will make all the difference to our task and the council should take advantage of what is on offer. Does anyone wish to add a point at this stage?'

No one spoke.

'Right then, I propose ending this meeting now

and reconvening two weeks from today, which will give us all time to read and think about the information on housing and the Greenwood Act that you've been given.'

Rathley looked at him in surprise. 'But surely–'

The mayor cut him off. 'You'll have a chance to raise anything else you wish to discuss at the next meeting. I am taking it upon myself to place a high priority on this matter of decent housing and slum clearance – and that will include decent sewage connections for all.'

Not much was said as people filed out.

'By hell,' Charlie said to the group he'd sat with as they paused in the paved area at the front of the building, 'Kirby told them good and proper, didn't he?'

Leah said in her usual quiet way, 'Yes, but will he have the numbers to do anything? It must still be approved by a majority in council. I was watching Rathley and I didn't like the look on his face. First he looked angry, then he exchanged smug glances with Higgerson, as if they knew something that would prevent any action being taken.'

Todd put his arm round his wife's shoulders. 'From what I've heard from several people, he and his cronies have been suspected of going after those who oppose them one by one, and accidents have happened. No one's been able to prove anything against them so far, but who else can it be?'

'Then we'll have to be careful how we do things, won't we?' Her voice was firm. 'I agree with the mayor. We can't let that slum continue to fester.

Our good doctor was telling me only last week that it's a miracle the small outbreaks of infection due to bad drainage have been contained to Backshaw Moss itself. Sadly there has been loss of life there, especially among young children and the elderly. But he's worried in case something happens that spreads to the rest of the valley.'

She paused to let that sink in, then added, 'How many more small children have to lose their lives before the council acts? I have a small child and a sister at the grammar school. I care very much about their safety.'

Who could disagree with that? Charlie thought. He too had a child and expected to have others. By hell, if anything happened to them because of the dilatory actions of certain councillors, he'd not be answerable.

They broke up then, each person looking thoughtful.

Charlie watched Todd say goodbye to Leah at her car, since she was driving herself home, then walk briskly back into town. As the first part of their way lay together, Charlie joined him. 'Not going to be easy.'

'No. But then, what is?'

'Aren't you going home?'

'I left my car at the sales yard. I want to check that the workshop has been properly locked up for the night.'

'Couldn't the new chap do that for you? You must trust him or you'd not have brought him here.'

'I always like to check such things myself. It'll be good having someone else to do that if I'm otherwise occupied, though. There were some rough lads loitering nearby as I left today. I told them to move on and they did, but I wonder now if they were there as a warning to me.'

'Rathley acting up already? Surely not?'

'Who knows? Don't say anything to Leah. I don't want her worrying. I phoned Deemer and he said he'd tell the new constable to check the Crimea Street area a few times as he patrolled the town centre.'

'Can't be too careful. What's the new constable's name again?'

'Hopkins. He looks about ten years old.'

'The new ones always do. Wet behind the ears. Deemer will pull him into shape.'

Charlie turned off towards his shop and left Todd to carry on to his workshop.

A lot to think about. And worry about.

He glanced at his watch and once he'd checked the workshop and got into his car, he drove straight home.

Marion had the evening meal ready early, to allow for Wilf coming at seven o'clock. It had been such a busy day, Charlie had forgotten that until now.

'I should have told him to come later,' he grumbled. 'I've not stopped all day.'

'He can't come later. It'll be too dark. Just wash your hands and we'll have a quick meal in the kitchen.'

11

That evening Wilf kissed his wife and children goodbye after tea. 'Wish me luck.'

'It's not luck that Mr Willcox is giving you this chance, love; it's the hard work you've put in over the years. I'm that proud of you, Wilf!'

Then one of the children called for her and she was gone. He'd have liked to cuddle her for a bit longer. He missed that sort of touching with two children always nearby. Not that he regretted adopting them, definitely not. They were a grand little pair.

He set off on his bicycle for Charlie's house. He'd seen it from outside, knew all the streets in his valley, could play them like a picture show in his brain because he'd tramped round them many a time on days when he had no work, just to get out of the house. But of course he'd not been round to the back of any of the big houses in Birch End, except for a couple where he'd done odd jobs.

The bicycle was a godsend, he thought as he pedalled down the hill from Ellindale, but he wished he had a car or better still a van to carry tools and materials round in. Maybe he could scrape together the money to buy one after this job was fully confirmed, or even ask for an advance on the money so that he could work more efficiently. Driving wasn't difficult. He'd kept up his skills and sometimes managed to borrow a vehicle for heavy loads.

Charlie Willcox might help him. He understood how things were with ordinary people, if anyone did. He and his staff were known for treating even those who used his pawnshops with politeness and for giving fair prices on goods pledged.

Wilf was surprised that the studio plans had gone through the council's planning department without a hitch. It was known that plans were sometimes refused when they were for builders other than Higgerson. That man's plans were never turned down, for all the shoddy workmanship Wilf had seen by his men.

He enjoyed watching skilled men work. You could learn a great deal from seeing how they did things. He'd been lucky recently, what with steady work, two grand little children to adopt and a wife who had stopped fretting about being childless. It was as if his life had turned an important corner.

He looked up at the sky as he dismounted at the gate, pulled off his cap and stuffed it in his saddlebag. Thank goodness it was fine tonight. It wouldn't have looked good to arrive looking like a drowned rat. He wheeled his bicycle inside the front garden, took a deep breath and knocked on the front door.

Charlie opened it and urged him to come inside.

The bicycle had been too hard won to leave where anyone could walk off with it. 'Can I put this round the back, please?'

'Yes, of course. You wheel it round. I'll go

131

through the house and let you in the back way instead.'

When Wilf went into the kitchen, Mrs Willcox was waiting with Charlie, looking eager. Her husband started to speak but she took over when Wilf asked her about one detail. She explained to him what she wanted, showing a clear understanding of what would be involved.

Charlie didn't seem to object to this, just shrugged and left her to do the talking.

She knew her way round a plan, all right, which some people didn't, explaining why the windows had been placed that way and how important light was to an artist. Wilf studied the drawings, then looked at the wall to which the new room would be attached and through which they'd make a door. 'Can I go outside and look at that part of the house from the garden?'

'Of course. I should have thought of that before we started talking.' She led the way.

After they came back inside, Wilf looked at the plans again, hesitating, not sure whether to make suggestions. Only, he did like things to suit their purpose, so he risked it. 'Might it not be useful to have a storeroom built on to the back for your art materials, Mrs Willcox? You don't want windows in that wall, so you could fit in quite a big one, with built-in shelves and plenty of space for your canvases and larger pieces of material?'

She frowned and bent over the biggest plan, the one showing the room and how it fitted onto the house wall and jutted out into the back garden. After staring at it for so long Wilf began to worry, she said slowly, 'Why didn't the architect suggest

132

that? It's a very good idea.'

He let out his breath in a whoosh of relief as Charlie looked at him and nodded encouragingly.

She turned to her husband. 'We'll have to get back to the architect and get this changed then run it past the planning department.'

'I can draw it up for you well enough to show them what you want and give the correct dimensions, if you have some paper,' Wilf volunteered. 'I've done it for a shed and coalhouse I built.'

'Is there anything you can't do when it comes to houses?' Charlie teased.

'I love constructing things,' Wilf said simply.

He and Mrs Willcox spent a delightful hour producing a better plan and working out the interior shelving for the cupboard. Charlie soon lost interest and went to sit in the living room and read the newspaper.

Once that was finished, Marion summoned her husband to say goodbye to Wilf and Charlie walked out with him, stopping at the front gate to chat.

'You made a good impression on my wife.'

'I did? She didn't sound exactly happy.'

'Oh, that. She always speaks sharply when it's to do with business. She's really good at what she does, you know, designing cards and letter headings and such. She has a real eye for it and is good at drawing. I just – never expected my wife to *want* to work. But there you are.'

'I can see that she's got a good eye from the way she helped me sketch out her ideas for a big storeroom.'

'Aye. If we go on at this rate, that storeroom will be as big as her studio and it'll cost me nearly as much.'

That made Wilf worry that he'd upset Charlie. 'You don't, um, mind the extra cost?'

A chuckle set his mind at rest even before his companion said, 'No, lad. What else is money for but to use? And if it makes my Marion happy, all the better. As long as she gives me another child or two, that's the main thing.'

'Aye. It's good to have children.' Even if you hadn't managed to create them yourself.

'Here's to the future.' Charlie held out his hand and the two men shook. 'I look forward to working with you.'

Wilf hesitated but it had to be said. 'Um. There's just one more thing. I wondered if you could see fit to advance me enough money to buy a van. It'll make a huge difference to doing the job, because I'll need to cart all sorts of bits and pieces to and fro. And you know I'll pay you back.'

Charlie stopped and Wilf waited, swallowing hard, hoping.

'I think that's an excellent idea. You and I need to have a little chat about it and sort out the details, and there's another idea I've had. Why don't you come and see me tomorrow at work? Two o'clock would be a good time for me if you're free then.'

'I can come any time. Can you give me a clue, in case it's something I need to think about?'

'I might like to help you set up a little building business. I've backed one or two people starting up and they've not let me down. I don't think you would, either.'

Wilf could only gape at him.

Charlie clapped him on the back. 'Don't look so shocked. I know nowt about building and I shan't want to poke my nose into that side of things, but I do know a lot about people, who's capable of running a business and who isn't. I'd make a good partner because I'd be able to get some things more cheaply than you ever could. And I'm sure that in the long term you'll make money for me as well as for yourself.'

He turned back towards the house without waiting for an answer. 'See you tomorrow.'

Wilf clutched the bicycle, making no attempt to get on it, going over what had been said in his mind. He gulped back the emotion as it sank in that this really was his big chance to do the work he loved and give his family a better life.

He rode slowly back and it was a while before he realised he was grinning like a fool. Well, who wouldn't grin when a man as well respected as Charlie Willcox wanted to go into business with you?

Enid looked at him in amazement when he told her about the job he'd been offered.

'Charlie Willcox wants to go into business with you? Oh, Wilf, love, would that be wise? People like us don't know how to run a business. What if things go wrong and we lose everything?' She looked round the little house.

Wilf looked round it, too. Every piece of furniture, every dish, was hard won. For a moment, fear tarnished his elation, then he shook his head.

'It won't go wrong, love.'

'You can never be sure.'

He put his arms round her. 'You can never be sure of anything, Enid love. All I know is I know how to do the job, and I do it well. I couldn't live with myself if I didn't have a try at this. It'd be like my wildest dreams come true.' The ones that had kept him going for all those years when he'd tramped round Lancashire and Yorkshire looking for work, sleeping rough many a time, trying to learn as much as he could everywhere he went.

And he had learned, taking any job offered. He'd always been good with his hands. He hadn't realised how good until he left the valley and saw the cack-handed way in which some people did things.

'We've the children to think of now,' she insisted. 'We can't *afford* to take risks.'

'Nay, lass, it'd be partly for them I'd be doing it. Why, I might even earn enough for us to send them to the grammar school. Who knows where they'd end up then, eh?'

'All they need is to build decent lives. Nothing fancy. I still don't think you should do it. Promise me you won't.'

He was horrified. 'Enid, don't say that!'

'I have to. It's a risk. You're better off letting other men take the risks in this world. You could lose everything. *Everything we own*, Wilf. If that took my home and children from me, I'd not want to go on.'

'Times are getting better. And this isn't a risky venture. I know exactly how to do all the jobs involved and I'd have Charlie Willcox behind me.'

'You might think you know, but even this is a bigger job than you've ever taken on before. And if you tried to get into building whole houses, you'd be lost. You haven't done *that* before. Besides, times aren't getting better for everyone. What you read in the newspapers isn't always true for us in the north.'

They didn't often quarrel, or even disagree, but he wasn't going to give in on this.

'You must trust me, Enid. I can do this. I know I can.'

'You can, if things don't get worse suddenly. But it's not worth the risk.'

He put his arm round her shoulders and said it again. 'With Charlie Willcox behind me, it's not such a risk. I might not make a profit, but I'd not lose everything. He hasn't made his money by choosing bad people to work for him.'

She threw his arm off. 'He isn't the problem. There's that Higgerson to think of as well. He's a lying, cheating fellow and he isn't going to like another builder setting up. What if he starts playing dirty tricks on you that ruin the job? What if he hurts the children? No, no! I can't bear you to take the risk, Wilf. I absolutely forbid you to do it.'

'And I can't bear not to accept the job. I'm definitely going to do it.'

She ran out of the room, sobbing.

They'd never slept on a quarrel before, but they did that night. He heard her crying during the night, faint sniffles and furtive movements to mop her eyes with the sheet, but he didn't try to comfort her. He'd be a fool to turn down this opportunity. He might never get another one like it. And anyway, he was good at building, he knew he was, putting the jobs together in his head, seeing clearly in his mind the order in which to do things, hearing people's praise as he did a job well.

No, he was right to do it, he was quite sure about that.

He hadn't even told Enid about buying a van. She'd go mad about that, too. She hated to get into debt.

He stifled a sigh and kept his back turned to her. He didn't want her trying to cajole him into giving up his dream.

12

The following afternoon Nick took Mr Slater out for another driving lesson. It went much better than the previous one and he added a 'treat' at the end, a quick trip up the gently sloping road to Birch End, so that he could show his client how to get the car moving safely when parked on an incline.

They went to a quiet lane Nick had discovered when checking out this area. It sloped gently, perfect for a beginner to practise on. He didn't think it likely there would be any other traffic round there, and even if another vehicle did come along, you could easily see it long before it got close.

Slater had a few attempts at hill starts till he

grew used to the necessary moves with the clutch, then he handed over control of the car for the journey back into the town centre.

'You're doing better today,' Nick told him.

'I am? Really? Well, it didn't feel like it. Driving is harder than it looks.' Slater patted the sweat from his brow with his handkerchief. 'Much harder.'

It was a good thing Nick was driving as they started back towards the main road, because just as they rounded the bend at the end of the lane, they saw a young woman ahead of them, struggling with two men. She appeared to be giving a good account of herself but it was a hopeless struggle – or it would have been if they hadn't happened upon the scene.

Both men cried out in shock involuntarily and Nick accelerated forward, jerking to a halt near the trio and flinging open his car door.

At the sight of the car, the two men had let go of their victim and even in the short time it took Nick to reach her, they'd scrambled over the fence and were running off across the nearby field. Only then did he realise he'd rescued the young woman he'd met on the train.

Hair tumbling across her shoulders, she bent to pick up the shoe she'd been using as a weapon and hopped about as she shook out some gravel and tried to put it on again.

He moved to support her while Slater picked up her handbag. 'Are you all right?'

'I'm a bit bruised and battered but so will they be.' She glared in the direction the attackers had taken, even though they were now out of sight.

'I'll recognise them again, I promise you.'

'I will too. Miss Melling, isn't it?'

'Yes. Nice to meet you again, Mr Howarth. Thanks for rescuing me.'

'I'm glad we happened along.' He spoke calmly, keeping an eye on her in case she showed any sign of fainting. But she looked furiously angry rather than overwhelmed. He gestured to his companion. 'This is Mr Slater, who has been taking a driving lesson with me. We didn't expect to encounter a damsel in distress, though.'

Mr Slater brushed dirt off her handbag and handed it to her.

She clutched it to her chest and looked round. 'Can you see my hat? Oh, there it is.' She bent and picked up the squashed lump of felt, studying it with a grimace. 'That won't be much use now. They've trampled it to death.' She stuffed it into her large bag.

'Come and sit down in the car, my dear young lady, till you've recovered. We don't want you fainting on us.'

'I'm not the sort to faint, Mr Slater, but I'm very angry indeed, and at myself most of all. I was warned not to go about on my own near Backshaw Moss but I couldn't believe anyone would attack me in broad daylight, and so close to those houses, as well!' She gestured to where a row of roofs showed beyond a line of trees.

Nick was puzzled. 'Why would anyone think you might be attacked? It's not a common occurrence round here. They didn't take your bag so it can't have been to steal your purse. You haven't been here long enough to have made enemies, surely?'

'I got on the wrong side of my stepmother's cousin and Mrs T, my landlady, says he prides himself on getting his own back on people who upset him.'

'The person you were going to stay with? Who is he?'

'Clarence Rathley.'

Mr Slater growled in his throat at the sound of that name.

Nick turned to him. 'Do you know this Rathley fellow?'

'He calls himself a businessman and got elected as a town councillor three years ago, goodness knows how. But I'd not buy anything from him or trust him in any way. He's a bully and a scoundrel, and a very poor landlord. He's got a few slum houses and he never does any repairs on them, if he can help it, and the tenants are terrified of his rent collector.'

Nick was surprised at the vehemence in Slater's tone. 'How did you manage to upset Rathley so quickly, Miss Melling?'

'We went to stay at his house, but I didn't feel comfortable because he kept looking at me in that horrible way some men do.'

She glanced down at her chest and it was obvious what she meant.

'I was given a bedroom away from the rest of the family and it had no lock on the door, which worried me. So I found another room with a lockable door because I just didn't feel safe.'

'Why would he think you'd, um, welcome his attentions? You don't seem that sort, if you don't mind me saying so.'

141

'You heard my stepmother on the train. From the way she talks you'd think I was immoral, yet all she's really fussing about is my manners, which she doesn't think are ladylike enough. Ha! Ladylike doesn't get the sheep shorn or the hens fed on a farm, does it? I think he must have believed I'd let him into my bedroom and ... you know...'

Mr Slater went a little pink at her frankness.

'Go on,' Nick said gently.

'I was right to worry. Someone did try to get into my room after everyone was asleep. I can't prove it was Rathley but who else could it be? Except for his chauffeur, who doesn't live in the house, the servants are all females and they seem scared even to breathe deeply when their master is around. Anyway, I threatened to crown whoever it was with a brass candlestick if he came into my room, and he must have crept away because there were no more noises.'

Nick looked at her in admiration. 'Well done. What did your stepmother say about it?'

'I didn't tell her. It'd be no use going to *her* for help about anything, and certainly not against a man she calls her *dear* cousin and acts as if he's king of the world. So this morning I left his house and moved into lodgings. He must realise that I guessed who was trying to get into my room, yet he had the nerve to forbid me to leave and he even tried to drag me back into the house by force. But I got away with the help of my new landlady's son. I'm at Mr Tucker's, now.'

Mr Slater nodded. 'Peter Tucker, a very decent young fellow. Um, did those young fellows who attacked you today say anything about why?'

'One of them said they were going to teach me to keep my mouth shut about my betters and that after they let me go, if I knew what was good for me, I should go back to Australia and stay there. How could they have known where I came from? I'd never even seen them before.'

'Well, you won't need to say anything for people to talk about your leaving Rathley's house after only one night,' Mr Slater declared. 'You won't be able to stop them gossiping because he's already known as a womaniser. It'll look bad for him that you moved out so quickly – and serve him right, too.'

'Why were you going to Birch End today?' Nick asked.

'I was going to Backshaw Moss, actually.'

'That's a bad place for a young lady on her own,' Slater said. 'You should stay right away from it.'

'The thing is, I found out I may have relatives there and I wanted to see if I could find them. I was warned by my landlady and her son not to come out here alone because of upsetting Rathley, only I didn't really think he'd send someone to attack me in the middle of the day, not in this day and age.'

The angry red in her cheeks was beginning to subside and she started brushing down her clothing, muttering something under her breath as she found a gap where a button had come off her blouse.

'Did those louts make any other threats?'

'No, but one of them kept trying to touch my –

143

um, my body till I managed to kick him where it hurts most.'

Nick couldn't hold back a chuckle. 'Good for you.'

'That's when he clouted me.' She touched the bruise on her cheek. 'I think I could have fought off one attacker, because our old stockman in Australia taught me a few tricks about where men are most susceptible, but two attackers, no. I screamed for help and bit one when he tried to put his hand across my mouth, but no one came. It's lucky you were driving past. I dread to think of what might have happened otherwise.' She shuddered.

At the thought of that, Nick lost all desire to smile. 'You must let us take you back into town, Miss Melling.'

'Thank you.'

'Did you say you were staying at Mrs Tucker's?'

'Yes. If you can take me back there, I'd be grateful.'

'It's the least we can do.' He helped her into the front passenger seat, which Mr Slater had insisted she take, studying her covertly. She still looked angry but definitely wasn't the fainting type.

As he set off, he asked, 'Do you mind if I take Mr Slater back to Willcox and Selby Motors before I drive you to Mrs Tucker's? It's more or less on the way and he's booked a taxi to take him home after his driving lesson. It might not wait for him if we're too late.'

'That'll be fine by me. Actually, if you'd kindly let me wash my hands and face, and tidy my hair properly at your office, I'd be further in your debt.

I'd rather people didn't see me looking quite such a mess. The road outside the boarding house is quite busy because it leads into the town centre. And Mrs T is going to say she told me so, I'm sure.'

He thought Miss Melling looked magnificent in her anger, with her cheeks rosy, her eyes sparkling and her dark hair falling in a shining stream over her shoulders. Today she seemed a different woman to the one on the train, more of a free spirit, as if her real self was showing – perhaps because she was away from that horrible, complaining stepmother.

When they got back to Crimea Street, Todd looked surprised to see Miss Melling get out of the car with her clothes awry and face bruised, in spite of her attempts to tidy herself up.

'This way.' Nick hurried across to the building, trying to stay between her and a couple of gawking passers-by.

Todd followed them into the kitchen. 'What's happened? Has there been an accident?'

'Not exactly. Miss Melling was attacked by two men as she was walking along that narrow road this side of Birch End, the one that's a short cut to Backshaw Moss.'

'*What?* We need to report the attack to the police, then.' He looked at her, frowning. 'I don't think I've seen you around town before, Miss Melling, and I know most people by sight.'

'No, you wouldn't have. I've just arrived from Australia.'

'Ah. Sorry you've had such a poor welcome to

145

the valley. I'm Todd Selby. This is my garage and car sales yard.'

'Pleased to meet you.' She looked at Nick. 'May I use your bathroom to tidy myself up?'

'What am I thinking of keeping you here chatting? It's at the top of the stairs. There's a clean towel folded on the shelf.'

She gave them a rather forced half-smile and disappeared, her footsteps echoing on the bare wooden stairs.

Todd looked at Nick. 'I've never heard of an attack in broad daylight before, even there. Were they trying to run off with her handbag?'

'No, they didn't even try to snatch it. It seems she's upset someone called Rathley and it sounds as if he sent them to frighten her.' He lowered his voice to add, 'Or worse. Do you know him?'

'Who doesn't? He's becoming rather notorious, though I knew *of* him, rather than knowing him personally until I went on the town council with him.'

There was a pregnant silence, then Slater said grimly, 'He'll overreach himself one day, that one will, and it can't happen too soon for me. I'd not do business with him, that's for sure.'

'I don't think I heard of him when I was a lad here,' Nick said. 'But I'll definitely find out about him now.'

'You don't want to tangle with him, Howarth. In fact, I'll point him out if we see him when we're out on our driving lessons, so that you can avoid him.'

Nick didn't say anything but he wasn't going to play the coward, and was now very determined to

146

keep an eye on Miss Melling. It didn't sound as if the poor lass knew anyone else in town to turn to for help.

There was the sound of a vehicle stopping outside and Slater went to look out of the front door, returning a moment later. 'That's my taxi. Will you be all right, Howarth? You don't need any more help with the young lady?'

'No. I'll make sure Miss Melling gets back to her lodgings safely. See you tomorrow afternoon.'

Still Mr Slater hesitated. 'If you think it'll help, I could spread the word about what's happened to a few people I know, ones who have no reason to love Rathley. They'll keep their eyes open for her, too.'

'That wouldn't hurt,' Nick agreed.

After Mr Slater had left, he put the kettle on with a wry smile at Todd. 'If all else fails, a cup of tea's usually a big help in settling the nerves. I'm sure Miss Melling will appreciate one.'

'So would I. I'll just phone Leah and tell her I'll be late. There may be something I can do to help, and at the very least, we should work out some way of keeping an eye on Miss Melling. The trouble is, Rathley was vouched for by a friend as being with him, so there's no obvious way of tying him to what happened today. There never is when something happens that seems suspicious. I've wondered about a couple of incidents that nudged business in his favour.'

Nick looked grim. 'That sort of person can get overconfident.'

'Well, Rathley hasn't been accused directly of anything so far and from what I've heard, ordin-

147

ary people are frightened to challenge him, given the sort of men he employs as rent and debt collectors.'

'It worries me, Todd. She's on her own here and who'd even know if she suddenly vanished? And anyway–' He broke off abruptly.

'And?' his companion prompted.

'I don't like to see young women treated badly. I have cousins and if anyone hurt them, I'd go after them.'

'Yes, and my wife has a younger sister. I'd feel the same.'

'I'm going to be out and about quite a lot, so I can keep my eyes open. It's surprising what you notice when you're giving driving lessons, because you often have to go slowly with beginner drivers. And you also have to be on the alert for what's going on around you to prevent your pupil doing something stupid. Pedestrians don't pay much attention to cars that aren't close to them, I've noticed. Nor do people in other cars.'

'What can you hope to see?'

'Who knows? I've got another advantage: I have really good vision for things at a distance. I can recognise a bird's shape when other people only see a dot in the sky. That comes in useful sometimes in my job.'

13

There were footsteps on the stairs and Jo came to join them, looking much tidier, with her hair in a low bun and the blouse pinned together. But the bruise on her cheek showed so clearly it made Nick's anger flare up again.

'You'll have to be very careful from now on, Miss Melling,' he warned.

'I will, I promise you. I hadn't expected anything like that to happen to me. From now on, I'll be on my guard, even in a small town like Rivenshaw.'

Todd joined in. 'Show me the town, small or large, that doesn't have its share of villains. I've never found one and I've seen quite a bit of the world. I've even been to Australia and may I say that it's nice to hear an Aussie accent again.'

She gave him one of those wide, relaxed Aussie smiles he remembered so vividly from his travels. 'My stepmother complains bitterly about the way I speak. Luckily I've never valued her opinion, so it doesn't upset me. But look, Miss Melling sounds terribly stiff and formal. We Aussies use first names more often than you Brits do. That absolutely horrified my stepmother but I prefer it, so please could you call me Jo?'

It was Nick she looked at as she said this, though, rather than Todd.

He responded at once, 'Like a cup of tea, *Jo?*'

149

'I'd love one ... *Nick.*'

Todd watched them smile at one another as Nick set out a cup and saucer in front of her and then put their usual mugs in front of himself and Todd. They were attracted to one another. You could always tell. Did they realise it yet, though?

She surprised them both by pushing the cup away before he could pour tea into it.

'That's another thing. I'd far rather have a mug like yours, if you don't mind. On our farm I used to drink good, strong tea with the men. There never seems to be enough to quench your thirst in one of those little cups and on the ship they made the tea so weak it hardly tasted of anything.'

Todd went across to the cupboard and got her a mug. 'Here you are, Jo.'

Nick poured her tea and she added a spoonful of sugar then sipped it with obvious relish.

'Are you sure you're all right?' Todd pointed to her cheek. 'Does that hurt much?'

'Nah. It's only a bruise. I've always been a tomboy so I'm used to them. But I'm still angry at myself for getting caught out.'

'I think we should talk about what happened,' Todd said. 'If you've run afoul of Rathley to the extent that he's sending men to attack you, you might find yourself in trouble again. As he's grown richer he seems to have decided he can get away with anything. Since you weren't intending to stay in Rivenshaw, perhaps you should cut your losses and go on your way?'

She got that stubborn expression on her face again. 'My father taught me not to turn tail and flee from trouble. He used to say, it'd only follow

150

you and attack from behind another day. Besides, I still have unfinished business here. I want to find my father's family. It was one of his dying wishes.'

Todd shook his head regretfully. 'Can't argue with carrying out someone's last wish, but take care how you go from now on, eh? No walking through the countryside on your own. And remember, in town you can always take refuge in here if someone comes after you.'

'I'll be here part of the time as well,' Nick added. 'The office for my driving school is in one of the front rooms and I'm living in the house for the time being, keeping an eye on Todd's place at night.'

'My wife and I live up in Ellindale,' Todd said. 'I think you'll get on well with Leah. She's a no-nonsense person too.'

'I'd like that.'

'Nick, we'd love to have you, too, and when she comes to tea, you can drive Jo up and take her back.'

'Both those would be my pleasure.'

Todd turned back to Jo, speaking slowly and emphatically. 'You shouldn't go out on your own after dark, and that even includes crossing the street to a neighbour's house.'

She grimaced but nodded agreement. 'I think I'll carry something to defend myself with in my handbag, just in case, a spanner maybe. Good thing I don't carry one of those silly little pouch bags that are fashionable for ladies.' She gestured to her leather bag that was big enough to be called a satchel.

'About your father's relatives – what makes you think they're living in Backshaw Moss?' Todd asked.

'Mrs T introduced me to someone called Kath Melling, who turned out to be a distant relative, and she thinks that's where they are.'

Todd made a disapproving sound. 'It's a dreadful place. These relatives might not be – respectable.'

Jo banged her empty mug down. 'I've come ten thousand miles and it wasn't just to look after my stepmother, so I'm *not* going back without trying to find them. If they live in a slum, they may be dreadful people, for all I know, but what if they're not? What if they're just trapped there because they're poor and can't find work?'

'It does happen.'

'My father and I used to talk about that, because they're going through hard times in Australia as well. He tried to help people whenever he could. Men on the tramp used to stop at our farm and ask to fill their billycan with water. He'd give them a meal as well. My stepmother didn't like that.'

She sighed and went on, almost talking to herself, remembering. 'Sometimes there were whole families on the road together, pushing handcarts with all their possessions in them and sleeping rough. Dad always gave them a good square meal and maybe a few shillings to help them on their way, and he let them sleep in the barn if the weather was bad. If I find that my relatives here are in need, I shall definitely try to help them, as he'd have done.'

She was not only a brave lass, but an intelligent

and caring one as well, Nick thought. Just let him catch anyone trying to hurt her from now on.

That intensity of his protective feeling made him suck in a sharp breath. Oh hell! He was even more attracted to her after a second meeting, and she was only here on a visit. And anyway, he had to focus all his energy on getting his driving school going.

Why did fate so often toss temptation your way at exactly the wrong times?

Todd was speaking, so he tried to concentrate on that but it took a huge effort.

'Well, let's make some plans, then.' Todd managed not to smile. When they weren't staring at one another, both his companions seemed to be lost in thought. They might have only just met, but they seemed connected in some way, as if they understood one another instinctively.

It had been like that with him the first time he saw Leah. Only she'd been married to Jonah then.

Jo wasn't married, though, and seemed alone in the world. Maybe ... oh, who knew? He wasn't going to interfere but he couldn't help hoping his newest friend would find someone to share his life. It wasn't money that made you happy but people. Well, it did if you were a decent sort.

Now he was the one getting lost in thought. He'd better pull himself together. 'If you'd like to go up to Backshaw Moss and look for your relatives tomorrow morning, Jo, I can come with you. I have no appointments and there's no car due in for repairs.'

Nick shot him a quick glance. 'I'll come too. In that place, two men will be better than one. We can put a sign on the door here saying *Back in an hour*.'

'All right. The sooner you and I find some clerical help, the better. I'll put an advert in the Friday newspaper.'

'I could help out till you find someone, if you like,' Jo volunteered. 'I worked in an office for a few years in Perth. I'm good with figures and paperwork. I kept the account books and did the correspondence for a haberdasher's shop. I enjoy organising things.'

Todd spoke without thinking and saw her face brighten. 'You sound like the sort of person we'd offer a job to.'

'Well, how about I help you out for a week or two? I'm planning to stay in the valley, if not in Birch End, for at least that long, whether I find my relatives or not.'

They both looked at her in puzzlement and Nick asked, 'Why?'

'Because I want to look round this part of Lancashire. I checked the history of the county in one of Dad's books and it sounds an interesting place. Did you know they opened the first co-operative store in the world – well the first of the modern sort – in a town called Rochdale in 1844? They have similar co-ops in Australia now because that way of organising a co-op has been so successful.'

'Are you interested in history?' Nick asked.

'Yes. About how ordinary people used to live, anyway. I don't care about lords and ladies, or

154

politics. We had a co-op store in the little town where I grew up in Australia, you see. Well, it was the only shop and people relied on it for most of their daily needs, the ones they couldn't provide for themselves on the farms, that is. The manager was a friend of my father's. When he found out I was coming to Lancashire, he wanted me to go and see the co-op in Rochdale and send him a postcard from there.'

She sighed and got a rather sad look in her eyes for a moment or two, as if she missed her home and friends. Well, you would, wouldn't you?

Todd looked at Nick, who nodded quickly. 'Did you mean that, because if so we'd be happy to have your help in the office, Jo?'

'Of course I did. It'll give you time to look round for someone permanent and it'll suit me to have something to do. I can't bear sitting around idly all day. It nearly drove me mad on the ship. My stepmother said I should take up embroidery. Ha! I'd rather go riding or work in the garden any day. My real mother used to laugh at my efforts and tell me I sewed like a one-armed kangaroo!'

'Won't helping us mean you have to stay here for longer than you intended?' Nick asked.

Todd watched her expression turn sad again.

'I don't have any close relatives to go back to in Australia, just friends and former neighbours, so I'm not in a hurry. I haven't got a booking yet. Actually, I'm not at all sure what I'm going to do with the rest of my life. My only relatives in Australia are over in Melbourne now and that's about one thousand, seven hundred miles away and foreign territory to me. And our farm's been sold.'

'Why didn't your father leave that to you?' Nick asked. 'Was it only rented?'

'No. He owned it. He might have left it to me if I'd wanted to run it, but I didn't. I like being outdoors, but I don't like killing animals I've helped look after and I'm not interested in growing crops. I can easily take the time to hunt for my relatives here *and* to help you.'

She didn't tell them she'd received most of the money the farm had brought, apart from the chunk that'd been left in trust for her father's second wife. He had said she should keep that information to herself, and especially not tell Edna.

Todd frowned. 'I don't know of any other Mellings in the valley, except for Kath's lot.'

'Turns out that I have distant relatives still in the area, as my father expected. They're called Tayner.'

He cocked his head to one side, then shook it. 'Tayner? I can't think of anyone by that name. It's unusual, so I'm sure I'd remember it. Are you certain these people live in Backshaw Moss?'

'Mrs T thought they did, but she didn't know exactly where.' She flushed as she added, 'There's a sort of cousin called Moira apparently. Kath said the rest of the family don't speak to her because she's, um, living off immoral earnings.'

'And you still want to find her?' Nick couldn't hide his surprise.

'I'd like to find out if she's been driven to that sort of life and wants to escape. If so, I can afford to help her. I have, er, a little money of my own and I'll have more if my stepmother gets married again, which I think she probably will, since she's

156

the clinging vine type.'

Todd whistled softly. He wasn't sure Jo understood how much trouble she could get into by mixing with people like this Moira. Respectable people might suspect Jo's morals, too, as Rathley already had. He didn't think she had an immoral bone in her body, she had such a frank, open face, but some folk seemed to look for faults in others.

'We'd better help you find out about her, then, Jo. There are only a few streets in Backshaw Moss but there are a lot of families crammed into one room each and some rough types, as well as people down on their luck.'

Nick chimed in. 'I drove through it when I was checking out the valley, looking for places for beginners to practise their driving in safety. I drove straight out again. Apart from anything else, there's a strong smell of sewage at the far end of it. I was surprised the council hadn't done something about that.'

'Well, if it isn't a big place, it won't take us long to look round it for my family, will it, and we won't have to put up with the smell for long?'

'We also need to discuss what's needed in our two offices, see if you fancy working here for a while. Are you sure you're up to discussing that after your upset today?' Todd studied her, but apart from the bruise her face was rosy and her eyes bright.

'Oh, yes. I'm feeling myself again now that I've tidied myself up and had a cuppa. I'd enjoy sorting out your offices.'

'Do you always decide to do things so quickly?'

Nick asked.

'If it feels right, yes. Why not?'

'How do you know you'll be safe working for us?'

'Well, Nick, for a start, *you* rescued me and then–' She broke off and shrugged. 'I don't know. I just feel Todd's a decent chap. Most people's character shows in their faces, don't you think? I met a lot of people when I worked in Perth, and got used to making judgements ... about men particularly. They were usually polite enough, but some of them weren't used to seeing a woman dealing with accounts and didn't think I could be capable, so they treated me as if I was stupid, talking slowly and more loudly than usual. There were only a few men who looked at me in *that horrible way* and I soon set them straight, I can tell you. I won't put up with that sort of treatment.'

Todd would have loved to be a fly on the wall when she was setting a man straight! He opened his mouth to speak but just then someone tapped on the front door, so as he was nearest, he got up to see who it was. He found a shabbily dressed man of roughly his own age standing there. 'Can I help you?'

'I was told there's a driving school starting up here.'

'Mr Howarth is the one setting it up. You'll need to talk to him.' He turned and called out, 'Nick. It's for you, about the driving school.'

'Coming.'

But he saw Nick hesitate in the doorway, turning back to Jo. 'Will you be all right if I deal with

158

this before I take you back?'

Her voice rang out clearly. 'No worries. I'll be quite safe in the kitchen.'

Someone yelled 'Shop!' from the front yard, so Todd looked out of the front door and yelled back to his friends, 'Looks like I've got someone wanting to look at cars.' Then he bellowed out to the customer. 'Just a minute, sir.'

Glancing at his modern wristwatch, he strode down the corridor to say to Jo, 'I can chat to you about helping out in the office after I've seen this client, if you don't mind waiting.'

'I'll be all right.' She grinned. 'Go and sell him a car.'

Jo watched Todd go and muttered, 'I wish I had a car here. I'd be able to do so much more, and I'd be safer, too.'

'You can drive, then?' Nick asked.

'Yes, of course. Aussie kids who live in the country often learn to drive as soon as they can reach the pedals. The younger ones stay on their own land, of course. They're not allowed on the road.' She grinned at him. 'Well, mostly they stay on their own land. When I came home to look after Dad, I drove his car all over the place, so I had a lot of practice. My stepmother thought it was scandalous driving around on my own. *She* wanted to hire a chauffeur.'

'Is there no end to the things you can do?'

She shrugged, then looked towards the front door. 'Go and find out what that poor man wants. He's waiting so patiently. I'll see if I can squeeze another cup of tea out of the pot. You and I can talk afterwards. There's even a newspaper I can read while I wait. After all, I've nowhere else to go.'

That sad little remark made him want to hug her, but she made a shooing motion with one hand, so he went to see what the man wanted, taking him into his office. 'Sorry to keep you waiting. Please take a seat. Did you want to book a driving lesson?' The man didn't look affluent enough to be able to afford that, not in his experience anyway, but you could never be certain.

His visitor took a deep breath, as if nervous. 'No, Mr Howarth. I wanted to ask whether there's any chance of a job. I used to teach men to drive in the army, you see, everything from cars to big lorries. I enjoyed doing it, too. There wouldn't be as many accidents if people knew how to obey the rules of the road.'

'I agree. Unfortunately I'm only just starting up, so I don't even have enough clients to fill my own days yet. There may be a job later on, though. You could ask again in a few weeks.'

'I can tell you about myself now and write down where I live. For future reference. Just in case. Um, if you don't mind.'

Nick saw even the faint trace of hope fading from his companion's face and felt sorry for him. He knew how desperate men could be about even the slightest chance of a job, so he said, 'All right. Good idea. We'll do that.' He wrote down the man's name and address on an office card and repeated the name. 'Silas Johnson. Right. I won't forget you if anything crops up, lad.'

He weighed down the card with the inkwell. 'We have a clerk starting soon, so she can file this.'

Then something occurred to him and he studied Silas once again. As Jo had said, you could tell a lot from someone's face and this man met his eyes with a direct gaze and held himself upright, every inch an old soldier. 'You look as if you know how to handle yourself if it comes to a fight.'

'Well, yes. Those of us who've been through the trenches don't forget how to fight.'

'I have another job you might be interested in, though it's only temporary.'

Silas leaned forward eagerly. 'Oh yes?'

'The young lady you saw in the kitchen has been attacked. She's a visitor, isn't staying in the valley for long, but I wouldn't mind finding someone to keep an eye on her for the next two weeks. I can't do it myself because I'll be out and about giving driving lessons. And also Todd may have the odd job for you in his workshop as well if you know anything about cars.'

'I do know a fair bit about motors!' The desperate gulp the man gave made Nick forget his vow not to spend a penny he didn't need to. He intended to make sure Jo stayed safe and it'd help this poor chap as well. Well worth it.

And anyway, two weeks' wages as a bodyguard wouldn't break his own bank. He'd lived with his brother and family and been very careful with his money over the past few years.

14

Jo didn't intend to eavesdrop but the sounds from the front office echoed down the hall to the kitchen and whoever Nick was talking to had a rather loud voice.

She quickly realised that he was trying to protect her by providing a bodyguard at his own expense. How kind of him!

It wouldn't cost a lot, because you could hire help cheaply in bad times and she wasn't staying here long, but Nick didn't look as if he had much money to spare, given the clothes he was wearing, and she had plenty. And of course, he'd have a lot of expenses starting up his business, however careful he was.

Should she intervene?

Yes, of course she should. She wasn't going to let him spend his money on her. But he was right. It would be a good idea to hire a bodyguard until she left. She'd hated feeling helpless when the two men attacked her. She didn't intend to give in to threats and run away like a frightened animal, but as a stranger she didn't know the valley and could quickly run into trouble, as she'd already proved.

She gave a nod, drained the last mouthful of tea and marched along the hall to the front of the building to confront the two men.

They turned to look at her as she stopped in the office doorway. 'Excuse me, but I couldn't help hearing what you were saying because words echo down the hall. You're talking about paying this man to protect me, Nick. Shouldn't you have discussed that with me first?'

'Sorry. I only just got the idea. But we do need to make sure you're not on your own when you go out and about, and I can't see an energetic woman like you sitting indoors for hours on end waiting for me or Todd to escort you around when we have a little time to spare.'

She couldn't help smiling at the very idea. 'You're right. I'd go mad. But I'd rather pay for the necessary protection myself. Silas, isn't it? I'm Jo, short for Josephine.' She held her hand out to the stranger and he hesitated briefly before shaking it.

'Pleased to meet you, miss.'

'Call me Jo. Us Aussies prefer to be on first-name terms.'

'You're Australian?'

'Yes.'

'One of my mates went out there after the war on something called a group settlement scheme. They gave former soldiers land. Eh, I'd have liked to go too, but my mam was getting old and there was no one else but me to look after her.'

'Well, she'd naturally come first, wouldn't she? Good on you for doing it. But Australia's a great country and it's not going anywhere. Maybe you'll still get there one day. Now, back to the present.' She turned to Nick and repeated, 'It *is* a good idea but I'll pay Silas's wages myself.'

He opened his mouth to protest but she folded her arms and gave him a determined look and he spread his hands out in a gesture of surrender.

'As you please. But you *will* do this, won't you?'

'Yes. I can afford it, if that's what you were worrying about. And what better to spend my money on than my own safety in a strange town?' She turned back to Silas. 'Is that all right with you, working for a woman, I mean, not to mention spending all day trailing round with me?'

'I don't care who I work for or what I do, as long as it's honest.'

'Good. You look like someone I can trust, so you're hired. Mind you, it'll only be for two weeks, possibly three.'

His whole bearing suddenly seemed more upright, his eyes brighter. 'Yes, miss, I mean Jo. Mr Howarth told me that. Um, I ought to know your surname as well, don't you think?'

'It's Melling. Now let's go over what I'll need you to do. I'm going to be doing some office work for Mr Howarth and Mr Selby, so I'll want you to walk here with me from my lodgings in the mornings and escort me back there in the evenings, then I'm afraid you'll have to hang around for most of the day. When I need to go out, you'll go with me – unless I'm with other people I trust, like Nick here, in which case there may be something you can do to help Todd in the workshop.'

'That seems clear enough. Do you know who wants to hurt you?'

'I think it's a man called Rathley. I can't prove it, but I don't see how it can be anyone else.'

His expression changed immediately to a dark

scowl. 'Then I wish I could afford to do this job without charge, miss, because that man has caused a lot of trouble for a good friend of mine.'

'If I can help your friend in any way, let me know.'

'There's a group of us keeping an eye on him, don't worry. We all go to the job club in Ellindale when we've no work. And that's another thing: Rathley's told everyone the job club is a waste of the town's money and he's tried to get it closed down, only Mr Carlisle owns the old house we use and the council doesn't have any power to close it down unless they can prove it's in a dangerous condition. Well, it isn't. Us lads have seen to that.'

'Good for you.'

'It's been a life-saver for us, that job club. It cheers people up to have somewhere to go, and we can learn new skills there as well.'

'Sounds like an excellent idea. You must tell me more about it when we're working together.'

Nick heard Todd's customer calling goodbye outside, so moved forward. 'Why don't you wait in the kitchen, Silas, while Todd and I have a chat with Jo about how she can help us in the office? Was there any tea left in the pot, Jo? Not for me, but for our friend here.'

'If you don't mind it being lukewarm.'

'I don't mind it stone cold,' Silas said frankly. 'It still bucks you up, tea does.'

'Well, it's only going to get thrown away, so drink as much as you want. There's milk and sugar on the table. There's plenty of that.'

They watched him walk down the hall.

'I like him,' she said. 'Good idea of yours.'

'I like the fact that he's a strong chap, an ex-soldier who knows how to fight.'

There was no arguing with that.

When the three of them were seated in Todd's office, he took charge. 'Tell us about the work you did in Australia, Jo, so that we can figure out the best way for you to help us.'

She explained what sort of tasks she'd done and it soon became clear how familiar she was with office work, not only with keeping accounts but with the many other tasks involved. In fact, she knew far more than they did about it.

'Did you enjoy that sort of work?' Nick asked. 'I'm not at all fond of doing accounts, myself.'

'Yes, I did – well, mostly. I'm good with figures. Is there any job on earth that doesn't have some boring parts to it, though?'

'Like tidying your desk.' Todd shot a rueful glance at his desk and the rickety old table next to it, both covered with untidy piles of papers, as well as odd pencils, a big bottle of ink, something lumpy wrapped in brown paper and a spanner he'd been using when he ran to answer the phone earlier.

'Aha!' He picked the spanner up and put it more prominently on the main desk so that he wouldn't forget it. 'I've been looking for that all over the workshop. I reckon the first thing you'd need to do for me here is tidy up and organise places to put things.'

'I can do that easily enough, though you'll need to buy a tall cupboard and a filing cabinet because I can't very well stack things on the floor, can I?' She turned to Nick. 'What sort of help would *you* need?'

'I'm not as untidy as Todd, I promise you, but I haven't even started to buy equipment for my office yet. Well, you've seen it. Practically nothing in there. I'll need account books and stationery, and I think I'll need a cupboard as well, but maybe we can buy a second-hand one, eh? The old table can continue to serve as a desk, if you don't need it back, Todd?'

'Good heavens, no. Though you may want to do something to even up the legs so that it doesn't wobble.'

'I can easily do that.' He turned back to Jo. 'I had someone wanting driving lessons before I'd really got going, you see, or I'd have at least made a start on the office before now.'

The two men looked at her so hopefully, she was reminded of two little birds waiting to be fed and couldn't help laughing. 'Leave it to me. I can do all that for you. I know what's usually needed and it can't be all that different here in England. Silas can come with me. He'll probably know where I should go to buy what's necessary.'

The men exchanged glances as if a question had been asked and nodded.

'You're hired, then,' Todd said.

'Thank you.'

'Er – just one thing, Jo: how much should we pay you?'

'You're asking *me?* How do I know what's the going wage here? The only thing is, I'd want the same as you'd pay a male clerk. I don't see why women get paid so much less for doing the same work.'

Nick looked at her in surprise. 'I've never heard a woman say that before.'

'Well, you have now. Single women have just as many living expenses as single men yet people pay them about half the wages. That's not fair. It took me a while to find a job where someone would pay me the same as a man doing that work, but my boss in Australia had just had a man mess up his accounts and orders, and he said if I could do it better, he'd pay me the same. He didn't think I would, just said it to shut me up, but when I proved myself he kept his word.'

Todd smiled. 'Fair enough. How about four pounds a week? No, if you're paying Silas to go about with you, we should contribute to that as well, because half the time you'll be on our business.'

'All right. It's only for two weeks, so we won't argue. I'll make sure you get good value for your money and I'm sure Silas will help out with anything he can here, rather than just sitting around watching me.'

'We'll need to make sure you have enough cash on hand to buy office supplies,' Nick put in.

'Petty cash, yes, for small items like post. But if there's a shop selling office stationery, maybe we'd better set up accounts for both of your businesses to buy there. Have you got all your bookwork started, Todd? You've been going a while, haven't you?'

'Um, yes. I have an account set up at Dyson's already – that's the name of the stationer's in town.

I haven't kept up with the bookwork very well, I'm afraid. I have kept all my receipts, at least. Leah's been nagging me about sorting it out.'

'Good. I can do that for you. When do you want me to start work? I'd still like to go looking for my relatives tomorrow morning, if you don't mind.'

'You can start officially tomorrow afternoon, then. Now, let's get you home again. I'm ready for my tea, even if you aren't.' Todd turned to Nick. 'Can you drive Jo back to her lodgings?'

'Of course.'

'And you'd better take Silas with you, too, so that he knows where to go and they know who he is. I'll lock up here.'

Nick went to fetch Silas from the kitchen and explain what was going on, then drove him and Jo to her lodgings.

'I hope you'll have enough sense to wait for Silas to arrive before you go out in the mornings, Jo.' He gave her a look that made that 'hope' an order.

She immediately stuck her tongue out at him and a snort of laughter escaped him, even though it was a serious matter. He'd never felt so much at ease with a woman before.

Mrs T opened the front door to them and stared in shock at the bruise on Jo's face. 'Whatever happened to you, lass?'

'Two men attacked me when I was out walking.'

'I thought you'd gone into the town centre. Surely they didn't attack you out in the street?'

Nick watched her wriggle uncomfortably under

Mrs T's searching gaze. Good.

'No, I felt like a brisk walk and I found myself near Birch End. I thought I'd be safe so near to the village, and in daylight.' As Mrs T opened her mouth to protest, Jo held up one hand. 'I know. It was stupid of me to get out of sight of other people, and I won't do it again.'

'See that you don't. And who are your friends?' She looked at the two men and waited. Once they'd been introduced and their presence explained, she looked a bit happier. 'Nice to meet you both. Good idea to get someone to keep an eye on her, Mr Howarth. If you're a friend of Mr Selby, I know you're trustworthy. He's a good man. Everyone likes him. And I think I've seen you around town, Silas, helping out at the market.'

'Yes. I've picked up a few odd jobs there. I've seen you, too, and heard how well you look after your ladies. Nice to meet you properly, Mrs Tucker.'

'Mrs T will do. Come down to the kitchen, all of you. Silas, you'll want to meet my son, because he's keeping an eye on this young lady as well. We'll both be glad to have someone looking after Jo all the time, very glad.'

'I'm not totally helpless,' she protested.

'You're a stranger and you don't even know your way round the valley properly yet, lass, let alone who to trust. Don't be surprised if my Peter tells you off about your rashness. He saw how Rathley went after his sister. You'd better get used to being careful from now on, lass, if you want to stay safe. Rathley's a madman about women who don't do as he wants. Only he's cunning with it and Sergeant Deemer has never found proof of him being behind what's been done.'

It felt strange to have so many people concerned about her safety, Jo thought as she followed Mrs T down the stairs to the lower floor. She hadn't had anyone to look out for her for years. She'd been on her own when she'd left the farm to work in Perth, though she'd made one or two friends there, of course.

And when her father fell ill and she went back to live at home, she'd been the person in charge of caring for him as he grew weaker – as well as having to deal with her stepmother. Edna had gone to pieces when her husband fell ill, which wasn't how Jo would have behaved if a man she loved was dying.

Stop going over all that! she told herself.

Mrs T smiled at them and gestured to some chairs set round a huge table. 'Sit down, do and I'll get our Peter.'

As they sat down, Jo caught Nick's eye and he winked, so she winked back. He was such a lovely fellow, she thought again. Pity he lived in England.

Now, where had that thought come from? What business was it of hers where he lived? She'd never see him again after she went back to Australia.

Unfortunately.

Mrs T's son had not long been home from work and had been changing his clothes and having a quick wash before he sat down to his meal, which was always served after that of the lodgers.

By the time they'd explained it all yet again, it was getting late and the lodgers had finished eating, so Mrs T insisted on feeding Nick and Silas as well as Jo.

'You said Janey's had to go home early because her mother's ill, so I'll just help you clear the table up there, Mum.' Peter followed his mother up the stairs.

She came back with some tureens on a tray. 'Plenty of leftovers today. Nice lamb stew, this is, but some of those lasses eat like birds. The food's still warm because it's been sitting on my new electric warmer.'

From the way Mrs T spoke, barely concealing her pride, Jo guessed this gadget must be a new possession. Electricity was certainly changing the world and making life easier for women. They didn't have it out at her old home, but she'd got used to its convenience in Perth.

Peter put a tray of dirty dishes in the scullery and pulled out a chair at the table opposite Jo. '*Promise* you won't go anywhere outside the town centre on your own till we sort this out.'

'Not you nagging me as well!'

'I mean it.'

'I've arranged for Silas to accompany me everywhere, haven't I?'

He continued to stare at her, so she rolled her eyes at him and said, 'Oh, all right. I promise.'

'Make sure you stick to that promise. Rathley is getting worse. He was acting so strangely yesterday morning when we picked up your luggage, it made me wonder if he's losing his marbles.' He tapped the side of his forehead in the universal sign for someone who was mentally not right.

After that warning Jo ate her food absent-mindedly, thinking of what might have happened the other night if she hadn't had the wits to find another bedroom. Or yesterday, if she hadn't had Peter to protect her. How would all this end? she wondered.

Then Peter nudged her and she realised Mrs T had spoken and was waiting for her to answer. 'Sorry. What did you say?'

'You should call in to see Mrs Fernby before you go up to Backshaw Moss looking for your relatives, Jo. The minister's wife may know where these Tayners live and how best to approach them. She does a lot of good work among the poor.'

'Yes. Good idea. I could stroll round to see her this evening. It's not far, is it?'

Nick gave her a stern look across the table. 'Thinking of going out on your own?'

'No. With one of you, if you've the time.'

'I'll come with you,' he said at once.

'So will I,' Peter said. 'I'll enjoy a stroll.'

Jo didn't feel as grateful as she should have but hoped she hadn't shown that. It was going to irk her to be always watched, she knew that already.

Silas ate his meal quickly and stood up. 'That was delicious, Mrs T. Now, if you don't need me any longer tonight, Jo, I'll get off home.'

'See you tomorrow morning at eight o'clock.'

'Yes. I won't be late.'

Mrs T got up with him, picking up a package and slipping it into his hand. Jo heard her say in a low voice, 'For your wife and children.'

His voice came out sounding choked. 'Thank you.'

When Mrs T came back, she sat down quietly and went on with her meal.

'That was kind of you,' Jo told her.

Mrs T flushed. 'It was just a few leftovers.'

'Silas looked a lot happier than he did earlier. It was good to see.'

'Chaps like him aren't asking for the moon, just a regular job,' Peter said. 'And even a temporary job lifts the spirits. Now, if you've both finished, let's go and visit Mrs Fernby before it's too late. You'll like her, Jo.'

15

The three of them walked through the streets at a brisk pace.

'You're a good, fast walker, Jo,' Nick commented.

'Dad used to say that. He told me to be sure to go for a tramp across the moors while I was here, said I'd love the soaring feeling you get when you're surrounded by wide open spaces. Oh, bother! I can't go out walking on my own now, can I?'

'I'll take you, if you like,' he offered. 'We call it "the tops", which is what the moors are, I suppose, tops of hills. I used to go out walking there sometimes when I was a lad, before we moved away.'

'I'd enjoy that very much. Thank you.' She smiled at him and couldn't look away for a moment or two.

He was the one to break the invisible connection. 'We might even be able to go during the week, if I have no bookings – and if the weather is fine.' He chuckled and added, 'I'm sure your employers will give you half a day off work.'

'Will you be working at weekends?'

'Saturdays, yes, once things get going. Not Sundays, though. That'd be frowned on, even though people who work full-time would love to have driving lessons then. I can't afford to upset people.'

'I'll go walking whenever it suits you.' She saw Peter watching them and felt her cheeks turn warmer. She could tell what he was thinking about the two of them from the knowing smile on his face.

She had a sudden wish that it was true. She'd gone out with young men a time or two but had lost interest in them after a while, and had come to the conclusion that she wasn't the sort to lose her head over a man and therefore was not likely to get married. But now she wasn't so sure. Maybe she'd just never met the right person. Only it was no use starting anything with Nick. She was going back to Australia after she'd finished here ... wasn't she?

She reined in her thoughts abruptly.

It took only a few minutes to reach the minister's house, a comfortable residence standing next to the neat, plain Methodist chapel with its tidy

175

churchyard and rows of headstones.

Peter gestured to it as he rang the doorbell. 'Largest chapel in the district, that is, first one to be built round here. A lot of mill owners contributed towards building chapels in the nineteenth century, because they thought it kept their workers away from boozing – and also because they wanted the children they would one day employ to learn to read and write at Sunday school.'

'It's far bigger than our church in Beeniup,' Jo said. 'Well, even Birch End is bigger than the town I grew up in. Only we didn't call Beeniup a village, even so.'

The maid opened the door just then. She nodded to Peter as if she knew him and he said quickly, 'It's your mistress we'd like to see, not Allan.'

'Oh, right. Please come and sit down. I'll tell Mrs Fernby you're here.'

She showed them into a room to one side of the hall, which was furnished with wooden chairs and a table, obviously a place for parishioners to consult their minister or his wife, or perhaps hold small meetings.

The minister's wife joined them shortly afterwards, so Peter introduced the others and explained why they were there.

She looked at Jo and hesitated, as if reluctant to say something.

Jo could guess what it was. 'I'm twenty-six, Mrs Fernby. I grew up on a farm and I do understand what the world is like. Which is not to say I approve of people behaving immorally.'

'Well, then, I have heard about your relative. It's not good news because she's living in one of the houses in Packman Alley, Number Three I think.' Another hesitation, then, 'The alley's behind the corner shop near the pub and all three houses there are apparently used for – well, immoral purposes.'

'Oh dear.'

'They call her Red Moira, because she dyes her hair bright red. She has a daughter who lives with her, but Tess is quite young. Most people would say she was too young to be plying that trade yet, but you can never tell. It always horrifies me when young girls are involved.'

There was a murmur of agreement.

'I was told that Moira is saving her um ... her daughter's innocence for the highest bidder, and that some men are already showing an interest.'

No one said anything and they avoided one another's eyes as that sank in. It horrified Jo and she could see the looks of disgust on the two men's faces.

She swallowed hard and stared at the ground, wondering how to help, then had an idea, not a pleasant idea but still, it might work. She forced herself to speak calmly, 'Then perhaps I can be the highest bidder and rescue the girl that way. What do you think?'

There was another brief silence as her companions took in her suggestion, then Mrs Fernby spoke. 'Who knows what people like that will agree to? I don't approve of you doing such a thing, but sadly, it may be the only way. It wouldn't be cheap, though. Can you afford it?'

'Yes, I can. I inherited some money recently.'

'What would you do with the girl?'

'I haven't even thought about that. I'd take her away from Rivenshaw, I suppose, maybe take her back to Australia where nobody knows her circumstances. I'll work something out once we discover exactly what's going on.'

'It might be best to get her as far away from Backshaw Moss as you can, if you can get Moira to agree to you taking the girl, that is.'

'I'll have to go and see her, persuade her. Surely she'll want a better life for her child?'

'You can't always be sure. She may think it is a better life than working in a mill or in some of the hard, dirty jobs on farms, which pay very poorly. I believe the higher-paid women of the mother's sort can earn a lot of money.'

Peter and Nick started speaking at the same time, stopped and Nick gestured to the other man to continue.

'You can't go into this Moira's home, Jo. It'll also be where she works.'

'How else can I speak to her?'

'I'll go and see if I can find her, persuade her to meet you—'

Jo shook her head. 'No! I'm going to find her myself and the sooner the better. Any suggestion about her daughter will come better from me than from either of you. I doubt she'd trust a man.'

Her two escorts glanced quickly at one another in dismay, then looked pleadingly at Mrs Fernby as if begging her to intervene.

'In that case, I think my husband and I had

better come with you, Jo. We can wait outside but if you leave the door open, our presence there will protect your reputation. I'll ask him now.'

She got up and left the room.

'You shouldn't go near that woman, relative or not,' Nick told Jo.

'I don't *like* the thought of getting mixed up in such a situation, but there you are. Sometimes you have to do things you dislike.'

They all fell silent until the door opened and the minister joined them.

'My wife has explained what's going on and I agree with her: we'd better go with you, Jo. We can all squash into my car.'

'No need. I have my car,' Nick said.

'It'll be better only to take one car into Back-shaw Moss at this time of day. Lads there have been known to throw stones at passing vehicles, goodness knows why, or try to break into parked cars. But they know mine by sight and leave it alone, because I go there to help people.'

Peter and Nick both looked relieved at this offer. Jo wasn't so sure about the idea. Wouldn't being confronted by a group of people upset Moira? Especially if one of them was the Methodist minister?

And why should this woman trust Jo, let alone allow her to take her daughter away? It was doubtful that she'd allow it straight away and if she cared about the girl, she'd want to get to know their new relative first.

It was so hard to know what was the right thing to do. Her father would say to be careful of rushing into something heedlessly. But she hated the thought of a young girl risking being caught up in such a trade. No, her father would approve of her saving the child, whatever it cost, she was quite sure of that, at least.

Nick sat on one side of Jo in the back of the car, looking unhappy. 'You shouldn't be doing this,' he whispered suddenly as the minister drove them up towards Backshaw Moss.

She replied in an equally low voice, 'If Mrs Fernby is right, this girl is in great danger of being forced into an immoral life. I have to save her if I can, Nick, surely you understand that? She's a relative. And actually, I'd want to help her even if she wasn't related to me. She's only a child.'

'I feel sorry for the girl, of course I do, but it's your safety and reputation that worry me most, Jo.'

'I'll do my best to look after both aspects.'

Mrs Fernby said, 'This is Backshaw Moss, the better part.'

Jo gazed out, first at one side then the other, immediately disgusted by what she saw. And this was the better part of the district!

They were driving slowly along between two rows of houses that looked ready to fall down any minute. Men were lounging on street corners, barefoot children were running round, and women in soiled pinafores, some with cigarettes in their mouths like the men, were gossiping in doorways. Windowpanes here and there must have been broken because the frames were filled by cardboard or wood. Washing still sagged on lines strung across the street, even though it was late. The clothes didn't look particularly clean, either. And rubbish lay everywhere. You could smell it as well as see it, even from inside the car.

The car slowed down still further, bumping along at a slow walking pace to avoid a group of men standing in the road, who scowled at the car and made no attempt to get out of the way. When Mr Fernby pulled up about twenty yards further on, the men turned to watch.

He switched off the engine and pointed to the right. At the other side of the road there was what looked like an alley. The opening was narrow, not much wider than the car, next to a small corner shop, which had half its window boarded up and only a few tins of food on display in the other half.

'This is Packman Alley, I'm afraid.' He paused to let them look round then asked, 'Shall I go and enquire for your cousin, Miss Melling?'

'If you would, please.'

Jo watched him cross the road, speak to an old woman leaning against the wall and slip her a coin. She pointed down the alley, slipped the coin down the front of her bodice and hurried away.

He returned to the car. 'The end door, she says, the blue one, and your cousin is at home, apparently. She – er – hasn't started work yet, thank goodness.'

'I'll come with you, Jo,' Mrs Fernby said.

Her husband shook his head. 'No, dear. I'd rather you didn't. I'd better do it, I suppose, though I've never met this woman.'

Jo could see his reluctance. 'She'll be less likely to speak openly if you're with me, Mr Fernby, given that clerical collar you're wearing.' And the disapproving scowl he was also wearing, but she couldn't say that. 'Nick, would you come with me, please, but stand back a little?'

'Yes, of course.'

Peter got out as well. 'I'll wait at the corner of the street.'

Jo walked down the narrow cobbled alley and knocked on the door at the end. Her heart was thumping and she hoped she wasn't showing how nervous she was feeling.

Bracing herself to do whatever was necessary, she knocked on the blue door again. And waited. Just as she was about to knock yet again, she heard footsteps coming closer.

A woman opened the door, frowning to see her, then looked past Jo towards Nick. The woman's hair was dyed an improbable shade of red and her face was plastered with make-up, but in spite of that, she looked pale and ill.

'Go away. This is no place for your sort an' I don't need my soul saving.'

'Are you Moira Tayner?'

'What if I am?'

'I think I may be a cousin of yours, second cousin anyway.'

'I don't care if you're cousin to the king, I won't put up with any lecturing and praying over me. Go away and leave me in peace.'

'I won't go away till you've heard me out.'

When Moira tried to close the door on her, Jo put her foot in the way, saying quickly, 'Look, I'm from Australia. My father died recently and he wanted me to find my relatives here in England.

And that means you.'

'Why in hell's name did he want you to do that? I've never even met anyone from Australia.'

'Because I don't have any close relatives left there and because he thought they might need help.'

'What sort of help? Are you going to dish out money to all your relatives? If so, you can give me some.' She laughed as if this was a joke and then started coughing, a horrible hacking sound.

'Can I please come in and talk to you, Moira?'

'No.' She continued to cough and tried once again to close the door, pushing at Jo and banging the door against her foot.

Jo didn't budge.

'Mam, you need to come inside and sit down.' A girl joined them, standing close to her mother and staring at Jo. She was plainly dressed, with her hair in two childish plaits, but that didn't hide how pretty she was. She proved she'd been eavesdropping when she added, 'And why are you trying to send this lady away if she's a relative and wants to help us?'

'That's my own business. You get back inside, love.' But turning sharply towards her daughter made Moira sway dizzily and she had to set her hand on the wall to steady herself.

The girl put her arm round her. 'Come and have a rest, love. I'll talk to this lady.'

Moira closed her eyes, then looked at Jo, and it seemed for a moment as if shame was warring with anger in her eyes, then her expression grew hard again. She tried to speak, but could only cough helplessly.

183

'She's not been well,' the girl said. 'Who are you again? Come inside and tell me why you're here.'

'Leave the door open,' Nick called.

The girl looked out of the door. 'Is that your husband?'

'No. Just a friend.'

The girl led Jo into a room that smelled strongly of some sickly perfume and gestured to a chair. Moira flung herself on the sofa, struggling not to cough.

'I'll have to get some of her cough mixture.'

'Just give me water to sip, Tess love. That cough mixture makes me feel dopey. I can't afford that when I'm working or the sods will try to cheat me.'

'You can afford to take a day or two off and get better properly. Let me look after you, Mam. I thought we'd agreed about that.'

Moira ignored that and stared at Jo. 'Why are you bothering? Your sort don't usually care about women like me.'

'I told you: because you're my relatives.' She explained how they were connected.

Moira considered this, head on one side, then nodded. 'Sounds as if you really are a relative, but I'm not going into a home for fallen women, thank you very much. They might be saving your soul but they don't do much good for your body. They treat you like slaves in those places and they'd separate me and my Tess, probably send her out to be a housemaid. They'd not even tell me where she was, in case I corrupted her. I've spoken to people who've been in them places, so I know what they're like.'

'Why do you think I'd send you somewhere like that?'

'Because that's what respectable women always try to do to women like me.' She sounded bitter and held out her hand to her daughter as she spoke.

The girl took it and cradled it in both hers, looking at Jo. 'No one's going to take me away from Mam.'

Jo frowned as she watched. The love between them shone out.

Moira looked at her with such understanding of what she was thinking that Jo didn't know what to say or do. Then it came to her. 'What if I took you both away from here to Australia? Together. The sea journey and the warmer climate out there would probably do your health a world of good, Moira.'

The woman looked at her very sharply. 'Have you got that much money?'

'Yes.'

'Hmm. But even if you paid our fares, how would we live when we got there?'

'I've enough money to keep you for a while once we got there, and in reasonable comfort, too.'

The woman couldn't hide her surprise. 'And you'd do that?'

'Yes. I could help you get settled. I only came to England to bring my stepmother back to live near her family after my father died. I'm going back soon whether you go with me or not.'

There was a long silence and Jo didn't interrupt, but stood patiently waiting.

185

Eventually, Moira looked up. 'Well, you have surprised me. I'll think about it, I really will. How do I get in touch with you?'

'I'm staying at Mrs Tucker's lodging house.'

'Ha! She'd have a fit if I turned up there. She'd slam the door in my face.'

'But if I told her what was going on, she'd let Tess or someone else bring a message for me, then Peter or Nick could bring me to see you again.'

Another of those long silences followed, then, 'I'll definitely think about it. I'm tired now. See her out, then lock the front door, Tess love. You're right. I'm not up to working tonight.'

At the door, Jo said quietly, 'She's not well at all. Has she seen a doctor?'

'No. She won't. She just gets cough mixture from the chemist in Rivenshaw.'

From Moira's appearance, Jo was afraid it was too late for a doctor to help anyway. She'd seen others look like this. She kept her voice calm. 'Come and fetch me if your mother needs my help, Tess. With anything. And talk to her about my offer. I meant what I said.'

The girl looked at her and Jo realised yet again how pretty she was. She was nearly as tall as Jo but was still dressed like a child in unflattering and shabby clothes. With a bit of luck they were in time to save her.

'I'm not leaving her,' Tess said suddenly. 'Whatever you want to arrange, I'm staying with Mam.'

'You sound as if you love her very much.'

'I do. She's protected me from ... a lot of bad things, things a lady like you wouldn't know

186

about. And at some cost to herself as well. She's been the best mother she can.'

Pity speared through Jo and sadness as it reminded her of her own loss. 'My mother was the same, always doing her best for me. She died when I was about your age. I envy you still having yours.'

Tess stared at her as if trying to see whether she meant this, then relaxed a little. 'Yes. I think you do understand. Part of it anyway.'

'And I really do want to help. We're family.'

'Hmm. We'll see. Action speaks louder than words. I'll let you know.'

The girl took a step backwards and closed the door.

Jo could only hope that she'd said the right thing.

16

Hobbs had been keeping an eye on the alley since he saw the car stop nearby. He moved further back into the shadows as he watched the trio leave. Who the hell was the young woman he'd seen and why would someone like her want to visit Red Moira? She not only looked respectable but had been driven here by the Methodist minister. Decent women didn't come to places like Packman Alley, let alone go inside one of the houses on their own.

Was she was trying to save souls? He grinned at

the thought of them attempting to do that with Red Moira. She'd soon give them what for. She could look after herself, that one could. Besides, that interfering Mrs Fernby would have gone inside with the young woman if that was the purpose of the visit, but she'd stayed in the car. The car hadn't driven away, though; it had waited for the younger woman to come out again.

He scowled in the direction the car had just taken. If you asked him, that particular minister's wife should keep her nose out of other folk's affairs. She'd encouraged his wife to defy him, damn her! And look what that had led to. Doris had got her sisters in to help and the bitches had thrown him out of his own home. He did occasional jobs for Mr Rathley but he'd not had much to do recently.

With nothing better to occupy his time and not enough money to sit boozing, he kept watch at the end of the alley for a good two hours longer to see if anything else happened that night. There might be something to be gained from this situation, but he'd have to tread carefully. Red Moira was another uppity woman and you had to be careful how you spoke to her, even if you only met her in the corner shop. Someone should have beaten some sense into her years ago.

If he could only work out what these people were planning, he might be able to take advantage of it, maybe sell some information to Mr Rathley. He stayed there to see if Moira opened up later, but though he waited until the corner shop closed, her lamp still didn't go on in the window next to the blue door and no one tried to go in. The only people coming and going in the dimly lit alley were customers calling at the other two houses.

He knew Red Moira charged more for her services than the other women did and had several regular gentlemen callers who were let in even when the light wasn't switched on, including Rathley. He'd watched them go in and out many a time. He knew more than most folk about what was happening in Backshaw Moss. You had to if you wanted to find work.

In the end the cold began to get to him, so he decided to give up for the night and walked along the street to the pub. The Packman's Arms was set back a little from the road and wasn't quite as tumbledown as the rest of the buildings round here. The place must be a ruddy goldmine, because it was full every night, even though people didn't have as much money to spare and had to make their drinks last longer these days.

It was past closing time now but the landlord rarely bothered to observe the legal hour for pubs to stop serving booze, at least when it came to regular customers. The front entrance to the pub was shut and locked, but that wasn't the only way in, as the locals well knew. And there was even a way to escape if there was a police raid because of the after-hours drinking. You could squeeze past the dustbins into a narrow passage between backyards. It led to Packman Alley.

Hobbs walked round to the back of the pub, showed his face to the doorman and was allowed inside. By counting out his pennies and half-pennies, he managed to buy a pint of beer but had to make it last so that he could stay in the warmth.

He sighed in disappointment and drained the last of the beer when the landlord threw everyone out an hour later. Old Ronald didn't like his customers all going out the same way, so like one or two others, Hobbs walked along the narrow ginnel to Packman Alley. He checked as he passed Number 3, he could see that there was still no light in the window, or anywhere else in the cramped little house.

Red Moira didn't often take a night off. She was up to something; he'd known that when he saw her going into the lawyer's office in town. Now, why would she do that?

He'd wondered whether to take that information to Rathley, but since he didn't know why she'd gone there, he couldn't see how that would benefit him. You had to be sure of what you were telling that sod. He'd had people beaten up for wasting his time.

It was common knowledge among certain people that Rathley had his sights set on Moira's daughter Tess. He liked them young.

What was Red Moira plotting? Why go to a lawyer? Did she intend to sell her daughter to someone else? Rathley would make her sorry if she did that.

A few people thought she might take the girl away before the inevitable happened, so fiercely had she looked after her over the years. But Hobbs didn't believe that. Why would she take her daughter away when the girl was worth a fortune to her here? No one could be that stupid.

He knocked on the door of his home and his wife stuck her head out of the window. 'Can I come back, love? It's a really cold night.'

'Have you got any money for food?'

'No, but I'll get some tomorrow, I promise.'

'Ha! I bet you had money for beer or you'd have come here earlier. You have kids going hungry, Kenneth Hobbs. You can't come back here till you can help feed them.'

'But Doris love–'

'I've got a big stick and I'll thump you good and hard if you try to get in. And my sisters are only two doors away. They'll come running to help if I shout for them.' She slammed the window shut.

When Doris got that sharp tone in her voice, he knew better than to argue. He spat in her direction and went round to the shed at the back of his friend's house, where he made himself as comfortable as he could on a pile of sacks, not for the first time. His belly rumbled with hunger, but it had been a choice between food or beer and a bit of company, and he knew which he preferred.

There was no help for it: he'd have to find some way of earning a few shillings for food. That would have its compensations. He ate better when he was living at home. His wife could make the pennies spin out to buy food for the family better than anyone he knew. But the sort of jobs he could find were hard work, and often mucky work too.

Still, going home would be better than sleeping here. He shivered. Much better.

He sniffed and pulled a face. Ugh! Had his friend's cat made a mess in here? No. It was the

191

drains again. They were always getting blocked up. Once they got bad enough, the council would do something about them, but not before they had to.

When Jo walked away from Number 3, she was glad to see her two escorts waiting for her. As she moved towards them, a man came into the alley, cap pulled down low to hide his face. She didn't like the furtive look of him and hastily turned her head away because she didn't want him to recognise her in future.

He stopped to stare at her but as Nick took a step towards him, he hurried across into the middle house.

'Hurry up, Jo. It's starting to get busy here. Don't say anything yet and keep your face hidden as much as you can. There's another chap over there and we don't want to be overheard.' He jerked his head towards a doorway near the entrance to the alley where a man was leaning against the wall in the shadows, watching them.

She heard the car engine start before they reached the vehicle and when she got in, her companions followed her without a word.

The minister set off straight away. 'I suggest we wait till we get home to discuss what you've found out. I need to concentrate on my driving on this narrow road and I may miss something you say that's important.'

Even after they left Backshaw Moss and the narrowest part of the road, they drove back down to Rivenshaw in silence. Jo was glad to have time to gather her thoughts together. Her mind was full of conflicting feelings about the situation and how best to help her relatives. Conventional morals said she ought to try to take the girl away from such a mother, but she'd seen their love for one another and would feel guilty doing that.

And anyway, the two women she'd met weren't poor helpless creatures needing to be guided and rescued, not in the way she'd expected, anyway. It just went to show how patronising her attitude had been before she met them. They both seemed intelligent to her and like many others with jobs so scarce, were fighting for survival in a hostile world. The hard lessons of that were written on Moira's face and on her daughter's to a lesser extent. Tess might be young but her eyes betrayed an understanding of life that was a lot older than her years.

The two women's love for one another reminded Jo of how she'd felt about her own mother. That made an instant bond between them – on her side at least – and because of it, she felt even more determined to help Moira and Tess get away and start a new life together, whatever anyone else said or did, whatever she had to do and pay to achieve that.

Surely that would be possible? Money didn't do much good sitting in the bank, after all, not when there were people she could help with it.

Once they arrived at the minister's house, they were ushered inside so that Jo could tell them what had happened. She went over it, trying hard to make them understand the love between mother and daughter.

To her dismay Mrs Fernby was adamant that the only way to save the girl and give her a decent life was to take her away from such a mother.

Jo didn't say it, but the discussion only made her more determined to help *both* women and not by shutting the mother up in a home for fallen women, either. In the end she said simply, 'Well, Moira is going to send a message to Mrs T's when she's made up her mind whether to accept my help. I don't think we can do anything till we hear from her.'

Mrs Fernby stared at her in surprise. 'But surely we ought to make plans for where to send the girl? I already know of a home for women like the mother near Rochdale, where the matron will see that this Moira woman leads a decent, hard-working life in future.'

Years of dealing with her stepmother had taught Jo to avoid making specific comments in advance about what she intended to do. 'My cousin hasn't decided what she wants to do yet and we can't kidnap the girl, after all.'

Mrs Fernby's voice grew noticeably cooler. 'We can get a magistrate to order that she be taken away from such a sordid background, under my supervision. I've done this before.'

'I've offered to take them both to Australia. They could make a new start there, as a lot of people have done.'

'*What?* But surely that would cost a great deal of money?'

'I have enough for the fares and what better way to spend it than on helping them?'

'The woman doesn't deserve it. Why, some

people would consider that more like a reward and it's wrong to reward immorality.'

'Well, we can't decide anything till we see what she wants.'

Peter intervened. 'I don't think there's anything further we can do about it tonight and it's getting late. Thank you for your help, Mr Fernby, Mrs Fernby. Nick and I will walk Jo back to my mother's house.'

Once they were away from the minister's house, Jo said, 'I upset Mrs Fernby, didn't I?'

It was Peter who answered. 'Yes, you did. She's a good woman but she has very strong views about immorality. Are you really determined to keep Moira and her daughter together?'

'Oh, yes. It'd be terrible to tear them apart.'

Nick looked at her determined expression and didn't argue. He was inclined to the same view.

They walked in silence until they reached Mrs T's house, then stopped. Nick didn't want to leave her yet, so he gestured to the low wall in front of it. 'Let's sit there and chat for a while. It's a pleasant night and I'm not ready for my bed yet.'

Peter gave a big yawn and eased his shoulders to and fro. 'Well, I'm sorry but I'm tired now. I had a busy day at work and it'll be the same to-morrow.'

'I'm still wide awake,' Jo admitted.

Nick saw her glance at him as she said that and said quickly, 'You and I could sit and chat for a bit.'

Peter took a step away from them. 'I'll leave you

to it and I'll tell Mam you won't be long, Jo. If you stay on the wall, in full view of the house, it'll be perfectly respectable to be out late together. My mother's younger lodgers often sit out here on summer evenings with their men friends.'

When Peter had left them, Jo found herself a smooth spot on the wall and Nick sat down next to her. 'It's a bit of a tangle with your relatives, isn't it?'

'Yes. Not at all what I expected.'

'What's she like to talk to, this Moira?'

'Sharp-witted, protective of her daughter. Tess is nearly as tall as me but she was dressed in very childish clothing and was wearing her hair in two plaits. I think it must be to keep her safe from men, but she won't be able to rely on that for much longer. If I'm not mistaken she's well on the way to having a woman's figure.'

'I've never met an immoral woman,' he said thoughtfully. 'I've seen them in the streets, of course, but that's all.'

'Moira's just a woman, not a three-headed monster. In other circumstances, I'd have liked her, I think, and I respect the way she protects her daughter.'

'Are you really going to take them back to Australia?'

'What else can I do, Nick? They can't settle round here, can they? My cousin Moira is too well known, from what Mrs Fernby said, even if she changes her ways. And I've no other close family to keep me here, after all. Kath Tayner's branch is quite distant from mine and though she was polite, it was clear that she wasn't really bothered about getting to know me.'

Nick gave in to temptation and reached out to take hold of her hand. When she didn't pull away, he said quietly, 'I'll be sorry if you go away.'

'Will you?'

'Yes. I'd have liked to get to know you better.'

'Oh.'

'If you were staying, would you have given me a chance to do that?'

'Yes.'

She was as straightforward about that as about everything else. He liked that about her, liked it very much. 'No young man waiting for you back in Australia?'

'No. I've met a few, even started seeing a couple of them regularly, only I got rather bored with them after a while. One of them would take me out to the park and then sit there in silence. The other had never read a book in his life unless forced to at school, and didn't go to the cinema, even. He worked long hours in his family business and that was all he could talk about.' After a pause, she added with huge scorn, 'Ironmongery! Nails and hammers.'

'Shows how stupid they were. I'd have made a lot more effort than that. You're the most interesting woman I've met in a long time.'

'That's one of the nicest compliments I've ever had. I find you interesting, too, Nick.'

Silence, and they both gasped in unison as they saw a shooting star whiz across the sky.

'It's supposed to be lucky to see one,' he said.

'Is it? I wouldn't mind a bit of good luck if I have to take Moira and Tess away.' Jo smiled rue-

197

fully. 'I've only just arrived, and I spent the journey putting up with my stepmother's fussing. I could have strangled her sometimes, the way she goes on and on about things that are unimportant. I wonder what my cousins would be like as travelling companions. They couldn't be worse than she was, that's for sure.'

'I hope you never find out what they're like. I don't wish them ill, but you'll be risking your own reputation if you get involved with Moira. Can't you just give them some money and send them to Australia on their own? Most people in the valley are good sorts. You'd easily make friends if you stayed here.'

'I might have done that if things were different. But I don't think Moira is very well, and what if she died and left Tess on her own in a strange country? That could be dangerous for such a young woman. I can't reconcile it with my conscience to run that risk. If you'd seen Moira, heard her cough, a really bad hacking sound that went on and on – well, you'd understand.'

'Could it be serious?'

'Yes. I think it could. She's so thin, even though I'm sure she can afford decent food. From the way she looked at me, as if afraid I'd say something, I'm fairly certain she knows that she won't make old bones. She seems to be trying to hide it from the girl. I'm not sure she's succeeded, though.'

'I can see why you're worried, then.' He admired her concern for her relatives at the same time as wishing she wasn't planning to get involved.

She spoke slowly and softly, as if expressing her

thoughts aloud, 'Life doesn't always let you do what you want, does it, Nick? And it can take people you love away from you suddenly. I've lost both my mother and father now. I can't just abandon Tess.'

'No, I suppose not.' He didn't speak for a while, but he kept hold of her hand and was glad when she didn't pull away.

In the distance, the town hall clock struck ten and she sighed. 'I think I'd better go into the house now. I'm sure I saw a curtain move. Mrs T is probably keeping an eye on us. I think I'll enjoy being old more than I'm enjoying being young, because I'll be able to do what I want without people scolding me.'

'I suppose so.'

She started to pull her hand away but he held on tightly. 'Please remember, whatever happens, that if you need my help, you mustn't be afraid to ask me. Whether I approve of what you're doing or not, I'll always be on your side.'

'Thank you. I'd never be afraid of asking you anything, Nick.'

'And Jo – please don't go away without telling me what you're doing and saying goodbye properly.'

'All right.'

'Promise.' He raised her hand to his lips.

Her voice came out choked and her hand trembled slightly as she reacted to his touch. 'I promise.'

He stood up. He wanted to kiss her, wanted it desperately, but there would probably be someone watching them from inside the house. 'Better go inside now or Mrs T will be coming out to chase me away.'

He watched her disappear through the front door, then murmured softly, 'Please keep that promise, Jo Melling.'

As he walked home, he prayed desperately that fate or whatever you called it would step in on his side for a change and let him get to know Jo.

Only a few paces further on, he stopped and faced up to it: he wanted to do more than merely get to know her. He was already sure that he wanted to court her.

How could he feel like that so quickly?

Perhaps because she was right for him. He smiled and nodded.

Mrs T was waiting for Jo in the hall. 'Come down to the kitchen and I'll make you a cup of cocoa while you tell me how it went.'

Another repetition, Jo thought with a sigh, but did as she was told.

When she'd finished describing her visit to Moira, Mrs T didn't say anything, but sat staring into space. Then she surprised Jo.

'I was at school with Moira. Friends with her till her father ran off with someone and her mother started selling her body to make ends meet. After that, my mother told me to stay away from Moira and she didn't come to school as often. Pity. She was a good scholar, could have become a teacher herself.'

'She seemed sharp-witted.'

'Mmm. She tried to get away, to manage without following her mother's example and went off to live in London. But she met someone there who left her with a child on the way. Women can be fools about men.' She shrugged. 'I'm sorry for her but I won't have her or the girl come through my door, let alone staying here.'

'I won't bring them. You don't know where I could take them, do you? Just for a few days?'

'Why would you need to do that?'

'If they have to leave that house suddenly.'

'From what I've heard, it's Moira's own house, so they won't have to leave it, whether she's, um, working there or not. Like I said, she's not stupid. I bet she'll have money put aside as well.'

'Doesn't she need a male protector to do that sort of work?'

'She's got one. Big Donny. Slow-witted young chap but strong. He's always with her when she leaves the house, going to the shops or whatever, and I've heard he sleeps in the scullery at night. She can call him if anyone gets too rough with her.'

Jo wondered how Mrs T knew all this but didn't interrupt.

'In return she's protected Big Donny from the sort of lads who hang around the streets and torment slow-witted folk.'

'Oh.'

'You'd better think carefully before you do anything, lass. I know you want to help her, but you'd be safest staying right away from her.'

'She's a relative.'

Mrs T sighed. 'I thought you'd say that. Well, be as careful as you can.'

17

That same evening, Charlie Willcox sat frowning into space for so long his wife Marion eventually poked him with her knitting needle. 'What's going on in that head of yours? You're plotting something. I can always tell.'

'I can't stop thinking about the council meeting and the notes the mayor gave us about previous attempts to deal with our pet slum, or rather about how the former council deliberately did *not* deal with it. That's left me with all sorts of things to think about, and I've gone through them till my head aches, trying to figure out what we can do about it.' He rubbed the side of his forehead as if to reinforce this statement.

'Go on.'

'It's a good job we've got some new council members ready to take action. Did you know there was a small outbreak of something suspiciously like cholera a couple of years ago because of the filth in that place? And the last council would only authorise a temporary clean-up, when what is really needed is a whole series of new connections to a proper sewage system.'

'No, I didn't know that. I'm surprised it's occupying your mind to such an extent, though, Charlie. You didn't even want to get involved with the council when the mayor asked you to stand for election, and you were grumbling all the time he was nagging you and insisting you do it.'

'Well, I've changed my mind. I'm glad now that I'm on the council. Very glad. We have a son and another child on the way. I don't want Arthur or the new baby catching something that kills them off. Infections can spread, you know, and our home is very close to Backshaw Moss.'

She looked at him in horror. 'Oh, my goodness, yes. You're right. And yet I didn't even know that had happened. How did I not find out?'

'They kept it secret, threatened any workers who spoke about it, and called it a temporary blockage.'

'Well, you and the others will have to *insist* the council do something about it now that we do know. Why else do we pay rates on our houses?'

He shot her a quick sideways glance. 'I thought you'd be annoyed if I got too involved. It'll mean me going out more often in the evenings.'

She gave him one of those soft, special smiles that few other people ever saw, then the sharp-tongued Marion returned and she followed up the smile with another poke. 'I *don't* want my children brought up in a valley run by corrupt men, and I particularly don't want them to risk falling ill because of that horrible slum.'

'Exactly.'

'So if you can do anything to help, I shall be on your side. And if you need my help, you have only to ask.'

He gave her a quick hug. 'Thank you. But I'd not dream of getting you involved, especially while you're in that condition.' He patted her stomach gently. 'These are ruthless men, love.

That sort of skulduggery and corruption seems to have crept up on us all.'

She looked at him anxiously. 'Does that mean *you* might be in danger if you try to make real improvements?'

'What? No. I'll be very careful, Marion, I promise you.'

'Make sure you are.'

'It's good that Reg has found out and is trying to turn things round, isn't it? It's the *right* thing to do. The honest thing. You know?'

'Yes. But you will move cautiously at first, won't you, Charlie? You have a tendency to dive into something feet first. Look how you bought that electrical goods shop, then had trouble turning a profit at first.'

'The shop's doing all right now. Better than all right. Harry Makepeace is a top-notch manager and electrician. And of course I'll move cautiously with the slum clearance. But what I've been thinking of tonight is that when it comes down to it, there's far more than bad drains involved. I drove round there and I think we need to knock down half the buildings in Backshaw Moss before they *fall* down and maybe kill somebody. We need to build new houses there, decent places where children can grow up healthy. Not big houses like ours, smaller ones, with rents cheap enough for decent, hard-working folk to afford.'

She stared at him in surprise. 'I've never thought to hear you talk like this before.'

'Like what?'

'Like a man who cares about doing the right thing for his town. Successful citizens used to do that more in the old queen's time, from what I've read. They called it their "civic duty".'

He wriggled uncomfortably. 'I'm no saint, but someone has to do it. I'm not on my own in this, you know.'

The soft look was back on her face. 'I'd be very proud if you helped sort out that horrible slum.'

'We'll do it and afterwards I hope people will think of that area as part of Birch End, not call it *Backshaw Moss* in that horrible, scornful tone of voice.'

'You know what? If you go on like this, you could end up as mayor, Charlie Willcox.'

He could feel himself flushing. 'Not me. Don't talk daft. I've enough on my plate. In the meantime, you concentrate on your new studio and on growing me another fine son.'

She leaned across to kiss him. 'Just be careful, love, that's all I ask.'

'Wilf is coming round tomorrow morning to discuss how he'll start.'

Charlie didn't tell her that someone had told him he'd only got permission to build on a room so easily because Higgerson, the main builder in the valley, wasn't interested in working on something that was for him, a man he didn't get on with. And since it was a small project anyway, Higgerson hadn't interfered. There had been two or three shouting matches between the two of them after Charlie had bought this house and then complained about one thing after another. With reason. Shoddy workmanship, cutting corners, all had been evident.

That was enough serious talk. Charlie switched

on the radio and they listened to a variety pro-
gramme together, laughing at the jokes and
humming along with the songs. He couldn't help
being aware of her staring at him now and then.
Well, he'd not only surprised her, but had surprised himself, too, with how angry he felt about
the mess just down the road from his home and
by how much he wanted to improve things. Not
just wanted to, but was determined to.

Marion went up to bed before he did, because
she got tired more easily at the moment. He re-
read the notes about council activities, shaking his
head sadly and feeling angry all over again. He
didn't like Rathley but as their paths hadn't often
crossed, he hadn't realised how many old houses
the fellow had bought or what a bad landlord he
was.

And as for Higgerson, who called himself a
builder, he shouldn't be given any more council
contracts. Definitely not. And if Charlie had any
say in it, he wouldn't get them, either. The houses
he built were not sound. If that man had anything to do with rebuilding that slum, he'd only
be building another slum of the future – and the
near future at that.

Charlie wished he had someone knowledgeable
about the world to discuss the situation with. As
he made himself a bedtime cup of cocoa, he
stopped for a moment, spoon in hand, thinking
about his older brother, who had also been his
best friend. He was deeply sorry to have lost
Jonah, and particularly now. Jonah had always
offered such wise advice, not poured it out all
over you at the drop of a hat but offered it gently

just when you needed it.

Would his new brother-in-law make a good substitute when he needed someone to talk things over with? He got on well with Todd, who could surely be trusted with private information and thoughts and who must have learned a lot travelling round the world as he had after the Great War. And he was a councillor too, now, an ally if needed.

It'd be worth having a preliminary chat with him about clearing up their valley. See how it went. Sometimes, when things were very important, you needed to get other people's opinions before you acted, particularly people who had similar morals to yourself.

He knew or knew of many of the better-off people in his valley, but he'd hesitate to discuss this with most of them. Though Finn who lived at the top end of Ellindale was another option. Finn was quite a philanthropist, though he hated you to say that to him and usually helped people quietly. Most folk didn't want to get involved in such 'messes', unfortunately.

A phrase he'd read somewhere came into his mind: *No man is an island.* He hadn't the faintest idea where it came from but it sounded like a poem, and it seemed to describe the situation with the council. You lived in a community, not on your own, and he, heaven help him, was one of the people elected to run certain aspects of his community's daily lives and interactions. And that meant helping put things right that had been wrong for a good long while.

It was a sobering thought. But he would never

put himself up for mayor, no way. What on earth had made Marion say that?

Charlie slept badly that night, which was rare for him. When he woke up, he decided the first thing to do was to have an informal chat with the mayor. After all, Reg had got him into this. Reg must have some idea about how to set about sorting it all out.

Next morning he phoned Reg at home before he went off to work and luckily caught him in.

'What can I do for you, Charlie lad?'

'I've been reading through those papers you handed out at the council meeting, and I'm surprised – no, more than that, absolutely *disgusted* by what I read. I had no idea things were that bad, and especially in Backshaw Moss. I knew there was some corruption around – well, there always is, you can never stamp it out entirely – but I thought it was only minor fiddling. I was too busy with my own affairs, I suppose.'

Reg made a sympathetic sound. 'Go on.'

'But it's not minor, is it? And it's in my own part of the valley, close to home. That shook me rigid, I can tell you.'

'It's in the whole valley, actually, but I think your local slum needs dealing with first and foremost.'

'Yes. I agree. How did you find out about it all?'

'When I became mayor, I found people at the town hall reluctant to give me full information about various matters, so I started poking around. You can find out a lot more if you stay at work after the clerks and other officials have gone home, and as mayor I had access to all the keys. Fortunately, the caretaker is an old friend of mine. I've known Paddy Blain since I was a lad. He kept what I was doing quiet, or I'd never have obtained the necessary information.'

'He's a good man.'

'I'd have done more about Backshaw Moss, Charlie, only I was saddled with a corrupt bunch of councillors, and I couldn't get a big enough majority to vote in the necessary improvements not to mention funding. You can't do anything without money and allies.'

'Have we got a majority now?'

No need to explain who the 'we' was. Reg was the one who had pushed Charlie and a few others into standing for council, popular people who had a lot of support. They'd all met privately a few times.

'Yes. As long as we all stay fit and well, we'll have the numbers, because not all the councillors are aligned with a side yet. Watch your back, though, Charlie.'

'What? You surely don't think they'll–'

'I'm not sure how far they'll go. I was attacked one night when walking home through the centre of town. Luckily someone came along and piled in to help me. I don't go out on my own at night any longer unless I'm in the car, and I carry a heavy walking stick.'

There was silence for a few moments as he let this sink in, then he continued, 'I think it's best for all our group to be on guard. Rathley and his cronies won't like their lucrative little schemes being stopped and they can be ruthless. Look, why don't you come round tonight and I'll show you a few more things I've unearthed? Make sure you're not followed and come into the house the back way.'

Charlie put the phone down but it was a while before he went to tell Marion what Reg had said about being careful, he was so shocked by how bad things were behind the scenes.

His wife was just starting to read the morning newspaper and looked at him over the top of her glasses.

When he'd finished going through what the mayor had said, the newspaper was on the floor and she had reached out to clutch his hand. 'You will take care, Charlie.'

'Oh, yes. Definitely. They won't dare attack me, though. I'm too well known.'

He hoped they wouldn't! He wasn't sure he'd convinced his wife about that, though – or himself. But he was going to follow the mayor's example and not walk anywhere on his own after dark. And he'd seen a heavy walking stick in one of his pawnshops. He'd take that for his own use.

This had only made him more determined to clean out the filth from his town, though, whether it was literal filth or disgusting people who behaved in a despicable manner.

His sons were going to live and grow up in a decent community.

Before she left for work, Jo asked Mrs T to send word to the car yard immediately if Tess or anyone else turned up with a message from Moira.

Mrs T grimaced. 'I'll do that, but no more. I

meant what I said last night: I won't take that girl into my house if she leaves her mother. I daren't lose my good name.'

'Yes, you made it plain and I do understand that.'

Silas was waiting for Jo outside the lodging house and together they made their way on foot to the office, not talking much today. She had seen Backshaw Moss yesterday, so intended to start work on the offices that morning. They certainly needed sorting out.

She was lost in thought most of the time but once she looked up and couldn't help noticing how carefully Silas was keeping an eye on their surroundings as they walked. His presence made her feel much safer. Who'd have expected this in England?

Nick was in the kitchen when they walked in and as he stood up, smiling at her, Jo found herself smiling back at him, in spite of her worries. She felt better just to be with him. She had been lucky in the friends she'd made here, very lucky.

'Did you sleep well, Jo?'

She told him the bald truth. 'Not really. I kept worrying about Moira and Tess, how to help them, you know?'

'We'll work something out.' He glanced at the battered clock on the mantelpiece. 'I have to go out to give a driving lesson at half-past nine. You can make a start on my office while I'm away, if that's all right?'

'Yes. Your office isn't bad at all, considering. I'll just check that the account books are up to date

211

and sort out all the official information so that we can find it easily if we need to check something. Then I'll move on to start work on Todd's office.'

'Thanks. I don't envy you sorting his stuff out. I don't know how he can find anything in that chaos.'

She chuckled. 'He probably won't be able to find anything for a while once I've sorted it out. My boss in Australia couldn't.'

Nick turned to leave, then came back. 'Do you think you can buy me the cupboard and other things later today?'

'I'm looking forward to doing that.'

'Don't forget to buy a desk and chair for yourself.'

'For my successor,' she corrected gently, seeing the disappointment in his expression, but she didn't want to raise false hopes. 'I might have considered staying here but I doubt I'll be able to do that now.'

He sighed and she quickly returned to the matter in hand. 'Any price limits on what I buy?'

'I want to spend as little as necessary, but make sure all the chairs are comfortable. No one can work well if they're sitting awkwardly. The items should look reasonable, too, not shabby.'

He looked round the office and frowned. 'It's going to be a squash fitting in here. I might ask Todd if we could clear out the back room behind this one, then I can move there, leaving whoever takes over from you in here to act as a sort of receptionist as well as secretary to both of us. What do you think?'

'It sounds like a good idea. You'll need to have

that back room painted, though. It must have been used as a place to dump things for years.' She couldn't help wishing again that she could stay, could get to know him better, could help him establish his business.

Todd was late, so she did what she could to Nick's office while waiting for him to arrive, even pacing it out to see where she might be able to put cupboards and where her own desk could be squeezed in. That finished, she was wondering whether to start work across the central passage in Todd's office when she saw his car stop in front of the workshop. Good. She could ask him exactly what he wanted.

He strode across the black tarmac to the house first. 'Hello. I'm a bit late today. I always make myself a cup of tea to start the working day. Come and chat to me while I put the kettle on. I'll make us all a cup.'

He led the way to the rear of the house, stopping at the sound of someone sweeping vigorously in the rear room and going to peep inside.

Silas looked up and grinned at him.

'What are you up to?'

'Making a start on this place, since we don't need to go to Backshaw Moss this morning now.'

'I didn't want Silas just standing round idle while I was tidying Nick's office, so he's been working on the back room, then Nick can use it. I was thinking of starting to sort out the papers in your office next. Is that all right, Todd?'

'As much as you can tidy up without cupboards to put things in.'

'Well, if you're going to be in for the rest of the

213

morning, Silas and I can go out and buy some office furniture for you and Nick. If you're going out, though, you might want us to stay here and keep an eye on the building and sales area. We'll do whatever suits you best.'

'I'm staying in the workshop. I want to check a few things on my own car. It was misfiring on the way here. What I usually do is lock up the house and put up a notice telling customers they can find me in the workshop. You've got your own key to the house now, haven't you?'

'Yes. Nick gave me a bunch of keys yesterday. If you'll put that sign up, we'll be on our way. Never mind the cups of tea.'

He went into his office and fished among the piles of papers, pulling out a rather battered piece of grubby white cardboard with one corner missing and words scrawled unevenly across it. He waved it at her triumphantly. 'Here it is.'

She nodded, making a mental note to buy some pieces of card and make a new sign. Maybe they'd even have some cellophane sheets for sale at the shop. People were starting to use it more and more to protect things, she'd noticed.

He gestured with one hand at the half-furnished office. 'As far as I'm concerned, the sooner you can get these offices sorted out, the better.'

'A cupboard and a filing cabinet for you. And proper stationery. Anything else?'

'A couple of better chairs than the ones I've been using, for customers to sit on. Nick can have the old chairs for his customers, if he likes.'

'All right.' That would save him some money, anyway.

At the door she paused again, to ask, 'Would you mind if we put net curtains up at the windows of both offices? I'll be in the front one all day every day and I don't really want to spend my life on view to the public. I'm sure anyone else working there would feel the same.'

He stared out of the window. 'I never thought about that. You're right, though. Order whatever you feel best.'

18

Jo was glad to get out into the fresh air again, but even though it was summer here, it wasn't what *she* would call pleasantly warm. She really must buy some warmer clothes to wear.

Silas showed her the way to Dyson's, and she paused at the door to ask, 'Do you know anywhere we can buy a second-hand cupboard and filing cabinet a bit like those we're buying for Todd? Nick hasn't as much money to spend and he hasn't got to know the shops well yet.'

Silas thought for a moment or two. 'We could try Willcox's main pawnshop. He has two places and the bigger one sells furniture from a huge shed out at the back.'

'The same Willcox who's part-owner of the car yard?'

'Yes. Charlie Willcox. He's an honest chap, firm in the prices he offers for goods being pawned and just as firm about his selling prices. I've

215

never heard of him cheating anyone, and he'd be as polite to a beggar as to the king.'

'Let's go there afterwards, then.'

They had no trouble finding the furniture for Todd's office. They were the only customers in the shop and the man who served her was clearly delighted with the sale, promising to have everything delivered that afternoon.

'Willcox's next,' Silas said. 'This way.'

Before they got there, however, they came face to face with two elegant ladies out shopping: her stepmother and Mrs Rathley.

Jo hesitated, not sure whether to stop and chat, and was relieved when Mrs Rathley solved the problem for her by stopping and holding out her hand.

'Jo. How nice to see you again. Are you out shopping?'

'Yes. Though it's to do with work, rather than my own needs. I've got a job as a clerk, the same sort of work as I was doing in Australia.'

Her stepmother gave her only the tiniest nod of the head and looked suspiciously at Jo's companion, so she introduced him. 'This is Silas, who's acting as my bodyguard.'

'Bodyguard!' Edna exclaimed, looking at her as if she were a liar. 'Why on earth would *you* need a bodyguard? If you'd come back to the house when Clarence wanted you to, you'd be perfectly safe.'

'I need a bodyguard because I was attacked while I was out walking on my own yesterday, so my employer decided I needed someone to keep an eye on me.'

Silas had tipped his cap to the two ladies and

was now standing watchfully beside Jo.

It was Mrs Rathley who looked more upset about this than her stepmother. 'Take care, then, Jo. There are some lawless people around.'

She couldn't resist saying, 'As *you* must be aware, Mrs Rathley.'

That made the older woman draw in her breath and look even more upset. She tugged her companion's arm. 'We'd better carry on now, Edna. We have an appointment with my dressmaker. Goodbye, Jo. Be careful.'

Jo stepped aside to let them pass. 'Goodbye.'

Once again, her stepmother merely nodded and threw her a sour look.

Silas waited till they were out of earshot to say, 'Mrs Rathley was upset when you told her you'd been attacked.'

'Yes. The poor woman must know what her husband is like. It'd be hard not to if you'd lived with someone for years, I should think.'

'She'd have to be very careful what she says and does with that one, every minute she's with him. That'd be hard.'

'I agree.' Jo glanced sideways, thinking yet again how perceptive and intelligent he was. What a pity he hadn't been able to find a permanent job.

Charlie went to look into the big shed at the back of his main shop, wondering whether to try to tidy it up a bit. He was trying to distract his thoughts from the problems with the council, but not succeeding very well.

When a man he knew by sight came into the shop escorting the young woman he recognised

217

from the incident outside Rathley's house, he waved aside the employee who'd started to move towards them. 'I'll deal with this, lad. Got to keep my hand in.' He moved across to the customers. 'Miss Melling, isn't it? I hope you're well.'

'Yes, thank you. Do you know Silas? He's making sure I stay safe.'

There was a slight pause as Mr Willcox's eyes narrowed and he studied her again. 'Good idea after your previous, um, difficulties. Now, how can I help you today?'

Jo explained what they needed and he laughed. 'I own a share in Willcox and Selby Motors, as you must realise, so I'll do you a far better deal on what you buy than you could get elsewhere. I have some quite good second-hand desks in my back shed, actually.'

Jo stopped at the doorway of the big shed, inside which there seemed to be absolute chaos, with so much furniture piled up one piece on top of another that it was hard to make your way through it, let alone search for specific items.

Charlie went straight to a narrow gap at one side and beckoned them to follow him along the cleared passage to the back. At the far end, he indicated some desks piled on top of each other. 'Could you please help me get those two desks down, Silas?'

The men manhandled several desks out to the yard and Jo went over them, pulling drawers out, running her hands over the surfaces. 'That one's far too big for Nick's office. He'll never need one that big because he'll be out in the car most of the time. This one might do, though, but we'll need a smaller desk for his secretary or it won't fit in.'

'His secretary?' Charlie asked. 'Isn't that you?'

'Only temporarily. I'm going back to Australia in a week or two, just giving Nick and Todd a hand in the meantime.'

'I see. If you don't mind me saying so, I love your accent, Miss Melling. I met a few Aussie soldiers in the war. Good men to have at your back, they were. Hearing you speak reminds me of them.'

'My stepmother is forever complaining about my dreadful Australian accent.'

'Don't listen to her. It's charming.' Chatting gently, he helped them to disentangle chairs and other smaller pieces of furniture from the mounds, putting some to one side immediately as too shabby, and after a few questions, getting together exactly what Jo had been looking for. He then added a few 'small pieces that haven't sold' at no cost.

When he named the total price, Jo stared at him suspiciously. 'Are you sure? That seems very cheap.'

'It is cheap, but then it's for a business and building I'm part-owner of, so as long as I cover my costs with just a tiny bit extra for my trouble, I'm happy. I'll have them delivered, shall I?'

'Yes, please. And thank you very much, Mr Willcox. Todd and Nick will be grateful. How soon can you get the things to us?'

'As soon as I can send the shop lad round to the chap who delivers things for me. In about an hour if he's not out on a job.'

'We'd better get back quickly, then.' She set off

219

at a brisk pace.

On the way back she stopped to buy a loaf from the baker's for their midday meal, which she called 'lunch' and Silas called 'dinner'. Laughing at the differences, they came out of the shop, and she couldn't resist lingering for a moment to look in the window of a small bookshop just along the road.

'I'll stop here on my way home and see if they have any second-hand books. I need something to occupy my time in the evenings. The other girls listen to the radio apparently, but I prefer to read.'

Suddenly Silas yelled, 'Get back!', gave her a shove that sent her stumbling helplessly to one side, then ducked down himself.

As she fell a brick whizzed past her, so close to her head that she let out a cry of shock. It hit the nearby shop window, smashing one of the panes at the level where her head had been. Luckily most of the broken glass fell inside the shop, not on her.

Silas straightened up, yelling, 'Get inside quickly!' as she started to stand up again. She ran into the shop but he set off after the man who'd thrown the missile.

The owner of the bookshop insisted she crouch behind the counter with him in case any more bricks were thrown and it seemed a good idea.

'Does this happen often?' she asked.

'Never happened before. Good thing I don't have a big plate-glass window, eh?'

'You don't seem all that upset.'

'The mess upsets me but it's an ill wind... That particular pane had a crack in the bottom corner, only don't remind anyone of that if the insurance man asks you what happened. I'll get a new pane of glass out of this without spending a penny.' He stood up. 'Look, I think we'll be safe to stand up now. That lad hasn't come back. I'm too old to crouch like this.'

They stood up and he continued chatting. 'Of course, I'll have to clear up the mess, but that won't cost me anything. I just hope whoever it is won't do it again or they'll drive away customers, and I definitely don't want that.'

She forced herself to continue chatting but kept wondering what Silas was doing, whether he'd caught the man who'd thrown the brick.

'Were you coming in to buy a book?'

'Just to look in the window. I was going to pop in to buy something on my way home from work. Will you still be open around six o'clock?'

'I can be open as long as you like because I live over the shop. Or you could search now.'

'I'm too upset at the moment to enjoy looking at books and anyway, I have to get back to work as soon as Silas returns. I'm at Willcox and Selby Motors, sorting out their office.'

'And you've got enemies, it seems.'

'What? But I thought that stone was aimed at your business.'

'I happened to be watching the world pass by, something I often do, and in my opinion, the lad was aiming to hit you. I'd seen him standing watching you from the other side of the street and wondered why. Also, I could see he was holding something under his jacket, so I kept my eye on him. The street was clear of people and he could have thrown the brick earlier without anyone seeing him. Only he didn't, did he? No, he waited till you were standing looking in the shop window. If that chap with you hadn't reacted quickly and pushed you out of the way, you could have been hurt badly.'

He pointed to where the brick was lying on the shop floor amid shards of broken glass and she froze, staring at him then back at the brick, shocked to the core as this sank in. So the trouble hadn't stopped. Someone was still trying to hurt her and it could only be Rathley. Was he actually trying to have her killed now? Surely he wouldn't go to such lengths to get back at her? Or was he making a big effort to get rid of her completely and send her fleeing back to Australia?

With a sick feeling in her stomach, she decided Rathley must have gone mad. He didn't seem mad when you talked to him, but this wasn't the act of someone in their right mind.

'I'm John Twomer, by the way.'

She realised the bookseller was looking at her expectantly and tried to pull herself together. 'Sorry. What did you say?'

'My name's Twomer.'

'Jo Melling.'

'Do you know who wants to hurt you?'

She nodded slowly two or three times. 'I think so. And this is his second attempt. But I can't prove anything so I won't say his name.'

He went to the door and peeped out. 'There's no sign of that young fellow coming back. You stay here in the shop, but keep an eye on the street while I put the kettle on. Call me if anyone approaches. You would like a cup of tea, wouldn't you?'

'Thank you, but no. I have to get back to work as soon as Silas returns.' Since there was no one in the street, she nipped outside and quickly picked up her shopping, annoyed to find the loaf was partly squashed. Then she went back inside.

'You should have let me do that.'

'I kept an eye out for anyone approaching. I wonder how Silas is getting on.'

'Your young man, is he?'

'No. A man hired to keep an eye on me.'

'Well, he's earned his money today, by heck he has.'

There were footsteps outside and Silas came back into the shop, panting and red-faced. 'I lost him. Some kids got in the way, and they did that on purpose, I think. But I'll recognise him again. I never forget a face.'

'Good. This is Mr Twomer, owner of the shop. My friend Silas Johnson. Mr Twomer saw the lad who threw the brick today and says he was watching us, choosing his moment. So that's an independent witness to identify him as well, if he's caught. I'd recognise the two men who attacked me yesterday and Nick would recognise one of them, too, so if the police ever manage to catch any of these villains, it won't just be one person's word against them.' It must have been Rathley who'd arranged the other attack and now this one. Who else could it be?

'Did you know this chap who attacked Jo

223

today?' Silas asked the bookseller.

'Not *know*, but I'd seen him before around town and I'd recognise him again: dark hair, lank and far too long and a lumpen, pasty face with a nose that had been broken...'

She clicked her fingers as that description struck a bell with her as well. 'One of the men who attacked me the first time, the shorter one, looked like that.'

'Perhaps they're the same person.' Twomer shook his head. 'I don't know his name, I'm afraid.'

Silas looked at him. 'Well, if you do remember anything else about him, Mr Twomer, you'd better let Sergeant Deemer know! We'll be reporting this to the police. Miss Melling could have been seriously hurt.'

She looked at him in surprise; she hadn't thought of telling the police. But of course they ought to. Then she smiled at the bookseller. 'We'll call in tonight on the way back to my lodgings and I'll buy a book or two, if that's all right. I see you have a tray of second-hand books.'

'I'll look forward to seeing you.' Twomer opened the door for them, tutting as some glass crunched under his shoes.

Silas went out into the street first, holding up one hand to keep Jo back and looking round carefully. 'I can't see anyone suspicious so we'll hurry straight back to Todd's house.'

They didn't speak, but saved their breath for walking as fast as they could.

In strange contrast, it seemed to be very quiet everywhere. People were probably eating their midday meals.

Jo had lost all appetite.

Todd was out but Nick was in the kitchen. He listened to their account of the incident and stared at her in concern. 'You could have been killed if that brick had hit you on the head.'

'Well, I wasn't. Really, I'm all right, Nick, but it's mainly thanks to Silas's quick action.' She couldn't help shivering at the memory of falling helplessly and the sound of smashing glass. She could see that Nick had noticed her reaction.

His voice became gentler. 'You're all right this time, thank goodness, but maybe you should go back to Australia as soon as possible.'

'And maybe not. I don't run away from problems.'

'Whether you leave or not, I agree with Silas about one thing: we're reporting this to the police, and to Sergeant Deemer himself not his constable. He's a wise old bird, not only knows the valley well, but has many years of police experience. Everyone respects him.'

'There's no need for that, surely?'

He placed one hand on her shoulder and stared earnestly into her eyes. 'There is *every* need, Jo. This is the second time you've been attacked and this one was life-threatening, as Mr Twomer will bear out. Are you sure you didn't recognise the lad who did it?'

'I'm afraid not. I'd know him if I saw him again, though.' She explained about him possibly being one of her previous attackers.

'We'll bear that in mind,' Nick said. 'Let's go

and report this right now. I'm trying to remember where the police station is. We'll have to rely on you for that, Silas.'

The other man hesitated, looking at Jo. 'Look, why don't I go and see Sergeant Deemer while you stay with Nick? She's still a bit upset, whether she admits it or not. Unless you have another driving lesson to give, of course?'

Jo sought for words to contradict him convincingly and couldn't find any. Who wouldn't be upset if someone had tried to hurt them like that?

Nick patted her arm again and then kept his arm round her shoulders. 'I'm free for the rest of the day. I agree that it'd be a better idea for you to go, Silas. You saw the whole thing and chased after the man, so you can tell Deemer much more about what happened. If he wants to see Jo, I'll drive her there later. You're right, she is a bit shaken up by it.'

Nick's touch was comforting and Jo stopped even trying to protest. They were right about her being upset. The attack had been so unexpected – and the brick had passed horribly close to her head. She shuddered again at the memory and allowed herself to lean her head against his shoulder, just for a few seconds.

'That's settled, then,' Silas said. 'Deemer knows my uncle and he knows me well enough to realise I wouldn't exaggerate. He'll believe me but I should think he'll come round to see you as well, Jo, just to check the details. He's very thorough, well respected. You can trust him. I'll tell him you'll be here all afternoon, shall I?'

'Yes. We have to be for the furniture to be

delivered.' She looked at the loaf and grimaced. 'I squashed the bread when I fell, I'm afraid, but I can still make you a quick sandwich with it.'

'Thank you.'

When Silas had left, Nick looked at her and smiled slightly at the same time as shaking his head.

'You might be a bit wobbly, but some women would have had full-blown hysterics at what happened.'

'When you grow up on a farm, you don't get time for having hysterics, whatever happens. It's that it was done *on purpose* that upsets me.'

'How did your stepmother cope with that sort of life? She doesn't seem at all like a farmer's wife.'

'She isn't. I found Edna impossible to live with. She thought I was there to act as her slave and wanted me to stop going outside with the dirty animals. We sold beef cattle mostly, you see. As if I wanted to avoid them. The calves are lovely little things. I don't think she ever went within twenty yards of the animals.'

'Go on.' He wanted to turn her mind to other things than the attack.

'I moved out within weeks of her coming to live there. I think Dad regretted marrying her by then, but of course he didn't say so. Though he seemed happy with one side of marriage, so she must have pleased him in bed.'

He was surprised to hear an unmarried lady mention this, but that was Jo for you, calling a spade a spade, so he replied to her comment just as straightforwardly. 'That side of marriage is very important, I think. Men's, um, needs seem to be stronger than women's.'

She surprised him by letting out a cackle of laughter, which showed he was succeeding in his attempt to get her to relax.

'Tell that to the cows when it was time for the bulls to mate with them, Nick. They seemed to enjoy it just as much as their partners did.'

His gasp of surprise was audible and she said quietly, 'I'd not have said that to anyone else, but I feel I can talk to you about anything. It's part of life, after all, so I don't know why people pretend it doesn't exist.'

'I don't know, either. And I feel that way about you, as well, as if I can say anything to you.' He ran one finger very lightly down her cheek. 'I'm very glad indeed that you weren't hurt today.'

Now it was her turn to draw in a sudden breath as his touch seemed to linger on her skin. She turned hastily to the rest of the squashed loaf. 'I'd better make us some sandwiches.'

But when she stole a glance sideways, he was still watching her, still smiling. And she couldn't help smiling back.

Silas returned nearly an hour later and said Sergeant Deemer would be calling in to see Jo shortly, which he did. Deemer was a burly chap, looking strong in spite of his thinning grey hair. He studied Jo carefully when he was introduced.

'Are you all right to answer some questions, Miss Melling?'

'I'm fine now, thank you. I was a bit shaken up at the time. You don't expect people to throw bricks at your head.'

'Silas told me about the incident. I hope you don't mind me going over it again. I have to make sure neither of you misses out any details.'

She answered his questions patiently, sitting across the table from him, while he laboriously wrote down her replies in a battered notebook.

After what seemed like a long time, he said, 'I think that's everything about this incident. If you remember any other details, do come and tell me about them, Miss Melling.'

However, Nick intervened. 'There's something else we ought to discuss in more detail, sergeant. I first met Miss Melling on the train and then when she was being attacked by two men in Birch End, my passenger and I were able to drive them off, thank goodness.'

'I was coming to that next, sir. Silas told me there had been another incident but he didn't know much about it. How about you both tell me what happened?'

They did that and the sergeant asked various questions then hesitated and looked at Jo. 'Have you any idea at all who might be behind this?'

She looked at him, not sure whether to say anything.

'You do have some idea, don't you?'

'Yes. But I have no proof, so I ought not to accuse this person.'

'You could tell me off the record. I won't note it down or take any action without proof but I'll be able to bear it in mind.'

So she had to go over her experiences at Rathley's house yet again, which made her shudder.

The thought that he might have succeeded in his attack had upset her ever since. If she hadn't been suspicious ... if she hadn't changed bedrooms... Ugh, she hated to remember it.

'I'll report the incident with the two men and ask around.

I won't forget what you've told me about the ... other possibilities. And please, miss, be careful for every single minute of the day. Never go out on your own, whatever anyone tells you.'

'I won't, sergeant.'

Nick had told her that, too. She might have gone out before the second attack, if something had seemed urgent, but not now. Oh, no. The second attack had shown her how serious Rathley was and had made her certain it was he who was trying to frighten her away, whether it could be proved or not.

Well, he wouldn't do it. Her father hadn't brought her up to be a coward but to face up to problems.

Shortly after Sergeant Deemer had left, the office furniture was delivered and that took Jo's mind off the attack, thank goodness. The men put the desks and cupboards in the positions she indicated, then she and Nick worked on filing his paperwork in the various drawers and putting his smaller items on the cupboard shelves.

Silas asked if anyone minded him standing in Todd's office, hidden by the curtains, while they did this. He'd be able to keep an eye on passers-by from there.

Jo paused for a moment. 'Do you think they'll

be checking this place out?'

'I would if I were after someone. I'd watch the place they worked very carefully indeed and find out about their patterns of behaviour for every hour of the day. So as I've nothing else to do at the moment, I'll continue to watch what's going on outside, if you don't mind. I just wish we had those net curtains you're going to buy.'

'Go ahead. You could be right.'

Nick went into the other office a couple of times during the next hour and looked at Silas questioningly, but on each occasion he shook his head.

When Jo started work on Todd's office, Silas moved to keep watch from the other front room.

'He's a good chap,' Nick said. 'And shrewder than most. If I had a job to offer him, I'd not hesitate to employ him permanently.'

'I wish you had one. I really like him.' But not half as much as she liked Nick. It really did feel as if she'd known him for years.

She couldn't help hoping he felt as strongly attracted to her.

19

Wilf went to look at a van in the afternoon after he'd spoken to Charlie. The latter had tipped him the wink about a good one that was for sale. It was a wonder the way that man heard rumours before anyone else did.

The van had apparently belonged to an older man, a jobbing carpenter who'd died suddenly of a seizure. His widow was now selling up, only keeping what she needed to furnish one room, so that she could go and live with her son and his family over in Rochdale.

To Wilf, the van looked as good as it had sounded, but Charlie had told him to let Todd look it over before buying it, so he got permission from the widow to take it out for a drive. Todd had offered to check any vehicle they might be interested in. Eh, folk could be that kind and helpful. It did your heart good to have friends like that.

If he ever managed to find a secure occupation, he'd help others, too, help them in major ways like providing them with real jobs, if he was lucky. Mind you, he'd had steady work for a while now, more than he could cope with on his own at times, so he'd been able to give odd jobs to others here and there, and that was a start. It always made him feel happy to see their faces light up.

He was doing rather well these days, if he said so himself.

Ha! He had to say it himself because his wife didn't trust that this run of decent jobs would continue and she insisted you'd jinx it if you crowed too soon.

He'd watched Enid grow more and more mistrustful of the future over the long years of searching for work and had hated to leave her to scrape by on her own at home while he went looking for work further away. Only he'd had no choice but to leave her, because he wasn't going on the assistance.

She had never known even when to expect him back because he took any and every job he could find. She said sometimes that he could have died while he was on the tramp and she wouldn't have been aware of it. The best he could do to answer that was carry a piece of card in his pocket saying who he was.

He brushed such memories aside. What good did it do to linger on the problems of the past? Watching Todd go over the motor and check the bodywork underneath for rust as well, he learned a point or two about what to be careful about when buying second-hand vehicles of any sort and he asked questions to make sure he understood it all properly. It was like that with everything in life, he'd found: you could often find something to learn if you kept your eyes open and weren't afraid to ask for an explanation. You never knew when the knowledge might come in useful.

Todd moved away from the van wiping the oil off his hands and smiling. 'You've got a good bargain there, lad. Snap their hands off.'

So Wilf went back to see the widow and paid her the full price she was asking, even then not needing to use all the money Charlie had thrust into his hand 'in case'.

'Shall I carry these into the house for you?' He pointed out the tools in a couple of heavy-duty canvas bags that were still sitting in the back of the van.

'You might as well keep them.'

This was a bonus he hadn't expected, so he slipped her another couple of pounds. 'No, you take it, love. It's only fair. They're worth all of that.'

233

Her voice wobbled as she said, 'Thank you, Mr Pollard. It all helps because I'm not eligible for the old age pension yet. Everyone says you're a decent man, which was why I did as Mr Willcox suggested and let you see the van first. And I'm glad I did.'

He still hadn't got used to people calling him 'Mr Pollard' instead of Wilf, and it always made him feel like an imposter.

She stared at the bags and reached out to pat one, as if saying farewell to it, trying to blink away the tears trembling on her eyelashes. 'Eh, my husband did some good work with those tools, but they're no use to the family now. My son-in-law's a good lad, but he's a clerk. Got a nice secure job but he wouldn't know a hammer from a saw, that one wouldn't. Even I can bang in a nail better than he can.'

It was as he was driving the van home that Wilf let himself face the next problem: Enid was going to be upset and he still hadn't worked out how best to convince her what he'd done would be all right.

He went into the house and began by saying, 'Sit down a minute, love. I've got some good news for you.'

He watched her sit next to the kitchen table, took a deep breath and said, 'I've done what I said I might, borrowed money from Charlie and bought a van. A real bargain, it was.'

'*What?* Wilf, you never.'

He nodded. 'Aye. I did. That's it outside. I haven't just borrowed the van, I own it now. *We* own it, I mean. Come and look.'

'I don't want to look at it. You can just give it back to whoever you bought it from and return the money to Charlie. We're in no position to buy a van. What if the work dries up again and we've no way of paying him back? What *were* you thinking about, Wilf Pollard?'

Her voice had grown shriller as she spoke and she finished by hurling the tea towel at him.

He batted it away, annoyed about her reaction, but trying to speak softly. 'Look, love, it'll pay for itself, that van will. I've done all the sums and–'

'Don't even try to convince me, because you won't do it. You know we agreed never to get into debt. Never, ever! We managed to avoid that through all these years of hardship and we're *not* starting now.'

'I need a van to carry my tools and building supplies. I'm doing bigger jobs these days, ones that make us more money. The van will soon pay for itself. Really it will. I've gone through all the figures. I can show you them if–'

Enid slammed one hand down on the table, making the cups rattle. 'You've got a handcart to carry your stuff in.'

'Enid, love, it's not enough. The handcart won't hold the bigger loads and it takes too long for me to get anywhere with it on foot. I hear about some good jobs further away from Ellindale and I could get a few of them easily if I had a van. I could earn more money, I know it. This is a lovely village to live in but it's right at the top end of a road that goes nowhere else.'

She continued to glare at him and he stared

steadily back, forcing himself to keep a calm expression on his face, though some men would have given her a good telling off, or worse, for what she'd said.

When she spoke again, her voice came out harshly, 'I won't let you do this to us, Wilf.'

'You can't stop me because it's done. I need that van and it's a bargain. I got Todd to check it out for me, just to be sure. I keep telling you, I'm not rushing blindly in. I know what I'm doing and Charlie agrees with me. The van's in excellent condition, Todd says, and it'll last for years.'

She looked at him with tears welling in her eyes and starting to roll down her cheeks, even though she rarely allowed herself to cry. But he wasn't going to give in on this, whatever she said or did, because he was right. She must have read that in his face, because she started sobbing loudly, leaning on the table and putting her head on her hands, wailing as if someone she loved had died.

'Enid, love, don't.'

She looked up. 'Don't you call me "love"! If you loved me, you wouldn't have done this. You promised. No debts, ever. All those years. Some weeks I hardly ate a thing to keep from borrowing money while you were away. And now you've broken your promise. I'll never trust you again if you don't give that van back, Wilf Pollard, never.'

He'd been prepared for tears but she was far more upset than he'd expected and when he tried to put his arm round her, she began screaming at him like a fishwife and shoving him away.

He looked sideways and saw the children. 'Hey. Stop that, Enid. You're frightening the kids.'

It took her a few moments to realise how terrified the two children were at this unusual behaviour. They'd retreated to the corner, cuddling up to one another, something they used to do when upset by their real parents. They were crying along with her, too, sobbing and hiccupping, though they couldn't really have understood why he and Enid were quarrelling.

She made a gulping sound, snapped her mouth shut then blew her nose and took a few deep breaths, before saying in a low voice, 'Take that van back. Please, Wilf.'

'No. I need it.'

'That's it, then. I'll never forgive you for this, Wilf Pollard. Never. Even if it works out, it'll be more by good luck than good management and you shouldn't be risking it. I'll not sleep a wink till every penny of that money is paid back.'

So he put his most secret dream into words. Surely she'd understand if he told her what this was leading to? 'Look, Enid, I've learned a lot during these years of going on the tramp and taking on any job I could find. I've always been handy at making things, but I know enough now to start up a proper business one day – building whole houses, I mean, not just things like sheds. I've seen how it's done, worked on every job there is, even if only as assistant to experts.'

She looked at him as if he'd run mad.

'Because of that, I was able to organise the renovations for Mr Carlisle up at Heythorpe House and he told everyone how well it turned out. Now Charlie's asked me to build on that extra room and when I make a good job of it – and believe

237

me, I will – he'll tell everyone, too, and other people will ask me to do bigger jobs.'

She didn't say anything, just continued to glare at him.

'The van is only a start, Enid. I'm going to be a proper builder and for that, I'll need a workshop, a yard and all sorts of things before I'm through. And if I have to borrow more money to get them, I shall, because I *know* I can do it. That dream has kept me going for years. You're not the only one who's had to go hungry, you know. And I did some rotten, filthy jobs when I was on the tramp. But I learned so much.'

She let out a laugh that was as harsh as a crow squawking. 'Don't be stupid. Doesn't matter what you learned, *you* can't turn yourself into a proper builder, however hard you work. You've not had the training, and you haven't got a family in the business to give you a start.'

'Have you so little faith in me?' That surprised him.

'It's what the world's like. People like us don't get rich. Not honestly, anyhow.'

'I shall. I'm really good with my hands, Enid, you've seen that many a time. And I'm good with my brain, too. I can do all sorts of bookwork now. I've even learned to do accounts.'

'That's not the point. We're still ordinary people and I feel lucky even to have this. My mother never had as much.' She waved one hand round the room. 'A decent life and enough food on the table for us and our kids, clothes to keep us warm in winter. We can put a bit of money in the savings bank, maybe, because bad times come and go. But we won't be able to do that if you get us into debt.'

'Is that all you want out of life? This!' He too made a sweeping gesture with one hand. 'A two-up, two-down house with an outside lav? Why, we haven't even got decent furniture, just old stuff that we've bought second-hand or I've made myself.'

'It does the job. I'm not greedy. It's the folk who try to overreach themselves who get into trouble. I've seen it time and again, but I never thought you'd do it to us.'

Wiping her tears away with one hand, she went across to comfort the children and Wilf shut up. It was clear she didn't understand, or more likely, didn't dare believe in a better future after all the lean years of making do. Even he hadn't realised how strongly it had affected her.

He could only pray that she'd come round, because he wasn't going to give up his dream. It'd kept him going during the long years of chasing work, that dream had. He'd had to sleep under hedges and in barns, as he tramped all over the north of England – because Enid had refused point-blank to leave the valley and move to the south where there was full-time work. Well, she wasn't going to stop him doing this as well.

Why, even Charlie Willcox believed in him and had invested money in him. That said something, didn't it?

After a few minutes of heavy silence, Enid took the children out to the lav and then put them to bed. She didn't even bring them to him for their usual goodnight kiss, and that made him angry.

He heard creaking in the room overhead, so she

239

must have gone to bed, too. It might be best to let her simmer down a bit before he went up to join her, he decided, and made himself a mug of cocoa. But it went cold as he sat there thinking and a nasty skin formed on top, so he poured the last of it away. He couldn't even settle to reading the newspaper.

When he did go upstairs, he stopped dead outside the door of their bedroom, sucking in his breath in shock. His work clothes for tomorrow were piled up on the landing, together with an old blanket and his pillow. When he tried to turn the door handle, he found it locked.

It was a simple lock he'd picked up somewhere for a few pence and they'd only put it on to stop the children walking in on them unexpectedly. He could have got his tools and opened the damned thing easily enough from this side, but he didn't. He'd leave her be tonight.

That wasn't just to give her time to calm down; now *he* needed to calm down, too.

She shouldn't have done that.

He'd let her have a day or two, if necessary, then insist they speak about this again. They never kept a quarrel going for long. At least they never had done before. Even if she didn't agree with him, she'd calm down when she saw how much more he could earn.

He might give her a little extra money to put in the savings bank. Surely that would make her feel safer?

There was a sound behind him and he saw Peggy peeping round the door of the children's bedroom.

'Mammy's been crying.'

'I know, love. She's upset about something. She'll get over it.' He gave the little girl a hug and tucked her back into bed beside her younger brother. Ronnie was fast asleep and didn't stir.

As Peggy snuggled down, he kissed her soft little cheek then stood looking down at the two of them, his heart full of love. What fine little creatures they were. He'd make sure they were well educated, give them hope for the future. They wouldn't grow up in poverty.

He went downstairs, carrying the things Enid had left out for him. You had to look at all the options, so he asked himself if he should give in to her to keep the peace. Was he really risking their future? Was he so likely to fail?

He shook his head. No, he wasn't. He had faith in his own skills and ability to work hard. She was wrong.

He made up a makeshift bed on the hearthrug. Enid had pegged it herself out of clean rags but it was a dull, limp thing. Not want more? Of course he wanted more than this for his family.

He lay in the darkness watching the embers turn slowly black as the fire died down. He had trouble getting to sleep because his thoughts were circling round in his skull like slow birds of prey.

Why did his wife not believe in him? Had he ever let her down when he promised something? No, he hadn't.

He didn't expect to get rich or to become a big, important builder, but he did expect to earn steadily and make a name for himself as a good sound builder of smaller houses. And one day he'd make his other dream come true: buy his own house, or better still, build it himself.

He had to admit one thing, though only to himself: adopting the two children had been a mixed blessing. He loved them dearly, they both did, but Enid had become so obsessed by them, after over a decade of trying in vain to create a child of her own, that she was terrified of anything and everything that might hurt them.

Eh, she'd stop the rain falling on them if she could.

He turned over on the hard floor, not quite warm enough, wishing he had another blanket. In the end he fetched his overcoat from the hook near the front door and spread it on top of the blanket.

But he woke with a start a couple of times during the night and couldn't help rehashing their argument in his mind as he tried to see how he could have done better.

He kept wondering how Enid would greet him in the morning – and what the best way would be to greet her.

20

Rathley walked into Packman Alley quite openly that night, sure that no one he met here would dare say anything about seeing him, just as he saw other men of the better classes here and never mentioned it, whoever they were. It was an unwritten code, protecting them all.

There was no light showing in the window of Number 3, but he pushed the door, expecting to walk straight in. However, it was locked.

After rapping impatiently on the window, he saw the curtain twitch and waited, quite sure that he'd be let in. But the door wasn't opened.

'Hoy! Let me in!'

'I'm not working tonight,' Moira called from inside.

'I'm not here for that. I'm here to talk.'

'I'm not well and I–' She started to cough and it went on for a long time.

He waited for her to catch her breath and speak, deciding he wouldn't be using her again. She was getting past it, still skilful, but he didn't like the sound of that cough. Anyway, it was more than time she let him have the girl. As they'd discussed before, he was quite prepared to pay handsomely for the pleasure of being the first.

He rattled the door, then went closer to the window. 'Damned well open up, Moira, or I'll break this down.'

'Just a minute. I'm coming.' As she spoke Moira looked at Tess, who was standing in the kitchen doorway. She made their get-away sign with one hand.

Her daughter nodded and disappeared into the kitchen. Moira let out a long sigh of relief. Tess was wearing trousers, as she did most evenings 'in case', though her shirt was getting a bit tight now. Better buy her another one tomorrow. The pawnshop would have something suitable.

It was getting harder and harder to protect her daughter because Tess had grown so fast recently towards womanhood.

The door rattled again.

'Just a minute.'

She watched Big Donny help Tess climb out of the kitchen window and shut it behind her, then go to sit quietly in his corner. Moira put one finger to her lips, asking for silence, and he nodded. He might be slow-witted, but he was strong and he would do anything to protect her. She reckoned she was the only person who'd been kind to him since his mother died.

She didn't often need his help, though, because she was careful not to upset people. Tonight she watched him sit down on the corner stool and relax against the wall, closing his eyes. She'd built up a fire, even though it was still summery weather, and the house was warmer than usual tonight. Well, she had been feeling 'shivery' all day. Donny didn't feel well, either, poor thing. He was still getting over a cold.

She sighed, wishing she didn't have to deal with Rathley but there you were. Life didn't often push you along the easiest path.

Taking a deep breath she moved towards the front door. She'd get rid of him as quickly as she possibly could.

It felt chilly outside after the overheated little house, so Tess walked briskly along the narrow ginnel that ran along the back of the houses and pub, intending to take refuge in her favourite hiding place in the park, the ramshackle bandstand where concerts were given sometimes on Sundays in the summer. The park was in the better part of Birch End, so there were rarely people around this late, unlike the streets near her home.

The air was so still, she could hear the faint sound of the town hall clock striking down in Rivenshaw, marking what she was sure would be a long hour or two of waiting till Donny came to find her.

She'd hidden some old sacks under the rickety bench at the rear of the bandstand and no one seemed to have disturbed them. The sacks helped keep her warm when she had to get out of the house. To her dismay, tonight some lads were kicking an old football around in front of the bandstand using the two lampposts in front of it as goalposts. She knew those lads. They threw stones at her sometimes in the street. She didn't want them to catch her on her own here or they might really hurt her.

She circled past them to get to the shrubbery on the far side of the wooden structure, silent as a ghost. She had another hiding place in the middle of this shrubbery, but no way of keeping warm there. She knew just about all the places to hide in Birch End.

As she bent to push the shrubs apart, a hand grabbed her arm and she let out a yelp of fear.

'I'm a policeman,' the man said. 'I'm not going to hurt you, lass.'

When she saw his uniform, her fear subsided a little. 'Oh. All right.'

'What are you doing out at this hour of the night?'

'My mam sent me out. She wanted to be private with, er, someone.'

'You're shivering. You should be home in your bed.'

'I have some sacks in the bandstand and I usually stay there, but those boys kicking a football about would have seen me. They like tormenting people.'

'Well, they ran off home when they saw me, and I'm going to send you home as well.'

'I can't go home yet. Please. I'll be all right now those boys have gone. I'll hide in the bandstand.'

'You'll be even better off at home at this time of night.'

'No. I won't.' Tess looked at him pleadingly. 'Mam's got a man visiting her. I come here sometimes when that happens. I'll go home soon.' She tried to pull away, but his hand only tightened on her arm.

'Oh, no, lass. I'm coming with you and making sure you get there safely. I don't know what your mother thinks she's doing, sending you out on your own at this hour of the night. What's her name?'

'Moira Tayner.'

'Ah. I see. I know her but I haven't seen you around. Anyway, it's going to rain soon, so I'm not leaving you out here.' He kept a firm hold of her arm and set off, dragging her when she hung back.

'Mam will be angry and *he* will be even angrier.'

'Who is he?'

She was too afraid to tell him that. 'I – um, don't know his name.'

'I'll find out when we get there. Come on.'

She wanted to cry as she stumbled along, it was so humiliating being taken home like this. And if the policeman saw him, Mr Rathley would get angry at her and her mother, and he'd probably hit out at them when the policeman had gone. He was noted for thumping women, didn't care who he hurt. He'd slapped her when she was smaller if she made a noise, but not lately – no, lately he'd looked at her in a way she hated. She'd rather have been slapped than see him do that any time.

Her mother kept saying that the day was getting closer when they'd have enough money saved to move away. It couldn't come too soon for Tess. Until now, she hadn't been caught when she went out to hide, because once she got away from the streets there weren't many people around.

How had she missed seeing or hearing this policeman approaching tonight? She tried one last time to plead with him to let her wait in the bandstand. Her mother would be so angry about this and *he* would be even angrier if he was still there.

She thought about that. He probably would be. He took a longer time to do the job lately.

Her mother had promised to keep her safe from him, whatever it took, and had managed it so far. Now, what was going to happen?

As soon as the front door was unlocked, Rathley pushed his way into the little house. Moira shut the door behind him and turned to face him. 'I'm not working tonight, Clarence. I'm not well.'

'I haven't come about you. It's the girl I want,

and I intend to have her this very night. I've waited long enough.'

'She's not old enough yet. She hasn't started her monthlies, even, so she's still got a child's body. You're rough. You could damage her permanently.'

He waved one hand dismissively. 'It always hurts them the first time. She'll recover. Now, fifty pounds and she's mine till I tell you I've had enough. I'll still let you keep her here, and you can carry on working, but if she learns to please me I might set her up somewhere a bit nicer. Mind, no one else is to touch her. And fifty pounds is my final offer, as I told you last time.'

'Tess needs another few months' growth yet. I won't risk her being damaged or she'll be no use to me after you've grown tired of her.'

'I'm *not* waiting any longer, woman. Get her ready. I'll break her in tonight.' Starting to feel excited, he fumbled in his pocket and brought out a bundle of five-pound notes, slapping them down on a low table.

'She's not here,' Moira said at once.

'I don't believe you.' Rathley moved towards the stairs and when Moira tried to bar the way, he shoved her aside so roughly she fell to her knees.

When she was alone, she picked up the money and hid it. If there was one thing she'd learned in this business, it was to have a good hiding place for money.

Upstairs Rathley explored the two bedrooms, the one Moira used for customers and the even smaller one her daughter slept in. The girl was nowhere to be found.

He went storming downstairs. 'Where is she?'

'Out at a friend's.'

'Then send that stupid creature you keep in the kitchen to fetch her. He was asleep when I went in. He doesn't even earn his keep.'

'He's got a cold. He's not well either.'

'Well, cold or not, send him to fetch her back.'

'He doesn't know where she is. He can only find his way to places he knows. Anyway, this friend doesn't know him, so won't let her leave. I keep my daughter safe, Clarence.' It was a moment before she added, 'You'll be glad of that one day, but not yet.'

Rathley glared at her, sure she was telling lies. She'd been putting him off for a while now. Perhaps she was trying to get another man to pay more for the girl. She'd hinted she might do that if he didn't pay what she wanted. Thinking of this possibility made him so furiously angry, he hit her as hard as he could, so hard she tumbled sideways across the room like a helpless rag doll.

When he took a step towards her, she jumped to her feet and pulled a knife out of her pocket. He jerked to a halt.

'Don't you dare touch me.' She raised her voice to call, 'Donny!' but it came out croakily and her protector didn't answer.

With a laugh, Rathley stepped forward again. 'Looks like he's gone out, too. Good. I'm going to teach you to obey me from now on.'

She waved the knife to and fro. 'If you touch me, I'll stab you where it'll hurt most. I mean it.'

He kicked out, taking her by surprise, his heavy boot again sending her flying sideways. She let out a little cry that cut off abruptly as she fell, but as he moved forward she didn't try to roll away or get up, just lay there, face down.

Puzzled, Rathley paused, wondering if this was a trick. Then he saw a trickle of blood leak from underneath her body on to the pale, threadbare rug. For a few seconds he couldn't move, couldn't think, because there was such a lot of blood. Where could that be coming from? He'd only kicked her. Kicks bruised you, not cut you open.

Bending, he rolled her over, gasping at the sight of the knife hilt protruding from her belly, feeling the warmth of her blood pulsing out on to one hand and on to his clothes where he was leaning against her. He edged backwards in case she lashed out at him, but she didn't move. She was still letting out faint, fluttery breaths but she wasn't conscious.

He looked round for the fifty pounds but it had vanished. Where the hell had she put it?

He hesitated, unwilling to search her body, then heard a footstep and turned to see Big Donny standing in the doorway to the kitchen, rubbing his eyes sleepily.

Rathley ran to the front door and fumbled with the handle, expecting at any moment to be grabbed by her huge protector.

But Donny had fallen to his knees beside his mistress, whimpering, and begging her to wake up.

Flinging open the door, Rathley stumbled outside and slammed it shut. He stopped for a moment to stare down at his hand and clothing. Those stains would give him away. The last thing he wanted was for people to link him to this – this damned accident. It was *her* knife, *her* fault, but people might try to blame him.

He had to get home quickly and get out of these clothes, burn them or something.

For a few seconds he couldn't move, then realised he was in luck and there was no one in the alley. He took a step forward intending to hurry off down the street, but heard footsteps and saw the long shadow thrown by a street lamp. Oh, hell! Someone was coming. He turned and hurried into the narrow ginnel leading off the rear end of the alley, breaking into a shuffling run. He was panting by the time he passed the rear of the Packman's Arms.

He was going to wipe some of the blood off on the wall, but then it occurred to him that someone might see it and work out which way Moira's assailant had gone. No, better if he didn't leave a trail.

He didn't allow himself to whimper, but he wanted to. Oh yes, he did. Because unless he found some way to keep his presence at her house tonight secret, they'd arrest him, charge him with murder and hang him, even though it'd been an accident.

And Big Donny would be able to tell them he'd been there, unless ... maybe he could find a way to blame the accident on the stupid fellow. If it was his word against the idiot's, they'd believe him ... wouldn't they?

He couldn't get over the irony that it really had been an accident. She'd fallen on her own knife. But who would believe that?

And what had she done with the money? He'd have to accept its loss, he decided. He wasn't going back to search. Only ... perhaps she had more money hidden away if she had a hiding place already? He'd have to think about that. He hated losing money.

He realised he'd stopped moving, but luck was still with him and although a woman came out of the back door of the pub and dumped some things in the rubbish bin, she was yawning sleepily and didn't even look round, let alone notice him.

He let out a long, slow breath of relief and took a moment to check that his clothes were tidy with his clean hand. He could feel the stickiness of the blood on the fingertips of his other hand and looked down in disgust at it, dark-looking blood in the faint light coming from the pub window.

He set off again, hadn't walked this fast for years and he was soon panting, so had to slow down. By using the back alleys and climbing over a stile into a field, he almost managed to keep away from people.

Only once was it unavoidable, so he hid his face from the young couple as he passed them. They were more interested in one another than in him, and didn't even spare him a second glance, thank goodness.

It was only a few minutes' walk from the slum to his own home in Birch End, but it seemed to take a very long time to get there.

Hobbs had been keeping watch on the alley again, for lack of anything better to do. He saw

Rathley come out of Red Moira's front door then stop and look round as if afraid of being seen. He hadn't looked afraid as he went into the house, had kept hammering on the door angrily. So what had happened to him inside?

There was enough light from the window for him to see that there was something dark on the hand that Rathley was holding awkwardly away from his clothes. It must be something dirty from the way he looked down at it. The watcher grinned. He'd always had good eyesight. Very useful, that was.

He couldn't see enough from here, though, to work out what sort of muck it was. Strange. Gentlemen didn't usually dirty their damned soft hands when visiting whores. From the horror on Rathley's face as he stared at the hand, it was something very unwelcome. Only a couple of things you wouldn't want on your hand came to mind but surely it couldn't be the worst one, which left only blood.

When Rathley set off along the rear ginnel, the man decided to follow him by the front route. He passed the front of Packman Alley and stopped at the other side of the pub. Yes, Rathley was there. He'd stopped. Hobbs hid behind a barrel, able to watch through the gap between it and the wall. He watched Rathley try to tidy himself without using that hand, then set off running. Well, trying to run. He was too old and fat to move fast.

Intrigued, Hobbs speeded up till he was close enough to keep an eye on Rathley but not too close. He smiled as his prey slowed down again, hearing him panting in the quietness away from the pub. What had set that arrogant sod sneaking out round the back of Moira's house as if he was scared of something? Why hadn't he left the alley the usual way?

Was there some profit to be gained from finding out? There must be, surely.

When Rathley detoured through two back alleys, and even climbed a stile to get through a field, heading towards the posh part of Birch End where he lived, Hobbs grew more puzzled – and more interested. Something was definitely going on. He'd never seen Rathley do anything except strut about like he owned the world before, but tonight the arrogant sod was terrified of something from the expression on his face. But what?

A young couple came towards him across the field, arms linked, eyes only for one another, and Hobbs quickly slipped behind a tree.

He continued to follow Rathley, saw him reach his own home soon afterwards and it was quite easy to get close to the house without being noticed. Instead of going in through the front door, Rathley went in through the French windows of a room at the side.

He switched on an electric light inside and the watcher crept forward thinking: *Thank you for that, Mr Rathley. Very helpful. I can see you much better now.*

The light was bright enough to shine on the hand that reached up to close the big windows. It was jerked back and the other hand was used. Yes, that stain was blood. Hobbs could see the colour now. Whose blood was it, though? Someone else's, obviously, because Rathley wasn't moving as if the hand or any other part of him was injured.

Had the sod hurt Red Moira badly enough to make her bleed all over him? He could be a rough devil with women, everyone knew that.

The curtains were drawn to cover every inch of the windows, so Hobbs risked going closer. As there was nothing wrong with his hearing, he recognised the sound of a key turning in the lock on the inside and bolts being clicked into place. He stayed watching the house for a little longer but the light went off inside that room almost immediately.

No lights were switched on downstairs but one appeared on the first floor, Rathley's bedroom, probably. It stayed on for a while, then was switched off.

Nothing more to be found out tonight, Hobbs decided. What could he do with the information he had about Rathley? There must be some way to turn it to his profit.

After a few moments' thought, he made his way back to Packman Alley to see if anything was still going on there. To his astonishment, he saw the new constable standing outside Red Moira's house as if he was guarding the place.

He edged closer to a small group of people who were watching from the end of the alley. 'What's going on?'

'Red Moira's been murdered,' a woman told him.

'Stabbed to death,' another added.

'*What?* Who killed her?'

'It must have been the idiot.'

One man shook his head. 'No, I don't think so. I was passing by and saw Donny come out screaming for help just as Constable Hopkins turned up with Moira's daughter. I heard the idiot shout, "He's killed her! He's killed her!" so it can't have been him who did it, can it? Well, he wouldn't have the wits to blame someone else for it if he had, would he?'

'What did the constable do?' the man prompted.

'He was just coming into the alley, so when Donny ran out he rushed along it into the house, dragging the girl with him, and after that all hell broke loose. He came out and yelled for someone to take a message. Some passers-by had stopped in the street to see what all the fuss was about, so he sent one man to fetch Sergeant Deemer as quick as possible and said to tell him there had been a murder.'

'Where's the daughter now?'

'Still inside the house. When she went in, she started screaming and wailing. It fair curdled your blood to hear it.'

'You'd be upset if someone had up and killed your mother,' someone else said.

The woman who was doing most of the telling about what had happened didn't look upset, though. She was excited by it all. Well, it wasn't every day you had a murder take place on your doorstep, was it?

'It's just like a show at the pictures,' she said with relish.

Hobbs let them speculate about what had happened, wondering how exactly Moira could have been killed, and stepped slowly back. He always preferred to be on the edges of crowds because then it was easier to get away. But he was shocked. Shocked rigid. He hadn't figured Rathley as being capable of murder.

Standing in the shadows between lampposts, he smiled as he thought about it. He knew who had murdered Red Moira and was probably the only one who did, because you couldn't make sense of what the idiot said.

This was his big chance in life and he intended to make the most of it. He'd get a lot of money out of Rathley for keeping quiet, enough to set himself up for life. Though he'd move away as soon as he had it, so that the sod couldn't arrange to have him killed, too. He might or might not take Doris with him.

No one cared much when a whore got herself killed, but a rich man would care very much about being hanged for her murder. How much exactly would he care? A hundred pounds' worth? Two hundred? A thousand even?

The mere thought of the money sent a happy shiver down Hobbs's spine.

21

Tess flung herself on her mother's body, but the policeman pulled her off. She couldn't believe Mam was dead, couldn't stop sobbing. Then she began to wonder what life would be like without the woman who'd loved and cherished her all her life. What would she do?

Life would be empty, that's what. Empty. As if she were on her own in a big, echoing room and didn't know which way to turn.

Who could have done this? Rathley? Surely not. But who else could it have been?

Why hadn't Donny stopped him?

And who was going to save Tess from *him* now. Her mother's cunning but false promises had been the only thing keeping him at bay for a couple of years.

When the sergeant arrived, it took him a while to calm the poor girl down enough to answer questions about her mother, but nothing she said could throw any light on the situation.

Then one question the policeman asked made her suddenly pay greater attention.

'Do you think Donny killed her, lass?'

'*Donny?* No, impossible. He adored her. She saved him from some lads beating him up and looked after him from then onwards. And he looked after her in return. He might have hit someone who tried to hurt her, but he'd never harm *her.*'

'You're sure of that?'

'Oh, yes. Absolutely sure. I'd stake my life on it.'

Sergeant Deemer studied Tess. He believed her. Let alone her words had the ring of truth, his many years of experience told him that the large, moon-faced man sitting sobbing in the kitchen wasn't violent and hadn't committed a violent crime, even by accident.

The trouble was, the sergeant couldn't imagine

that most other people would believe Donny innocent, especially the new district inspector, who was an arrogant sod and seemed to think he knew everything about a valley he only visited occasionally. Everyone knew Donny acted as Moira's protector. Who else could have got near her?

There was one important piece of evidence that Deemer could bear witness to personally, though: there was no blood on Donny's hands or clothes, not one drop, though the body had clearly been moved and there was a lot of blood on the rug. But would that be enough to save the poor chap?

As far as Deemer could work out from looking at the scene, Moira had fallen face down after being stabbed, and then been turned over. And there was a smear of blood on the rug next to her, not a splash but a smear, as if someone's hand had brushed the rug as he handled the body.

Just then the undertaker arrived to collect the body, and he had to take Tess into the kitchen while they did what they had to. She was so upset, he didn't probe further. He had his own thoughts about the situation, but he had to have proof to do anything about them.

'Can I go with her?' she asked.

'There's nothing you can do for her now.' He didn't mention that they might have to carry out an autopsy. It seemed obvious how Moira had been killed but the magistrate might want something else checking. You could never tell with magistrates.

He stood between Tess and the door into the front room and only after they'd carried away the body did he let her leave the kitchen.

There wasn't only her to think about. There was Donny. The more he thought about it, the more he worried that if he left the poor chap free to roam the streets, other people would cause trouble and shout things out at him, or worse. Donny was slow-witted and would have to be shut away and looked after somewhere safe, for his own good. The trouble was, there was nowhere for folk like him in the valley.

He went to the door and watched the under-taker's van move away, then turned to the constable. 'We'll look after Donny at the police station till we find out what happened. He's so upset, he doesn't seem to know what he's doing.'

'Donny won't make sense for days,' Tess put in. 'When he gets this upset, it takes him a long time to calm down. Only my mother could soothe him.'

'Will he listen to you?'

She wiped away more tears and sniffed, fumbling in vain for a handkerchief, so he gave her his.

'He might listen to me. But what would I tell him?'

'Well, first I want you to ask him if he saw who did it.'

She followed the sergeant back into the kitchen where Donny was huddled in his corner, rocking to and fro, covering his head with his hands. 'Donny, listen to me. Listen. Shh now.'

When she tried to hold his hand, to comfort him, he pushed it away, and howled like a dog, shouting, 'She's dead. He killed her. She's dead.'

The sergeant gave up. That was all they'd been

able to get him to say, over and over again, the same few words, the same howls of anguish. Who was the man Donny was talking about? Why would someone have killed Moira? She'd kept herself to herself and given him and his police constable no trouble, in spite of what she did for a living.

He took the lass back into the front room because Donny was still sobbing and moaning in the kitchen. 'Have you got any relatives you can go to, Tess? I know there aren't any close ones, but would you have distant relatives who could take you in? You can't stay here, especially on your own. Apart from the fact that you're only a child, the murderer might come back.'

Tess looked at him numbly, finding it hard to concentrate because she kept wondering whether to tell him that Rathley had called that evening. But she didn't want anything to do with *him,* and anyway, what reason would a rich man like him have to kill her mother? She felt as if her head was full of cotton wool, couldn't decide about anything.

'Relatives?' Deemer prompted.

'The Mellings don't speak to us and the other Tayners have left the valley, gone south somewhere for work. Anyway, they hated Mam, you know, because of what she did. They'd not take me in because of that.' She didn't even have to think twice to work it out.

'We'll have to put you in an orphanage if there's no one to look after you.'

'No!'

'There's no choice.'

Tess thought desperately of who she knew and a picture of Jo's lovely smile and kind offer came into her mind. 'There's Jo.'

'Jo who?'

'Jo Melling. She's a distant relative.'

'The young woman who came here from Australia?'

'Yes. She came to our house looking for her father's relatives. I don't know her well but we're definitely related. She said we were the closest left in England and she offered to help me and Mam leave here and go to Australia with her, so maybe she'll help me now.'

There was no one else, no one in the whole world who really cared about her now.

'We'll ask her, then. Why don't you go and pack your clothes? Whatever happens, you won't be allowed to stay here on your own. Who's your landlord? I don't think I know that.'

'Mam bought this house for herself years ago, so that no one could throw her out. I suppose it'll come to me now.' Tess began sobbing again. 'Don't take me away. I want to stay here. It's my *home*. Donny will look after me.'

When Deemer sighed and patted her shoulder, she knew what he was going to say.

'You're a minor, Tess. You have to have a grown-up to look after you. And Donny doesn't count as a grown-up, let alone he's not making any sense tonight. Do you know where this Jo Melling is staying?'

'At Mrs T's lodging house.'

'Good. We need to take Donny to the police station first, to keep him safe, then we'll see about you. Will you be all right riding in the back of my car with him?'

'With Big Donny? Of course I'll be all right. He'd never hurt me and he's *not* the one who killed Mam, either.'

Her utter certainty about this reinforced the sergeant's own feelings about the childlike man.

But who else could have committed the crime? The constable was a smart lad and he'd had the wit to ask the neighbours and people who came to gawp if they'd seen anyone hanging around earlier that evening, but no one had, or would admit to having seen anyone, more like.

Once Tess had packed some clothes, Deemer locked up the house, leaving it guarded by two lads he'd hired on the promise of five bob each if they kept an eye on it till morning. One was to stay at the front, one at the back. He breathed a sigh of relief as he opened the car door for Donny and Tess.

Donny was still too upset to think straight and if Tess hadn't had the idea of giving him her mother's best shawl to hold, they might have had trouble persuading him to leave the house and get into the car.

When they arrived at the police station, Donny continued to cuddle the shawl as if it were a live creature, but he did as Tess told him, going into the cell, sitting down and rocking to and fro, crooning to the shawl. He didn't even seem to notice when they locked the door on him.

'That chap never killed anyone,' Deemer told his constable.

'He doesn't look capable of killing but you

263

never know.'

'I'm quite sure of it. But I think he's in danger. It's my guess the real murderer will want to keep him quiet. Donny can stay in that cell till I can work out what happened. Nobody is getting away with murder on my patch.'

The constable gaped at him. 'It's like you see in films, isn't it, sarge?'

'Sort of. Only in real life it isn't as easy to solve crimes. Now, I'm going to take that poor lass to find her cousin. You're not to tell anyone what I'm doing or where we're going. If they ask, just say I've gone out to have a look round and you don't know where Tess is. Your job is to keep an eye on Donny – and you be kind to him, mind.'

'Where exactly are you going, sarge?'

'I told you: I'm taking this poor lass to find her cousin. After that I'm not sure.'

That was all he'd say to his young constable. It seemed safer.

Sergeant Deemer drove her round to Mrs T's to find Tess's cousin, and Tess waited in the car while he woke up the landlady.

Tess watched and saw the woman hesitate when he spoke earnestly and gestured to the car. After a moment or two, the woman nodded, so Tess went to join them.

Mrs T sent them downstairs into the basement kitchen while she went up to the next floor to fetch Jo. She tossed over her shoulder a grudging, 'You might as well sit down, I suppose.'

But Tess had seen the look Mrs T gave her and she knew already that she wouldn't be welcome to stay here. It was always the same, only before she'd had her mam to go home to.

When the landlady returned with Jo, the sergeant explained what had happened.

Tess watched her cousin. What would Jo say? Would she turn away from her as well?

Jo looked at the sergeant in horror. 'I can't believe it!' Then she turned to Tess. 'Oh, you poor thing!'

The kindness in her face made tears well in Tess's eyes again and when her cousin hurried round the table and put her arms round her, she couldn't keep back a whimper of relief.

'The lass says she doesn't have anyone else to turn to but you,' the sergeant said. 'Was I right to bring her here?'

'Of course you were. I'll look after her.'

When she heard this, Tess couldn't help it, she started sobbing again, clinging to Jo, who stayed close, the only person who'd ever cuddled Tess apart from her mother.

Mrs T cleared her throat to draw their attention and everyone looked at her.

'The girl can't stay here, sergeant. I'm really sorry, but people won't want to lodge with me if *she* is in the house. Let alone what her mother was, there's been a murder. It's not only the morals, they'll be afraid she'll attract more trouble.'

'Just let her stay till the morning, then,' Jo pleaded. 'She can come into my room. No one need see her.'

Mrs T hesitated then shook her head again. 'I'm sorry, but no.'

Tess listened to them in dismay, wondering if

this reaction would make a difference to Jo. People had always treated her scornfully. Most of the other children did at school and so did the teacher. If her mother hadn't insisted on her keeping their secret, she'd not have continued going to school and facing the daily humiliations. And even though she was a good scholar, the teacher never praised her.

But the secret had helped keep *him* away till her mother could save enough money for them to get right away from Backshaw Moss. They had both been prepared to do anything necessary to stop him, had often discussed what life would be like afterwards.

How would she get away from *him* now? She knew where her mother hid the bank book and some money in case of an emergency, but would she be allowed to take that? And even if she did have money, where could she go? She might be able to keep herself in food and clothing, but a girl her age couldn't stay in her home alone, with no one to protect her, she knew that better than anyone. It wouldn't even be safe to stay in the valley, whoever she was with, not with *him* nearby.

She saw Jo look reproachfully at Mrs T, who flushed but still continued to shake her head.

Jo's voice was very chill. 'I presume you'll let her sit here in the kitchen until I've packed my bag? Or is even that beyond your charity?'

Her question won a sigh and a reluctant nod.

'Then I'll go and do that. I'll send for my trunk later.'

The sergeant intervened. 'If you can be quick about it, Miss Melling, I'll take you wherever you

266

want to go. *And* help you with your trunk.'

Tess noticed Jo give a tiny sigh of relief.

'Thank you. I know someone in Rivenshaw who may give us temporary refuge.'

'I'll wake my son and he'll help you carry down the trunk,' Mrs T said.

'The sergeant and I can manage,' Jo said. 'I'm not a weakling.'

She didn't say where they were going and Tess didn't ask. Well, she didn't believe anyone in the valley would let Red Moira's daughter stay with them, so it must be outside the district. But she felt so weary and unhappy she couldn't seem to ask about anything. It was an effort even to stay upright. All she wanted to do was curl up somewhere and weep her heart out. She felt like a little child, wanting her mammy, couldn't seem to get beyond that.

But the sergeant did ask about it, 'Where are we going?'

Jo threw a scornful look at the landlady. 'I'll tell you when we're away from here.'

Mrs T flushed scarlet at this sign of mistrust, but folded her arms across her chest and said only, 'Better go and pack, then. I'll stay here.'

'I'll let you know when I've packed and you can come up and help me,' Jo told Deemer and he nodded.

No one spoke as they waited. The sergeant came to sit next to Tess and Mrs T put a kettle on the gas stove. 'Cup of tea, sergeant?'

'No, thank you.'

'I'll make one for the girl as well.'

'But you won't take her in, a child who's just lost

267

her mother. I thought better of you, Mrs Tucker, I did that. So I don't want your tea, thank you very much.'

Tess was surprised that the sergeant was helping her like this, though her mother had always said he was 'all right, for a policeman'.

It seemed a long time till Jo came back down the stairs with a Gladstone bag and a suitcase. 'Can you carry these for me, Tess love? Sergeant Deemer, I'm afraid my other luggage is quite heavy.'

'We'll manage.'

Tess took the bags from her cousin, setting them down by the door and standing beside them.

Mrs T didn't say anything, so Tess didn't either. What was there to say? She'd lived through some bad times, but this was the worst ever.

When the sergeant and Jo had brought the trunk down, they lugged it outside and put it into the boot of the car.

Sergeant Deemer came back for the large suitcase and Tess followed him out, carrying the other two bags even though they were quite heavy, so eager was she to leave. It was quite a squash to get them all in as well as the luggage but she didn't care. She wasn't coming back for anything, not if Mrs T didn't want her.

No one said goodbye and Tess half expected Mrs T to slam the door after them, but it was closed very quietly before they'd even left. And locked.

She wondered if she'd heard the faint sound of weeping from inside the house or just imagined it. Why would Mrs Tucker weep?

22

Before he started the car, Deemer asked, 'Why didn't you want to tell Mrs T where we were going, Jo? She'd not come after the lass. She's not that bad underneath, just frightened for her livelihood.'

'I don't trust her now. But that's not why I think we should try to keep Tess's whereabouts a secret. Until we know who killed her mother, I think she'll be safer staying hidden.'

'You're probably right, but you'll have to tell me, though, or I can't take you there.'

'Well, of course. I trust you absolutely, sergeant.' She lowered her voice, even though they were inside the car with the doors shut. 'I think Nick will let us stay with him at Willcox Motors. There are empty bedrooms and since I work there, I have a key to the front and back doors. I can let us in without waking the neighbours then go upstairs and wake Nick to ask him if it's all right to stay there.'

'Right. Good idea.' Deemer started the car and set off, driving slowly down towards Rivenshaw.

'Why should this Nick let me stay?' Tess asked. 'No one else in the valley would.'

'He's a kind man and I feel quite sure he'll let us both stay there. Don't forget I'm homeless too, now.'

'Mrs T would take you back if you were on

your own.'

'But I wouldn't go back because I'd not feel comfortable with her, knowing how heartless she is. Besides, I'm not on my own. I'm going to be looking after you from now on, if you're agreeable.'

Tess sniffed back tears. 'I don't understand why you're doing this when you hardly know me but I'm very grateful and – I promise I'll try not to be a bother.'

'I'm doing it because you're the closest relative I've got and because you're still a child. You need me ... and I need you as well. I'd like to have a family again, you see, even a family of only the two of us. I've never counted my stepmother as family. I can't stand the woman.'

Silence, then Deemer said, 'You're a lucky girl, Tess.'

'Then you'd better know the whole truth before I start feeling too hopeful.'

Jo stared sideways at her in the moonlit darkness of the car's interior. 'What do you mean?'

'I'm not a child – well, not exactly. I'm sixteen. My mother had me when she was working in London, and she didn't come back here till I was ten, only she told everyone I was seven. I've kept pretending to be younger than my real age ever since, especially lately.'

'Why lately?' Deemer asked.

'To stop that horrible Rathley man coming after me. He likes to, um – he likes young girls. It's a good thing I've always been small for my age, isn't it? But I've grown a lot in the past few months, so we knew that couldn't go on.'

Deemer made a sound of deep disgust in his throat as he heard the name Rathley. 'We've heard that about *him* and young girls before but we've never been able to get anyone to complain or give evidence. He's been very careful to pick on people who daren't betray him. We'll catch him out one day, though. I've been keeping my eyes open for a while and asking others to do the same. I can't abide nasty devils like that.'

They all fell silent, contemplating Rathley and his unnatural behaviour with the same instinctive disgust.

A minute or two later, Deemer said, 'So you're sixteen, eh? Well, I'll be blowed. I'd never have guessed you to be that old. What were you going to do when you couldn't pretend any longer?'

'Mam's been saving her money for years and we were planning to run away quite soon and start a new life. She was going to get her lawyer to sell the house after we left.'

'She had a lawyer?' He sounded surprised.

'Yes. He took her on for my sake.'

'Do you know his name?'

'Yes. But I'll tell you that later. When things are more settled. When I'm more sure of what's going to happen.'

Jo didn't press her. 'I can't stand Rathley, either. He came after me the one night I stayed at his house. He thought I was a poor relative, you see, and because my stepmother disapproved of me and said unkind things, he must have thought I had loose morals as well. I left their house the very next morning. Edna will probably go on saying bad things about me, though.'

271

'You should threaten to sue her for slander if she does,' Deemer said.

'I may do if she doesn't stop. If Tess and I stay here, that is.'

The girl slipped her hand into her cousin's. 'You understand what it can be like, then. Rathley offered Mam fifty pounds for me, more than the other men offered by far.'

'Other men?' Jo asked in surprise.

'There have been others, but Rathley offered most. Mam kept putting him off but she took his little bribes to keep me safe. She never could resist money. I wouldn't go to him for fifty thousand pounds. She told me to climb out of the kitchen window whenever any of those men came to see her and she taught Donny to lock the window after me. I always hid in that little park just up the hill. There isn't usually anyone around so late. After whoever it was had gone, she would send Donny out the back way to fetch me. That's why your constable found me there tonight, sergeant. I was waiting for it to be safe.' She pressed one hand to her mouth, struggling against tears.

'It's a good thing you did slip out tonight or you might have been killed, too. Well, well. That explains a lot. I wonder if–' But the sergeant broke off and didn't finish the sentence.

Just before they entered Rivenshaw he slowed down and stopped by the roadside. 'You seem sure Nick will help us, Jo.'

'I am. He and I – well, we seem to understand one another, even the first time we met.'

'Hmm. I don't know him well enough yet to guess how he'll react, because he left Rivenshaw years ago and has only just come back, but I know Todd and Charlie, who work with him, and they'll both be happy to help a lass in trouble, I'm sure, whoever she is. You're wrong to say no one in the valley would help you, Tess. There are some very decent folk living here.'

Jo glanced at the girl, sitting beside her on the back seat, looking desperately anxious. 'Is that all right with you, love, hiding there, right in the centre of town? I don't think they'll expect to find you still around, you see, and I can tell anyone who asks that I sent you away to a friend's for safety.'

'I don't care where I go as long as I'm with you.'

'Is there any way we can get to the car sales place without being seen?' Jo asked the sergeant. 'I can live there openly because I work for Nick, and Tess can hide upstairs till we figure out what to do next. I know it'll be boring, Tess, and you'll have to be very careful not to be seen at the window, but you'll be safe there and we'll be together.'

'I'll be happy to be bored as long as I'm safe.'

Deemer joined in. 'If anyone tries to start up a hunt for you, I'll only tell them I know where you are and that you're safe.'

Tess and Jo let out a deep sigh of relief at the same time, then gave one another faint, sad smiles.

Deemer put the car into gear and set off again. 'Why don't we go round to the rear of the house? There's a back laneway for coal deliveries and such, and I'll switch off the car's lights before I drive along it? If anyone looks out to see who's driving around in the middle of the night, they'll recognise my car and not think anything of it because I sometimes do keep an eye on my town at night. If they ask me what I was doing, I'll say I was just checking that everything was quiet.'

'You're being so kind,' Tess said suddenly. 'I didn't expect that.'

'It's my duty to keep you safe, lass, and to find your mother's murderer. You can be sure I won't stop looking for him till I've succeeded.'

'Good for you, sergeant,' Jo said.

'Right then. That's what we'll do. There's enough moonlight for me to see where I am. The fewer people who notice us going into the house with Tess, the better.'

As they drove past the front of the car sales yard, they could see that the building was dark, with no lights showing apart from a blurred reflection in one window of a street lamp.

Deemer drove as quietly as he could round to the back alley then switched off his car lights. It was dark there and as far as they could tell, no one was awake in any of the houses that were homes as well as shops.

When he stopped at the rear of the car sales place, he looked back but no lights had come on in the houses they'd passed. 'Go on, lass. Ask Nick if you two can stay there.'

Jo got out and went to the back gate, grunting in annoyance when she found it locked. She didn't have a key to it, either.

'Oh, to heck with it!' she muttered, hitched up her skirt and climbed up the gate, using the handle as a step. She'd been a real tomboy as a child and her skill at climbing trees stood her in good stead now. And if the sergeant saw more of her legs than was decent, too bad.

She sat for a minute astride the top of the gate studying the other side, then waved to Deemer, swung her second leg over and clambered down into the backyard.

Deemer chuckled. 'She's a lively one, isn't she? You're lucky you've got her, lass. Don't let her down.'

'I won't. I'm used to being careful what I do.' Tess leaned forward as she thought of something. 'You'll look after Donny, won't you? He can't look after himself, but if you give him simple tasks he's a hard worker.'

'Yes. I'll see he's all right. Maybe find a farmer that'll take him.'

'Don't tell him where I am, though. He blurts out anything he thinks of, regardless of who can hear him.'

'No. I'll not even be telling my constable that. The fewer people who know your hiding place, the better.'

Inside the house, Nick was awake because he'd heard a car slow down and stop for a few moments outside at the front. Who would be driving around at this hour of the night? The town centre was usually quiet after midnight. He decided to check, but by the time he'd got up and looked out of the window, the car had driven off.

He was about to get back into bed when he heard the sound of an engine from the rear of the house. It had to be the same car. He ran to look out and realised that someone was driving along the back lane without lights.

Well, if they thought they were going to break in and steal something, they'd find they were making a bad mistake.

He grabbed his dressing gown and ran down the stairs, picking up a chunky walking stick from the hall stand. It was the work of a minute to leave the house by the scullery door instead of the main back door and he let out his breath in a soft, 'Aah!' as he saw a figure sitting on top of the back gate.

He couldn't make out the person's details because the gate was in deep shadow, but as he saw the figure jump down, he crept across the backyard and pounced on the intruder.

To his surprise he found he'd got hold of a woman. He dragged her out of the shadows into the moonlight, recognising the face instantly. 'Jo!'

'Nick. Oh good. That saves me waking you up. We need help. Can we come in?'

'We?'

'Let's get everyone inside, then we'll explain. Sergeant Deemer is in the car with Tess. There's been trouble, really bad trouble.'

'If I can help, you have only to ask.'

She smiled at him. 'I know.'

He gave her a quick smile back and slid back the bolts holding the gate, finding a key for the padlock. As soon as he'd opened the gate, the car door opened and Deemer got out, followed by the girl who'd been in the back seat of the vehicle.

Jo pushed past him and put her arm round the stranger, leading the way into the house.

'What the hell's going on?' Nick asked the sergeant in an undertone.

'There's been a murder. Tess's mother.'

The shock of that took Nick's voice away and he followed the other man into the rear of the house in silence, reaching out automatically for the light switch.

Deemer grabbed his hand. 'Don't put the lights on.'

'Can we sit down and get the fire blazing up a bit?' Jo asked. 'Tess is very upset.' She took off her coat and wrapped it round the girl's shoulders.

Nick went to get a coat for Jo from the hall stand then joined them at the kitchen table, listening in amazement to the tale of the night's doings. When it was finished, he didn't wait to be asked, because it was obvious why they'd come. 'You and Tess are welcome to stay here, Jo, but we've not got any spare beds, only a couple of rolled-up flock mattresses, and thin old things they are, too.'

'Thank you. I knew you'd help us. And we can put the mattresses on the floor, make do with them. If I'm staying here openly, we can buy me a bed, and Tess and I can share it.'

'Will it be possible to keep Tess's presence a complete secret?' Deemer asked.

'If she's careful not to go near the windows, yes. But Todd and Silas will have to know, of course, because they might see something or even bump into her. And I think Todd will want to tell Charlie Willcox, who's his business partner.'

'We won't be able to keep my presence here a secret,' Jo said. 'Nor should we try.'

Nick looked at her anxiously. 'What will people think? An unmarried woman staying here alone with a man? It'll ruin your reputation.'

'That doesn't matter,' Jo said, then added brightly, 'We could pretend we're engaged.'

'You'll still get a bad name.'

She looked at him, shrugging, 'I'll just have to put up with it. Tess's life may depend upon us keeping her safe.'

'There is one thing we could do.'

'Oh, what?'

He took her hand, ignoring the others, rushing in he knew, but he felt so certain she was right for him. 'This is a terrible time to ask you to marry me, but I think I'd have got round to it quite soon anyway. Will you do that, Jo, marry me? I wasn't going to ask you so soon, though it didn't take me long to be sure of my feelings for you.'

She wanted to say yes, wanted to very much. Because she'd fallen in love with him just as quickly. But she didn't just have herself to think of. 'Can we just pretend and see how things go? I have a feeling none of this is going to be easy and I don't want to tie you down. If the sergeant can't catch the murderer, I may have to take Tess back to Australia to save her life and – and then I can't just think of myself. I'm sorry.'

'I'm sorry, too. I don't want you to go away. And I meant it. I do want to marry you. And if that includes Tess, it's all right by me.'

As they stared at one another, their expressions betraying their love, Tess moved forward. 'I can't let you sacrifice your happiness for me, Jo. I'm not worth it.'

Jo turned to her young cousin. 'It's too early to talk about sacrifices. Let's see how we go, eh? We can start off pretending, then if things go all right, we can ... all of us think about it for real.'

She turned back to Nick. 'You're just starting up in business, something you've been dreaming about for a while. I hope me staying here won't spoil it all for you.'

'I don't think you would spoil anything, Jo. You are important to me.'

'Maybe if things work out, we can get married. But I'm not rushing into anything, so it's just a pretend engagement.'

His voice was firm. 'For now. Till it's safe for me to ask you again. I *am* going to marry you, whatever it takes.'

Behind her Tess gave a sentimental sigh.

Jo wanted to sigh like that, too. His words made her feel loved, as did the way he looked at her, but she had Tess to think of now as well as herself. She couldn't abandon the girl if it was too dangerous for her to stay in Rivenshaw. And she didn't want to put Nick in danger.

But oh, she did wish the engagement were real. She'd never met anyone she felt so right with.

How could you know so quickly? She hadn't expected that.

When the first signs of dawn turned everything in the kitchen grey, Wilf felt relieved that he could get up and do something useful, tired as he was after a night sleeping rough in his own kitchen.

He found some live embers where he'd banked up the fire at the back of the grate and watched

279

the cautious little flames creep out of the gaps and snatch at the lumps of coal. They grew slowly bigger, just as his dreams had.

He heard sounds from their bedroom and turned to watch the door but Enid didn't come down to join him and share a pot of tea. He usually ate his breakfast earlier than her and the kids, enjoying a quiet chat with her in the peace of early morning.

Eh, it wasn't like her to keep a quarrel going.

Half an hour passed and his anger at her rose steadily as he sat there alone, waiting, glancing at the clock far too often. In the end he made himself a thick jam butty and ate it in angry, snapping bites, then picked up his tool bags and left the house in the new van.

He wasn't going to beg for her forgiveness, because he had done nothing wrong. And he definitely wasn't giving back the van – or abandoning his dreams.

How long would it take Enid to simmer down, though?

Surely she wouldn't stay angry for more than a day or two?

Wilf spent most of the morning working, finishing off some small jobs, then drove to the older part of Birch End and stopped outside a tall, elegant terrace. It always looked to him as if someone had started building decent houses here and then stopped suddenly. The change hadn't been a good one, because they'd thrown up some rows of much smaller houses, so that as many as possible could be crammed in on the piece of ground.

He usually stopped to study the outside of the houses when he passed by because these were the sort of homes *he* would like to live in.

He knew Mrs Morton at the end house was living on a pittance these days, thanks to her son's stupidity with the money she'd lent him. Garrard Morton had killed himself out of shame, which had made the situation even worse for his poor mother.

Wilf had recently noticed a couple of problems with the windows, which would become serious if left as they were, so he knocked on the door and offered to mend them for her.

'I'm afraid I can't afford it, Wilf.'

'I can spare an hour or two. You helped me by giving me odd jobs when things were bad, so I'm happy to help you in return now. Come winter you'll get leaks if those problems aren't fixed.'

She inclined her head. 'Oh. Well, I'll be very grateful for your help, then. If I can ever do anything for you in return, don't hesitate to come to me. I may be growing older but I'm still able to get about. Mona and I manage very well considering.'

'I'm sure you do. Have you heard from your daughter-in-law lately?'

'No. She's remarried and wants nothing further to do with me. I can't work out why she blames me for my son killing himself.' She paused to control her trembling lips. 'Anyway, I'd be grateful for your help, Wilf.'

He repaired the worst leak temporarily, but he'd have to come back with the things to do it properly. He would also do a couple of other small jobs here over the next week or two. It'd be a shame to let this lovely house deteriorate.

When she protested, he said, 'I'll just do it whenever I'm in the area and have an hour or two free. I'll expect a cup of tea from you, mind.'

'You'll deserve it. And a piece of cake or biscuit to go with it.'

'I won't say no to that.'

She was dabbing at her eyes as she closed the door.

Not wanting to go home yet, Wilf ate his sandwich and decided to go and show Charlie the van and tools. He was, he admitted to himself, reluctant to go home.

Charlie studied the vehicle and its contents, then slapped the side of the van with one hand. 'The chap who told me about it was right, wasn't he? It's a grand little van and the tools have got to be worth a lot more than two pounds.'

Wilf smiled. 'I'm right set up about it all, I must admit.'

'Come in and have a cup of tea with me to celebrate. And I've got some shortbread fingers in the biscuit tin.'

'I never say no to a cup of tea.'

They went into the back of the shop and sat in Charlie's office, waiting for the woman who worked there to bring them some tea.

'What did your wife say about the van? I bet she was pleased.'

Wilf didn't know what to tell him, then decided on a brief summary of the truth. If Charlie was going to go into business with him, he deserved to know how things stood.

'Actually, she's upset about it.'

'What the hell for?'

'She hates getting into debt.'

'You'll have that van paid off within six months, Wilf lad, probably less, if I'm any judge.'

'I know I will, but she can't seem to believe that. The bad years have made her very nervous about money.'

Charlie stared at him in compassion. 'Eh, I'm sorry, lad.'

'Yes. So am I. It'll all work out in the end and she'll realise I'm bringing in more money than before, but it'll take a while. I'm not giving up my plans.'

'No. You shouldn't do. You're a clever chap and you'll get on in the world, given half a sniff of a chance.' He added with his usual cheeky grin, an urchin's grin for all Charlie was in his late thirties, 'And what you earn will make me a bit of extra money as well. Ah, tell your wife not to worry. I'll help you find plenty of jobs now you can travel further.'

Wilf forced a smile. He'd known Charlie would find him jobs. They'd shaken hands on it, hadn't they?

The woman brought in tea, and Wilf forced himself to eat a couple of pieces of shortbread.

He wasn't giving up his dream. Not for anyone or anything.

But deep down he felt sad, very sad. He'd so wanted to share that dream with Enid, to rejoice together over every step taken. Even a stranger like Mrs Morton had been pleased for him.

23

That morning, Jo woke with a start, unable for a moment or two to figure out where she was. Then last night's horrors came flooding back to her and she allowed herself to lie in bed for a little longer, praying for the strength to do whatever was necessary to help her young relative.

She looked round and grimaced. How many more strange beds was she going to wake up in before she found somewhere to call home again?

Well, this was undoubtedly going to be a difficult day, but she couldn't put off facing it any longer. She got up and hunted in her luggage for her dressing gown so that she was decently covered before she left the bedroom.

Peeping into the back bedroom to check on Tess, she was pleased to see that the girl was still asleep, though the tangle of bedcovers bore witness to a restless night. No, not child, young woman. She must remember that.

The bathroom still felt damp, presumably from Nick's ablutions. He must have been very quiet, because she'd heard nothing. She tried to be quiet, too, so that she'd not wake Tess. After freshening herself up, she got dressed in the first skirt and blouse that came to hand, dragging on a cardigan over the top of them, anxious to talk to Nick before Tess got up.

When she reached the kitchen she paused in the

doorway to watch him. He was frowning into space. What a nice, comfortable sort of face he had! She'd not be afraid to tell this man anything. She didn't know why she felt so sure of his help and support, but she did.

Suddenly seeming to sense her presence, he turned to stare solemnly across the table at her. 'Are we still engaged?'

'Do you want to be?'

'Very much. And you?'

It was out before she could stop herself. 'Yes, very much indeed.'

His face brightened. 'That's a good start to my day.'

She tried to face facts. 'I may still have to go back to Australia because of Tess. I can't desert her. And I doubt she can make a decent new life here.'

'I've been thinking about that. If you do have to go back, I'm coming with you. I'm not going to abandon you, not now, not ever.'

'But you've only just started your business here.'

He held out his hand in a mute invitation to join him. 'You're far more important to me than any business, Jo, surely you know that? I lay awake last night, thinking about Australia, and though I admit I'd rather stay here, I'll not do that if it means giving you up.' He put a mock fierce tone into his voice as he added, 'And you won't change my mind about that, whatever you say or do.'

She walked forward and took the hand he was offering. How could she not? 'Oh, Nick, I hate to ask you to make such a sacrifice.'

'You didn't ask me. I volunteered. And it may

not be necessary.' He pulled her to sit on his knee and gave her a sweet, gentle kiss.

And heaven help her, she kissed him back.

'How about we buy a special licence and get married next week?' he asked.

She gaped at him. 'That quickly?'

'Yes. I'd do it tomorrow if we could but if I remember the marriage laws correctly, you have to wait seven days, or is it seven working days? I'll have to find out.'

He eased her off his knee and stood up. 'Now, let me pour you a cup of tea and offer you a slice of toast. That's all I have in my nearly empty pantry for breakfast, I'm afraid, but the strawberry jam is delicious.'

'Sounds fine to me. I'll do some shopping later and put a few more provisions into the pantry here. What time does Todd get into work?'

'About nine o'clock, but he's coming in a little later so that he can spend some time with his wife. He has a meeting after work, you see. He's on the town council and that keeps him busy.' He grinned. 'He's still madly in love with her. It's lovely the way he talks about her.'

She looked out of the window. 'It's not going to be very warm today. Look at those dark clouds. Good thing I bought a card saying OPEN. We can put it in the window and keep the front door closed.'

'You're good at details, aren't you?'

'I try to be. Now, let's get that toast made. I'm good at being hungry in the morning, too.'

The gas cooker was quite new and had a built-in grill at eye level, so they had no need to light a fire to do the toast. That was real progress for you, she thought, admiring the cooker. Such equipment must make millions of people's daily lives easier. Then she smiled ruefully and mentally amended it to 'millions of *women's* lives'.

There was the sound of footsteps on the landing and Jo ran to the foot of the stairs to stop Tess coming down to join them. 'Stay upstairs! You could be seen if anyone came into the house.'

'Even this early?'

'I'm afraid so. It'd look strange if we kept the door locked on a working day, wouldn't it? We can't take any risks when dealing with a ruthless murderer. Oh, and don't flush the lavatory if you hear anyone else downstairs.'

'All right. Do you have a book I can borrow?'

Nick came to stand in the hall, looking up at Tess. 'There's a makeshift bookcase of planks and bricks in my bedroom. You're welcome to borrow any book you fancy. I have a few Agatha Christies. I really enjoy her Hercule Poirot detective stories. Have you read any of them?'

'No.'

'Then you might like to start with *The Mysterious Affair at Styles*. That was her first book.'

'Thank you.'

Jo took over. 'In the meantime, how do you like your tea? I'll bring you up some and a couple of pieces of toast as well in a few minutes.'

'Tea would be wonderful, but I'm not hungry.'

'Force a piece of toast down, though,' Jo coaxed. 'You have to keep up your strength. We don't want you fainting on us.' The poor girl looked so wan and unhappy, Jo couldn't help it. She ran up

287

the stairs to hug Tess, then pushed her gently towards the bedroom. 'Remember, don't show yourself at the window, either. Best to keep the curtains drawn, I'm afraid.'

Tess nodded and went slowly back into her room, her whole body drooping.

Jo shook her head sadly as she walked downstairs again. 'This is going to be very hard for her, Nick, sitting around doing nothing, on top of mourning her mother.'

'At least she'll be safe here.'

'For a while, yes.'

He put his arm round her waist as they returned to the kitchen and they stood together by the window as they chatted.

'The quicker Sergeant Deemer catches the murderer, the better. That poor girl won't be truly safe until the villain's behind bars. Does she have any idea who'd been visiting her mother that night, Jo? Was it Rathley or one of the other men interested in the girl?'

'It's my guess she does know but she gets upset when I ask her. I think she's afraid of him. I'd guess it was Rathley, though, wouldn't you? It's a terrible thing to lose your mother, but how much worse must it feel to know your mother's been murdered?'

'I think we should tell Deemer we believe she knows something.'

'It would feel like a betrayal and I'm only just starting to gain her trust.'

'Better to feel betrayed than be murdered like her mother, don't you think?'

Jo nodded reluctantly.

The sergeant was coming to the same conclusion as he finished off his breakfast. His wife, bless her, knew him well enough not to interrupt his thinking by trying to chat.

He was certain Tess was holding something back and unfortunately the slow-witted man he was keeping at the police station for his own safety couldn't seem to talk sense, still kept repeating, 'He's killed her.'

Someone had to have seen Moira's last visitor, who had to be the person most likely to have killed her, but who apart from Big Donny? The daughter had been at the park under Constable Hopkins' eyes at the time of the murder and couldn't possibly have seen how it happened or who did it.

But who was the customer who'd driven her from the house? The trouble was, prostitutes didn't usually sit around and chat to their customers. They wanted to get rid of them as quickly as possible. So two or even three men might have visited Moira while her daughter was out.

He'd been considering seeking help from a couple of men in Rivenshaw who passed on information to him occasionally for small sums of money. He could suggest they keep their eyes and ears open, and ask around carefully, not saying why they were interested. Maybe he'd offer to pay them twice as much as usual for any piece of information that proved useful. Yes, even the inspector would surely approve of doing that if it led to a conviction.

When he opened the front door of the police

station, which was attached to his house, Deemer saw Constable Hopkins walking down the street towards him and nodded approvingly. The lad was a good timekeeper, never late without a good reason, and had the makings of a good policeman. You could always tell.

He sent Hopkins straight out again to take a walk round the town centre and see if he could find the informants, whom he also knew. It was usually easy enough to find them, because they spent a lot of time loitering near or in the town square, offering to carry bags for travellers coming out of the railway station or to run errands for shopkeepers, anything to earn a penny or two.

The constable was back within half an hour, looking pleased with himself.

'I found both men, sarge, but neither of them was near Packman Alley, so they didn't see what happened or who went in there. They said they'd ask around, though, when I told them you'd pay a bit extra to get genuine information quickly. It made them eager to help.'

'Good. I'm going back to Moira's house now. I intend to check every inch of it. You'd better come with me. Two pairs of eyes are always better than one. I'll lock this place up. If something's urgent, people can knock on the house door and leave a message with my wife. I reckon catching a murderer is a lot more important than finding lost objects or even lost pet dogs.'

'I agree, sarge. What about Moira's daughter? Will you allow her to go back and live at home once we've gone over the house?'

'No, of course not. She's too young to live there

on her own. I've left her with a family I trust and no, I'm not going to tell you who that is. I'm not going to tell anyone. We don't want the murderer going after her, do we?'

'I'd not reveal the information,' the constable said indignantly.

'Better if you aren't *able* to let anything slip.'

'Will the inspector let you keep it secret where she is?'

'He won't know I've done it unless you tell him. I'm trusting you about this, lad. Just keep telling folk you don't know where the daughter is. The more people hear it, the more they'll believe it. Even if I get in trouble about it later, you won't, because I won't let on that you ever knew anything. Loyalty works both ways.'

He didn't trust the inspector, though, reckoned the man couldn't see anything beyond the rule book and the end of his own nose. How he had gained such a high promotion baffled Deemer.

Hopkins gave a solemn nod, looking so young and fresh-faced, so untouched by life and tragedy that Deemer felt sorry for what he would see and do as a police officer over the years. He wondered how that would affect Hopkins. It wore some officers down. You could never quite tell who'd stick it out.

'Well, let's drive up to Moira's house, then, eh lad?'

When they got to Packman Alley they found no sign of the two lads who'd been left to keep watch on Number 3. Deemer frowned. 'Not like them lads to leave a job without being paid.'

When he touched the front door, the only way into the house, it swung open, even though he'd locked it and taken away the key. 'Someone's broken in.' He bent to check the lock. 'Scratched. They picked it. It must have been someone those lads are afraid of.'

'Tread carefully when we–' He pushed open the door, which led straight into the living area. 'Oh, hell!'

Deemer walked grimly round the inside, followed by a shocked young constable. Everything was in chaos. Someone must have searched every drawer and cupboard in the place and simply tossed their contents on the floor. Broken crockery and spilled sugar in the kitchen, powder and lipstick and an upended slop bucket – ugh! – in the main bedroom.

'They were looking for something, lad, not just burgling the place.'

When they came downstairs he began to go through the mess on the floor.

'What do you think they were looking for, sarge?'

'I don't know. But it doesn't look to me as if they found it. They've searched every nook and cranny, not missed a single shell even. If they'd found what they wanted early on in the search, they'd not have continued, would they? What's more, there are objects here they could have sold, but they haven't bothered with them. So they weren't here to burgle the place.'

'Whatever it was must no longer be here, then.'

'I don't know. They could have taken it away or it could have been exceptionally well hidden. I wonder if the daughter knows what it might be and where her mother hid her valuables. Have to ask her.'

'I felt that sorry for the poor lass yesterday, skriking like a babby, she was, sarge.'

'You'd have cried if your mother had been murdered. But I felt sorry for her, too.' The sergeant sighed. Death came soon enough without dealing it out on purpose. No one had the right to take a life.

He paused for a moment to think it through. It wasn't likely to be a poor man who'd come visiting. Poor men wouldn't be able to afford Red Moira's prices. But rich or poor, if her visitor had done it, he deserved hanging and Deemer hoped to see the day that happened. He'd feel a failure if he didn't solve this crime and the nearer he got to retirement, the less he wanted to leave something undone behind him.

Only a few more years to go. What he'd do with his time then he'd not been able to work out, but you had to retire at a certain age, whether you wanted to or not. Stupid, that was.

Todd left work early to go to a special meeting of the council that evening, so they could lock the front door. But even with that done and the curtains drawn, Jo wouldn't allow Tess to join them downstairs.

What's more, she insisted that tomorrow they had to create a hiding place for the girl in case someone broke in. Anyone who'd stab a woman and leave her body sprawled on the floor wouldn't hesitate to do the same to her daughter.

After tea, Jo sat chatting to Nick for a while, then went up to collect Tess's meal tray and have a little chat.

She found the girl weeping and not much of the food had been eaten.

Tess looked up at her from the bed, wiped away the tears with the back of one hand, then started sobbing. More tears ran from her swollen red eyes and she dabbed at them with a soggy handkerchief.

Jo sat beside her and gave her a cuddle, shushing and rocking to and fro as if Tess were a small child. Gradually the tears subsided but Tess still kept hold of her hand.

'What started this off, love?'

'I was sad about my mother, then I started worrying about what *he* will do now.'

So there was definitely some information Tess hadn't shared with anyone. 'Who do you mean by "he"?'

'Who do you think?'

'Rathley?'

Tess nodded. 'He was there last night. That's why she sent me out to hide in the park. Mam always does that when he visits. Even when it's raining you can shelter in the bandstand, you see.'

'Ah. Does – did he visit your mother often?'

Tess shrugged. 'A couple of times a week.'

'But if he, um, takes pleasure in your mother's company, why would he kill her?'

'It might not have been him, only...' Her voice trailed away.

'Only what?'

'Only Mam wasn't well. She kept coughing. She

said she'd not be working at all last night. He might have ignored that, though. I've heard people talk about him. If he sets his mind on doing something, then you're best letting him do it or he'll make sure you regret it.'

'Is that so?' She stopped talking and waited, hoping to encourage further confidences.

'He wants to use my body, Jo. He's been waiting for me to grow up. She persuaded him to wait till I'm older. That's why I had to dress like this. He was offering her fifty pounds if I was untouched, but she promised she wouldn't let him do that to me. She's been saving money for ages and we were nearly ready to run away. Didn't I tell you that she'd even arranged for the lawyer to sell our cottage for her if we left suddenly?'

Another pause and a sigh that ended on a sob. 'Even so, it doesn't make sense for Rathley to have killed her, it just doesn't. I keep going over and over it in my mind and I can't work it out for certain. Why would he do that when he wanted me alive? All I know is, I don't want him to find me. That's another reason I haven't said anything to Sergeant Deemer. I don't want to draw Rathley's attention to myself.' She shuddered and crossed her arms in front of her chest protectively.

'Well, as long as you stay hidden and don't give yourself away, I doubt Rathley will suspect that you're here.'

'I hope and pray he doesn't.'

When she went to bed, after a few pleasant moments chatting quietly to Nick, Jo found it hard to settle to sleep because she couldn't forget what Tess had told her. She too loathed Rathley and didn't trust him. And he'd come after her because he was angry at her. She could believe he'd killed Moira, but surely he'd have done it in a way that didn't implicate him?

Tomorrow she'd definitely tell the sergeant what Tess had said.

24

Todd slipped into Reginald Kirby's house the back way, meeting up with his wife and Charlie just before he got to the gate.

'The conspirators gather!' Charlie struck a melodramatic pose.

Leah gave her brother-in-law a mock slap. 'Don't be silly. This is serious.'

He gave her his usual broad smile. 'Doesn't mean we can't enjoy it.'

'Well, keep your voice down.' She stood on tiptoe to kiss her husband's cheek. 'Did you have a good day, Todd love?'

'Not really. Everyone's talking about the murder.'

'What murder?'

'Where have you been all day?'

'Working on a new flavour of fizzy drink. You'll have to test some for me when we get home.'

'Always happy to do that.'

'Has there really been a murder in our valley?' she prompted.

He told her about Red Moira, but it was the

thought of the woman's daughter that caught Leah's attention. 'What on earth is that poor girl going to do now? No one will want to take her in with a mother like that.'

'Who knows? She seems to have vanished off the face of the earth.'

They were still waiting for a couple of people to arrive, and of course the murder in Packman Alley was the main subject of conversation for everyone in the meantime.

The lawyer Henry Lloyd, coming in last, heard the words 'Packman Alley' and insisted on them going over it all again. He looked so shocked, they asked what was upsetting him, but he shook his head and didn't explain.

Then even Charlie settled down to listen quietly as Reginald explained what he wanted to do and why.

'I think we need to focus on public health first. There's been another outbreak of fever in Backshaw Moss, not a serious one this time, thank goodness, but bad enough to make Dr Fiske worry about the drains and the drinking water once again. He says if the council does nothing about them, it'll keep happening and next time it could be really bad, maybe spread right round the valley.'

Leah nodded vigorously. 'I agree with him. I think it's more than time for the council to do something about it.'

'I tried and failed to get funding for improvements to the sewage system last year. However, with all of you now on the council, maybe we really can do something. If you agree with me, that is. I'm assuming I can count on your support for a new proposal?'

There were murmurs and nods from every member of the group.

'The whole of that slum needs dealing with,' Todd said. 'Half the buildings look ready to fall down and the place is a festering sore. It's all right for you folk in the posh part of Birch End, Charlie, but the ordinary folk in the main village deserve better.'

Charlie pulled a face. 'Actually, we're starting to get affected by those drains as well. Marion was complaining about the smell only last week, and I've smelled it, too.'

Reginald raised his hands in a gesture of help-lessness and frustration. 'There you are. I've had several other people complain directly to me lately. They've tried complaining to the council sanitation officers, but they've been told there's no money to improve anything. There's a man called Jackson in charge of that at the moment, who's afraid to upset anyone, a real weakling.'

'I've met him,' Charlie said. 'If you made a rule that everyone had to stand on their head and sing the national anthem backwards every hour, he'd enforce it.'

'That sort of attitude won't get us anywhere. Since you're new to the council, you may not rea-lise that our town could have been making a start on improving this sort of thing years ago under the Housing and Town Planning Act of 1919. But for nearly fifteen years, they've fiddled around and done practically nothing, mainly thanks to people like Rathley and his builder friend Higgerson.'

He paused to let that sink in and went on,

'We've got rid of Rixom from the town hall now, thank goodness, but there are others who need dealing with, too, who either obstruct progress for their own benefit or are terrified to do anything, like Jackson. Higgerson's houses are shoddily built, but no one dares call him out about it, and they pass inspections, goodness knows how. Other builders don't flourish in Rivenshaw, except in a small way, because Higgerson's been awarded the contracts to every major building development for over a decade, as well as being allowed to do whatever he wants on his own building projects.'

'That man would cheat his own mother out of her last sixpence without blinking,' Todd said feelingly. 'He tried to pay me only half what he owed me for repairing his car last month, then had the nerve to threaten to take me to court if I insisted on charging so much. I told him he needn't bother because I'd be taking him to court for non-payment – so in the end he paid up "under protest". Well, he's free to get his car *and* his company's lorries repaired by someone else from now on, and so I told him.'

Charlie nodded. 'He throws together houses that look nice enough from the outside, but there's a lot of faulty workmanship and skimping on materials that shows up when people are living in them. I should know. I have one of his houses and it's cost me a fortune to set things right be- cause you can't get him to admit that he's respon- sible.'

'Well, we can make a start now on necessary improvements and repairs, and we have you on board, Henry, in case we need to go after someone legally.'

'Always useful to have a lawyer on your side,' Todd said.

'Yes, but most important of all we need a majority on the council.'

'Are you sure we do have a majority? Jane Sowerby is a bit of a ditherer.'

'She'll vote with us,' Reginald said. 'Her son works for me and has promised he'll make sure his mother does what's necessary. Pity her husband died. He'd have stood for council and made a better fist of it than she will. She's a bit of a fool but her heart's in the right place.'

He picked up some folders and handed them round. 'You can each take one of these away with you and read the contents before the next council meeting. To sum up the overall situation, the 1919 Act *allowed* a start to be made on slum clearance but it's mainly been used for greenfields development, as far as I can make out from speaking to people from other local authorities, and that's what we can aim for.'

Reg nodded, looking smug. 'The recent Greenwood Act of 1930 *requires* councils to act, which is going to be a big help to us because even our worst backsliders on the council will have to agree to doing something.'

'How do we start?' Charlie asked.

'With your support I'm going to make this recent outbreak of diarrhoea an excuse to call an emergency meeting about Backshaw Moss. I shall propose that we do something about the sewage and water supplies, but for the main works we'll have to find some land to build the new council houses on. I've marked on the plans in your folders where there's a farmer willing to sell us a couple of his smaller fields and if we buy those we'll be able to erect new houses built to standards properly controlled by the council, ones that are both affordable and suitable for those in need. None of this one-room-and-share-an-outside-lavatory stuff. And we'll make sure people other than Higgerson get a look in on doing the building.'

'Does the council have the funds?' Todd asked.

'There's enough to make a start and grants can be obtained according to the number of persons being helped, not the number of buildings demolished. There are a hell of a lot of people crammed into Backshaw Moss, you know, far more than is safe. I hate to think what would happen if any of those ramshackle buildings caught fire, and we'll just have to pray that nothing will go round until the new houses are ready. But if we've improved the sanitation and water supplies to the present dwellings, we can hope things won't get out of hand. The sort of grant we can get will make a big difference to what we can afford to do.'

'Higgerson will still try to get any new building contracts,' Charlie said gloomily. 'And he usually manages to do it.' And the trouble was, it'd take a while for Wilf to become a builder. He'd have to see if he could find some way of making sure Higgerson didn't get every contract, and that he did good, sound work. Hmm. That wouldn't be easy.

'Well, this time Higgerson's friends haven't got a majority on the council and I intend to keep a very careful eye on what happens at the town

301

hall. That is...' he paused and looked at them, 'if I have the firm promise of ongoing support from all of you.'

They all murmured and nodded, and Henry said, 'I agree. If we stick together, we can surely manage to make some progress. No one could sort out all the problems in the valley at once, but if we can make a start, other things can be dealt with later.'

'How do we choose who gets the first houses and so on?' Leah asked.

The mayor smiled. 'How about you start up and chair a small sub-committee to see what can be arranged, Leah? I'll guarantee some funds from council – but don't go overboard. There won't be a lot of money.'

She looked at him in near panic for a moment, then took a deep breath and said, 'Very well. I'll do my best. But I'd appreciate some advice from you about how to set about it. I've not been in charge of a committee before.'

'I'll certainly help all I can, but my secretary will be the person to ask for practical help with the details. Miss Brayburn knows more about the ins and outs of council workings than anyone at the town hall.'

By the time the meeting broke up, the various new councillors were feeling moderately optimistic about their ability to make a difference to their world.

Reginald watched them leave, then went to pour himself a whisky. It was going to be harder than his colleagues perhaps realised, because Higgerson and friends were not afraid to play dirty.

But this time, surely, he'd found a group of supporters who would not be deterred and were younger than him and enthusiastic. They'd be able to defend themselves if necessary, he was sure, even Leah, who had her husband beside her, and loyal workers at her fizzy drinks factory during the day. The important thing was to get the reforms started.

He'd definitely warn them about the possible dangers next time. For the moment, let them get used to the idea of major change being needed in Backshaw Moss.

He raised his glass and looked at the ceiling, saying aloud, 'I need your help, Lady Luck. I hope you're going to be on our side this time.'

As an afterthought, he added, 'And it wouldn't hurt to have Miss Brayburn supporting our efforts, either. That woman baffles me. Which side is she on?'

Darned if he knew.

It wasn't till he was on his way home that Henry Lloyd let himself think about the murder of his client and how it would affect him, as her lawyer. He'd liked Moira Tayner, in spite of what she did for a living. She was a sensible woman who was making practical provision for the future. He wished more people were like that.

Who'd have thought that he'd have to do as she asked so soon, though?

He'd forward the letter she'd entrusted to him to the person named tomorrow morning. And he'd keep his eyes and ears open because no one had seemed to know what had happened to the daughter and he needed to know that.

Well, you couldn't hide anything for long in a small town. Deemer seemed to be involved and Henry had a great deal of respect for the sergeant. If anyone could solve the crime, it'd be him. And he probably knew where the daughter was.

What a sad thing to happen, though!

He hoped the murderer would be caught quickly. It made everyone uneasy when something like that happened right on their doorstep.

Henry didn't say anything to his wife about the part he'd have to play in the events. He was always scrupulous about client confidentiality.

But his first thought in the morning should be about that poor woman, and as soon as he got to his rooms, he would do as she'd asked and post the letter.

Would the person it was going to respond?

Who knew? He hoped so.

Hobbs had been sent to watch the mayor's house and had noted down who went in, licking the lead of his stub of a pencil to make it write indelibly, and laboriously printing his own random spellings of their names in a small, grubby notebook. He knew who these people were. Oh, yes. He knew all the better-off folk, especially which ones might slip you a shilling for doing a little job or taking a message for them.

He hoped he wasn't getting these folk into bad trouble, because they were kind, the sort who helped those worse off than themselves. Only, if he didn't get some money today, his own kids would go hungry, and they were more important than anything. So he continued to watch and take note.

As he waited, he tried to find shelter from the drizzling rain till they'd all come out of the house again and driven off in their cars. But the tree he was waiting under dripped steadily on to him and he could only stand there in misery.

Chilled through, he watched them drive off in their comfortable cars, then picked up a brick and hurled it through the front window of the house. That cheered him up. Even if he hadn't been instructed to do it, he might have vented his anger that way.

He waited only to see the glass shatter and cascade everywhere, then ran off down the street. He dearly loved smashing windows, had discovered that pleasure as a lad. It made such a satisfying sound, not to mention leaving a mess for rich sods to clear up. Even the kinder rich sods needed waking up now and then, he reckoned. What did they know about being hungry?

To be paid to smash a window was a real bonus to the job.

If what had happened in the past was anything to judge by, something had started up again and he would be earning a good bit of money in the coming weeks – and breaking a few more windows, he hoped. The man paying him had ordered this before. It was an ill wind!

He went to report what he'd done and hand over the list of names.

'I think I'd better employ you as a general handyman and cleaner from now on, so that there's a reason for me to be seen speaking to you, Hobbs.'

'Yes, sir. Thank you very much, sir. I'd really appreciate a proper job, sir, and I'll try my best to give satisfaction.'

'See that you don't let me down, whatever I ask you to do.'

'I'd never let you down, sir. Never, ever. I've always done what you asked, haven't I?'

A grunt was his only answer, and a dismissive wave of the hand.

Hobbs could have danced his way down the street, except it'd have drawn attention to him and he never thought it wise to stand out in a crowd. Eh, his wife was going to be over the moon about him having regular work. Maybe she'd show him a bit more affection now.

Pity about having to spy on them nice folk, but there you were. You had to look after yourself and your family first, second and third in this world.

25

The following morning Jo went upstairs to spend a few minutes chatting to Tess. She kept an eye on the battered old clock ticking away on the mantelpiece and after a while said, 'I'd better get to work now.' She picked up the breakfast tray, reluctant to leave the girl alone but she had to act normally in the office.

She planned to spend the morning sorting out

more invoices, receipts, brochures and miscellaneous rubbish in Todd's office, while he worked on some car repairs in the workshop. It was taking longer than she'd expected to set his office to rights, not only because she kept getting interrupted but also because his idea of filing had been to put the papers and letters into neat piles, regardless of what they related to, and stack them at the back, on the floor.

Silas arrived just before Nick left on a job and alternated between chatting to Todd in the workshop, prowling round the house and occasionally strolling along the street. He came back inside at one stage and said, 'It's a good thing you've had those net curtains put up. I can watch from the window of Nick's office without anyone out there realising.'

'It didn't take Todd long. They're only threaded on poles. But they do the job.'

An hour later, he crossed the hallway to consult Jo. 'Look, I've seen the same chap saunter past here several times, and why would anyone do that? I have his face firmly fixed in my mind, but I don't know him. I'm wondering whether it'd be a good idea to follow him and see where he goes. What do you think?'

'Excellent idea.'

'But that would leave you alone here. I'm not sure Nick would be happy with that.'

'I'll be fine. We're keeping the back door locked all the time, so no one can get in that way. And if anyone came in the front way and caused trouble, I have Tess upstairs. She'd come running to help me if I yelled. Yes, and there's Todd working nearby as well. I have good lungs, believe me.'

He grinned at that. 'I believe you.'

'I don't think there will be any trouble here, though, not in the daytime on premises where people are going past all the time and customers stopping to look at cars.'

'That's what I was thinking. OK. I'll nip out next time I see that fellow go past and follow him. Be careful, though.'

'I will.'

It felt strange to be left on her own and she enjoyed the peace. So much had happened since she came to Rivenshaw that she'd hardly had a quiet minute to herself. Nick was giving two consecutive driving lessons that morning and picking up the second client in Birch End. It seemed as if people were starting to become aware of his driving school, because they had another lesson booked for later in the afternoon as well.

He'd been reluctant to leave her, and said he wouldn't have done without Silas. She was wondering whether that protection was actually necessary, and if it hadn't been for the murder would have refused to spend her days so closely watched. She could usually take care of herself anyway and was on her guard now, thank you very much. She always kept something nearby that she could use as a weapon.

Only now that she didn't have Silas with her, she began to feel uneasy. Strange how his presence had made her feel safe to relax. With a sigh she gave in to her fears and went to lock the front door. She was within earshot if someone knocked. Better to be safe than sorry, and her father had always taught her to trust her instincts.

When Todd came across to see her, he looked a bit surprised that Jo had to unlock the door for him. 'I see you're taking care.'

'Yes. Silas has gone out for a few minutes. He won't be long.' She assumed Todd was just after a cup of tea, as usual. 'I'll put the kettle on, shall I? I'm getting thirsty myself.'

'Where's Silas gone? Surely he shouldn't leave you on your own?'

She explained.

'Well, as it happens, I've not come across to make a pot of tea but to see you about something. Can you come across to the workshop, Jo? You could follow me in a couple of minutes carrying a mug of tea as an excuse. The thing is, Deemer is there and wants to see you but he doesn't want anyone to know that, so he's pretending he has a problem with the car.'

'Oh. All right. I won't be long.'

'Tell Tess you're going out and remind her not to open the door to anyone, however hard they knock. Silas has a key, doesn't he?'

'Yes.' Jo nipped up to tell Tess what was going on, then locked the front door behind her as she left, carrying a cup of cold tea. In case anyone was watching, she shouted, 'I've brought you a drink, Todd!' as she passed the police car parked just inside the workshop with its hood up.

At the back Deemer was waiting for her, standing behind a car that was up on the lift above the inspection pit.

'If you like lukewarm tea, be my guest.' She held

out the cup but Deemer grimaced and shook his head.

'I never say no to a cuppa.' Todd took it from her then moved to one side, sipping it as he listened to them.

Deemer spoke quietly, even though there was no one close enough to hear them. 'Jo, I need to speak to Tess. Someone's broken into their house and searched every single drawer and cupboard. It probably happened early yesterday morning and the whole place is in a right old mess.'

She was horrified, 'Oh, no! Something else to upset that poor girl. What did they take?'

'Nothing, as far as we can tell. Actually, it didn't seem like a burglary to me, because they went through every single drawer and cupboard. There was a rather nice clock standing on the mantelpiece, which had only been moved to one side, probably to check underneath it or in the back. Burglars would definitely have taken that away with them. It'd fetch a quid or two. No, I think these people were searching for something.'

'I can take you across to see Tess now.'

'I don't want to be seen going in or people might guess why. I wondered if she could put your clothes on and come across to the workshop pretending to be you.'

A woman wouldn't have made that mistake, Jo thought. 'Tess is shorter and thinner than I am, so that wouldn't work. My clothes would drown her. I don't know what else to suggest, though. Whether you go in the front way or the back, you'd be seen. For all we know, someone might be watching the house right this minute.' She told him about the man Silas had followed.

'I'll have to come in the back way after dark then, though I wish I could find out what she knows now.'

Todd put the mug down and came to join them. 'I might have a solution. There used to be an old house here, as you probably know, sergeant, but it fell into ruin decades ago. Eventually someone knocked it down and built the workshop here.'

Deemer nodded. 'I remember the old house well. My kids and their pals used to play pirates and robbers and all sort of games inside it when they were small, till one of them got injured by falling masonry. They had a den in the cellar, I remember.'

'Well, it's still there, right underneath this workshop. More to the point, it connects with the cellar in the house and it's still safe to use.' Todd pointed underneath the car he'd been working on. 'The entrance is at the end of the inspection pit. It must have been easier not to fill in the cellar when they built this workshop, so they left it as it was and put in that little door in case it needed maintenance.'

He pointed to the door. 'You have to crouch to get into the cellar, but that's easy enough. I have the key to the door.'

Deemer peered into the pit. 'Imagine that. You'd never guess it leads anywhere, would you? You're sure it's safe?'

'Seems fine to me, the brick walls are still sound and the rafters are solid ash. They'll last till the end of the century if they're left alone. I check the cellar every now and then, just to be sure, because I don't want the floor of the workshop caving in on me. We run some heavy vehicles across it, after all. There are a few cobwebs and some of the paving stones are cracked, that's all. There's nothing stored there now, of course. Too hard to get things in and out through this little entrance. I might use the cellar one day if the business expands and make an easier way in.'

'How do you get into next door's cellar?'

'There's a door at the far end. You only have to walk through it.'

Deemer slapped Todd on the back. 'Good lad! That'll solve the problem nicely. If you'll help me get down into the cellar – I'm not as spry as I used to be – Miss Melling can meet me at the other end inside the house.'

Jo wished she could have gone through with Deemer. It'd have been interesting to explore a secret place. There seemed to be more cellars in England than in Western Australia. 'I saw the door to the cellar on our side, just beyond the pantry and opened it to see what it was like. But I didn't have a torch and there was no sign of an electric light, so I didn't go down into it.'

'I can lend you a torch, sergeant,' Todd offered.

'Thanks.'

Jo moved away from them and picked up the empty mug. 'I'll go back to the house now and take Tess down into the kitchen to meet you, sergeant.'

Deemer shook his head. 'Better if you leave her upstairs and I go to her. I don't want anyone seeing her through the window, not even a glimpse.'

'There are net curtains at the front now,' Jo said.

'Not in the kitchen,' Todd pointed out. 'There could be someone in the back laneway.'

She shivered at the idea and was about to leave when she had a sudden thought. 'Why don't you spread out the sergeant's overcoat over something at the back of the workshop, Todd, so that it'll look as if he's taking a nap? Especially if you put the helmet at the side.'

'Good idea. Did you enjoy plotting games with your friends as a child?'

'Never had much chance. There weren't many kids nearby in the country and when you lived on a farm, you had a lot of chores to do.' She grinned and looked mischievous. 'No, any plotting I come up with is from reading boys' adventure books. I used to play-act them out in the paddock when I was younger, pretending to be an explorer or something like that.'

He smiled. 'I can just imagine you doing that.'

'Yes, well, I'd read anything I could lay my hands on in those days. *The Boys' Own Paper* put out some really exciting stories, much more fun than girls' magazines. And then there were comic books like *Batman*. I loved that one. I even read my dad's newspaper as soon as I could, though I didn't always understand what the articles were about.'

She was clearly reliving some happy memories. 'I was definitely a tomboy. You should have seen me climb trees. I used to beat most of the boys at it – and I probably still could.' She looked down and swished her skirt. 'If it wasn't for this sort of thing. I wore trousers a lot on the farm, not fashionable ones like you see on film stars, but men's working trousers. They're a lot easier to live with, believe me.'

Both men smiled at her indulgently. It was fairly obvious that she wasn't a languid lily of a woman, as the sergeant thought of some females. Jo absolutely exuded energy and determination. She strode through life, not ambled.

Tess was sitting on the bed staring blankly into space, her arms round her raised knees, a book lying unheeded on the floor nearby. She looked up when Jo came into the room.

'Sergeant Deemer will be coming to see you in a minute or two.'

'Won't people see him coming and guess I'm here?' She looked terrified.

'No, they won't. There's a cellar connecting our house with the workshop. He's coming in that way and then he'll talk to you up here, out of sight. I've locked the front door, so no one can get in without us knowing.'

'Oh, thank goodness. Will you stay with me?'

'If you want me to.'

'Yes, please. Do you know what he wants to ask me about?' She hesitated, then told Tess about the burglary, which brought tears to the girl's eyes.

'We'll find out the details from the sergeant. I'd better go down now and bring him up to you.'

'Can I come and see where he comes in from? It might be a place for me to hide or a way of getting out if there are any problems.'

Jo was surprised at how afraid Tess was. It must be Rathley. Well, just let the man dare try to hurt that girl. There were a few people looking out for Tess now.

She didn't say anything except, 'Good idea, Tess. But don't linger downstairs.'

Leading the way, she opened the cellar door then took out the torch Nick kept in the kitchen drawer, in case they needed it for the adjoining cellar, though there was a switch and one light bulb dangling from a wire in the middle of the ceiling in this part.

Tess followed her down the steps, past a pile of coal dumped in the cellar through the coal chute. The space was large but contained little except a few empty shelves and a pile of broken boxes with a small axe nearby. Some of the boxes had already been chopped up into kindling for lighting fires.

Jo tried to get her bearings but wasn't sure exactly where they were in relation to the house. 'Now where is the way in from the workshop, do you think?'

Without hesitation, Tess pointed to a side wall. 'It has to be there if it connects with the workshop.'

'You've a better sense of direction than me. Let's see if we can find the door.'

It was Tess who found a set of shelves that swung outwards and opened it to reveal the sergeant approaching, using a torch.

'Ah, there you are, ladies.' He frowned to see Tess.

'I'm just showing my cousin the cellar in case she needs somewhere to hide.'

'Or in case I need to escape,' Tess put in.

'Good idea. But we'd better go upstairs for our little chat, then Jo can unlock the front door and maybe even open it once we're out of sight. It'll look strange to have it locked in the daytime and the weather seems to be brightening up now.'

Jo waited to unlock the door till the others had gone up the stairs, but as Silas returned just then, she was able to let him in and go up to join Tess.

He'd come back from his walk looking thoughtful, but brightened when he saw the sergeant looking down over the bannisters. 'I've got something to report, sarge.'

'If it's not urgent, let me talk to the lass first then I'll come down and listen to what you've found out.'

Jo pointed to a book, 'If anyone comes in to book a driving lesson, will you deal with them, Silas? We write down the lesson times in this. I've made a grid of times available.' Then she went up to join the others.

She pinched a chair from Nick's bedroom for the sergeant, who sat astride it facing its back, as men often did, while she sat next to Tess on the bed.

He explained about the break-in, then said firmly, 'It's time for you to tell me who came to see your mother the other night, lass.'

Tess looked mutely at Jo, who nodded encouragingly.

The girl began to speak in broken bursts. 'It was Rathley. That's why I went off to hide in the park. There isn't usually anyone around at that time of the evening, but that night there were some lads kicking a football to and fro, so I couldn't get to

316

the bandstand without being seen. Your constable sent them home and – and then he found me hiding among the bushes.'

'Rathley's a filthy swine!' Deemer muttered suddenly. 'I can't abide men who go after children. I don't hate many people, but them sort I do.'

'Who doesn't? They're disgusting.' Jo took Tess's hand and patted it.

'What time was that about?' the sergeant asked. 'Tell me as exactly as you can.'

Tess frowned for a moment, working it out, then told him.

Deemer thought this slowly through. 'And Hopkins found you before you had time to hide for long?'

'Yes. I hadn't even got down among the bushes yet.'

'I have the exact time he found you from his notebook. There wouldn't have been time for your mother to entertain another customer except Rathley because Hopkins took you straight back home.'

As this sank in, the two women stared at one another in shock and Deemer seemed to swell up in disgusted indignation. 'He's weaselled out of other charges, but I'll nab him for this, if it's the last thing I do. Only I have to make sure I obtain good evidence. People with money can hire lawyers and get away with things ordinary folk can't.'

He asked a few more questions then stood up. 'Right. Better get on with my day. Be very careful, young lady. You could be in even greater danger than I thought. I'll go and see what Silas wants

317

now. I hope he's found out something useful.'

As he waited for the sergeant Silas spent the time checking out the entrance to the cellar next door, then putting a couple of candles and a box of matches on a rickety old shelf just inside it. Always best to be prepared.

When Deemer came to join him, his expression made Silas ask, 'What's happened now?'

'We're putting pieces of the jigsaw together.' The sergeant hesitated, studied Silas as if he could read his very soul, then explained.

Silas nodded once or twice. 'Then here's another piece of the puzzle. There's a man keeping watch over this place. I saw him passing several times, going in both directions apparently, so I followed him. He went to the back door at Rathley's office and was let in.'

There was dead silence, then Deemer asked, 'What's his name?'

'I don't know. But if you stand near the front window with me, you'll probably see him pass by and you might know who he is. He won't be able to see us.'

They had to wait nearly half an hour for the man to walk past again, and they could both see how he slowed right down and studied the place. By then Nick had returned from his second driving lesson and was watching with them.

When Todd joined them, wondering what was keeping the sergeant, he too stayed to keep watch in case he could identify the man.

'We'll be having a party in here next!' Silas joked.

Finally, Jo came in as well. 'You're not leaving me out.'

Before she could say anything else, Silas called suddenly, 'That's him! The tall one with his cap pulled right down.'

The watchers all stood still and the man conveniently stopped. He seemed to be staring at Nick's car.

'I don't know him, but I won't forget what he looks like,' Nick muttered.

'I don't know him either, but I've seen him mooching around the town centre every now and then,' Todd said. 'So he can't be in regular work.'

Deemer smiled, not a nice smile, either. 'I know him. He's been in trouble with the law a few times, Hobbs has. Normally someone like that wouldn't have any connection with a reputable businessman, so what's he doing calling on Rathley? I'll find out, believe me. When I want to speak to him, I'll pounce, but for the moment I'll hire someone else to keep an eye on him. The watcher watched, you might call it! I know just the chap to do it, as well.'

He looked at the others. 'No mention of this to anyone at all. I think, and pray I'm right, that they're just keeping an eye on Miss Melling in case she leads them to her cousin. But one murder's been committed, so make sure you're protected at all times as well as your cousin, Miss Melling. No walking across the yard to the workshop on your own even, from now on.'

She grimaced. 'All right.'

It was starting to add up, Deemer thought as he used the tunnel to go back to the workshop. He'd

319

gather enough incontrovertible evidence then pounce.

As he got into his car and left the workshop, he thanked Todd loudly for repairing it before driving back to the police station.

26

Wilf started work straight away at Charlie's. That was a blessing because it got him out of the house for most of the day, away from the arguments and sharp remarks.

He and Enid were sharing a bed again, mainly because there was nowhere else in the small house for him to sleep. But there was still a coolness between them and she slept on the edge of the bed, trying not to touch him. He didn't know how to bridge this distance.

He quickly noticed that she was skimping on their meals, not just one meal but all of them, going back to what he thought of as 'famine eating', mainly bread and dripping or margarine. This puzzled him because he was bringing home more than enough money to buy decent food for everyone. Why the sudden change?

He raised the matter that evening, waiting till after the children had gone to bed. 'I'm still hungry, love, and so are the little 'uns. You didn't give us enough to eat today.'

'They haven't complained.'

'They wouldn't. They got used to going hungry

before they came to live here. And they're still afraid of upsetting us.' He sometimes wondered whether the poor little souls would ever feel secure.

'Well, it's only till we've paid off the money we owe. You can use the money I save for doing that. They'll manage on what I'm giving them for a while.'

He gaped at her. 'You'd let the children go hungry because you've gone stupid about money.'

'No, because *you* broke your promise to me. So it's your fault. And you'll pay for it, too. None of us are going to be eating lavishly till we're out of debt. I'm determined about that.'

'I won't let you do that, Enid.'

She raised her chin defiantly. 'You can't stop me.'

'Oh, can't I? Well, we'll see about that. I'll–'

She turned her back on him and banged a pan she was holding down hard on the wooden draining board, then banged it again. Her attitude made him so angry, he didn't let himself finish the threat he'd been going to make, but walked out of the house and slammed the door good and hard behind him.

If he hadn't left, he'd have started yelling at her and that'd have upset the children. He'd never hit her and never would, because he despised people who hit those weaker than themselves, but deliberately making little children go hungry had brought him as close to it as he'd ever come.

When he got into the van, he sat for a few moments clutching the steering wheel tightly and trying to calm down. It wasn't easy. He'd do better if he could take his mind off their quarrel. Since it was still light, he decided to go and replace the temporary repair on Mrs Morton's window and see to her leaking kitchen sink at the same time. He always thought better when he was working with his hands.

On the way he stopped at the chip shop and bought himself a bag of chips slathered in salt and vinegar, eating them quickly and with no enjoyment, but at least satisfying the residual hunger in his belly.

Mrs Morton opened the door herself, looking surprised to see him there so late in the day. 'Good evening, Mr Pollard. What can I do for you?'

He hesitated, then told the truth. 'I needed to get out of the house, so I thought I'd finish off that little job in the kitchen for you. Is that convenient, Mrs Morton?'

'Of course it is. I'm grateful for your help. Come in. It's Mona's evening off, so she's out at the cinema and I'm on my own.'

When they got to the kitchen, she asked hesitantly, 'Would you like to join me in a glass of sherry?'

He looked at her ruefully. 'I don't know that I've ever drunk sherry before, Mrs Morton.'

'Then I'll give you a small amount before I fill your glass. It's not to everyone's taste and I don't want to waste it. My husband and I used to drink it for a treat and I grew to like it. I still have a few bottles left from better days.'

'I'd like to try it, but after I've finished the job, if you don't mind.'

'I don't mind at all. Um, I won't be in your way if I stay in the kitchen, will I? It's warmer in here because I didn't light a fire in the parlour. The evenings are getting a bit chilly now, aren't they?'

'You won't be in my way at all, Mrs Morton.'

He started on the job and she sat at the table reading the newspaper. It wasn't everyone who could sit quietly and not feel the need for conversation, he thought. The silence and the tidy room with colourful plates and sparkling glasses arranged on the shelves of the dresser were calming, he found, and his anger began to fade. For some reason, he'd always felt comfortable with this kind lady.

Half an hour saw the job finished, then he washed his hands and accepted a seat opposite her at the table. She poured him out a scant half inch of pale amber liquid in a pretty glass with a criss-cross pattern etched into its sides.

'Try it, Wilf, just a sip. One doesn't use sherry to quench one's thirst, but to enjoy the taste.'

He took a cautious sip and moved the liquid round his mouth to get the full flavour. When he swallowed it, he saw her watching him and nodded at the glass, saying quite truthfully, 'I like it.'

'Good. I'll pour you a proper glassful, if you have the time.'

He nodded. He definitely didn't want to go back yet.

'Do make yourself comfortable.'

She poured for him then picked up her own glass and took a delicate sip, staring at him across the table. 'Do you want to talk about whatever's bothering you? I like to think I'm a good listener and it sometimes helps to unburden yourself. Not if you don't want to, of course.'

He stared back at her, seeing nothing but kindness in a face that was still attractive in spite of its wrinkles. 'I'm at odds with my wife and don't know how to sort it out. We don't often quarrel, but this is a big disagreement.'

'Go on. I can still remember what it was like to be married and I doubt anyone gets on well with their spouse all the time.'

He told her about his quarrel with Enid then took another sip, letting silence settle between them. If Mrs Morton had any advice to offer, he'd listen. If she didn't, well, she was right: it had been good to put the problem into words. It had helped him to see it more clearly.

'I don't think you can do much except perhaps give the children extra food yourself. Buy them a few treats.'

'Yes. That's as far as I'd got.'

'I have an idea! Why don't you bring the whole family here to tea tomorrow? I'll give them a good, filling meal. Only if you'd like to, mind.'

He was astonished at this invitation and blurted out the first thing that came into his head, 'But we're not – well, the sort of people a lady like you invites to tea.'

She stiffened. 'If you don't wish to come, just say so. I shan't take offence.'

'I'd love to come – as long as we wouldn't be imposing on you.' He watched her relax again.

'Far from it. To tell you the truth, I'm rather lonely these days. And for some reason, I find I can talk to you, Mr Pollard.'

'I feel that I can talk to you, too, Mrs Morton.'

'It happens sometimes that two people can bridge what others might see as a wide gap between them, and even become friends. My only son is dead and though he was married, he had no children. I never did manage to bridge the gap between his wife and myself, though, and she hasn't been near me since the funeral. I have no close family left now and most of my friends have died over the past few years.'

'I'm sorry to hear that.'

'I'm seventy and in excellent health for my age. My mother lived to be ninety-four and I hope to do the same. That would be a long time to be lonely, though, don't you think? So if I want things to change, I must do something about it, get to know new people.'

'Well, we'll come to tea with you happily.'

She positively beamed at him, which made him feel certain she really wanted them to visit her and wasn't just doing it out of pity. 'What time?'

'Come at half past three and we'll eat around four o'clock. I'll make sure there's nothing too fancy for the children to manage.'

'Thank you. For everything.'

After the last driving lesson of the day, Jo and Nick had left Silas to keep an eye on the house and cars and gone to the town hall to book their wedding. Very fortunately, they could both lay hands on their birth certificates and Jo had her passport with her as well. Unfortunately, they had to queue for nearly half an hour.

'We'd like to book a wedding,' Nick said when

it was finally their turn to step up to the counter.

The clerk was a sour-faced young man who looked down his nose at them while they went through the formalities.

'You are resident in this town and have been for the past seven days?'

Nick lied without hesitation. 'Yes.'

When they both gave the same address, the young man let out a scornful sniff and Nick almost told him to be more polite. Not worth it, he decided.

But the fellow continued with the same attitude, not troubling to hide an even deeper scorn when Nick asked about the quickest way to get married. He didn't want to wait a month.

'It'll cost you three pounds ... sir. And you'll still have to wait a week.'

It made Nick furious to see Jo flush and look embarrassed on what should have been a joyful occasion, so he put his hand down flat on the form the clerk was filling out and said firmly, 'Stop looking at us like that.'

The clerk gasped and took a hasty step backwards. 'I beg your pardon?'

There was no one else waiting, so Nick said, 'To put it bluntly, we are *not* living in sin, which you seem to have assumed, though what business that is of yours, I don't understand. My fiancée is from Australia, as you can see by her passport, and she had nowhere else to stay, so she's sleeping in another bedroom at the house where I live. If I could marry her today, I would, because I love her. As it is, we have to wait till your little rule book tells us we can wed.'

Jo dug him in the ribs and he realised he was frightening the clerk. Well, serve the stupid fellow right for being so cheeky.

'I'm not – I wasn't – please, sir, I can't fill the form in if you keep your hand over it.'

Nick took his hand away and glanced quickly sideways at Jo, whose cheeks were still pink but who now had, if he wasn't mistaken, a twinkle of amusement in her eyes. He winked at her and turned back to the young chap. 'Go on.'

'You wish to marry here in the town hall, did you say, sir?'

'Yes, here.'

'I'll need to check that there's a free half-hour on the day that you become eligible.'

'I shall be very annoyed if there isn't.'

Another stiff silence as the clerk took a smaller book from the side of the counter and bent over it. 'Oh, yes. That'll be fine. Ten o'clock in the morning. Is that all right?'

Nick looked at Jo, who nodded and said, 'Yes.' She was looking more at ease and there was definitely a smile twitching at the corner of her mouth.

As they walked out, she took his hand and pulled him to a halt, saying in a false, girlish voice, 'My hero! You jumped to my defence like a knight of old.'

Heedless of passers-by, he kissed her and they walked slowly back, hand in hand. It was good to be with someone who had a similar sense of humour. Where would you be if you couldn't laugh at the silly things you sometimes encountered as you passed through the world?

Wilf drove home slowly and got back to find Enid still up at well past her usual bedtime. When he looked at her, he could see she'd been crying, so said simply, 'Let's not quarrel any more, love. We'll be careful with money but truly, I'm earning more *because* of that van, so it's paying for itself.'

'I can't bear to be in debt. I just can't, Wilf.'

'I know it upsets you. But the debt will be paid off by Christmas, I promise you.'

'And you won't borrow money again?'

He had to think for a minute because he only made promises he intended to keep, but had to shake his head. 'I can't promise that. I can only promise not to do anything rashly.' He held up one hand to stop her protesting. 'Let's leave it like that for now. I want to tell you what I've been doing tonight.'

He explained about Mrs Morton and her invitation and that definitely took his wife's mind off money.

'We can't go to tea with a lady like her!' Enid seemed horrified rather than pleased at the prospect.

'Of course we can. She's lonely, she doesn't have much money, and even though she's a lady born and bred, somehow I've made friends with her. I bet you'll like her, too.'

'She won't like us if the children spill their drinks or break something.'

'I don't think she'd mind. She's sounded wistful whenever she's asked me about my family, and she told me how deeply she regretted not having any grandchildren.'

Enid was so bemused by the idea of going to tea with a lady, she forgot to be stiff and chatted about it as they got ready for bed.

She snuggled down with a sigh and fell asleep almost immediately, but Wilf lay awake for ages. Had Mrs Morton known the invitation would have this effect on his wife? he wondered. She was a wise old lady, that was sure.

He was looking forward to going out to tea there and it'd do the children good to meet someone new and enjoy a completely different experience. Enid would wrap them up in cotton wool and stand guard over them every minute, if she could. She didn't even let them play out unless she was standing at the doorway. He wanted to take them out and about, so that they could get used to the world and learn how to deal with it. He and Enid had argued about that, as well, come to think of it.

Surely the outing would do Enid good? She'd not been looking well lately, seemed to have lost weight, and she'd always been thin, couldn't afford to lose more. But when he'd asked, she'd insisted she was fine, just a bit tired, that was all.

He'd have to keep an eye on her. She seemed to think only of the children these days, and might be neglecting herself. She was neglecting him, too, in her thoughts and in her deeds. She didn't even want to make love when they went to bed in case the children heard.

And what was the point of doing *that* anyway, she'd added bitterly, when they couldn't create children by it?

He'd need to sort out that side of their life with

her. A man had his needs and Wilf certainly didn't want to go elsewhere to satisfy them. Besides, the loving brought you closer together. She used to enjoy it. Other people didn't stop once they had children. Why should he and Enid?

He sighed and turned over, but it was a still night and he heard the town hall clock strike twice more before he began to feel sleepy.

The hours seemed to pass slowly for Tess, all alone in the bedroom. By the time Jo and Nick closed the office each day, she felt as if she was going mad with boredom. There was a limit to the amount of time you wanted to spend reading, however interesting the books. She'd always wished she could read all day long, but now she had the time to do that and had found she grew restless after a while, wanted to move about, *do* something, talk to people.

In the evenings, the other two still didn't let her come downstairs, were very insistent on that, but they brought up the wireless and either listened to it with her or sat and chatted.

'I wonder what Sergeant Deemer is doing about Rathley?' Nick asked idly when some rather boring organ music came on the radio.

'Making plans to catch him, I hope,' Tess said with a shudder.

'Be patient. He's a good policeman.'

She didn't say how hard it was to be patient, how much she missed her mother's company. They were being kind to her, and sensible. She had to be sensible, too.

The other two went to bed earlier than Tess

would have wished. She was more used to late nights. She lay in her narrow bed, wide awake still, and soon there was complete silence from the other bedrooms.

Suddenly she thought she heard a faint sound outside in the backyard and sat bolt upright. What was that?

When the sound came again, she flung back the covers and jumped out of bed, holding back the curtain and peeping out of the window. To her dismay, she saw two men at the back gate, one in the process of climbing over it. They were as clear as anything in the bright moonlight.

At that moment the one on top of the gate glanced up and pointed towards her bedroom window. Oh no! He'd seen her.

She stepped back, letting the curtain drop and rushing into Nick's bedroom. She shook him hard. 'Nick, wake up. There's someone breaking in at the back of the house. Nick!'

He jerked fully awake as Tess's words sank in. 'What did you see?'

'Two men, one of them climbing over the gate.'

'Damnation! Go and wake Jo.'

Nick got out of bed, and cursed under his breath. Why did they make pyjama bottoms with that embarrassing gap in the front? He turned his back to her, pulled his trousers on hastily, and snatched at his sweater, dragging it down over his head as he ran next door.

One quick glance out of the back bedroom window showed him two figures, one actually in the backyard, the other sitting on the top of the gate.

They seemed to be arguing about something.

'Let's see if they still hang around when we switch on lights everywhere.' He didn't wait for the two women's agreement but started doing that.

'Come on, Jo. We'll do the same downstairs.'

She'd grabbed her dressing gown and didn't wait to get dressed but followed him down the stairs, calling over her shoulder, 'Stay back, Tess. If they see you clearly in the kitchen, they'll know they've found out where you are, which is probably what Rathley is looking for. If they see only me downstairs, they'll probably recognise me.'

'If they try to break in, you must phone the police station for help, Jo.' Nick picked up a heavy walking stick that had been in the hall stand. He'd kept it handy to help defend himself, if need be, when he was living here alone. You couldn't be too careful in town centres, with valuable cars parked just underneath your bedroom window.

'I'm not leaving you to fight on your own. I can fight alongside you.'

He spun round. 'No!'

She looked very determined. 'Dad always insisted I know where a man's weak spots are. I haven't forgotten what he and the stockman taught me about defending myself. We lived in the country, remember, and there were no police nearby.'

Another voice said, 'I can help, too.'

They both turned to look at Tess, who had followed them down and was standing in the kitchen doorway.

Nick sighed. 'Please go back, Tess. The one

thing we're agreed on is that we don't want them seeing you.'

'I think they've seen me clearly enough to recognise me already.'

'What? How did that happen? Surely you didn't put the bedroom light on?'

'No, but I was still half asleep and didn't realise how brightly the moon was shining on that side of the house, so I pulled the curtain to one side to peep out. If I could see them clearly, they must have been able to see me equally well, don't you think? Anyway, one of them looked across from the top of the gate and pointed towards me, then they started to argue.'

'Do you really think they could see you clearly enough to recognise you, though?'

'Probably. I could see them clearly enough to describe them and recognise them if I met them again.'

'Oh, hell. We'll have to find you somewhere else to hide, then.' He turned back to the kitchen window, half expecting it to be smashed at any moment. But nothing happened. He couldn't see clearly with the kitchen light on so called out, 'Switch the light off again, Jo.' When she'd done that, he moved across to the window and peered out.

There was definitely no one in the yard now.

'They seem to have gone.'

'Do you think they'll come back?'

'They may do. I wasn't worried about security before but I am now. There's hardly anyone living in this street, if we have to call for help. It's mostly shops. We'd better contact Deemer straight away, not wait till the morning, and get his help to keep you safe. I'll go into the office and phone him.'

'I'm sorry!' Tess looked distressed. 'It's all my fault for being so stupid. I wasn't thinking clearly when I went to look out of the window.'

Jo put an arm round her shoulders. 'It's done now.'

They heard Nick's voice coming from the office.

'Let's go and eavesdrop,' Jo said, but before they could do anything, there was the sound of a phone being put down and footsteps coming along to the kitchen.

'He's on his way,' Nick said.

'Just Sergeant Deemer?' Tess asked.

'Yes.'

'Won't he be bringing anyone else with him? What if several men come back to capture me?'

'You've been watching too many American gangster movies. Where will anyone find a group of villains at this hour of the night in Rivenshaw? I reckon those two were it.'

'I've hardly watched any movies. People didn't like associating with me because of Mam, so I only went out to go to school or do our shopping. Most of the time I stayed at home.'

Jo could have wept at what a dreadfully limited life the poor girl had led. 'That's going to change once we've caught your mother's killer, Tess. I'll take you to Australia and no one there will know anything about your background. You can make a fresh start, have friends, do what the other girls do.'

'Would you really do that?'

'Definitely. Would you come?'

'Yes.' Tess's gulp was audible and they could both see how hard she had to struggle not to cry.

Jo's eyes met Nick's and she tried to show him how sorry she was to have to offer to do this. But from what the girl had said, she was afraid there was no way Tess could make even a half-decent life for herself in any part of the valley.

Nick moved to put an arm round each of them. 'Since Jo and I are planning to get married, we'll all go to Australia together, if it's the best thing for you, Tess. But first we have to help Sergeant Deemer catch a murderer.'

Jo looked at him, couldn't help asking, 'Are you sure?'

'Of course I am.' His smile was tender and warm in spite of the problems they were facing, and she felt unable to protest further. Why should she? Marrying him was what she wanted most in the world.

Tess was watching them again. 'I love the way you two are with one another. Your love shines out. It makes me feel there's good in the world as well as bad.'

They all fell silent for a moment, then Tess said, 'Yes. We must help the sergeant catch him. For Mam's sake. I won't feel right if he gets away with it.'

Jo tried not to show it, but it was she who had tears in her eyes now. How wonderful that Nick was prepared give up everything to be with her. How wonderful what Tess had said!

They had to make things come out right, of course they did. But afterwards she wanted to spend her whole life with this man.

27

Sergeant Deemer put down the phone and went next door for a quick check of the one and only cell in the police station attached to his house. Big Donny was sleeping as peacefully as the child he still was mentally. The poor fellow had given them no trouble, didn't seem at all violent.

On the rare occasions when the cell was occupied, Deemer's wife took the prisoner's meals through from the house. She felt the same about this poor chap, couldn't see him starting trouble.

But although the sergeant felt quite sure Donny wasn't the one who'd killed Moira, he was keeping him here for his own protection. And his dog always slept in the police station at night or when it was unattended, so he had no doubt anyone trying to get in would be noticed and stopped, one way or the other.

He drove to the car yard and saw Nick open the front door to him. He glanced round before getting out of his vehicle, wondering if anyone was still hanging around. He hadn't seen anyone lurking in the streets on his way here. In fact, the town seemed unusually quiet, yet it felt as if something terrible was hovering, ready to erupt. Or was he letting his imagination run riot about this?

He followed Nick quickly inside and listened to him and the two women explaining exactly what had happened, then he and Nick went outside at the back to look round the yard. There were scratch marks on the gate, which Nick said hadn't been there before, probably from where the intruders had clambered over, but the padlock was still intact.

'I'm a bit old to climb over gates,' Deemer said. 'I brought the key.'

Nick unlocked the padlock then the two men went out to have a look along the laneway.

As they were standing there, someone made a faint hissing noise nearby, where a row of dustbins was standing in deep shadow.

Deemer spun round. 'Who's there?'

'It's only me, sarge. I don't want to show myself, though. Me an' Piper was following them men tonight, keeping an eye on them, like you said we should.'

He recognised the voice at once. His informer. 'Did you see who they were and where they went, Larry?'

'Yes, we saw who they were. And since they were on foot, Piper's following them. I said I'd keep an eye on this place. He's coming back here to tell us where they went. He might be away a while if they've gone up the valley, though. He knew one of them, you see, said the chap's called Hobbs and lives in Backshaw Moss. He does jobs for Rathley sometimes, but never says what, but Piper says everyone knows he's paid to go after people who've upset Rathley.'

'That doesn't surprise me. Seen anything else?'

'No, sir.'

'Mr Howarth and I will go back into the kitchen and wait for him.'

'Right. I'll stay here.'

'You don't want to come inside to wait?' Nick asked. 'You're welcome.'

'Not yet. I'll keep watch here. Me an' Piper will slip inside when we're sure he's not been followed back. Can't be too careful if that Rathley sod's involved.'

'You're doing exactly what I wanted, Larry lad. Well done, both of you.'

There was a snigger from behind the dustbin. 'Fancy me being praised by a policeman!'

'Fancy me having something to praise Flash Larry about,' Deemer muttered as he followed Nick into the house. 'He's a cheeky devil, that one.'

Further up the hill, Piper was following the two men towards Birch End, and doing it well, he thought. Suddenly someone jumped out and grabbed him as he passed a gateway in the drystone wall that edged the fields. He yelled out in shock and struggled hard, trying desperately to get away.

He would have managed it, only another man grabbed him from behind and they were both big chaps. So Piper tried cunning instead.

He stopped struggling and as they stepped cautiously back a little to stare at him, he held up his hands in a gesture of surrender. 'Hey up, lads! No need to thump me. It's only me, Piper.'

'I can damn well see who it is. What I want to know is why you were following us.'

'I was on my way home when I saw you and wondered what you were doing. If there's anything profitable going on, I thought I could maybe help. I'm a bit short of money at the moment, you see.'

The man he didn't know said doubtfully, 'Do you really know him, Hobbs?'

'Yeah. He's all right. Not on the side of the law that I've ever seen.'

Piper held his breath, beginning to feel hopeful.

'Should we take him with us, see what Mr Rathley wants to do with him?'

Hobbs punched his companion in the arm. 'Shut up, you idiot. You're not supposed to mention that name. We found out what our man wants to know, which is where the girl is, and we're *not* sharing the reward for that with anyone.'

For a moment, Piper's fate hung in the balance and he waited, wondering whether these idiots would give him any other useful information.

'I reckon we'd best let him go and say nothing. Rathley's a chancy sod and he might not pay us because we got seen.' Hobbs turned back to their captive. 'But if you try to follow us again, Piper, or whisper one word about who we're working for, I'll make sure you regret it.'

'I'd never go against you, Hobbs. You know me.'

'It's a good thing for you I do. Now get off home and don't come following me again.'

Piper didn't wait but set off running down the hill as fast as his legs would carry him. But once he was out of their sight and sure they weren't following him, he couldn't help smiling. He knew who they were working for now, and they could be forced by the police to answer questions about him. Deemer really wanted to find proof if Rathley was involved in something against the law. 'If!'

Piper sniggered as he hurried along. Quite a few people were aware of the way Rathley did things. It was proof that was lacking.

He frowned for a moment. Would Hobbs really come after a chap he'd grown up with and hurt him on Rathley's say-so? Nah, he didn't think so. But he wasn't risking it. People did all sorts of things when desperate for money, as he'd had to do himself. Though he drew the line at beating people up.

As he reached Rivenshaw, he couldn't help smiling again. Money for old rope, this little job was, and all on the side of the law.

He and Flash Larry would laugh about that for years. Good money it was, too, considering.

It was a full hour after he'd left before Piper returned to the alley, moving cautiously along it till Larry hissed to warn him he wasn't alone.

'I wasn't followed. I made sure of that.'

His friend stepped out from behind the dustbins, grinning so broadly his teeth showed white in the moonlight.

'Everything all right here?' Piper asked.

'More than all right, it's going fine. The folk here called in the sergeant because they saw Hobbs and his mate, so I told Deemer what we'd seen. He said he was pleased with what we were doing.'

Both men sniggered as they always did at the thought of a policeman being pleased with them.

'Deemer's gone inside and I said we'd join them there once you got back. They offered us a cup of tea an' I could murder a hot drink.'

'Do you think he's trying to trick us?'

'Nah. I sneaked into the yard now the gate's unlocked and listened at the kitchen window. He's desperate to find out what's going on and to nab Rathley.'

There was dead silence for a minute or two, then Piper whispered, 'Do *you* think Rathley killed her?'

'Who else would have wanted to? She was all right, Moira was. No enemies that I knew of. I reckon he was after that girl of hers.'

Piper whistled softly. 'I been wondering about that sort of thing.'

'Yeah. Stinks, doesn't it? Now, tell me exactly what you found out before we go in. I don't want any surprises once we're with Deemer.'

When he heard, he whistled softly. 'Come on. He'll give us extra for that, I reckon.' He hesitated then added in an even lower voice, 'I'd be glad to see that Rathley fellow locked up, as long as I'm not known to be involved. I don't like chaps that go after children, either. It fair sticks in my gullet.'

'Only you can't turn Rathley down when he asks you to do something, can you? He's got too many friends in high places.'

'I don't think Deemer is a friend of his.'

'No, but he's not in a high place, is he? Anyway, come on. I'm looking forward to a warm drink.'

Deemer looked up as he heard the click of the back gate opening. 'Here they come. I hope Piper's discovered something. Tell Tess to stay upstairs and not make a sound.'

He watched Jo slip out, look up towards the landing and signal to Tess by putting one finger

341

to her lips, then he went to open the door. 'Easier to come in this way, isn't it, lads? Want that cup of tea?'

'If there's one going.'

'You play fair with me and there'll be more than tea going.'

The two men grinned at one another and followed the sergeant into the kitchen.

When Piper went through what he'd found out, the sergeant let out a satisfied grunt. 'You did well.'

Jo had a sudden idea and said, 'I think those men you followed, Mr, um, Piper, saw Tess at her bedroom window. Is it possible ... could we persuade them to capture me, thinking it's her? I know we don't look a lot alike, but if it's in the dark and it's someone who doesn't know us well, we could maybe fool them for a short time.'

Nick shot her a quick look, as if he didn't like where she was going with this, as did the two men.

Deemer shook his head. 'Very kind of you to offer, but we don't use innocent people as bait in traps. And I'd not let any young woman fall into Rathley's hands.'

'But it might take you ages to trap him, and if they take me and tell him they've captured her, he'll have to show his hand to get her, won't he? Then you can pounce.'

'No!' Nick exclaimed. 'The sergeant's already told you it's too dangerous.'

'Not if someone keeps watch on me from a distance.'

Deemer's voice was very firm. 'No. Definitely

342

not. I'll ask you two men to keep an eye on him and if you help me *prove* Rathley murdered Moira, I'll give you a tenner each.'

Their mouths fell open in shock at this generous offer.

'Why are you so sure it was him as killed Moira, sarge?' Piper asked.

'I've got other information. He was seen going into Packman Alley that night at the right time. No one else was around. No one else had time to visit Moira before my constable took Tess home. But he's wriggled out of trouble before, so we have to prove it beyond doubt.'

'Now you're talking, sarge.' Larry turned to Jo. 'I think better after a nice cup of tea, if you don't mind, an' I like it with three spoons of sugar, please missus.'

She only just managed not to smile at his cheekiness and pushed a plate of biscuits across the table to them before pouring the tea. They were both thin, looking as if they hadn't eaten well for years.

When the men had left, Nick asked why Deemer was so sure of these two and the sergeant spread his arms in a helpless gesture. 'I reckon in better times, those chaps wouldn't have been crooks. They're decent in their own way, keep their word and if they take on a job, they do it. An' they're not violent, that I've ever heard.'

28

On the Saturday afternoon, Enid washed the two children, then dressed them in their best clothes, wishing aloud that they had better things to wear. She brushed their hair that morning and plaited Peggy's, tying a red ribbon near the end of the plait. Standing back, she smiled down at them.

'You look lovely. You'll be good today, won't you, my darlings?'

They nodded, then Enid turned to Wilf, who was dressed in his best suit. She sighed and brushed a few specks of fluff off the front lapels. 'You need a new suit. This one is literally thread-bare. I'll ask Vito look out for one about your size being pawned.'

'No. This'll do for the time being and when I do buy a new one, it really will be new – and so will your best dress.'

'Don't talk daft. I don't need new clothes, just respectable, hard-wearing ones. I'd rather save money than spend it. This outfit was a real bar-gain. It'll last me for years if I'm careful.'

He shook his head over that. She was certainly respectably clad, but the rusty brown skirt and jacket didn't suit her pale complexion at all and looked as if they'd belonged to her grandmother. Even he, who knew nothing about women's fash-ions, realised she ought to be wearing lighter colours, blue to match her eyes maybe. He liked her in blue. And surely her skirt should be shorter? Other younger women's were. It seemed as if Enid had stopped trying to look pretty since they adopted the children, as if she no longer cared about herself.

She'd stopped laughing and having fun with him, too. He missed that.

He still wondered if she was quite well. But he'd asked her again today and she'd nearly bitten his head off, all her attention being focused on making sure the children looked their best. He'd keep his eyes open from now on, though, and drag her to the doctor's if necessary. Like most mothers, she placed her own health last in the family: breadwinner, children, mother, that's the order it went in when it came to paying for a doctor's advice. Well, not in his family, thank you very much.

'Come on, then. I'll drive us down to Birch End.'

'We could walk and save the petrol,' she ventured.

'It'd use up four people's shoe leather and the children's clothes will get dusty.'

'Hmm. I suppose you're right.'

He heard her mutter, 'This time,' which wasn't fair but he said nothing.

The children were excited to have a ride in the new van and insisted on clambering into it themselves. They sat on the old sofa cushions he'd put in the back, one at each side, and then they held on to the loops of rope he'd fixed to the sides, beaming at him as he closed the back doors of the van on them.

He drove there carefully with such a precious

cargo on board, whistling cheerfully, looking forward to the tea party. Surely that would cheer his wife up a bit.

Enid said nothing, sitting stiffly beside him, clutching her worn old handbag, which she'd tried to smarten up with black shoe polish, but whose leather still looked scruffy and battered. Why couldn't she spend just a few shillings here and there on improving her appearance? It didn't take much to make a difference if you bought second-hand and they weren't scratching for every farthing now.

They all stood still after they got out of the van, staring at Mrs Morton's large, comfortable house. 'This row of houses wasn't built by Higgerson,' Wilf said. 'You can see the difference, can't you?'

'It's one of Roy Tyler's, isn't it?'

'Yes. He was a good builder, but he's neglected his business since his son died in an accident on a building site.' Some said it was no accident, but Wilf didn't tell her that. 'Roy still does small building jobs but he used to be the biggest builder in the valley. Pity.'

He stared a moment longer, then took Ronnie's hand. 'Come on, everyone.' Leading the way up the steps to the front door, he rang the bell.

The maid Mona opened the door today, smiling at them. 'Do come in, everyone. The mistress is expecting you. I'll hang up your coats, shall I?'

When she'd done that for the adults, she bent down and spoke directly to the children. 'And who are you two? What are your names?'

'Peggy.'

Ronnie hid behind his sister, so the girl whispered to Mona, 'He's Ronnie but he's only little an' he's a bit shy.'

'Well, you're a clever sister and I'm sure you look after him.'

Peggy nodded vigorously.

'Give me your coats and hats, then.' As Mona finished hanging them up, a door opened to one side and Mrs Morton came out to greet them.

'I couldn't wait any longer to meet the children. And it's so silly for me to sit in state in the parlour waiting for you to be shown in when you're just the other side of the door.'

Mona shook her head fondly, as if she'd half expected this, but said nothing.

Wilf had to put his arm round Enid to get her to move forward, introducing her and the children, then going into the parlour with their hostess.

He heard Enid sigh at what they saw. Well, it was a lovely room, a bit old-fashioned but with good, well-polished furniture and pretty ornaments, with little lacy mats under the vases on side tables. And there was a highly polished brass fender in front of the fire, a beautiful piece of work, that. Eh, it must be wonderful to live in a place like this.

One day, he said to himself. *One day. If I have to drag Enid into it screaming.*

Next to a low table in the bay window there was a wicker laundry basket full of toys. Mrs Morton pointed to it. 'These toys are a bit old-fashioned because they belonged to my son when he was little. It always seems so unfair at tea parties to expect children to sit and do nothing while the

347

grown-ups chat.'

She beckoned to the two children and Wilf wasn't surprised when they went to her without hesitation. She had a knack of setting people at ease.

'These are for you two to play with. You can do what you like with them.'

They looked at their mother, as if asking for permission to do this.

'I don't want them to break anything,' Enid said hesitantly.

Wilf realised suddenly that she was the shyest person here, not the children. How strange.

Mrs Morton smiled at her reassuringly. 'They're old and mostly soft toys, Mrs Pollard, and they've already been played with a thousand times. There's nothing left to break, and if there was, it wouldn't matter. Come and sit down on the sofa with me so that you and I can have a nice chat and get to know one another.'

But it was Wilf and their hostess who did most of the chatting. Enid listened and nodded from time to time, but it was clear that she was keeping an eye on the children, still worrying about what they might do.

Wilf shot Mrs Morton a quick rueful glance when his wife wasn't looking and she gave a slight shrug, as if to say it didn't matter.

When the clock chimed four, Mona came in to say tea was ready and they all followed their hostess into another room at the back of the house.

'I thought the children would be more comfortable eating their tea in the morning room than trying to balance plates on their knees,' Mrs Morton told Enid. 'It's where I eat most of my meals these days.'

'Oh yes. Thank you. I do agree, but I'll make sure they're careful.'

Wilf could see his wife looking round as if to check for traps. If only she'd relax a little, she might enjoy herself as the children were doing.

Mrs Morton handed round dainty sandwiches and miniature pies that seemed made for small hands. The children ate heartily and so did Wilf. He hadn't had such a good meal for ages. Enid picked at her food and continued to focus most of her attention on the children, occasionally interrupting to tell them to do this or not do that.

Their pleasure visibly declined at this constant bombardment of instructions and in the end Wilf could stand it no longer. 'Leave them to eat in peace now, Enid, and finish your own food. It's too delicious to do anything but enjoy it.'

She threw him a quick scowl and after that sat mainly silent, still only picking at what was on her plate.

When they'd finished eating, Mrs Morton swept them back into the parlour, where the grown-ups were offered a glass of sherry and the children a glass of the wonderful ginger beer made by Todd's wife at her small fizzy drinks factory.

Wilf was touched that Mrs Morton had spent some of her limited spare money on this treat, because Spring Cottage Mineral Waters were more expensive than ordinary fizzy drinks, aimed at people who still had money to buy fancy stuff, rather than ordinary folk.

'Thank you, Mrs Morton. The kids will love

that. Better give Enid a taste of sherry first, like you did me. She's not had it before and she might not like it.'

It was soon clear that Enid didn't really like the sherry and didn't know how to say so politely, so Wilf took the glass off her and said, 'I think you'd enjoy a ginger beer more than this, wouldn't you, love?'

She nodded, looking embarrassed.

Mrs Morton immediately poured her a glass of fizzing ginger beer.

Wilf tipped the remainder of Enid's sherry into his own glass and winked at his hostess. 'Too good to waste.'

She raised her glass to him in a toast to that.

When a break in the conversation and silence from the bay window area made him look towards the children, he saw that they'd fallen asleep, curled up together on the thick, soft rug.

'Eh, I wish I had a camera,' he murmured. 'What a picture they make.'

Mrs Morton spoke equally quietly, 'I have a little Brownie camera and I think there's some film still in it. If we switch on all the lights, it may be bright enough to take a snap.'

She tiptoed round, getting ready, then raised the camera and took a couple of snaps, then turned round and photographed Wilf and Enid. 'There, that's my film used up. I'll have to take it to the chemist on Monday to be developed. If the photos turn out all right, I'll get you copies.'

'Thanks. I'd like that.' Wilf looked towards the children, wondering if he should wake them.

'Let them sleep,' Mrs Morton whispered. 'It's a

long time since I've had the treat of watching a sleeping child, and your two are such dears, waking or sleeping. You keep them very nice, I must say, Mrs Pollard, and they have excellent manners for children so young.'

Enid softened visibly at that double compliment, but she still seemed overawed by her surroundings and left Wilf and Mrs Morton to carry most of the burden of conversation. Not that it was a burden. Their hostess was very easy to chat to.

When the children woke up, they said their goodbyes and thanked Mrs Morton, then put on their outdoor clothes.

Wilf drove them slowly home, feeling the tea party had gone well. He glanced at Enid. 'Mrs Morton's a lovely woman, isn't she?'

'Yes.'

'And the food was delicious.'

'Yes.'

'What the hell's the matter now?'

'I'm tired, that's all. I was worried the whole time we were there in case the kids broke something or showed us up.'

'Mrs Morton wouldn't have minded. She's lonely. Couldn't you see how much she enjoyed having us?'

'Enjoyed showing off how rich she was, more like.'

He was astonished and didn't even try to answer that unfair comment. He was deeply disappointed in Enid's behaviour today. What had brought on this reaction to the visit and why the suspicious attitude?

As she got the children ready for bed, Enid grew even more tight-lipped as Ronnie and Peggy discussed the visit and excitedly re-lived it. It was as if she didn't want them to be happy anywhere but at home, with her, Wilf thought. What had those years of hardship, together with her inability to have a child, done to her?

He was at his wits' end as to how to deal with her lately. Whatever he did seemed to upset her. All he knew for certain was, he wasn't having Ronnie and Peggy shut up in the house for the rest of their childhoods. Nor were any of them going to go short of food if they had enough money to buy some.

29

On that Saturday afternoon, Clarence came into his wife's bedroom and said abruptly, 'I'm making arrangements to visit a certain house again and stay overnight. Probably on Monday.'

He laughed, a nasty harsh sound. 'And I'm fed up of trying to pretend about what I need. If you weren't so useless in bed, I wouldn't have to get my pleasure elsewhere, so why should I hide it? All men have these needs, you know, and so do normal women. Which you're not.'

He grabbed her suddenly by the throat, something he hadn't done for a while, and squeezed hard. She couldn't breathe and this time she thought he was going to kill her. She panicked, scrabbling at him, making gurgling noises. But he didn't let his grip slacken until she had stopped struggling and was sagging helplessly against him.

'Let that be a warning to you, Gertrude. Not a word to anyone about what I do, especially the servants. I don't want word of my absence from home to get round. I'll probably stay overnight, have a few drinks and come back on Tuesday. As far as you're concerned, I will have been at home all Monday evening and in your bed all night, and so you'll tell anyone who asks.'

She nodded out of sheer terror and at long last he pushed her away. She staggered to one side, rubbing her throat, which felt bruised, wondering why he was suddenly acting like this. What had got into him lately? He was acting like a madman.

He smirked. 'You'll need to wear a high-necked blouse for a few days. I don't want you bringing Edna into this, either, so make sure she doesn't see it. But every time *you* look in the mirror, that will remind you of your duty of obedience to me.'

She forced herself to nod and lower her gaze in a submissive way. Did he really think the servants thought he shared her bed on these occasions? They were well aware that he never slept in her bed and that he spent the occasional night away, especially her personal maid.

And inevitably Edna knew, too. His cousin was a fool, but not blind. He was only keeping her here because he wanted to find a way to get his hands on her money, Gertrude was sure.

He was humming loudly as he left the house

and got into the car to be driven to his office.

She watched him go from her bedroom window, filled with loathing. He didn't usually work on Saturdays, so she knew something was being planned. She rubbed her neck, which was still throbbing painfully.

It was time to do something about him. She couldn't go on like this.

All she could think of was to get word to that nice sergeant about this and hope he could trap her husband. She didn't want any of the staff involved in taking messages, and certainly not Edna, so would have to find a way to see Deemer herself.

Clarence could easily have killed her tonight. Perhaps one day he would. Unless she stopped him for good.

She summoned her maid and showed her the bruised neck, telling her that Mr Rathley had just done it, telling her that she was frightened for her life.

'I daren't defy him, ma'am. I just daren't.'

'I know. But I wanted someone to know.'

She made sure the blouse slipped and Edna saw the bruising later, telling her, too, what Clarence had done.

'I don't believe it.'

'Who else could have done it, do you think? I couldn't do it to myself and I haven't left the house this morning, have I?'

'Oh. Oh, no! What did you do to make him so angry?'

'You don't need to make him angry when he's in this mood. He *likes* hurting people. You'll find that out one day. He's been surprisingly kind to you so far. One day he'll pounce on you, it's inevitable, and you know what men want from women when they're in that mood.'

Edna turned white and hardly said a word for the rest of the morning.

Because one of Rathley's men was married to his cousin Lallie, Piper wondered if he could manage to find out for Sergeant Deemer what was being planned and when for.

Piper had warned Lallie against marrying Bill, but she'd been mad for him in those days. Pity she'd not listened to his advice. Bill had changed after they married. He wouldn't gab to anyone else about what he was doing, but Piper knew Bill didn't bother to keep his mouth shut in his own home, confident that his wife was too afraid of him to tell anyone.

Lallie had told Piper once or twice how Bill had forced her to tell the police he'd been at home with her when he hadn't. Now, he always told her to stay at home when he was about to do what he called 'a special job', usually for Rathley.

Would Bill be involved this time? Only one way to find out: ask Lallie. Piper couldn't visit her at home because Bill had forbidden her to let him into the house. So, it being Saturday, he went into town and before long saw her walking slowly and wearily along with her shopping basket over her arm. He'd guessed correctly.

She looked upset and no wonder. She had a big bruise on one cheek. He could see it even from twenty yards away. She hadn't seen him, so he nipped down a side street and hurried along it, overtaking her then bumping into her, seemingly by chance, as she left the main street.

'Hello, Lallie love. Haven't seen you for a while. Let's get out of sight and have a chat.'

She looked round, saw no one she recognised and followed him into a gateway.

'Eeh, what did you do to your poor face?'

'What did *Bill* do, you mean. He hit me again. He's drinking more heavily than ever and I can guess where he's getting the money from to do that, but he ought to make sure me an' the kids are fed.'

She touched her cheek and her eyes filled with tears. 'He gets rough when he's been drinking and wants a meal. If there's nothing to eat, he thumps me – as if it's my fault he's not given me any money for food.'

'You'd be better off without that one.'

'You don't have to tell me that. You were right that I shouldn't marry him, only I daren't try to leave him now. He'd kill me if I did.' She sighed and it turned into a sob. 'I wish he were more like you, Piper. Your wife's a lucky lass.'

He heard her stomach rumble. 'Short of money for food again, are you, love?'

She nodded and rubbed her belly as if it hurt. 'I've only enough to buy a stale loaf. If they have any cheap ones left, that is. If there aren't any, he'll clout me again.'

'I haven't got much to spare, but would a shilling be any use to you?'

'You know it would. Eh, I'm that grateful, Piper.'

'If you can't help a cousin, who can you help?

Um, do you want me to keep an eye on Bill? You don't want him spending time in jail, do you? He'd come out twice as mean.'

'Would you? You saved him getting caught last year and even he was grateful once he'd recovered from the drubbing you gave him.'

'He deserved a pummelling, hitting you like that. You wouldn't know *when* he's planning to do whatever it is this time, would you?'

'Must be Monday night. He's told me to stay home then and not go gossiping next door. I've not to let anyone into the house an' to keep the curtains drawn. I expect he'll want to claim he was at home all evening if things go wrong. I live in fear of being sent to jail myself for lying under oath, and then what would happen to the children? I wish he'd drop dead, I do indeed. I could live with Mum and Dad and manage better on my own.'

Piper slipped her a sixpence and two threepenny bits. 'Let me know if he changes the day he's doing whatever it is or I'll not be able to keep watch on him.'

'Thanks, Piper. I will. I'm that grateful to you.' She tried to summon up a smile and failed, so walked away.

He stayed in the gateway watching her go till she was out of sight. How old she looked these days, yet she was the same age as his own wife. If he could help lock that sod up in jail along with his brute of a master, he'd be a happy man.

It had made his stomach churn angrily seeing the big bruise on his cousin's face today. Lallie had been such a pretty lass once.

In the large, comfortable house in Birch End, the clocks seemed to be ticking more loudly than usual for the rest of that weekend – or at least, so it seemed to Gertrude. The hours passed so slowly, there were times when she could have screamed.

After her husband came home from his office on Saturday, she watched him covertly, acting meekly, seeing how he enjoyed this. She kept wondering exactly what he was intending to do on Monday night. Some poor woman would suffer for what he called pleasure, she was sure.

On the Sunday, he retreated to his smoking room and refused to go to church.

When she and Edna got back from the morning service, he was still there, so they sat in her little sitting room instead of the best parlour. As usual, Edna wittered on about nothing. His cousin seemed to get more foolish by the day. But at least that saved Gertrude the trouble of finding something to talk about.

'Cousin Clarence's mood seems to have improved,' Edna said suddenly. 'I overheard him talking to a man who came to the side door yesterday quite late in the evening and he sounded pleased. You can hear a lot if my bedroom window is open.'

Improved, Gertrude thought. I don't think so. It took only a little prompting to obtain more information from her foolish companion. 'What was he pleased about?'

'He seems to be planning a surprise for someone called Tess and the man who came is involved. Who is she? We don't know anyone called Tess, do we?'

She knew who this Tess was, but didn't intend to admit that. 'No. I think it's, um, the wife of one of his business acquaintances, a man he wants to keep happy. Don't say anything. Clarence hates to think anyone has overheard him and he'll get very angry with you, even though it's his own fault for having such a loud voice.' She was wondering whether he was starting to go deaf, and serve him right if he did.

Edna shuddered. 'Oh no, I won't, not now that you've warned me.'

'Good. This surprise – did you hear when it's supposed to be happening?'

'Tomorrow night, I think. But I believe someone's coming to see him tonight to go through the final details.'

'Then we'll go to bed early and leave him to it. That's always the best way to deal with him.' So the outing he'd told to her was about to be confirmed, was it?

Now she had to prepare for going into town alone. 'By the way, I have to see my dressmaker for a fitting tomorrow. I won't take you with me because I want to visit a former servant afterwards and their house is very tiny.'

'I could walk round the town centre while you were visiting them.'

'I don't know how long I'll be. And their house is on the way home, so I'd have to come back to get you. Best if you stay here this time.'

Gertrude went on with the rest of her day, hoping she looked as calm as usual. She'd certainly had years of practice at concealing her feelings.

Could she do it tomorrow, betray her husband? That might make her a social pariah. She fingered the scarf hiding the bruises on her throat. Yes, she could. She couldn't take any more from him, had to find a way to change things permanently. Oh, how she longed to live in a happy, peaceful home! Even if other ladies shunned her, she would be better off.

Clarence acted as if he were a king here! But she knew he was hurting innocent women and children whenever he went out, which seemed to give him a terrible sort of pleasure. She'd felt helpless to prevent that. He was more like the devil than a king, she always thought.

She studied her companion. Edna's presence seemed to annoy Clarence at times and yet he hadn't allowed his wife to arrange to find a house for his cousin to rent because he was wallowing in Edna's open adoration of him. What the silly woman needed was another husband to fuss over. Some women weren't capable of living lives of their own.

Gertrude was beginning to worry that if Edna didn't find someone, Clarence might make her his mistress and insist on keeping her living with them. She didn't think she could put up with that. Everyone had their sticking point, didn't they?

Was anything beyond him? She knew he'd been visiting that whore who'd been killed recently and she suspected he'd had something to do with that. She'd seen him come back towards the house on foot late that particular night, puffing and panting as if he'd been running, looking worried – more than worried, afraid. She'd never seen that look on his face before.

His clothes had had blood on them and he'd told the maid to burn them. But Gertrude's maid had told her about that and she'd told her maid it'd be wasteful. Far better to put them in the poor box instead, and she'd do that herself. If the master asked, they should just tell him the clothes had been disposed of.

She hadn't given them away, though. She'd hidden them in an old trunk in the attic. Evidence that he'd been involved in the whore's death, that was.

She was hoping Deemer would be able to use it and that it would help free her from her brute of a husband.

On the Sunday evening, once Edna had obediently gone to bed early, Gertrude crept into the empty bedroom next to Edna's and, like it, above Clarence's so-called smoking room. No one was supposed to know that people visited him there. He seemed to think that the other occupants of the house were all blind.

She waited, sitting by the partly open window in the darkness. She was just starting to think Edna must have been mistaken about someone coming to see Clarence tonight when a shadowy figure slipped across the garden to tap softly on the door below her.

She leaned forward and was able to hear some of the conversation between this person and her husband because it was a warm night. Clarence must feel very secure to leave his windows and door open like this. But he didn't realise how loudly he always spoke.

'It's all arranged, sir. Tomorrow night we'll raid that car sales place. Three of us should be enough, even if there's someone guarding the woman. If it's the same girl you're after, we'll snatch her. After all, there's only one man living there.'

Gertrude felt sick with disgust as she listened. Was he planning to kidnap another young girl and ravish her? He'd done it once before that she knew of, and he'd had that horrible gloating look on his face then, too. Usually he went with willing older women but some nastiness inside him made him do strange things, like nearly strangle her. He had a dangerous streak in him.

He hadn't had the house just outside Backshaw Moss then. He'd bought it afterwards and used it from time to time. She'd gone for a walk once when he was away on business and had a look at it. There were no close neighbours. Heaven help an unwilling woman trapped out there.

He seemed to think no one knew about it or when he went there. But she did. She had become good at eavesdropping, in sheer self-preservation. And some of his men must know too. Blind arrogance, that. A weak point, she hoped, that would one day trap him.

There had been a big fuss and hunt for the first girl he'd kidnapped and her parents had not stopped searching for her. It had been a month before she'd been found wandering on the moors, half out of her mind with terror.

According to the local newspaper she'd been kidnapped by tinkers and was frightened but unhurt apart from a few bruises. She and her family had left the valley the next day, however, and had never been heard of again.

All Clarence's doing, she was sure. He must have paid that family off. But he hadn't killed that girl, had he? Someone had killed the whore, though. Was it him? Or another man?

It was definitely time to go and see Sergeant Deemer and confide all her worries in him, ask him what to do with the bloodstained clothes. She knew from the way Deemer looked at her husband that he didn't like Clarence, to put it mildly.

Gertrude sat there in the darkness for a long time after the man left. Did she have the courage to act?

Yes. This time she did. She couldn't live any longer with the burden of knowing what her husband was doing.

If this didn't get rid of him for good, she'd flee. She had enough money of her own to live simply in some remote place. Anywhere would be better than living with him.

On the Monday morning, Gertrude went out to see her dressmaker, then took another route home, hurrying along back laneways, where she hoped not to meet anyone she knew.

She had told Edna she was visiting a former servant, but in fact she went to the back door of Sergeant Deemer's house. She was about to knock when she heard someone approaching in the laneway, so let herself in. Bad enough if someone had seen her in a laneway and told Clarence; life-threatening if he heard she'd gone into the police station.

Inside the hall, she leaned against the wall, trembling. Mrs Deemer came out of the back room, staring at her in shock.

'I'm sorry to just walk in. I have to see your husband, and I didn't want anyone to notice me coming in here. It's very important but has to be kept secret.'

Mrs Deemer nodded and patted her arm, speaking soothingly, as if to a child, 'Come into my sitting room, Mrs Rathley. I'll fetch him to you then no one will see you talking to him.'

The sergeant came in, unable to hide his surprise. But what she told him brought an expression of intense satisfaction to his face. 'Aaah! You've done the right thing, Mrs Rathley. I don't know exactly what he's planning, but if I'm sure it's for tonight, I can have watchers placed here and there. Do you know about the cottage he uses sometimes for his pleasures?'

'Of course I do. And it'll be there that he takes whichever poor woman he's decided to use.'

'Your information adds more pieces to the jigsaw puzzle I'm putting together.'

'There's more. He told the maid to burn the trousers and waistcoat he was wearing on the night that woman was killed. They had blood on them, you see. I told her I'd give them to charity, but I hid them in the attic instead. Any of the servants will recognise them as his if you need to identify him as being involved. Will they be of any use to you?'

That brought another 'Aaah!' after which he looked at her very solemnly. 'Very useful. What I don't understand, though, is why you're betraying him now, if you've been unhappy for a good while.'

For answer she uncovered her neck and showed him the bruises. 'This isn't the first time, but I hope it'll be the last. It was worse than before. I thought he was going to kill me. I couldn't breathe for a few moments, was near to passing out.'

He closed his eyes for a minute, looking upset. 'I'm so sorry you've had to face that, my dear lady.'

She couldn't prevent her voice from wobbling. 'Years I've had of it, but never this bad before. Mostly he ignores me. I'm sure it's only the existence of my family nearby that has kept me alive. I told him once I'd given them a letter, in case anything happened to me. If I hadn't done that, I'm sure he'd have killed me by now and found a younger, more co-operative wife.'

'You'll testify against him in court, if necessary?'

'With the greatest satisfaction.' She glanced towards a clock on the mantelpiece. 'I can't be away for too long. Is there anything else you need to know?'

'You've no idea exactly what he's planning?'

'Not more than I've told you already.'

'Thank you for doing this. Can you get home safely?'

'I'd be grateful if you'll look out and tell me when the way is clear for me to leave here the back way without being noticed.'

Gertrude got into town without meeting anyone

she knew and went into the chemist's. There she asked for something to help take away a bruise. She didn't show him her neck, but wanted an excuse for being out on her own for so long, so also bought some lotion for the hands, for Edna as well as for herself.

Then she braced herself and went back home, fear juddering in her belly as she walked through the front door.

But though he was in the house, not at his office, Clarence didn't seem to notice that she'd been out nor did he come near her. She heard him pacing to and fro in his smoking room. Like a rat in a cage, she thought.

He had his lunch taken in to him, saying he had paperwork to attend to, and ordered that his dinner be taken there as well. Thank goodness. She didn't want to see him, was still nervous about what she'd done.

Edna noticed her agitation, however, so Gertrude told her she had a sick headache and had visited the chemist for help, which was how she'd found the lotion as well. That distracted Edna, as expected.

'That was so kind of you to buy it for me, Gertrude.'

'Don't say anything to Clarence. You know how bored men get about such things and how they resent us spending money on cosmetics. But we women have to look after ourselves, don't we?'

'Oh, yes. Douglas was just the same, didn't realise how much effort it takes for a lady if she wants to present a good appearance.'

'You're right. I think I'll lie down and rest for a

while, if you don't mind. It's the only thing to do when my head is like this. Next week I'll start introducing you to families with single gentlemen or widowers in them.' She winked.

Edna beamed at her.

Gertrude spent the afternoon in bed and it seemed to go on for ever, so she joined Edna for the evening meal.

The evening dragged past just as slowly, but eventually it was time to go to bed and she went into her room, locking the door after her maid left her in utter relief at having got through the day.

As she lay sleepless on her bed, she prayed this had been her last day of living with him.

That was in the hands of fate now. And Sergeant Deemer.

30

Rathley had sent men to look for the girl in every possible place in Birch End and Rivenshaw, and had come to the conclusion that the men who claimed to have seen her at the car yard must have been right. He hadn't believed them because he knew from chatting to a young town hall clerk he was cultivating that Jo Melling was staying there. He'd thought they must have mistaken her for Tess.

But where else could Tess be? Perhaps both young women were staying there.

Jo was another person on his list. That insolent young woman would learn what it cost to defy him. Oh, yes. It was something to look forward to, but that was for another time.

In the end, he decided to send three men he'd employed previously on delicate matters to see whether the girl really was at the car sales yard, with Hobbs in charge. If they found her, they had orders to use whatever force was necessary to capture her, but were not to seriously hurt anyone. If they didn't find her, they were to capture Jo instead. He'd keep her in his house outside Backshaw Moss for a while, chained up. He smiled. He'd enjoy seeing her so helpless. Then he'd get rid of her when he tired of her.

He had to have a younger woman. It had been too long. No one in this town would dare accuse him of anything, he was too important. And anyway, Gertrude would say he'd been with her. He'd make sure of that.

He reminded Hobbs that they mustn't let their faces show or say who they were working for. Really, he'd rather not have had to send them to a place in the town centre, where there might be nosy parkers looking out of windows nearby or taking a shortcut down the back laneway.

If they went there late in the evening, but before the pubs closed, they ought not to meet anyone in the laneway behind the house. He hoped it was Tess they found. She was younger.

He pictured her and smiled. So soft and ripe for the plucking. He might even keep her as a mistress if she learned to please him, because she didn't have a mother to interfere now. Moira's death had been a lucky accident for him, really, and all her own fault.

And though people talked about that whore being murdered, he knew he was innocent, so he didn't feel at all guilty about having been present when she'd had her accident. No one would ever know about that, of course, because the clothes he'd been wearing that night had been burned and his wife knew nothing at all about any of it.

He told Hobbs to take the girl to his cottage near Backshaw Moss and to go there and get it ready for occupation first, with some simple food and tea-making materials.

Once they'd captured her, one of them was to come to his home and fetch him. It was close enough to walk to the cottage, if he took the short cut along the public right of way. He'd bought the cottage partly for that reason and partly for the way it was hidden by the slope and some trees, and out of earshot of the nearest houses. He'd put up big *No Trespassing* signs and there were already high fences.

He supplied the men with something to prevent her struggling. Always the best way. He didn't want her to struggle because they might mark or hurt her.

He reserved that pleasure for himself.

Tess had overheard enough snatches of information to know something was going on. She'd already decided to find something to protect herself with, just in case. It'd make her feel safer. When she saw Jo stroll over to the workshop to take a mug of tea to Todd, she decided to act now.

She knew Jo wouldn't linger there but this was a perfect opportunity to find something, because Silas had nipped out to the corner shop. He'd be back in a couple of minutes, so she didn't waste any time. She ran down to the kitchen and found a drawer of kitchen oddments that were not likely to be missed, scrabbling through it till she came upon an old paring knife whose blade was bent and slightly rusty.

It was still sharp enough for her purpose, which was to protect herself. Her mother had often carried a small knife for the same reason, only *he* had used it on her mother instead. Slipping it into her pocket, Tess went back to her bedroom and got there just in time. She heard the front door being unlocked and Jo returning, then Silas coming in.

Her heart was pounding as she wrapped up the paring knife in a rag ready to slip into her waistband that night. Then she waited and the day seemed very long indeed, even worse than the previous days she'd spent here.

One thought never left her: she intended to make sure her kind cousin wasn't hurt. She was nimble and if Jo left the house, she'd follow. She knew how to creep about unnoticed at night, because she'd often had to do it when her mother had customers.

Her cousin was so stubborn that she might even go against the sergeant's orders.

Against his better judgement, Nick accepted a warm invitation to join one of his customers at a nearby pub for a drink to meet several of his friends who were thinking of learning to drive. It might bring in several customers for driving lessons, so Jo told him to go. She'd be fine with all the doors locked.

He frowned at her. 'I'm not sure.'

'Just go for one quick drink. It needn't take more than half an hour. After all, Sergeant Deemer said he'd make sure the policeman on night duty walks past regularly.'

'Well, I'll be half an hour at most. You make sure you do keep every door locked. I'll sneak out the back way, too, so that if anyone's watching they won't know I've gone out.'

He'd walked past the pub a few times because it was only two minutes' walk away. It seemed to be frequented by decent folk.

Nick slipped into the pub and joined his customer, a very pleasant man, whose friends seemed equally good-natured. He accepted a half pint and sat down with them.

When another man joined the group, he had to stand up as they re-arranged the seats. As he did so, he caught sight of the reflection in the big mirror on one wall of a man wearing his cap pulled down low standing in the entrance hall staring into the room where Nick was.

The man turned away.

After chatting politely for a couple of minutes, Nick looked up again and was horrified to see the man again staring into the room. Why was he doing this? Were they planning to try to capture Tess? They must have seen him leave the house, though he'd tried to keep to the shadows.

When the man saw Nick looking at him he again

turned away, but that was it, Nick decided. He shouldn't have come and he was going straight back to make sure Jo was all right. Her safety came before trapping Rathley, and Tess wouldn't be able to protect her.

He left the pub the back way and tried to get home without being seen.

Jo chatted to Tess, then when the younger woman fell asleep, went down quietly to the kitchen and began to read one of Nick's books.

She found that she was sleepy too, so let the book fall into her lap and closed her eyes, just for a minute or two.

She was woken by a cold draught of air coming from the back scullery but before she could do anything, someone grabbed her by the hair and a hand covered her mouth, preventing her from crying out.

She struggled desperately, but whoever it was had a cloth that smelled of something that made her head spin. Chloroform! She panicked, renewing her efforts to get that hand and cloth off her face.

But it grew harder and harder to struggle and she could feel herself losing consciousness.

Despair filled her as everything faded away.

Tess had been listening from the bedroom, and yet she knew nothing about the break-in till she heard some faint sounds from inside the kitchen. Then she heard some scrabbling noises and what sounded like a chair falling over.

Worried, Tess crept further down the stairs. She

was even more worried when she heard the outside door open and someone go out into the yard. Was it Jo? No, why would Jo go outside when they had agreed to keep the doors locked at all times?

She ran into her bedroom and peeped out of the window, horrified to see two men carrying an unconscious Jo out of the yard and off down the alley while a third one closed the gate carefully behind them. Why wasn't Jo struggling? Did they really think they'd got Tess?

Had they killed Jo? No, if this was for Rathley, he would want her alive.

There was no way Tess could rescue her cousin, but she could follow them, find where they went and get help.

If only Nick hadn't gone out!

She slipped out of the house the back way, using all the skills she'd learned over the years of trying not to attract attention as she followed the group of men.

Jo was still not moving and to Tess's dismay, the men stopped at a car, shoved their captive in the back any old how and drove away.

She ran after it for a little while, hoping to see which way it went. It left the town centre by a less frequented road, which led only to one part of the valley, just beyond Backshaw Moss.

But where exactly were they going? There were too many people in the crowded slum for them to be taking Jo there.

Tess ran back to the house and to her relief saw Nick standing in the kitchen looking out of the back door.

He grabbed her and pulled her quickly inside.

'Where did you go and where the hell's Jo?'

'Some men have taken her. I don't know what they've done to her but she was unconscious. I followed them along the laneway, but they had a car so I lost them. I think they took that back road which goes near Backshaw Moss. I'd recognise the car again.'

'Then we'll drive after them and search the area till we find them. If necessary, I'll rouse people from nearby to help me hunt for her. I'm not leaving her in their hands.'

'Shouldn't we get Sergeant Deemer?'

Nick hesitated. 'Yes.'

But it was the sergeant's wife who answered his knock and she said her husband was out on a job. When Nick explained what was going on, she said she'd call in someone else to help. She knew who her husband used in emergencies.

'I'm not waiting. They went up towards Back-shaw Moss.'

She grabbed his arm. 'That'd be where that horrible Rathley man has a cottage.'

'Send whoever it is after us and tell them about the cottage. I'm going to look for their car.'

As they set off again, Tess kept thinking, *Please let her be all right. Please let them not hurt her.*

Jo moaned involuntarily as she tried to open her eyes, and someone again put that stinking cloth over her mouth and held it there forcibly. She felt the dopiness clouding her brain again so held her breath, trying not to take in any more of the evil-smelling fumes. She managed to do that till she was nearly bursting and at the same time she tried to feign unconsciousness.

She felt woozy and didn't think she could hold on much longer, when suddenly the cloth was taken away and she was able to take a shallow breath.

A man's voice said, 'She should sleep for a good half-hour now. Go and fetch Rathley now, Bill.'

'What if someone sees me driving up the road to his house and chases after me?'

'You put your foot on the accelerator and leave them behind, then ditch the car somewhere and run off across the fields. Pity if that happens. It's a good car, and someone's left things in it we can sell later. We fell lucky when we stole that one.'

'Rathley won't like us doing that.'

'It's a damn sight easier to use a car than a handcart or try to carry her all that way. She's a lot heavier than I'd expected.'

'She's not going to be a child much longer. She has nice, firm breasts. I had a quick feel. She's definitely becoming a woman.' He chortled. 'And in more ways than one tonight, eh?'

Jo felt fury sizzle through her at the thought of someone pawing her unconscious body and that made her feel more alert. These men were obviously sent by Rathley and still thought she was Tess, which showed that they didn't really know what she and her cousin looked like.

What else had they done to her while she was unconscious? Jo wondered. Fear churned through her, but she continued to lie quietly because they hadn't tied her up and they might do that if she let them see that she'd regained consciousness.

She might have a chance of escaping if she was

lucky. No one else was going to rescue her because they wouldn't know who had taken her or where.

She'd been so sure she could manage this. But it had all gone wrong.

The car stopped and she heard the door open, felt fresh air on her face, longed to take deep breaths of it, but didn't, just continued to lie still, taking slow, shallow breaths and keeping her eyes closed.

When a man picked her up and started walking, she had difficulty staying limp, she felt so vulnerable.

Could she find a way to escape? She had to.

31

Deemer drove up to Backshaw Moss with his men by a roundabout way before it grew dark that evening. He felt sure if Rathley had arranged anything for tonight it'd be at his cottage.

He knew all the little farm lanes in the area – well, he knew the whole valley, didn't he, because he'd grown up here? He was able to park in a lane near the rear of Rathley's house and slip across a field to the cottage's large garden. There was a fence and a sign forbidding trespassing, but the gate wasn't locked and there was no one around to see them slip into the garden.

He and his men found hiding places among the overgrown shrubs. Piper also did a quick reconnoitre round the cottage because he was quieter at moving around than Constable Hopkins. He checked that it was unoccupied and said he'd seen a loaf and some other bits of food on the kitchen table.

He was proving very useful. Ironically enough, the man would probably make a good policeman, Deemer thought with a wry smile.

It was over two hours before anything happened, but the food had made the sergeant sure they were on the right track.

He sucked in a long slow breath of satisfaction when he saw a car draw up outside and some of the men Rathley occasionally used get out.

Breath hissed into his mouth as one of them lifted Jo out of the car and carried her into the house. How had they managed to capture her, and why was she unconscious? Should he take his men in to save her straight away? This wouldn't have happened if he had other men he could call on for help at times of crisis, as he'd asked to arrange several times. It'd have been money well spent and the mayor had supported the idea, but the former council hadn't, damn them.

Well, trying again was for another day. For the time being he had to deal with it somehow, so he sent Piper to see what he could find out first.

The man came back as noiselessly as he'd gone, making Deemer jump as he suddenly appeared beside him.

'She's alive, sarge. I saw her move, then they covered her face with a cloth and she stopped moving again.'

'Is she tied up?'

'No. And they're not taking liberties with her or hurting her, either.'

'Thank goodness. I bet those sods are using chloroform. Now, we'll have to go in quickly. We don't want them hurting her and–' He broke off as one of the men came out and drove off in the big car.

The constable looked at him. 'We should follow him but we can't just leave her there, can we, sarge? I don't like to think of her in their power. She's a nice lass, was kind to me and my mate.'

'I'll go and keep an eye on them and yell if we need to go in.' At the sergeant's reluctant nod, Piper left again.

Deemer fought a battle with his conscience and the conscience won. It'd be nice to catch Rathley in the act of kidnapping, but Jo's safety was more important. 'We'd better get her out of there and–' He broke off as he heard the sound of a car. 'Is that it coming back?'

It was. The same car. It pulled up in front of the cottage.

'Wait till we see who gets out,' Deemer ordered.

It was Rathley.

'Aaah!' The sergeant smiled and whispered, 'Be ready to go in.'

Rathley's voice floated across to them, surprisingly loud for a man supposed to be here secretly. 'Get rid of that car *now*. You were a fool to steal it. One of you take it into Rivenshaw and damned well walk back here. Do you want some nosy parker seeing it here?'

Then he went into the cottage.

Scowling, the man who'd driven the car said

something to another man waiting by the door, then got back into it and drove off on his own.

'That one's leaving,' Piper pointed out unnecessarily. 'Pity! He'll probably get away.'

'That one who's driven off is small fry. It's Rathley we want,' Deemer said.

'Well, there are only three left, including him, so we outnumber them. And there's plenty of moonlight, thank goodness. They'll not get away from us.'

He sounded to be enjoying this, Deemer thought sourly. He wasn't. He was too worried about Jo getting hurt if there was any fighting.

He took a deep breath and gave his orders. 'Larry, go and stand guard at the front door and us three will go in the back way. Remember, keeping that lass safe is the most important thing, even if that means letting one of them escape.'

They all nodded, looking eager and excited.

Excitement was greatly overrated, Deemer decided sourly.

Nick drove up the hill with Tess in the front seat beside him. He took the direct route, driving straight through Backshaw Moss, but when he saw a car parked by the side of the road just outside it, with the headlights and engine still on, he slowed down. A man was peering into the boot, bent over as if searching for something, so engrossed he hadn't noticed them approaching.

Tess shouted, 'Stop! That's the car they took Jo away in!'

'You're sure?'

'Oh, yes. Definitely.'

He jammed his foot on the brake and jumped out. The man looked round and Nick saw that he'd been collecting a pile of small objects, piling them on a travel rug in the boot.

The man yelped in shock and tried to flee, but couldn't get away fast enough. Nick brought him down in a flying tackle. The struggle was short and sharp because he was terrified about what the others might be doing to Jo if he was delayed.

To his surprise, Tess joined in, producing a rusty knife and brandishing it at the man's throat so that he stopped trying to move and stared up at her, leaning his head as far away as he could from the blade.

'I'll be happy to use this if you don't tell us where my cousin is,' she said in a loud and very fierce voice.

'Cousin?' He stared at her, then exclaimed, 'Oh, hell! You're the one Rathley wants. Not her.'

'Yes, you've kidnapped the wrong person.'

Her grip on the knife had slackened a little and the man tried to jerk away, but Nick grabbed the arm nearest to him and twisted it behind the man's back. The pain made his captive moan and stay still.

'We need to tie him up,' Nick said to Tess. 'Either that or knock him unconscious.'

'Or kill him.' She sounded vicious and quite prepared to do that.

The man twitched at that and went rigid, his eyes wide and scared.

'See if you can find something in that car to tie him up with, but keep your knife handy.' He shook his captive. 'Whose car is this anyway?'

The man scowled and said nothing, so Nick increased the pressure on the arm.

'Ow, stop! I don't know whose it is.'

'Stolen?'

'Yes.'

Tess found a length of rope in the car and Nick used it to bind the man's wrists behind him.

They dragged their prisoner to their own car and shoved him into the back, and since she turned round in the front seat and continued to hold the knife at the ready, he didn't make any attempt to escape from the rough bindings.

'You've captured the woman I love, who is also this lady's cousin,' Nick said. 'If you don't tell me where she is, I'll not hesitate to let my young friend use her knife on you.'

The chill tone and another wave of the knife by Tess made the man volunteer information quickly.

'She's at Rathley's cottage. Go to the end of this lane, turn right and then first left. It's not far away, but it's set back from the road behind trees so it's not easy to find.'

'I hope you're telling the truth. Let's find out.' Nick put his foot on the accelerator.

Rathley went into the cottage and through to the kitchen, which was lit only by an oil lamp. 'Ah.' He advanced towards Jo, his eyes gloating and lingering on her body before he even looked at her face. He waved one hand dismissively at the men. 'You can go now.'

'You said you'd pay us.'

'You can come to the office for it tomorrow.'

'My family needs to eat tonight.'

381

Grumbling, Rathley fished in his pocket and took out two pound notes.

'And one for our friend,' Hobbs said.

Rathley slapped another one down on his hand, then shoved them out of the door and locked it.

While he was doing that, Jo tensed, ready to fight him in any way she could.

When Rathley turned back to her, she moaned and stirred slightly as if still dopey, keeping watch on him through half-closed eyes.

He took off his coat and laid it neatly on the back of a chair, then took off his belt and kicked off his shoes.

Fumbling to unbutton his flies, he came closer and studied her face, letting out an exclamation of rage. 'What the hell are *you* doing here? I sent them to get Tess!'

She opened her eyes fully and got ready to use the knife the men had missed finding in her waistband. 'Well, they kidnapped me instead.'

'I don't want you tonight. You're too old.' Then he shrugged. 'But as you're here, you'll have to do.'

'You're a pervert!' she yelled at him, trying to edge into a position to make a run for it. 'Not a real man at all. A rotten creature who should be locked away from normal people for good.'

Rage made his face even uglier and he raised one arm to strike her. 'I'll show you how much of a real man I am. If you're the only one available, I'll make do with you tonight.'

She brought out the knife and slashed at him, managed to catch the arm that was reaching out to her, at the same time trying to get towards the door.

But he caught her skirt and yanked her back.

Outside Deemer let the two men who'd come out of the house move away from it, then signalled to his men to stop them.

They were about to fight when they suddenly recognised the two uniforms. Hobbs groaned and stopped dead. 'It's the police.'

'It'll make things easier on you if you give yourself up,' the sergeant said as the men hesitated. He unhooked the handcuffs from his belt and shook them suggestively.

Hobbs sighed and held out his wrists.

The other man tried to run away and ran into Piper's fist instead.

Deemer pointed to Larry. 'You and Piper keep an eye on these two. If they make any noise, knock them senseless.' He turned away and crept up to the nearest cottage window, in time to hear Rathley threatening Jo and trying to grab her. But she pulled a knife out of her waistband and slashed Rathley with it, buying a little time and heading for the door.

Unfortunately the kitchen door was locked. The constable didn't wait to be told but threw himself against it and the door burst open.

As Deemer entered the cottage he yelled out, 'Leave her alone,' and Rathley whirled round with a shocked expression.

Jo moved quickly across to stand near Deemer, shuddering and gulping.

Rathley stilled as he saw who'd come in, then had the nerve to smile. 'I'm so glad you got here, sergeant. I was just trying to rescue this young

383

lady and was afraid her kidnappers would return.'

'He's not rescuing me; he's the one who arranged to have Tess kidnapped, only his men captured me instead by mistake,' Jo said loudly.

Everyone was standing still, watching Rathley.

Deemer scowled at him. 'Don't try your lies on me, Rathley. I heard your threats just now and so did my constable.'

'You mistook what you heard.'

'No. We didn't. And there are two of us who heard you.'

Just then another car drove up and braked hard in front of the cottage. They heard Nick's voice yelling, 'Keep your eye on him, Tess.'

The front door was flung open and Nick pushed in past Larry, now standing in the hall.

He paused briefly to scan the scene in the kitchen, sagging in obvious relief when he saw that Jo was all right.

As she ran into his arms, he pulled her close, saying, 'Can someone go and keep an eye on the man we captured on the way here, please sergeant? He's in the car and Tess is holding him at knifepoint. She wants to ask Rathley a few questions about her mother's death.'

Nick glared at the older man, who looked down his nose at the lot of them and said scornfully, 'You'll not be able to prove anything, sergeant. I was *not* kidnapping this young lady. I was rescuing her from these villains. And who'd believe anything a whore's daughter said?'

Deemer jerked one thumb at his constable. 'Go and keep an eye on the prisoner in the car and send the girl in. Nick will help me if Rathley tries to escape.'

When Tess walked in, she had eyes only for Rathley and no one tried to stop her going towards him, knife still in her hand. 'I'm sure you killed my mother because I saw you arrive that night before I escaped through the kitchen window. And Big Donny saw you, too.'

'Don't be ridiculous. I admit I visited your mother regularly, but she was alive when I left that night.'

'Then why were your clothes covered in blood?' Deemer asked.

Rathley looked shocked, then said quickly, 'I don't know what you mean.'

'We have the clothes. Evidence.'

'You can't have. I told them to burn–' Rathley stopped, suddenly realising that he'd betrayed himself.

'You might be richer than most criminals,' Deemer said in great satisfaction, 'but you're just as stupid when cornered. Out of curiosity, why did you kill her?'

'I didn't. She pulled a knife on me and when I shoved her away, she fell on it.'

Deemer blew out a puff of disbelief. 'Was that the best story you could think of? No one is ever going to believe such a feeble tale.'

'But it's the *truth*.' He looked at Tess. 'You must know that your mother carried a knife.'

She looked at him, a long slow look, then smiled and shook her head. 'Mam didn't approve of violence. She would never have carried a knife, let alone threatened to use it on a customer.'

Rathley turned back to Deemer, saying frantic-ally, 'This girl is a liar. I told you the truth! Moira's death *was* an accident. She fell on her own knife.'

'Tell that to the jury. See if they believe it. I don't.' Deemer looked at the others. 'We'll take them all away and lock them up now. Will you see that the young ladies get home safely, Nick?'

'Yes, of course.'

Deemer called in the other men.

'If you leave first, Nick, I can lock up and make sure nothing here is touched. Who knows what else we'll find. In my experience perverts do like their toys. Perhaps there's even something from that other young girl who went missing.'

He had been watching Rathley and saw the fear leap into his face, saw him turn pale and start sweating. Knew there was something to find.

'You'll not get out of this,' Deemer told him. 'I'd not be surprised if they hang you for murder.'

That thought gave him intense satisfaction. He'd like to see justice done to this rotten excuse for a human being.

At the station, he woke Big Donny, who took one look at Rathley and cowered back.

'He can't hurt you,' Deemer said gently. 'We're going to lock him up and let you out.'

When that was done, Donny lingered. 'He can't get out, again, can he?'

'No, he can't.'

'He won't kill me like he did Moira?'

'What?'

'I saw him. He killed her. There was a lot of blood. It was on his clothes. He killed my Moira.'

Deemer nodded to his constable in great satisfaction. 'Donny's calmed down. If we can keep him calm, he'll make an excellent witness. Take him into the house. My wife will look after him.'

He turned to Rathley and smiled. 'Another witness.'

'You can't take that idiot's word against mine.'

'I don't think Donny is clever enough to lie. And as I said before, there are the bloodstained clothes.'

'I want to see my lawyer.'

'Oh, we can't wake the poor man up in the middle of the night. We'll call him after we've brought in the inspector and a magistrate. They'll let you see your lawyer when you're safely in prison.'

'But it really was an accident.'

Deemer rolled his eyes. 'You can say that till the cows come home but no one's ever going to believe you.'

He closed the door on the area where the cell was and went out into the reception area. He felt tired but thoroughly satisfied with his night's work.

Murder should not go unpunished. And this one wouldn't. The evidence was too strong. Even if Rathley didn't hang, he'd be locked up in prison for life. As he deserved.

As for the men Rathley had employed, he'd find them tomorrow, if they were still in the valley. If he'd had more men, they'd be here in handcuffs now.

Nick drove the two cousins back down the hill.

'That's done, then. You're safe now, Tess.'

'Yes. Thank you for all you've done.' She hesitated then went on, 'I still won't be able to live in the valley, though, will I? No one will ever forget what my mother was.'

'I'm afraid you're right,' Jo said sadly.

'I'll find somewhere else to live. Mam had some money saved and I know where she hid it, so I'll be all right, Jo. You two mustn't spoil your life for me. You don't really want to go back to Australia, Jo, and Nick doesn't want to leave his business.'

'You're too young to be left alone. Family look after one another. We can all go to Australia and make a new life. No one will know about your mother there.'

Tess gave her a sad smile. 'I don't really want to go so far away.'

'I don't think you'll have much choice,' Jo told her gently. 'People have long memories. But the final decision about where exactly to go is for another day.'

'When Jo and I get married,' Nick told the girl, 'we'll be a family wherever we are.'

'But you've only just started that business,' Tess protested. 'I can't ruin your lives.'

'There is no choice,' Jo repeated.

'I can save up and start another business,' Nick said. 'The people you care about are more important than anything else.'

They didn't speak after that till they got back to the car yard, then Tess said she felt too exhausted to stay up any longer if they didn't mind and went to bed. The other two sat quietly for a while.

Jo yawned but wanted to tell him one thing.

'You won't have to wait and save up again, love, even if you can't get your money back from what you've spent here. My father left me quite a lot of money, you see. There's enough to set up a business in Perth *and* buy a house.'

'I can't take your money.'

She reached out to put one finger across his lips and stop him talking. 'Once we're married, what's mine will be yours and vice versa. The money isn't important. As you said, it's the people who count.'

He looked at her, then kissed the finger and pulled her close. 'Then it's not going to be as bad as I thought.'

'No.'

Later she admitted to him, 'I don't really want to go back to Australia. I've met some lovely people here, but there you are. You can't always have exactly what you want.'

'Well, we both agree that Tess deserves a better life, my darling. We won't be able to go anywhere until after the court case, and by then we'll be married.'

She yawned and he pulled her to her feet. 'Go to bed now. I'll check that everything's locked up then follow you upstairs. Sleep well, my darling.'

32

A man got off the train in Rivenshaw two days later and made his way to the rooms of the lawyer who'd written to him.

He was shown into Henry Lloyd's office and hardly waited for polite greetings to be exchanged to ask, 'Does she know?'

'No. I thought you might like to tell her yourself, Mr Litten. When I got your telegram yesterday, saying you would be able to come, I told her I had her mother's will and asked her to come and see me about it. Let my secretary get you a cup of tea while we wait for her.'

At two o'clock promptly, they heard the outer door open and the voice of the secretary.

The man looked at Henry. 'I'm feeling rather nervous. She has no idea I even exist.'

'No, none at all.'

They stood up as someone tapped on the door and looked in.

'Show them in, please, Miss Lawton.'

Jo and Tess came into the room, followed by Nick.

Henry moved forward, his attention mainly on Tess. 'I'm so sorry about your mother, Miss Tayner. Come in and sit down and I'll explain about her will and what she asked me to do if anything happened to her. She knew she was ill and wouldn't have long to live, you see.'

When they'd done that, he said, 'I'd like to introduce you to Mr Litten, who is involved in your mother's will. He has something important to tell you.'

The stranger nodded and said in a deep voice, 'I received a letter from your mother a couple of months ago, Tess. We'd known one another in London when we were both much younger. She told me she was dying, which grieved me deeply, but she also gave me some very good news–' He broke off, looking suddenly nervous. 'I believe it's good news anyway and I hope you do, too – she told me that I had a daughter, that I'm your father.'

Tess gasped and turned chalk white. '*My father!* She always said you were dead.'

'Your mother and I had a serious falling out and before we could resolve our differences, she left London. I don't think she knew then that she was expecting our child. I came to the north to search for her, but she apparently went elsewhere for a few years before returning to Rivenshaw. And by then I'd given up searching, given up hoping, too.'

Tess swallowed hard. 'That's what she meant.'

They all waited, looking at her, waiting for her to explain.

'She said if anything ever happened to her, I was to read a letter she'd left and do as she asked in it. I was going to look for her letter in our house in the same hiding place as she kept our savings, only I felt too exhausted to do anything yesterday.'

'You seem sure the people who broke in won't have found it,' Nick commented.

'I am. Sergeant Deemer would have noticed if

391

they'd found the place. We always knew her way of earning a living could be dangerous, so we always kept enough money there to run away.'

She paused and looked at him. 'You don't need to worry about me, Nick. I'll be all right.'

Mr Litten joined in again. 'Now that I know I have a daughter, I'd like to look after her.' He turned to Tess. 'I want to get to know you. I'm very happy that you exist, but I've missed so much of your life, it breaks my heart. I wish Moira had told me. And ... oh, I'm so glad I have a child.' His voice broke and he covered his face for a few moments with one hand, trying to control his emotions.

Tess could feel tears welling in her eyes, too, because it was clear he meant this. 'Won't your family mind you getting to know me?'

'I have no one at all close to me. My wife died a few years ago. After one stillborn infant, we never managed to have any other children. It was always a sadness to both of us. I wanted to come to see you as soon as I got Moira's letter, but she said she'd take you away and hide again if I tried. She didn't want to see me ever again and I was to wait till she died. She was always very stubborn. And I'd hurt her greatly. I never told her I was already married, you see, when we met. I let her hope for too much because I was a coward, because I didn't want to lose her.'

'Oh.' Tess turned to Jo, looking as if she didn't know what to say next.

'I'm Tess's cousin,' Jo explained. 'I'm from Australia and I was going to take Tess there to live with me. She clearly can't stay in the valley, not in a place where she's known as Moira's daughter.'

He turned back to Tess. 'You could come to me instead. I live in a small village in Wiltshire. We'd have to say you're my goddaughter, and you've been orphaned, in order to keep everything respectable. I can't think of anything I'd like more than to have you with me. But you will need to think about it, perhaps.'

Tess clutched Jo's arm and a few tears escaped her control and ran down her cheeks. 'I don't know what to say.'

There was silence, then Jo said, 'You don't need to decide now. Is it all right if she takes a little time to get to know you, Mr Litten?'

'She can take as much time as she needs.' He turned back to his daughter. 'But Tess, I really would love to have a daughter to care for and love. I get very lonely and don't feel like getting married again.'

'You can stay with me for a while, Litten,' Henry offered. 'Spend time with Tess. Go for walks. Talk.'

Jo had been studying Tess's father. She liked the looks of him, but thought he looked very sad beneath it all.

She wouldn't push Tess into anything, but perhaps, if everything went well, she and Nick need not give up their lives here.

Tess stood up. 'I don't want to sound rude or ungrateful, but so much has happened, Mr Litten. I can't take it all in, somehow, can't take a decision that important yet. I need some quiet time to think. And I need to read my mother's letter. She and I were very close, because we had no one else.'

He inclined his head. 'But perhaps you could spend time with me each day. If we get to know one another, perhaps it will help you to decide what you want to do.'

She nodded and let Mr Lloyd show them out. At the front door of his rooms, he said, 'I like the looks of Litten, Tess, if that's any help. And he came here straight away when I let him know your mother had died. And don't worry about your house. I can sell it for you.'

When they got outside, Tess looked pleadingly at Jo and Nick. 'I need to go home now, to my own home, and find Mam's letter. Everything's tangled up in my mind.'

'We'll go there straight away,' Nick said. 'But we daren't leave you alone.'

'Not even if I had Donny with me?'

'I'm afraid not. He's strong but not clever enough to think quickly.'

She looked at him. 'You hadn't intended to go to Australia until Jo found me, had you? You'd saved up for years to open your driving school. I've heard you and Jo talking about it.'

He shrugged. 'I can start another one in Australia, I'm sure, now I know Jo has some money. So don't let that influence you. Do what your heart tells you.'

'I did like him. He seemed gentle and kind.'

'Well, get to know him a little better before you decide. But it might be the best solution of all for you.'

The house in Packman Alley looked forlorn, somehow. To women standing in the doorway of one of the other houses stopped talking to stare at Tess, then one called, 'Sorry about your mum, love.'

'Thank you.'

Sergeant Deemer had given Nick the key and Tess took it out of his hand to open the door. They followed her inside and shut the world out.

'Where do you want to start?' Jo asked.

'The hiding place is upstairs. I won't be more than a couple of minutes. I'll call out if they've found it.'

She came down shortly afterwards carrying a package. 'They hadn't found it.'

'Where was it?' Nick asked.

'In a false panel under the windowsill. You'd never have guessed it was there, it was so cleverly done.' She was clutching it to herself. 'Would you mind if I went back upstairs to read this on my own?'

'Not at all.'

When she'd gone, they looked at one another. 'I don't know whether to hope she goes to live with her father or not,' Jo confessed. 'I don't want her to feel obliged to if she doesn't take to him.'

'I think she should. He seems nice and prepared to love her. And if we're still in England, she can always come back to us if she's unhappy with him.'

'You are such a kind, caring man.'

He smiled and pulled her to him for a kiss. 'I'll always help your cousin, but it's you I care about most of all. I love you so much, Jo. And I can't wait to marry you.'

She smiled at him with that cheeky expression he loved. 'Yes, but I haven't had a *proper* proposal yet, have I?'

That startled him for a moment or two, then he saw the mischief in her eyes, so plonked himself down on one knee and took her hand, trying to look lost in love. 'Dearest Jo–'

She tugged at his hand. 'Get up, you fool. I was only teasing you.'

'No, I like it down here. And I want to do this properly.' All the mischief suddenly vanished and he gave her such a loving look, she could hardly breathe.

'Jo, darling, I love you very much and I can't wait to marry you, either.'

Only then did he stand up and kiss her till the world started spinning and she had to clutch him. When he pulled away, she dragged him back by his shirt front and kissed him again.

They both said the same thing at the same time, 'Not long till our wedding now.'

Then they didn't say anything till Tess came back to join them, just stood close together, holding hands.

Upstairs, Tess carefully opened the tin box and took out the wallet with the money in it and found a letter underneath it, on top of her birth certificate. The certificate said 'Father – John Jones, deceased'.

'You should have told me the truth,' she whispered aloud, then opened her mother's letter.

'And you should at least have put him on my birth certificate, Mam.' She began to read.

My dearest Tess,

If you're reading this, I'll be dead. I've known for a while that something was wrong, and I've been in such bad pain, so don't grieve for me too much. We all have to die.

I ought to have told you before now that your father is still alive. He's called Gregory Litten and he lives in Wiltshire. He has a large house and land – and he never told me he was married, not in all the wonderful months we were together. I have never been able to forgive him for that.

However, you will need someone after I'm gone, so I've written him a letter and asked Mr Lloyd to let him know when I die. I think Gregory will look after you. He was a decent fellow in most things, even if he did deceive both me and his wife.

I've never understood how a man can say he loves two women, as he did, because I've only ever been able to love one man.

If he wants you, go to him. He'll keep you safe from Rathley.

I have always loved you, never regretted having you.

All my love,
Mam
PS If he doesn't want you, I think your cousin from Australia will look after you.

The PS was hastily scrawled at the end in pencil. The rest was written in her mother's beautiful copperplate handwriting in ink.

Tess raised the letter to her lips and kissed it. 'He wants me, Mam, so I'll go to him as you ask.'

She wept for a little while, then made herself stop and count the money. *Two hundred and six pounds!* And there was a bankbook with more in it, a lot more. She couldn't believe her mother had saved that much.

In the end she scrubbed her eyes, tidied her hair and went down to tell her cousin that she'd decided to go to her father, not only because it was what her mother had wanted but because he seemed like a really nice person.

Epilogue

Nick and Jo had expected to have a very quiet wedding with only Todd Selby and Charlie Willcox as witnesses. But the two men brought their wives along and Tess couldn't be left out. She brought her father.

When they said the words that made them man and wife, Jo's heart overflowed with joy and from the expression on Nick's face, he felt the same.

She saw that Charlie's eyes were suspiciously bright and he blew his nose rather loudly. His wife gave him a nudge with her elbow.

Once he'd finished blowing his nose, he grinned at the newlyweds. 'I've booked a room and a meal at the hotel. A wedding is something to celebrate.' He turned to Tess and added, 'And so is having a new father.'

'What he hasn't said,' Todd added, 'is that he's invited a few more people to the celebration.'

Charlie shrugged. 'We need a party to cheer us all up.'

Jo didn't care who came to celebrate with them. She was married to Nick, and that was all that mattered. She exchanged happy glances with him. It was good to celebrate with friends, but it would be even better when they were alone together, and when they could set about making a good life together here in the valley.

She was quite sure it would be a happy life in anything that depended on them and their love.

Inside the hotel, Tess stayed very close to her father, feeling shy, worried at how people would react to her presence. For once, however, she was smiled at by the other guests, spoken to kindly, treated in a way she'd always envied when she watched other people.

At one point during the meal, her father said, 'By the way, I can arrange for Big Donny to come and live on the farm I own and rent out. I think he'll be happy helping with the animals, don't you?'

Tess looked at him, already feeling love creeping into her heart. He had only to find out she wanted something to get it for her. Her new clothes were pretty and suitable for a sixteen-year-old, and Donny would be safe. 'That would be wonderful. He does his best but he's rather timid really, unless someone upsets him.'

'That's settled, then.'

In another corner, Charlie and the other councillors had temporarily forgotten that this was a wedding gathering and were speaking in low voices about the next council meeting and planning how to make progress in getting rid of the slums at Backshaw Moss.

'We'll do it,' Leah said, and they all nodded.

Further up the hill, Wilf was sharing a pot of tea with Mrs Morton, having just finished the last of the urgent repairs for her.

'I don't know what to do about Enid,' he confessed. 'She seems only to want to stay at home and look after the children.'

'The hard times have affected her, as they have many people. You'll have to bring her to tea again. Maybe if she gets used to coming here, she'll relax a little. You have.'

He grinned. 'Strange how comfortable I feel with you these days.'

'And I with you.'

'Well, go on. What's the latest gossip?'

'They say Mrs Rathley has been a much happier woman since her husband was arrested.'

'I'm not surprised.'

'And I hear that our local driving instructor and the Australian lass are getting married today.'

'Yes, I heard that, too. You can't keep anything secret in this town, can you? I don't really know them, but I like to see people in love, whoever they are.'

'No, you can't often keep secrets. I heard two women talking about them in the shop. I hope they'll be very happy. Later on someone else pointed them out to me in the street. You'd think a person from Australia was a strange new animal from the way she talked. But I must say, they looked like an old married couple already.'

In Birch End that evening, Charlie poured himself the small nightly glass of sherry to which he was becoming addicted and sat down to chat to his wife.

'It was a good wedding, wasn't it?'

'Delightful.'

'And Wilf will be making a start on the walls of your studio next week.'

'Good. And what will you be getting up to next, Charlie Willcox?'

He grinned at her. 'Who knows? But times are getting slowly better and now that I'm on the council I want to help our valley prosper again.'

'It won't be easy going.'

'But it'll be very worthwhile.' He raised his glass. 'To the Valley: Rivenshaw, Birch End and Ellindale. May all of us who live here prosper.'

She yawned and stretched. 'And while we're all waiting to prosper, your unborn child and wife need their sleep.'

He chuckled, set the glass down and went up to bed with her. It took him a while to get to sleep as he reviewed the events of the last few weeks. It had all ended happily.

Our valley will prosper again, he thought as he grew drowsy and fell asleep with a smile on his face.

CONTACT ANNA

Anna is always delighted to hear from readers and can be contacted via the Internet.

Anna has her own web page, with details of her books, some behind-the-scenes information that is available nowhere else and the first chapters of her books to try out, as well as a picture gallery.

Anna can be contacted by email at
anna@annajacobs.com

You can also find Anna on Facebook at
www.facebook.com/AnnaJacobsBooks

If you'd like to receive an email newsletter about Anna and her books every month or two, you are cordially invited to join her announcements list. Just email her and ask to be added to the list, or follow the link from her web page.

www.annajacobs.com

We do hope that you have enjoyed reading this large print book.

Did you know that all of our titles are available for purchase?

We publish a wide range of high quality large print books including:
Romances, Mysteries, Classics General Fiction Non Fiction and Westerns

Special interest titles available in large print are:
The Little Oxford Dictionary Music Book Song Book Hymn Book Service Book

Also available from us courtesy of Oxford University Press:
Young Readers' Dictionary (large print edition) Young Readers' Thesaurus (large print edition)

For further information or a free brochure, please contact us at:
Ulverscroft Large Print Books Ltd., The Green, Bradgate Road, Anstey, Leicester, LE7 7FU, England. Tel: (00 44) 0116 236 4325
Fax: (00 44) 0116 234 0205